MANIPULATION BY DEGREE

A NOVEL BY

CHARLIE BURNETTE

MAIN STREET RAG PUBLISHING COMPANY
CHARLOTTE, NORTH CAROLINA

This novel is a work of fiction. Any references to real events, businesses, organizations, or any locations, are intended to give the fiction a sense of reality and authenticity. All names, characters, places and incidents either are the product of the author's imagination or are used fictitiously. Any resemblance to actual persons, living or dead, is entirely coincidental.

Library of Congress Control Number: 2009936183

ISBN 13: 978-1-59948-196-8

Produced in the United States of America

Main Street Rag
PO Box 690100
Charlotte, NC 28227
www.MAINSTREETRAG.COM

To Marcia,
my inspiration

and
Taylor, Aylie, Bax and Hagan

My deepest gratitude to these folks who contributed to this work:

Lynn Barnes, Nicki Barnes, Betty Beamguard, David Benson, Bob Bristow, Mary Ann Brookshire, Margaret Burnette, Kathy Cockerham, Duane Christopher, Craig Faris, C.R.A.V.E., Harriet Goode, Brian Hamel, Thelma Hamilton, Dana Harkness, Gwen Hunter, Janice Hyatt, Todd Lowe, Bob McCleave, T. F. McDow, Jennifer Marquis, Nan Morrison, Scott Oliver, Terry Roueche, Allison Rushing, Alan Ryder-Cook, Marie-Helene Ryder-Cook, S.C.W.W. Rock Hill Chapter, Van Shields, Robert Scoville, Julie Spell, Brenda Weiler, Chris Wellborn, Earl Wilcox, Janice Wiley, Jenny Lynn Williams, Gilda Zeitz.

CHAPTER ONE

A Chicago Brothel
1945

The rusty mattress springs squeaked out a sad song in Sid Murck's ears. His fifty-five pound body rolled away gently. He wanted to throw up but knew better. At six years of age, Sid had cried out to his mother often, but she never answered.

Sid grabbed his knees and tucked his head slowly as he watched the man struggle with his zipper. A single tear fell from his eye and soaked into his unbuttoned tweed wool pants. He jerked slightly as the man rubbed a hand across the silky smooth side of his face.

"You're better than any woman in this place, kid. See ya next time."

When the man left and the door closed, Sid sobbed with both hands over his face so no one could hear. He prayed God would save him from the torture each night brought. He learned the prayer out on the street, taught by a woman dressed in black and white. His mother told him nothing good would come of those Catholic people except free clothes. But the prayer felt warmer than the threads around him, so he used it as a shield to ward off what he couldn't understand.

The small room was quiet except for the pounding and moaning muffled by the walls on either side of him. The brief silence became his hideout until a prostitute claimed it to turn a trick with her next customer. He calmed himself for the tears to dry, took a few deep breaths and waited for the knock.

The lingering stench of cheap perfume and aged body fluids followed Sid out into the hall connecting the same-sized bedrooms. His short, uneven steps spared some of his pain as he rounded the corner, until nine-year-old Bert Keller startled him. Bert towered over him with a mostly-toothless grin.

"You nothin' but slime, Sid." Bert laughed with an undertone of hatred that rattled Sid to the core. His shame was no secret among those seeing him pulled into the room. He shook as Bert forced his hand down into Sid's pocket, pulling out a quarter and a nickel.

"Gotcha some tips, hey. I'll keep it fer you."

Sid swallowed his words. The pain of Bert's fist in his gut was fresh and clear in his mind from the last time Bert stole his money.

Wanting to be the good boy the prayer lady talked about burned in his heart. He felt if somehow somebody could see the kindness inside him, life would get better. But the Starlight choked his dreams everyday, and his gentle way was at odds with everything that touched him.

He grew tired of looking for someone who cared. Sid's emotions calloused each night as the worst off the street paid Rosie Murck, his own mother, to work him into a back room between the regular ladies. In the Starlight, the only home he'd ever known, he watched soldiers and draft dodgers alike celebrate the end of the Second World War, waiting a turn to put their exclamation point to the event of the century.

His momma controlled the action, and he heard her boast that the end of the war was good for business. But the war tossed in his mind without a clear notion of what it meant. Talk of guns and blood painted his vision, and the mention of peace seemed an empty promise from where he stood. Rarely did the Starlight soften its brutality long enough to give him a ray of peace, his war.

A parade. A celebration. An unusual sight for the neighborhood caught Sid's clear brown eyes. After looking out, he climbed down from the wooden chair which boosted him to eye level with the small glass window in the front door of the Starlight. A strange rush of excitement overtook him. He looked backwards, slowly, to see if he was being watched.

A small whisper of freedom flowed through him as he stepped out the door into the sounds of happiness. The mid-afternoon sun highlighted the rainbow of colors moving under the clear sky. The cool air tasted almost like candy. His legs tingled as he stretched them along the crowded sidewalk, striding with an unfamiliar joy.

He settled into a small space by the curb between two ladies in large overcoats. They warmed his thinly covered arms as he watched a flower-laden float of clowns pretending to be German soldiers with bad aims. The crowd roared with laughter, and the parade moved forward.

Across the street, a set of eyes beckoned to Sid with a look of helplessness. A teary-eyed girl, with blazing red curls blowing in the crisp autumn winds, stood alone among the roars of victory. He slipped between rows of dressed-up elephants, and felt his heart pounding as he got closer.

"What's da matter?"

Her eyes met his. "I'm lost." She was an inch shorter than Sid and spoke with a voice so soft and clear that he wanted to smile.

"I'll help ya. We'll find yer home," Sid said as cheerfully as he could. "Where do ya live?"

"Somewhere over there."

Sid patted her slender arm as he looked in the direction she pointed. "Then that's where I help ya to. We'll get there, safe and sound." Sid watched her innocent face, now relieved, beaming trust for him. Virtue came over him knowing he'd save her, become her protector. Offering her something he longed for himself gave him a sense of purpose. He felt a new warmth inside until the abrupt sting of his mother's hand, crashing across the back of his head, snapped him out of what was making him feel good.

"Get ya stinkin' no good chops off dat red-headed jail bait. Ya be makin' time, it'll be on my time," she bellowed in her deep, raspy voice.

As she dragged him by the back of his shirt through a band of marching American Legionnaires towards the oppressive walls of home, he could only think of the girl with the curls. What would happen to her?

Rosie's bathrobe barely covered the large breasts she liked to shake near the Starlight customers' faces. Sid saw jaws drop on the parade watchers' expressions as she, without a care, flashed a bit of what she called her glory. Rosie's fading brown hair and once firm curves bounced across the busy street as she pulled Sid along. He pretended to be invisible as he hid in her shadow.

He wondered why his mother hated him. He wasn't "sickly" like she accused him of being, but things he saw and heard often caused him to lose his meals.

In his mind, he could mostly block out the men. But he couldn't understand why his mother wasn't treated better. Through the walls he heard the men yelling mean names at her most every night, telling her to do things. It made him think of a picture book he once saw in a doctor's office as he waited for his mother, who had caught something from one of the johns. He flipped pages of circus animals jumping to whips.

Though his mother cared nothing for his misery, he wished he could spare hers. Together they could stop the pain, but she would never let him.

"You's part of the money. Stay where ya be," she'd say, never looking in his eyes. Sometimes he thought being dead would be easier than being hers.

Chicago
1951

Twelve-year-old Sid Murck looked over the shoulder of Bert Keller down on one knee in a wet, downtown alley. Beneath Bert was a pool of blood extracted by a homemade knife from a passing victim. As Bert went through the bleeding man's wallet, his voice jumped an octave, "Man 'o man, there's got to be eight hundred bucks in here."

Bert called Sid the lookout. He hadn't volunteered for the job. But getting beat-up had taught him to shut up and do as told. For over six years, Bert had caused him to feel nothing but shame.

Sid knew his cut of the money was nothing, the same cut he got on Bert's last job, which rounded up six dollars and forty-three cents. The words still played loudly in his head. "Hey, Pecker Head, six stinkin' bucks ain't no money, not for stiffin' a man." Bert was the only person who called him a pecker head, and he hated it. Rage welled up in him like a shook-up soda, a time for change.

Bert's mother, Marie Keller, was a whore at the Starlight and worked for Sid's mother. As long as Sid could remember, Marie let Bert do anything he wanted, and he seemed to grow meaner as Sid's mother grew greedier. He lashed out blood-spilling smacks to Sid's nose anytime he hesitated to follow along. Sid, in his soul, didn't know what he was, or where he was going, or what he was supposed to be. But he knew he was no pecker head.

Sid knew better than to look to his own mother for help. She stayed drunk every day. She woke up in the early afternoon and passed out shortly after closing time. She told him he was nothing but a nuisance, until she found he could make money, and putting an extra twenty bucks in her bra while watching the occasional offbeat customer drag him into one of the back rooms fit the business. "He's just a kiddie and won't 'member this," he overheard her explaining to the other ladies.

But since the age of nine, he became an asset of a different kind to Rosie, watching her money. He made sure, even after the pills and booze, she had it the next day. Yet, Rosie gave Sid no protection from Bert, who always got his way.

The bloody wallet still lay in Bert's hand as he rose from the victim's body. Sid's fingers caressed the rough grain of the ash wood nestled in his hands. The alley was cold and dark. The rain splattered in the blood upon the pavement. Years of hate fueled Sid beyond his hesitation. With all the strength of his eighty-six pound frame, Sid drew back and slammed the lead-filled bat across the back of Bert's head. Sid could hear the dull sound of skull fracturing. The crunch of bone was like the sound of breaking crackers into his meatless soup. Bert's body flipped forward, and his head bounced twice on the alley pavement. He brought the bat down again and dropped it between the two lifeless bodies.

Eight hundred fifty dollars slid into Sid's pocket, making a bulge at his hip. He felt guilty, alone and sick as tears mixed with raindrops. He walked from the alley, which smelled of raw meat, reflecting on Bert's promise to kill Sid if he ever crossed him.

He parked his feet in the middle of the street, daring the next car to smash him, give him his due. He thought of Bert killing for pocket-change, and considered the people Sid saved who'd done nothing wrong. He felt the pile of money bulging in his pocket and decided to get out of the traffic.

Minutes after freeing himself from Bert, Sid walked into the front door of the Starlight, and stepped into the big open room with the bar to the left. Sitting on his usual stool at the end of the bar, he could see the whole room back to the hallway connecting the four bedrooms. Rainwater dripped from his jet-black hair and clothes. He took long, slow breaths through his nose, trying to look calm.

The Starlight had a soured smell about her. The cleaning rarely got into the corners or under the cabinets. Sid often found dead rats rotting away but learned the odors were part of his upbringing. During business hours, the beer and liquor, along with what the customers wore to smell better, masked what stunk around the bar. But regardless of the time of day, the odors of the ten-by-ten foot bedrooms in the back scared him.

About midnight, he spotted Marie Keller coming through the dimly lit opening of the back hall and step into the much brighter big room. She squinted her eyes and walked directly to where Sid sat.

"Where's Bert?"

"Don't know. Yah know Bert, won't let me hang out 'cause he says I'm a punk. He took off a couple hours ago. Said he was goin' to finds some action."

Marie laughed and adjusted her underclothing. "Yuh, that sounds like 'em. He'll be 'round in a bit." She gathered the arm of her next customer.

Rosie and Sid slept in the attic space above the Starlight. A single flight of unfinished steps rose from the back right corner of the big room to a plywood door, which opened into the attic. Their two worn mattresses laid directly on the splintered wooden boards that made the floor and were used only after business was done. He cleaned himself around the bar only when he had time.

Sid did his usual lockup at 3:10 a.m. once he settled the account of the last john. He went upstairs to bed after carefully storing away the eight hundred fifty dollars with the other monies he'd taken from the Starlight. His mother was already there, passed out, face up, legs hung over the sides of her mattress in two directions. She never said good night.

His head settled into his tattered feather pillow, and he felt strangely better and in control. Pillow was his only friend. As he had done through the years, he confessed his fears softly into the fibers of his confidant. It knew so well how Sid begged his mother. "No more Momma. No more of those men." It knew the sheer terror of Rosie's answer. "Ya nothin' but a bastard. Ya wanna know what that means? It's like bein' trash with nobody to claim ya. If I feed your sorry ass, ya be doin' 'sactly what I say do. Now quit ya yappin' and earn your keep."

Pillow knew Bert Keller and the beatings and gut wrenching ways he dominated Sid. It shared what bothered Sid most about Bert. "Hey, guys, come on over. Sid, why don't you tell the boys what you let those wrinkled old men do to you at the Starlight?" It soaked up Sid's pain when he was too ashamed to speak, as Bert told the story in unforgiving details, until the older boys laughed in his face.

But Pillow never showed unkindness. It was soft and listened without judging. Sid had spun its comfort into a protective hammock. It swung gently in his mind and even had room for his mother.

Sid eased his face into the middle of his ally. "You shoulda seen me tonight. I took care of Bert, just the way we talked about. Things is goin' to get better."

He slept for about four hours and started listening for the hourly chimes from the wind-up clock, which sat on a shelf behind the bar. He counted the exact number of snores his mother belted out between the chimes.

At nine o'clock, the morning sun started to warm the upstairs. A few minutes later, a loud knock on the door downstairs startled him. He gazed across the room lit only by a lamp with no shade. Now lying crossways over her mattress, his drunken mother mumbled something about money in her sleep. He stood and stepped across the room. Layers of old makeup and semen from the previous night covered her face. Except for the fact that her chest rose and fell with each breath, she had the appearance of having suffered a cruel death. The knock came again, followed by a terrible cry.

"Get up, Rosie, somebody's at the door in the big room." She didn't move. Sid lightly kicked her side. Her right eye quivered as the parting lids gapped apart. Strands of mucus, like the covering on a slug, hung between her eyelashes.

"Ya little piece of crap. Can't ya see I'm a sleepin'?"

Sid ignored her anger. "Ya hafta get up. There's someone cryin'." Slowly Rosie crawled to her feet, appearing as if her joints were nearly frozen.

Sid followed her step for step down the stairs from their living quarters into the big room, watching her grimace in pain with each placement of her feet. Across the room, over four round tables surrounded by low-back, wooden chairs, he could see Marie Keller peering through the small glass pane face high in the front door, crying hysterically.

"What da hell's goin' on?" Rosie asked as Sid unlocked and opened the door.

"My baby's dead."

Marie shook like the junkies Sid had seen on the street. He flipped a switch, turning on the wagon-wheel light fixtures hanging over the tables as Rosie grabbed Marie by the arm and pulled her in.

"Come in and calm yourself down, you want a brewski or somethin' stronger?"

After three shots, Marie was steady enough to describe what happened. Sid sat beside Rosie, carefully listening to the sobering details.

"Them cops knocked on my door two hours ago. I hadda go down to the morgue. There laid Bert with his head bashed in. Oh, Rosie, it was somethin' awful. Them cops say it was a strange crime. It looked like Bert had done killed a man. Bert had a knife, other man dead, but that don't explain how no baseball bat hit poor Bert in the back of the head. Cops say they checkin' fingerprints but, cause of all the rain and alley dirt, they not real sure nothin' would show up."

Sid knew there would be no prints. He carefully wiped off the bat and never touched the knife. He looked at Marie. "I'm sorry. Bert was a good person. It's jest not right for us to have loosed him that way." Sid surprised himself with the honest sound of his own words. He looked forward to sharing it with Pillow. Marie wailed, ran over, and hugged Sid, the most affection a woman had ever given him.

The three attended the funeral the next day. No one else came except the preacher who wouldn't get paid. Sid sat on a wooden, folding chair in a part of the cemetery with no headstones. He listened carefully to the reverend's words, thinking to himself the message could work for anybody.

"Bert," Sid said when the reverend forgot who was lying in the unfinished pine box. As they walked away hurriedly after the final nod, avoiding any gestures of payment, it occurred to Sid he probably knew Bert better than anyone.

A few hours after the funeral, seated at the head of the bar, Sid pondered the pain he'd caused. Maybe the killing was wrong; Bert could've changed, though deep in his heart Sid knew better.

He was caught off guard as Marie made her entrance, batting her eyelashes at the paying customers. She barely looked at him as she passed. Then he understood. Any grief he'd made for Marie was gone. It was Saturday night, and business was very good at the Starlight.

Monday afternoon Sid heard the school bus' brakes squealing one door down from the Starlight on W. Armitage Avenue. Children's laughter reminded him once again his mother had better use for him than attending the sixth grade. Except when the truant officers came around, Sid never attended. But school or no school, he was finding he could out think everyone he was coming across, and running the Starlight with a tight fist felt right.

The four rooms in the back had a double bed and table in each. The going rate in the spring of '51 was twenty-three dollars. Sid watched each john pick one of ten girls, except those being used. As the chosen one walked arm in arm with the customer, Sid wrote down the time from the clock on the mantle. When forty-five minutes passed, he'd knock on the door, but rarely did it take more than fifteen. Forty-five or fifteen, it still cost the same, and Sid's hand reached out to collect the fare. Handling the money became a welcome change for Sid since it got him out of the backrooms with the men.

Monday nights were slow. Often the ladies would play Bingo, waiting for a john. Cardboard cards and punched-out rounds to cover the numbers spread across the tables. The ladies would sink low in the chairs, backs bent, legs spread and made Sid call out the letters and numbers.

Sid practiced remembering each call, storing every one of them in his mind. When a lady shouted "Bingo," he'd never look at the master card to verify the winner. But no one seemed to notice.

One Monday night, in the middle of the game, a john, dressed like he had a bunch of tipping money, strolled through the front door. The ladies sprung to attention like an army troop Sid had seen in *Life* magazine. Their chests were out, chins held high, and work-look on.

Rosie bolted ahead, grabbed the man by the arm, and pulled him past the tables toward the back rooms. Sid got tickled listening to the ladies bickering over Rosie's ball-busting ways. When she finally pranced out of the back hall, Sid expected a fight.

The others were glaring angrily in Rosie's direction as she began to speak. Sid noticed the man was already dressed and following not far behind.

"Stop yer bitchin'. I'm so good... could do it in my sleep," Rosie shouted.

Sid couldn't help but laugh as the man's jaw dropped, and he began complaining.

"Do it in your sleep? Hell, Rosie, you might as well do it in a coma. A watermelon has more action. Next time my money's gonna grab one of those tighter asses."

After taking the fee from the john still rolling his eyes, Sid started reflecting on where all the money went. Before Sid taught himself some rough ways of adding and subtracting, Rosie handled the money. She would lose three-quarters of it by morning and wouldn't remember where it had gone. By age nine, Sid would take the fee for each trick and divide it half to the broad and half to the house. The only legal trade going on was the bar. Beer was a quarter, liquor half-a-dollar. An expired business permit hung on the wall behind the bar, as if to lend authority to the Starlight.

The irritated voices of the ladies, still mad at Rosie, blended into one high pitch as Sid focused on Tim Stevens. Tim was the bartender, and Sid had watched him long enough over the years to learn that only half of the money made it into the cash drawer. It needed to stop.

"Maybe Rosie needs to know 'bout them bills you stuff in your pocket."

"Geez, Sid-Sid, ya don't hafta go messin' with the old lady on that."

"Why not? It ain't yuh money, now was it?" Sid argued in his squeaky-soft voice.

"Hows about a pop? On the house," Tim offered.

"Not ya pop to be givin'."

"Then get your skinny ass outa here," Tim scolded, but sounded worried.

"That's a good idea." Sid turned and walked towards the tables. Rosie was still arguing about who gets to greet the customers at the front door.

"Hold it," Tim shouted.

That's all Sid needed. He made a deal with the grizzled bartender. Tim got two nickels out of every dollar, and Sid got one. He would watch Tim, closely.

Where Sid lacked in body bulk, he made up for in smarts. But life in the Starlight beat him down. Memories sapped his confidence. He tried to forget, but doubts and fears sneaked up on him daily. What wouldn't leave his mind, he shared with Pillow.

"Why don't I walk out of here? Why should I think she'll change and need me?"

Yet, somehow he still needed his mother's approval. The hope of it kept him imprisoned.

Sid managed the Starlight well, adding to his stash of money every night. By his thirteenth birthday, he had put back over two thousand dollars. To his mind, the payment was his just due for running the place since age nine, without a single thanks, while his mother tended to the back rooms. He couldn't stand thinking about what his services before that were worth.

Sid learned the story of the Starlight over the years, usually coming during chit-chat among the ladies on slow nights. Sid leaned forward sitting on his stool, the one at the end of the bar, placed his elbows on the shiny wood, and heard tales of the Starlight.

The old loblolly pine building used to be part of a big warehouse, constructed in 1916 to get a bunch of square feet at little cost. During the Great Depression, the warehouse space got carved up according to the needs of anyone who could produce green rather than promise. At a firmer and tighter age, Rosie solicited enough cash to buy a share of the warehouse, which became the Starlight. Funny thing to Sid, Rosie named it on a night when she was making a living with no roof over her head. She said if she ever got her own place, that would be the name.

Several of Rosie's better customers had carpentry skills. Cheap pine two-by-fours and thin cedar boards formed the four back rooms and the bar. Some street vendors rounded up rugs, shelving, and accessories and sold them to Rosie at bartered prices. The Starlight looked like more than she was.

A warm spring night brought in a familiar face. The man staggered, and Sid's clear brown eyes, filled with fear, followed him cautiously, fighting the shame that came with memories of nights in the back bedrooms.

"Where's Rosie? I need tuh talk to her," he said slapping a twenty-dollar bill on the bar. By the time Rosie emerged, Tim had served him two scotches straight up.

"Hey, ole girl, it's been a while."

Sid watched her smile her work smile, nod her head as the man spoke, and cut her eyes sharply in Sid's direction with a look of confusion. He couldn't hear what the man was whispering in Rosie's ear until she broke off, shaking her head.

"Listen, he don't do that no more. I'll get you a nice girl who'll make ya feel bunches better."

"Naw, Rosie, you know I like da boys. Now you listen here; I've got a chunk of cash in my pocket the size of your left tit. If he does r-e-a-l good, you get two hundred." He grinned as he flashed a large roll of green bills from his pocket. A chill ran up Sid's spine.

"Come here, Baby," Rosie hollered. Sid nervously followed his mother to the stairway corner of the Starlight. She leaned back on the rough, unsanded cedar-paneled wall, moving side-to-side, scratching her back. He could sense the dollar signs jumping in her head as she thought about what to say to him.

"Listen, yuh need to do it. Dis is big money. Might even be a few bucks in it for you."

Sid pleaded, "Momma, don't do this to us."

The back of Rosie's hand caught the side of his face like a wet towel slapped upon the bar. "Yuh gonna do what I gonna tell yuh to do."

Sid thought of throwing her aside. He was stronger and could easily have fled the place. He didn't exactly know why he'd stayed so long, except he kept wishing life as he knew it could change. His eyes met hers, willing to dismiss everything in exchange for his mother's love. As he searched her face, the deep lines and crevices held nothing but hate for him. She turned her back and hollered. "Room two's about through."

As she motioned the man toward the back, it became clear to Sid that now was the time. Sid's final walk felt like fate. As he turned left, Marie Keller was leaving room number two, and he searched her face for some concern. She raised her eyes to the ceiling as they passed.

As the customer stripped down to his shorts and reached to comb his fingers through Sid's unevenly-cut, greasy hair, Sid could nearly hear the man's heart racing. With the man's hand caressing the smooth skin on the back of his neck, Sid pulled away, saying he had to go to the bathroom.

"Hurry up, Sonny. Poppa's really lookin' forward to this."

Sid shut the door behind him and walked down the hall past the bathroom. He stopped at the opening leading into the big room and spotted Tim Stevens pouring a drink. Business as usual, no one giving his situation a second thought.

Sid quickly retrieved Pillow and entered the utility closet beyond the bathroom in the back hall. He had worked his plan through his head a thousand times. The details danced crisply and strongly through his mind. *Get the money box, put it by the window, open the window, pick up the matches and the deep metal cup.*

He poured the gasoline, being careful not to spill any on himself, into the cup and returned to the room. His companion, stretched across the bed, begged for personal attention. The smirk on his face said all Sid needed to know.

With a practiced motion, Sid sent the cool liquid across the man's lap, scratched and flipped the match. Whoosh.

Sid watched shock cover the man's face as the match's flame ignited a bluish rainbow. The scream of terror sounded no different than the usual screams of pleasure.

The flames jumped at Sid as he lurched back and out the door, slamming it behind him. The fumes burned in his nostrils as he headed back to the utility room, but he didn't care. He grabbed his money box, tucked Pillow under his other arm, and hurdled the windowsill to the ground. Pumping his small, muscular limbs, he sprinted out the alley and down the street. Somewhere behind him, he heard someone scream "fi-yerr." He didn't turn. He didn't flinch.

He rounded the corner on N. Burling Street and ducked into a hidden place under a stairway halfway down the block. He fought his need to think of the fire, and the Starlight, and his mother, but he couldn't stop it. His mind raced with mixed feelings between the bad he'd done and the freedom he felt for the first time in his life.

Sirens and flashing lights filled the night. Firefighters' voices echoed through his hiding place.

But he had to watch. Slipping out, Sid wiggled around what seemed to be less than bothered men with water hoses.

"Doubt we'll get any out. The place is going up like a hay barn."

Wedged into a drainage ditch, Sid could feel the heat of the fire jumping as he'd never seen before. The fire looked like a show, performing its colors. But inside, where he couldn't see, he imagined. He thought about the ladies, his mother, his home. He remembered back to a time when two drunken sailors, waiting their turn with a lady, argued over who was tougher. Finally they both took turns holding their hands over the open flame of a cigarette lighter. Sid wondered if the bitter, yet sweet, smell of burning flesh would rise from the Starlight and cover the city. He watched and thought as long as he could stand it, and went back to his hiding place.

He rolled his face over and over again into Pillow, saying farewell to the only good thing in his life. Its mushy threads held his past of tears and hurt. The money was different. It would spend tomorrow, his tomorrow.

Sid hugged Pillow with all his might, let it go and walked out from under the stairs into the midmorning sunlight. The smoke still rose steadily in the distance over the Starlight. At noon, with box in hand, Sid purchased a one-way Trailways bus ticket to Detroit. Before departing, he checked the newspaper racks and found the "Trib." The fire had come too late to make the morning edition. As he boarded the bus, he stopped and turned towards the airborne soot of his past. He tried to smile, but it wouldn't come.

The bus was clean, and its seats were large, padded, and covered with cloth. It felt strangely comfortable. He found a button on the side of the seat's arm and reclined himself. Looking at his olive-skinned arms, he remembered the chat among the women, on a slow night, about his color. They all agreed it came from his father's part of his coming about. But nobody could remember who fit the description.

The long trip gave him time to think. Sid figured he'd parked all of his troubles of the past in room two before he left. *Rosie's gone, my worry's gone, nothing left but somethin' better.*

A new pillow, he thought as he glanced over his shoulder. A well-contained tear escaped, glistening as it ran down his face, as he missed his old one.

He wanted to forget Chicago and his place in it. A new name might be safer. Although he'd dodged a juvenile record, if something came up about the fire, he didn't want to be traced.

CHAPTER TWO

Detroit
1952

The bus depot, dirty, smelling like a stale beer, gave Sid an eerie feeling. Heads followed Sid and his box. He read their eyes with a learned ability to know what was lurking behind them, a sharp sense honed over the years, sitting at the end of the bar. The minute a john came through the door, figuring whom he'd pick and what he wanted, seemed easy as Bingo.

Eyes around the depot beaconed for what Sid refused to give. He knew the risks, and might need to move fast. He decided the money box was too bulky and pulled a paper sack out of an overflowing trash can. But the eyes kept following him. Even the Starlight had nooks to find a glimmer of privacy. He had to think.

The feet he could see under the plywood stalls in the men's restroom were not moving. He sloshed through an inch of brownish water, which looked to have come from the broken plumbing, and waited for someone to leave, freeing up a little space for him to move his money into the bag. A man with a familiar slant of eyes exited one of the stalls. "You need some help there, young fella?"

Sid ducked gracefully under the man's arm and locked the shabby door behind him. Noise echoed above the toilet as he considered his next move. He'd picked Detroit at the Chicago bus station remembering one of the Starlight ladies saying if she ever got the hell out of the windy city, she'd go there. But Detroit looked worse than the Starlight from where he sat.

This town's got to be better than this bus station.

He pulled his thoughts together, slid the newly bagged money down the front of his tattered brown wool pants, waded out of the stall, past the eyes, and into the street. He started to walk. Feeling hungry and lost, he considered spending some of his money, but thought better to hold on to it.

The wind blew briskly, causing his cheeks to burn, and after several miles of storefronts and stacked-up apartments with laundry hanging from porch rails, his feet hurt. He turned on Elizabeth Street, and a truck went whizzing by. A man down the street flailed his arms angrily. It looked like something to check out. He hurried down to the man still yelling as the truck faded.

"What's wrong, sir."

"I leave the store for two stinkin' minutes, that delivery jerk slips in, dumps this chicken on the side of the road, and leaves. Lazy bum's job is to load it in my cooler, all eighteen cases. I swear he hides around the corner 'til I step out."

Sid nodded to the red-faced, older gentleman and picked up a box of frozen chicken.

"What do you think you're doin'?"

"Mister, I'm tryin' to help yuh before your chicken goes sour. I don't expect nothin' for helpin'."

He watched the slightly bald-headed man look suspiciously over him and wipe his arm across his moist head.

"Okay, then jump on it."

Sid made quick work of the containers of chicken. As the last box was stacked up and the cooler door secured, Sid waited patiently for the out-of-breath man to speak.

"Thanks son, do ya have a name?"

"Yes sir, my name is Sidney Wright. I see yer floor could use a little sweepin'. Would yuh mind if I borrowed that broom in the corner?"

Sidney felt better as the man laughed, mopped the remaining sweat off his brow and introduced himself as Harold Brown, owner of Brown's Grocery.

"Well, I'll be damned, ya go right ahead there, Sidney."

He rolled up the sleeves on his second-hand, cotton Oxford shirt, which still smelled faintly of gasoline, and started sweeping, then mopping and waxing the maple floor boards. The floor gleamed. Without asking, Sidney grabbed a duster and had all the shelves cleaned by sunset. Harold never stopped watching him, even while serving customers. He spent the last hour straightening a shelf of canned vegetables.

Seeing the store hours posted on the front door, he knew closing was at eight, a time Sidney figured would move his life in one direction or another. He took a deep breath and waited for Harold to speak.

"Son, it's time for you to be a headin' home."

"Mr. Brown, I don't got a home."

"What da you mean you don't have a home? Who are ya mother and father? Where do they live? Where'd ya spend last night?"

Sidney was ready. "This is a little bit hard to tell ya, but my mother died when she had me. My father raised me but never had no use for youngins. Said when I turned fifteen, he was awashin' his hands of me. Turned fifteen yesterday, he told me to hit the road, and I hitchhiked into the city. That's when I come by yuh store."

"Ya mighty small for fifteen. Are you bein' straight with me?"

Sidney looked him in the eyes with all the trust he could muster, "I'm tellin' the truth. You were kind to let me work here with you today. I'd go home right now if I hadda home. I don't. But I don't hafta impose, so maybe I can find a spot out on the street."

Harold Brown's hardened face melted in front of Sidney.

"You'd be mince meat by mornin'. Tell ya what I'll do. There's a cot and bathroom in the back. Since I don't really know you, I'll have to padlock you in which means you can't mess with anything in the store. You can't get out 'till mornin'."

"That's more than fair, I'll hafta work extra hard tomorrow." Sidney put his hands on his thin hips, and looked around the store. "Looks like I've got a bunch of cleaning." Harold smiled.

"Alright then, Sidney, you best grab an apple or two over there in produce before I lock you in."

Sitting on the floor with his back to the cot, he tried to focus, but the pace of the last couple of days drained him. He relaxed and fell asleep in a strange place without trying.

Sidney began his day at sun up. He cleaned most every surface in the store by closing time, and felt a stirring of pride as Harold beamed and claimed it hadn't looked that good since the day he opened nine years ago. Sidney felt a warmness flooding his chest, which confused him. He quickly forced a new thought to make the feeling go away.

Sidney took the same sleeping arrangements that night. He soaked up musty smells from baskets of cornhusks and old vegetables, waiting to be thrown out the next morning, which differed from the crisp and delicious aromas inside the store. His eyes roamed the rough concrete floor, his tiny bed, and the large metal door with its padlock on the other side. The sound of it being locked almost made him feel protected. As he chewed on the store's beef jerky, it troubled him to be comfortable.

Deliveries came the next morning. He spent the next day and a half restocking shelves. As he stocked, he paid close attention and quickly learned the layout and merchandise in the store. By the fifth day, he helped customers as Harold worked in the meat market. Mrs. Brown handled the cash register on Saturdays, the busiest day. She first seemed suspicious and nervous, but Sidney still liked her. He knew how to work his eyes and soon her doubts left her expression. Acting as a fifteen-year-old polite young gentleman instead of a thirteen-year-old fire-burning thug took some effort. Gaining her trust was refreshing.

"Mrs. Brown, you must be very smart to push those keys so fast and never break your beautiful fingernails."

When the front door was locked on Saturday, Sidney stood in front of the Browns' glowing faces, got a twenty-dollar bill and a hardy handshake. An emotion filled the air. Sidney felt it but couldn't understand it.

"I don't expect no money. You give me a bed when I don't got no place to sleep."

They insisted he keep the money. He did.

The Browns were both in their fifties and slightly overweight. Sidney thought the grocery business lent itself to their growing waistlines. But their hearts seemed pure, and he watched something special between them. A gentle touch, a smile, or a soft meeting of their eyes during the day showed Sidney a caring he'd never known. What really started bothering him was watching the Browns give candy away to some children, explaining their parents couldn't afford to pay.

Why give it for nothing?

The weeks passed, and Sidney got better around the store. Work strengthened him, and good food put weight on his once-skinny frame. The padlock disappeared, and he sensed the Browns growing closer, a little like Pillow.

The bathroom in the back had a small shower, sink, and a looking glass. For the first time in his life, Sidney bathed every day. He found an old pair of scissors, used to cut produce twine, and neatly trimmed his hair each week. The well-groomed, handsome face that looked at him from the mirror gave him his first stirring of self-confidence.

Harold Brown left a magazine by the cash register with pictures of boxers working out. Sidney discovered a long rigid piece of pipe and made a pull-up bar in an upper corner of his back room. With a wide board, a sawhorse, and a piece of leather, he put together an elevated sit-up bench. Between the reps in his make-shift gym and occasional sprints out on the streets of the neighborhood, he began to layer muscles.

During his first days at the grocery, Sidney rarely glanced at the newspaper racks outside the store. Sweeping the front walk one day a headline jumped into the corner of his eye. "Arson

Suspected In Chicago Fire." He walked away, not wanting to know his mother's fate.

Conversations with the Browns turned toward children, and he learned they couldn't have any of their own. He sensed they wanted him to fill an empty hole, but he quickly put it out of his mind. *I don't want nobody to need me.*

Soon he was taking meals with the Browns, and began asking questions about the business.

"Why not put some of the candy by the cash register? The kids have to just stand there starring at it. When they start screaming for it, the mom'll just buy it cause her ears are hurtin'."

"That's not a bad idea, Sidney, might work."

"Yeah, it will work, and I got more ideas. You're not against makin' money, are ya?"

Meals turned into brain storming about the store and turning a profit, and the Browns showed happiness with his drive and smarts. But they caught him off-guard when they announced he would enroll in school.

"Sidney, you'll never get opportunities in life unless ya finis' school. Work the store after school and on Saturdays."

He first argued he didn't need school. He sampled it in Chicago and found he learned more on the outside. But the store's books Mrs. Brown kept baffled him. Numbers stretched far longer than what he'd figured at the Starlight. He thought, *if I don't catch on to this math stuff, I might not be able to keep up with my own money.*

Over twenty-four hundred dollars sat in a secret place behind the dry goods in the back of the store. *My life's savings. If the schooling helps me with my money, maybe it's a good thing.* He went along with the Browns, and at the end of the summer he enrolled as the fifteen year old "Sidney Wright."

The school placed him in the ninth grade, all the kids were older, and textbooks read like a different language. During the first few weeks, his tongue stumbled as he tried to answer questions. The others laughed. But they also laughed when he wore the jacket the Browns bought him for the upcoming winter, on a warm fall day. Spending too many cold days with no decent coat made him not take a chance. *I can always learn to talk right.*

He was bent on turning his shame into something better. He wrestled every night with the questions and answers. Lying on his metal frame cot, with its lumpy mattress, he searched for his place in life. His mind drifted between losing and winning. A fire started to burn in him, torching thoughts of being no good, and the struggle made it tough to sleep.

Sidney reached deep into himself, trying to understand, and didn't always like what he found. He could hurt others or hurt himself. There wasn't much of a middle ground, like two people fighting inside him, both strong. A workable union, but he started pulling for the one that would hurt others as a way to protect himself.

Every school subject became not so much as a chance to learn but an opening of what the world should offer him. Slowly he caught on, and by Christmas break, grades improved. After work at the store, he studied tirelessly, and when exams finished in spring, his report card stated he ranked fourth in the class.

Summer brought a change in Sidney's life. He moved into his own room in the Brown's house, and started helping with the store books. With his new library card, he checked out a book called *Retailing at a Profit.* He read it twice.

He avoided the natural callings of summer and focused on beefing-up sales at the store. Content not to fish or hike, he entertained himself watching customers react to his moving items around the store.

Yes Mam, BLT... all the stuff right by your hand... that's it... okay, now the tomato... got ya.

The Browns seemed worried. "Sidney, feel free to invite friends over, have some fun."

"I've got too much to do 'round here."

The changes he made at the store saved costs and made the Browns more money, for which he got their praises and a bonus. The bonus felt good.

He started the tenth grade with keys to the Browns' grocery and house jingling in his pocket. Grammar slowly improved, and he practiced daily with store customers. By October, his money totaled twenty-eight hundred dollars, *not enough*, he thought.

B obby Depew became a turning point in Sidney's life. Bobby was sixteen, a hundred eighty-five pounds, and six feet two inches tall. He played starting defensive end for the junior varsity football team but was kicked off for throwing a punch at the head coach. As Bobby later explained, "don't like nobody gettin' in my face." He liked having things his own way, and Sidney noticed the teachers were afraid of him.

As Sidney crossed the school's activity field, Bobby had a small, squirming boy pinned to the ground. "I'll bust your head open as easy as wipin' the snot off my nose."

Sidney took a deep breath, walked up, and broke into the action, acting like he was in charge. "What's the problem here?"

Bobby cut his angry blue eyes in Sidney's direction. "You better mind your own stupid ass business, or you'll be next. This chump stepped on my samwich, and now I got no lunch."

"I didn't mean to," the kid squealed.

Sidney's mind raced through the choices. "Hold it. You can buy a sandwich in the cafeteria fer a quarter. Why don't ya ask him if he's got a dollar? Then you can get a sandwich, a profit, and you don't get blood on that yellow shirt of yours."

Sidney watched carefully as Bobby hesitated, looked at his shirt and then at the kid, "You got a dollar, punk?" Trying to fight back the tears, the kid checked in his dampened pants pocket and came up with seventy-five cents. Bobby looked at Sidney.

"Still a good deal," Sidney said. The kid was saved.

Bobby walked past Sidney, and mumbled, "Thanks." Sidney walked briskly and caught up. Bobby's frame cast a huge shadow over him.

"If you was thinkin' smart, you'd use one of them quarters and buy me a sandwich. You're still ahead, and I'll help ya out again."

"Right chump, the only samwich you'll get is my knuckles down your throat."

"Look, I just put money in yer pocket and kept ya from gettin' throwed out of school. I can help you more, you know, do the thinkin' for you."

Sidney got a ham and cheese and the beginning of what might be bigger plans. Although Sidney never stopped studying, his new acquaintance opened new possibilities. Between Bobby's overwhelming presence and Sidney's brains, they started pulling down slick deals around town. Sidney quickly learned that Bobby's mind was quite simple. Pulling the right strings was as easy as knowing what made Bobby happy. Sidney wouldn't take chances. If the situation wasn't right, he'd back off. He taught Bobby early on to do exactly what he was told. Sidney made the Bobby Depew who couldn't get away with anything into the kid who seemed to skate on water. His skates were Sidney. But Sidney cautiously molded each job so that if it went bad, Bobby took the fall.

"Bobby, Bobby. Don't think about nothing 'cept what I say. It won't go bad 'cause I already figured it out for you."

They took in over three hundred dollars within the first two months and split it fifty/fifty. Sidney's easiest take started when he found a case of empty high-end gin bottles behind a liquor store. Thinking it through, Sidney sent Bobby into the liquor store to buy a half-gallon of very cheap gin. Sidney cut the gin in half with water and filled the premium bottles. The liquor stores were closed on Sundays, and Sidney peddled the bottles at a ten-fold profit.

Sidney amused himself watching fellow students and got satisfaction figuring out their motives. The key was using it to his advantage.

Christina Swensen, the daughter of the minister of the largest Lutheran church in Detroit, flirted constantly in front of her locker on the tenth grade hall. Sidney found sound traveled well from her locker to his, just around the corner. Talks between Christina and her new boyfriend, a defensive tackle on the varsity team, started to make Sidney think.

One chilly afternoon, in the mostly-empty hall, Sidney got his chance. Between the giggles and heavy breathing, it sounded like Christina was getting rubbed in the right places.

"Not now, baby. I'll meet you in the boiler room under the gym in fifteen minutes. Nobody ever goes there."

He quickly left to get Bobby while juggling parts of the plan in his head.

The high school, located in the central city, had been constructed in the twenties. Steam pipes popped and clicked in a funny rhythm during colder weather among the thick brick walls, high ceilings, and pine flooring. The gym was on the downhill slope of campus, and the heating systems were just below it.

On the way, he stopped by a coach's office at the top of the steps, quickly opened the door with a flat piece of metal, and borrowed an empty camera.

Sidney sized up the steamy hot room and moved a gym mat to an open space between the large iron boilers. He settled into a damp and musty corner and waited until Christina came through the door, laughing with her friend.

Christina wasted no time in baring her firm and pointed breasts. She jiggled them side to side. "Think you can handle these, School Boy?" They fell upon the mat. Sidney watched as they rolled and stroked. He wasn't aroused, seeing the deed in far more interesting ways in the back of the Starlight. He thought it junior varsity at best.

Christina's voice went from high pitched and tickled to a hard low moan. Sidney's years of listening at the Starlight told him when things were right. He leaped from his position and walked by. "Nice tits, Christina. Bet the preacher will like the photos." Sidney shattered the intense moment like a rock thrown at a storefront window.

"Do something," Christina screamed at her flustered partner. He followed Sidney's calculated walk, pulling up his drawers and pants. Outside the boiler room door Sidney stopped and turned, with Bobby looming several feet behind him.

"What ya doin', man... look, this is none... hey, you got to keep your... why's he standin' behind ya?"

Sidney raised his hand to the much larger lover of Christina Swensen as if to say, stop talkin', it's time to listen.

"Bobby back there don't know nothin' about this, but he's here in case you get out of hand or if sump'n ever happens to me. What you guys has is a little problem. I got some film," Sidney said, holding up a black raised-skin Polaroid camera.

"Make no mistake, the Reverend will know it was you and his little girl. But we can avoid this happenin' so simple. I could cares less about ruinin' her little Lutheran reputation. Seventy-five bucks will make your problems all go away. Go back into the boiler room and talk to her. You tell her what I said, and she'll have no trouble roundin' it up. Get the dough and meet me at John's Hotdog Stand in two hours, and it's all over. Don't show, and it's all beginning. But remember, Bobby's with me and that could be a bigger problem for you guys."

Sidney got the money as planned. He'd studied the players and knew they would talk about how it was his word against theirs and question whether he really had a picture. Neither would recall a camera flash, but in the heat of things, they wouldn't know for sure. He figured she would call the shots and not take the chance.

He'd heard this kind of a deal called "blackmail." Library books labeled it "extortion," but he liked "shake-down" better. He felt stronger when Bobby helped.

Over the next year, Sidney put together more than a dozen shake-downs and dickered down Bobby's cut of the money each time. By the winter of 1955, over fifty-eight hundred dollars rested behind the dry goods at Brown's Grocery.

Sidney knew the Browns, deep in their hearts, considered him family, but as time marched on, he kept a cold distance from them. Sidney felt his body changing, with a burning need to wrap himself in the softness of girls he noticed at school. He dealt with these feelings mostly at night, on his own terms.

Sidney appreciated the Browns for all they'd taught him. The Starlight years brought day-to-day disappointment. But the Browns never let him down, never walked away. He struggled with the urge to hitch his feelings to them, always fearing losing control. He focused on his money instead.

Sidney's birthday, March 6th, brought celebration at the Brown's house, but Sidney's cake always burned two candles too many. As he blew out eighteen candles, he noticed an uneasiness with the Browns. He wondered what 1955 would bring.

"Sidney, we've got mixed feelings about some things," Harold Brown began, looking guilty. "An attractive offer has been made to buy the store. We could take the money and fulfill our dream to buy a place on Lake St. Clair. You're eighteen, smart, and probably don't need us anymore, but we want to do right by you."

The news jolted Sidney. *They're checking out.* It reminded him of a john, paying Sidney for the tab, leaving and not looking back. *They're done with me,* he thought.

"We don't want to hurt you, and we have some ideas that we want to talk about. Let's go out for a milkshake and work some things out to jump-start your future."

Sidney acted calmly and forged a big thanks to the Browns for all they had done. He politely told them he needed to study, and they should go on without him.

"No, Sidney, come join us."

"Not now. Go on and have your shakes, maybe bring back a malted-chocolate for me."

As he hugged the Browns for the last time, he could feel their love for him. He hugged them a little longer than usual and a warmness, peacefulness came over him. He tried to ignore it.

Sidney made a plan as he rattled his keys in his pocket, listening for the car to back out the drive. He knew the Brown's home and grocery inside and out. Mrs. Brown kept her better jewelry behind a shoe rack in the back of her bedroom closet. He removed the wooden box and took eight pieces. He knew their value because, over the last year, he had taken them to an upscale pawn shop across town to get an appraisal. Although the pieces were worth two thousand, he knew he would only be able to get eight hundred in a hurry. He put them all in his pocket. By the time he left the Brown's home, he had rounded up an additional two hundred thirty-five dollars in cash, one hundred twenty-five dollars in sterling silverware, thirty-five dollars in porcelain figurines, and a small antique clock worth twenty dollars. He put all the items, along with a few clothes, in a suitcase. As he headed toward the front door, from the corner of his eye, he noticed a reflection. Mr. Brown's gold wedding band lay beside the kitchen sink. Sidney recalled the laughs he and Mrs. Brown shared over Harold's bad habit of leaving the ring when he washed his hands. Sidney hesitated, put down the suitcase, and sat on the edge. Closing his eyes he thought of the Browns, but rekindled his resolve that they abandoned him. He rose and stuffed the band into his pants pocket. *Another twenty-five bucks.*

Five minutes later Sidney stood inside the grocery. He took a deep breath of the familiar smell created by the meat, produce, and aged lumber. A comfort swept over him like the place was a dear friend. He paused looking over the shelves and aisles which had nearly become a part of him. But he had to finish what he started. He found eighty-three dollars and forty-two cents in the cash register, along with a few silver dollars and gold coins Harold Brown kept under the counter. He picked up a few snacks for the road and left the store as quickly as he had come to it the first time. He needed to get out of town fast. Dressed comfortably, with his jet-black hair combed back behind his ears, he headed for the bus station.

Sidney figured the Browns would call the police, but he wasn't sure. He hoped they would report him.

They got plenty, and it won't break them. They'll forget it before they reach the banks of St. Clair. Come to think of it, they need to call the police... they'll need a report to collect the insurance... maybe get more than it's worth... maybe I did 'em a favor.

Sidney glanced over his shoulder from the window seat of the Trailways bus. Detroit faded behind him. He liked to think the

Browns as necessary pawns in getting his due. Guilt, dressed up as fear, kicked at Sidney's heart. He could deal with fear.

Not one bit of regret. He spent the next ten hours convincing himself.

CHAPTER THREE

Birmingham
1955

S idney strolled into City Bank and deposited three thousand dollars. He felt a bit cheated as the bank clerk explained his money would only earn 2.35 percent. He wanted to ask what they planned to do with his money and how much the bank would make off it. But he stopped himself, not wanting any more questions about the identification he'd shown the clerk.

He stuffed the receipt into the pocket of the light wool pants Mrs. Brown had made for him using a paper pattern and skipped skillfully down the bank building steps into his new city. He was sixteen, worth exactly $7,960.22 and bursting with excitement. He had overheard a Brown's Grocery customer claiming how much better the climate was in Birmingham compared to Detroit, but when he got off the bus two hours earlier, what caught his attention were people speaking like he wasn't a stranger and their voices being much slower, almost syrup-like.

He wandered through the steel-manufacturing district, observing the billowing smoke stacks and the workers flooding out of the doors of the plants at quitting time. *You won't catch me inhalin' that soot for no peanut wages,* Sidney decided.

He rented an apartment in a steel mill village and did a few odd jobs for pocket change. But life was moving too slowly, and paying rent felt like buying nothing. Soon he stumbled into a new idea. After the workers got paid on Friday, many played poker, and Sidney started watching.

The men played in halls set up in make-shift shelters. The mostly-unbathed workers carried a stench. The odors reminded Sidney of a sleazy man in the Starlight, but he ignored it. He felt in control and was more interested in the workers' paychecks, which had not yet made it home.

Sidney overheard one poker player defend the game. "The old lady'll give me a whole lot of lovin' when I get home with double my pay."

Sidney had been a quick study. The first two weeks he merely sat back, soaking up the winners' actions. Fifty-two cards, four suits, and a learnable number of combinations bounced in his mind. He closely watched eyes.

What good is a decent hand without a feel for the eyes behind the other hands?

The third week he started playing, and it hurt to lose more than he should.

Take it slow, I'm learning.

By the fourth week, Sidney was filling up with confidence. By carefully sticking to the odds and watching faces, he started winning. When the other players drank, the pickings were easy.

Sidney's real problem was dealing with folks who thought a blunt fist trumped a sharp tongue. Several close calls made him narrowly escape the poker game with his profits.

He found the only empty chair in the place at a table of eight. He eased slowly into the chair and sized up the competition. The other players apparently all worked the same shift at the same mill. Drunk and mean, two, named Joe and Frank, were so tall they had to duck their heads to walk under the low poker hall ceilings to make it towards the piss troughs.

Sidney noticed the bad smell of what surely was a week's worth of mill shifts layered over the skin of the players around his table. He felt out of place with his well-groomed hair, clean wool slacks, and white cotton shirt. After raking in a net gain of sixty-eight dollars on eighteen hands of straight poker, the game turned ugly.

"You damn slick-handed grease ball. Ain't no way yah wiped out all my boys unless you padded the deck." Joe stood and flipped the cheap ladder-back chair in reverse.

Sidney unbuttoned his sleeves and submissively pushed them to his elbows. "Come on ya'll, there no cards up here. You could've won easy as me, no big deal."

He paused hoping his reason would win out but heard nothing until one of them shouted. "Beat the hell out of 'em Joe."

Sidney swept up his earnings and rushed towards the nearest door. Exiting to the back alley, he felt Frank grab him by the collar of his shirt and jerk him to the ground. Pounding came from several directions until his mind went blank. When he climbed off the dirt, he'd bought a nasty gash over his left eye. The money gone, he felt frustrated and alone.

The next week he tried to be upbeat as he spoke into the rotary phone, "Bobby, how ya doin'? You remember me... Sidney? I need some help, man."

"You need help? Some teacher with a nice ass kicked mine out just fer lookin'. Then I got this two-bit job shoveling scrap metal at some car factory till some nit-wit cut my heel."

"Let me guess, Bobby, you decked him."

"Smashed him like a maggot."

"Here's your deal, Bobby. Round up some bus fare and get on the next one out to Birmingham. By sun up, I'll be waiting to pay you back, and you'll go bonkers for the rest of it."

As Sidney knew, Bobby agreed without asking a question, an easy sale.

Bobby stepped off the bus in Birmingham, and Sidney noticed he'd put on a ton of weight. His belt rode higher containing the bulge and his shoulders looked like the mountains in the backdrop of Birmingham. Bobby stretched, looked around the parking lot, and threw his canvas bag over his shoulder.

A smiling man passed by. "How ya'll doin?"

Bobby looked confused. "What's that about, he queer or something?"

"Southern hospitality, they call it. Takes a while to get used to."

"What's to do here?"

"Let's walk."

Sidney spoke of his plans for Bobby as they strolled up Ore Avenue towards the sign hanging above the sidewalk. Bobby seemed quite impressed as Sidney explained he bought the eight-unit apartment complex he was living in for thirty thousand. Putting three thousand dollars down, the owner carried a note for the balance at five percent interest.

"Vulcan Apartments, that's your new home. You'll run this place for me."

"Hey, they're all on one level, not stacked up like in Detroit."

"Yeah, each unit has two bedrooms, a kitchen-living room combo and a bath. Best part is all these people pay me to live here."

"So what do I get out of this?"

"You get to live with me in Apartment "A" for free. On top of that you get ten bucks every week, and I buy the groceries."

"All I can eat?"

That question made Sidney nervous, but he laughed it off. "Okay, all you can eat."

"I'm ready to start," he said as Sidney unlocked the door to his apartment, and Bobby headed for the refrigerator. Sidney rubbed the scabbed-covered cut over his eye and wondered if he'd made the right decision.

The next morning, he finished touring the gray asbestos-siding units with Bobby. The eight connected apartments were lined along the right edge of the narrow lot, and each door opened towards the parking area. He took Bobby to the office at the rear of the property, and felt relief knowing he could wash his hands of daily apartment problems and deal with more important things. But it wasn't long before he was dragged back into the fray. Bobby's first encounter with a delinquent apartment renter was to break the tenant's little finger.

"The guy says he's going to sue me. You think that helps things?"

"I'll break both legs, so he can't walk to the lawyers."

"It's called business, Bobby. I can't put his broken finger in the bank. Get it? The idea is to get his money, not that he gets mine."

"Sorry. It's just that he was gettin' in my face."

"It's okay. I'll smooth his feathers, give him a few bucks, and send him on his way."

Bobby, for the most part, served Sidney's purposes since the poker hall fight. He imagined, as days passed, Bobby becoming his puppet, but he didn't always respond to the string Sidney pulled.

"And that's fer bustin' my buddy's head open." Bobby hovered over Frank in the same alley where he took Sidney's money.

Sidney shook his head as they walked home. "Bobby, sixty-eight bucks, and you had him cornered. Why didn't you ask him for it before you cold-cocked him and took his billfold?"

"He had it coming."

"Only use your fists when the bottom line calls for it. Try and remember that."

Sidney believed he had a bigger future than poker. He knew full well that anything he learned from his brief stay in high school had paid off. Understanding some basics, if nothing else, helped him figure the gambling games. He wondered what college courses would do for him.

He enrolled in a local branch of the University of Alabama and took a full load of courses. Everything he learned turned into ideas about life, his life. He spent hours on grammatical skills and bettered himself every day.

Christopher Bonn studied art at the University. His black hair resembled Sidney's, but he stood three inches shorter. Sidney had seen him around, even spoke in passing. Thin and lanky, he casted an unimpressive profile, but his brilliant green eyes projected power, almost spell-binding, capturing Sidney's attention.

Sidney looked up from his lunch, in the noisy cafeteria, and saw Christopher standing at the table.

"Mind if I join you?"

Sidney pointed to the only other chair. "Sure, buddy, what's going on?"

"For starters, our play is about to fall apart."

"Why?" Sidney asked as he took a bite of his barbeque sandwich, slaw bleeding from the sides.

"We're in dress rehearsals, and half the cast is threatening to walk out before the show opens."

"So what's your part?"

"I have the lead, so it's not my problem."

"What's the lead, and why is there a problem?"

"You're naive. Most theater people have egos the sizes of barns."

"Does the lead not have to answer questions?"

"Okay, okay, I've got the biggest part, so I'm supposed to get the most attention, and it rubs the ones with the two-bit parts the wrong way."

"It sounds like the little people want the tail to wag the dog."

Christopher laughed loudly. "That's pretty close to it. So what's your deal, Sidney?"

"Guess you could say I'm a businessman trying to get a little education."

They talked until the time of the next class, and Christopher offered him a ticket to the play the following night. Sidney looked at the rectangular cardboard-like ticket in his hand. "What's this worth?"

"Keep your money. The lead gets comped a whole hand full of tickets. Don't sweat it."

"Comped? As in complementary, a compliment... free?

"Something like that."

"I'll try to make it," Sidney said.

Fine arts caught Sidney by surprise. As he entered Wallace Hall, he was impressed with the architecture and took a seat toward the back. The play, "A Man for All Seasons," proved stimulating. Christopher magnificently played Thomas More as if it were a personality transformation. He unfolded to the audience the spirituality of More and his intense commitment to the law of king, state, and God.

The words tumbled in Sidney's mind forcing new thoughts. He found himself on his feet when the performance ended with a full-house standing ovation. Not only was Sidney entertained, but fully intrigued. He took a cab back to the apartment that night, his head full of possibilities for the quite-talented Christopher Bonn.

The next day at lunch, he saw Christopher waving his arms across the cafeteria. Sidney motioned him over.

"Did you get a chance to see the show?"

"I sure did, you eased right into the shoes of your character. How long have you been doing this?"

"Since diapers, Mom tells me."

Sidney watched several other theatrical performances involving Christopher. They became friends, and lunch at the university cafeteria became their routine. One day Sidney looked across the table at Christopher's sad face. He saw a measure of desperation in his eyes. Sidney leaned forward, lowered his chin and spoke softly. "What's bothering you?"

"You know acting is what I love, but there's no money in it."

"Then why do it?"

"It's my life."

"So where does your money come from?"

"I guess you'd say from my dead grandmother. My dad left Mom, my sisters, and me back in the fifth grade... left us flat... broke. It's tough growing up like that. Guess my grandmother made it up to us. Her will and testament cut my father out and left everything to Mom. Not a lot, but it helped. Anyway, that money is used up. Looks like I'll need to take a leave from school, probably take a job at one of those godforsaken steel mills."

"How much money will keep you in school?"

"It'll take four hundred dollars to get me through this semester and another eight hundred to get through the year."

Sidney reached into his pocket and laid out twenty twenty-dollar bills, neatly stacked halfway between the two of them. "What on God's earth are you doing?"

Sidney looked intensely at Christopher. "First of all, God's got nothing to do with this. Secondly, this is a loan. Thirdly, if you'll give me a chance, I would like to invest this money for you tonight."

With a look of confusion and reluctance, Christopher agreed. Sidney explained carefully that he should watch at a distance, don't get involved in the investment, and don't change his mind in the middle of the process.

"Listen, Christopher, I can see some apprehension on your face, but consider this: it's a mystery, just like a good play. Trust me. It'll be far more intriguing than a steel mill."

"So, where do I meet you tonight?"

"Downtown. Corner of 20th Street and Morris Avenue, at eight-thirty."

That night it was Christopher's turn to be impressed. The smoke-filled room had piles of money on the table. Christopher's investment broker skillfully held, then folded, and then doubled up. The action became child's play to Sidney, amused as he caught glimpses of Christopher looking nervous, then amazed, as money started to pile up on Sidney's side of the table. Close to midnight he announced they were quitting, picked up the pile, and eased it into his blazer pocket.

He led Christopher to an all-night coffee shop. After ordering eggs, grits and coffee, Sidney slid the stack of bills out of his pocket to the top of the table.

"Ballpark, how much do you figure you won tonight?" Christopher asked.

"Count it. If there's not sixteen hundred in that pile, to the penny, you better re-count."

"How do you know, Sidney? Cash flew around that table faster than I could watch it."

"It's just a matter of focus, my friend. So there's your twelve hundred dollars. You owe me four hundred which I'll collect right now."

"That's ridiculous, it's all yours."

"Christopher, as one friend to another, I compounded your money for you. Accept it as a gift. Who knows, I may need a favor one day."

Christopher looked cautious for a moment, as if the "favor" comment sounded like a debt. Then he shrugged his shoulders, smiled, and put twelve hundred dollars in his pocket. Sidney picked up the check and, with a wink, handed it to Christopher.

CHAPTER FOUR

Birmingham
1958

S idney carefully scanned the headlines of the *Wall Street Journal*. Leaning a shoulder on a wrought iron lamp post outside a newsstand on Second Avenue, he flipped the pages until he spotted the article.

Sidney's newest passion, financial markets, occupied his mind constantly, and the business courses at UAB weren't satisfying his appetite. Developing a list of target companies, he found ways of getting resource information. If he didn't find what he needed, he did his own investigation.

Folding the newspaper under his arm, he considered the next move. By the time he drove his '53 Ford he'd just purchased back to the apartments, he had a plan.

The next day, he opened two accounts with different brokers. One carried his somewhat legal name, "Sidney Wright." The Browns secured him a Social Security card after they enrolled him in high school back in Detroit. The other account contained a name Sidney made up, "Fred Parham." He bought a suitable counterfeit driver's license and Social Security card from a printer south of Birmingham.

He put one thousand dollars into the legitimate account and made some conservative stock purchases. He anxiously watched the market daily, and after the first month, the account increased by two dollars. *What kind of life is this? It won't get better unless I make it better.*

I.F. Electronics, a small publicly traded company in Huntsville, Alabama, was located a couple of hours north of Birmingham. This young, growing company, specializing in aviation electronics, captured Sidney's attention.

He learned the Department of Defense was involved in upgrading the electronic security of all its aircraft. In addition to I.F., two other U.S. companies could deliver the technology, product, and service. Word was the Department considered all three companies as candidates for the upgrade. Of the three, I.F. was the smallest and youngest but still a legitimate contender for the contract, which was worth over eighty million dollars. But the "Street" considered I.F. a long shot. Sidney's own research convinced him I.F. wouldn't get the business.

The company's stock traded around a dollar fifty. Investors cautiously bid up the price to a dollar seventy-five after I.F. became a contender. Sidney bought on a dip at a dollar sixty-five, and five thousand shares landed in the account of Fred Parham.

On Friday, May 8, 1958 at 1:05 p.m., Christopher Bonn walked into the front office of I.F. Electronics. He displayed credentials to the receptionist. "My name is Davis McClure. I'm with the United States Department of Defense and have a rather urgent matter to discuss with Mr. Weatherford."

Wayne Weatherford was the executive vice president of I.F. and had been extremely anxious for I.F. to get the defense contract. Wayne had met with Department officials on several occasions. He was heavily invested in the company and had stock options maturing in the near future. He routinely left for lunch at noon and dined with his wife of six months at their nearby home. He returned at one o'clock and liked to nap in his office for thirty minutes before getting back to business. As planned, Wayne returned to his office moments before Christopher arrived.

The receptionist repeated verbatim what Christopher Bonn said, and the Defense Department official was promptly escorted to Mr. Weatherford's office. "Hello, Wayne, I'm sorry to drop in on you unannounced. You, of course, know my boss Bill Gregory."

Wayne's eyes opened widely. "Of course. Bill and I have been through a lot of details concerning your tech upgrade. He's a very capable fellow."

Christopher promptly continued the conversation without missing a beat. "Yes, he is, and he likes to do things in person. This morning he had a death in his family, or he would have been here instead of me. He has entrusted me to deliver to your company some very exciting news. To cut to the chase, you got the contract."

As a smile covered Wayne's face, Christopher continued. "Bill didn't want you to have to hear it from some other source. The Department will announce its decision Monday morning at ten o'clock. Since your company has already received the terms of the contract and found it agreeable, we'll sign the documents later that day."

Wayne seemed ready to explode with satisfaction. "That sounds great, Mr. McClure."

"Congratulations to you, and Mr. Gregory told me to tell you the same. He seems to think a lot of your company. See you Monday."

Insider trading in 1958 was pretty common, although technically illegal. By two o'clock that afternoon, the news spread like wildfire. Tips to family members and friends were handed out like candy by executives and other employees. Company phone lines were tied up, and many of the I.F. Electronic people left the plant to secure stock positions for themselves. By the end of the day, Wayne Weatherford had exhausted most of his liquid resources and then thought of flowers for his bride. They would celebrate that night.

Fred Parham made an arrangement with his broker to watch the market ticker tape that afternoon. I.F. Electronics was showing unusually high volume. By 3:00 p.m. on Friday, the shares climbed to four dollars and twenty-five cents. At 3:50, the bid price reached six dollars and fifteen cents. "Sell all five thousand shares," demanded Fred Parham. His broker followed his instructions and promised a cashier's check on the next business day. Sidney Wright, posing as Fred Parham, picked up a check for $30,750 at 9:15 a.m. on Monday. He cashed it an hour later.

Sidney enjoyed reading the Wednesday edition of *The Wall Street Journal*, which had a prominent article on the extreme price swing of I.F. Electronics over the past three trading days. There was no definitive reason given other than the speculation of obtaining the defense contract. The other potential companies for the contract complained to their respective Pentagon sources and, by 2:00 p.m. Monday, the Department of Defense issued a public statement that no company had been selected. By close of Tuesday's markets, I.F. traded at a dollar and fifty cents.

Sidney soon learned I.F. didn't get the contract, and within a couple of weeks Wayne Weatherford quietly resigned. Sidney gave Christopher Bonn another twelve hundred dollars for his excellent performance. He hadn't felt such a rush of excitement since he collected a ham and cheese sandwich from the overpowering Bobby Depew back in Detroit.

Twenty-two thousand dollars, four times what the average steel worker would earn in a year, and Sidney netted it in less than a week. He had yet to pay any significant taxes, and his newly earned financial status made him extremely cautious. He would focus on protecting his money as much as making more.

Over the next year, Sidney continued to excel in his studies and saw Christopher most days. Bobby kept managing the apartments, and most of the money found its way into Sidney's pocket.

CHAPTER FIVE

Birmingham
1959

B obby Depew never excelled in personal grooming. Somehow, deep inside, he believed himself to be a handsome fellow. Despite the fact that he took few baths and maintained a mild odor, his long wavy blondish hair fell nicely on his face.

Bobby nearly fell out of his chair when Paula appeared at the apartment office to inquire about a place to rent for her and her roommate, Donna. Paula was virtually everything Bobby wanted in a woman. She had breasts the size of cantaloupes, which she carried firmly as if they had their own purpose in life. Tall and thin, her smooth legs rose magnificently toward her thighs, and her hips swung gently from the rear as she walked. They put Bobby into a trance.

Bobby rented her Apartment "G" without a second thought. When he forgot to ask for the required rent and deposit, Paula mentioned it. "Oh, don't worry, I'll come by and collect it later."

She said they would move in at noon the next day, and Bobby stood waiting the whole morning for the Chevrolet Bel Air Paula drove. When it arrived, it appeared to be packed full of clothes and stuff. Bobby walked toward the car with his shoulders back, trying to profile his physique. She would be the first tenant he would bother to help move.

The previous night, Bobby wouldn't stop talking about Paula moving into "G." He felt like a kid again on Christmas morning. "Sidney, you gots to see this gal. It is the most beautifulest creature on earth."

"Well, Bobby, what makes you think she's interested in you?"

"You can just tell. It's the looks in her eye. I must has what she needs."

The next morning, Bobby was caught by surprise when Sidney and Christopher left classes early, showing up at the apartments to watch his new found craziness. He ignored their gentle ribbing and kept watching the parking lot through the office window.

Bobby had very little interest with the likes of Christopher. He thought of him as being too smart and too smooth. But Bobby depended on Sidney. If Christopher was okay for Sidney, he would be okay for him.

As Bobby grabbed the door handle on the driver's side of the Bel Air, something felt wrong. Her profile was not the same. Suddenly two hundred and thirty-five pounds of Bobby's greatest nightmare came gyrating from the vehicle. He froze.

"Hello, you must be Bobby. Paula and I are moving into Apartment "G." You are so sweet, you were going to help me unload the car, weren't you?"

A loud groan, sounding like a large dying animal, came bellowing out of Bobby. A long silence hung in the air as he sized up this woman.

Donna's hair was thin and grew in patches on her scalp. The small amount of hair was an unattractive rust color, resembling the iron veins running through the local hills. Bobby grimaced as he realized her hair was her best feature.

When in motion, her obesity jiggled around her awkward frame. Her twenty-something face contained the craters of severe acne that must have haunted her throughout her teen-age years. Her feminine traits, if she had any, were lost among the pockets and folds. Although her scalp suffered in producing hair, the rest of her body was a breeding ground.

"I guess I got no choice," Bobby finally mumbled.

Bobby turned to see what was causing the spewing of laughter behind him. Christopher and Sidney's sides seemed to be splitting with agony, and he glared at them as they stumbled back into Apartment "A", where he and Sidney lived. He rolled his eyes when Donna giggled about his friends being big party boys.

He hurriedly emptied the contents of the car with the gracefulness of a steel worker handling angle iron. As he finished, he felt Donna's hands rubbing his back through his shirt, sopping wet with sweat. He pivoted away from her and headed back to Apartment "A." Bobby found Sidney and Christopher rolling on the floor, howling at the ceiling, and he was mad as hell.

"You think this is funny?" The laughter started all over again and continued until they looked drained.

"So. Was that the girl?" asked Sidney.

"Hell no, it's her roommate. If I'd known that ugly broad was part of the package, they'd be livin' some place else."

"So where's the bombshell?" Christopher said.

"She's working. I'll tells you this, I'm not gonna deal with that roommate. That lard-ass woman already 'vited me for supper."

"So what did you tell her?"

"I told her I don't eat."

Bobby turned red as Sidney started chuckling. "What do you mean you don't eat, everybody eats."

"Not with that overgrowed heifer."

Donna became Bobby's misery. Most evenings, after work, Paula had a date or some other plans. Donna was always around. Bobby figured out she learned his schedule and committed his phone number to memory. She shadowed him and ruthlessly ignored his insults. She was sucking the air out of Bobby.

"Listen, Donna, I gots to run this apartments... you know, collecting rents can get ugly, and you might want to gets out of the way."

"But, Bobby, let me talk to your delinquent people. All they need is a sweet voice and pat on the back. I'll get your money for you. I like being a part of your life."

"Go on back to your own place. I'm the manager here and don't want your help."

"Well, you think about it... honey."

But Bobby couldn't get Paula out of his mind. He overlooked Donna's irritation for the chance of connecting. Occasionally, Bobby would catch Paula at home. Her polite, sensual voice made Bobby think she had a thing for him. Bobby knew dropping by piqued Donna's passion, but it was worth the risk.

"Bobby, why don't you grab a bowl of this great cabbage and beef soup Donna fixed. Just sit over there by the TV with her. I've got some things to do."

"That's alright; I'll just sit here and watch you eat."

Donna drummed in. "Oh, Bobby, you big old teddy bear, I'll fix you a bowl. You sit right down here beside me, and we'll stay out of her way."

Bobby's revolving circus was keeping Sidney and Christopher in stitches. His nightly update seemed like the highlight of the day for the two.

"Think this is some kinda soap operation, or whatever them shows are called? I oughta bust both your chops if you got nothin' better to do than hee-haw at my stinkin' luck."

Despite the fact their dickering in his love life was irritating, he couldn't help noticing Sidney, for the first time, laughing and acting happy. Bobby found it refreshing.

Bluff Park was not really a park but rather a winding road along the top of a mountain ridge, overlooking the skyline of Birmingham. Along the way, there were lots of stops for no-cost romance, and the Shades Mountain overlook opened up beyond a tree line. Bobby asked to borrow Sidney's car one evening, without a lot of explaining. Bobby was glad when Sidney asked no questions.

Excitement rose as Bobby navigated the Ford along the mountain ridge with the handwritten note in his pocket. The words ran back and forth in his mind, fueling his anticipation.

Dear Bobby,

I think about you a lot, but you know Donna's kind of in the way. If you want to know how I feel about it, meet me at Shades Valley overlook tonight at nine o'clock. You won't be sorry!

Love,

Paula

He bathed and brushed his teeth for the occasion. Every inch of her beautiful body passed through Bobby's imagination. His heart pounded hard inside his chest as he pulled the car along side the Bel Air and stepped through the trees and into the moonlight. A single silhouette appeared below him in the dark, lying on the rocky ledge. He carefully walked down the path leading to her. Big ideas bounced inside his head.

"I want you so bad. Come to me now." He knew that voice.

"What the hell is goin' on?"

"Oh, Bobby, your letter was so sweet. I'm ready for you," Donna sighed. He watched her sit up, rise, and hurry her large frame up the rock to hug him.

"Where's Paula?"

Tears welled up in Donna's eyes. "I thought you cared for me."

"I don't give a shit about you. Your fat ass has been in my way for too long, and I'm takin' care of you once and for all."

Anger inflated Bobby like a balloon. Bobby grabbed the volumes of Donna, threw her over his massive shoulder, and headed for the ledge.

"No," Christopher screamed as he and Sidney jumped from their hiding place to rescue Donna. Sidney could almost feel heat from Bobby's anger which seemed to propel Donna towards the cliff's edge and the deep void beyond it.

"Don't do it," Sidney ordered as they reached grasping range of Bobby's arm.

Their hands, inches from Donna, came up empty as her body fell over the ledge. Her scream of agony followed.

Sidney was pissed with Bobby, but more with himself, and found Bobby sitting on the ledge with his hands over his face.

"Sidney, I'm sorry, man, but why did you hafta do that to me? You know how that woman makes me crazy."

Sidney put his hands on Bobby's shoulders. He knew Bobby was right, and he blamed himself.

Sidney suddenly sobered from the humor of the last month. He needed to deal with the crime scene. Fortunately, there had been no other cars except the Ford and Donna's Chevrolet. He sent Bobby home with Christopher in the Ford. The full moon gave enough light for Sidney to negotiate the cliff face down to the shaking body. He retrieved the handwritten note, which lured Donna to the overlook, along with her car keys. The rocks had injured her badly. She sobbed in pain, and he felt a degree of sorrow. Her only vice had been nothing more than an attraction for Bobby Depew. The injustice of the whole matter swept through his mind as his gloved hands rubbed the sides of her face.

Sidney gently closed his eyes and imagined himself as a six-year-old in the back of the Starlight. A dark shadow filled his head and stoked fires of hatred. With a firm grip and snap of Donna's neck, her suffering ended.

Newly fallen autumn leaves provided good cover. She shouldn't be found for months. Her car was deposited miles from the body, and Sidney walked home in silence and frustration. The next morning Christopher and Sidney retrieved Christopher's vehicle, bought with the I.F. money, from the place where they had hiked to the overlook. Sidney instructed Bobby, in no uncertain terms, to remain in his apartment. Bobby seemed to have learned his lesson.

Sidney needed to know what information Paula had and stayed close to the apartment office. Under the circumstances, it would be better to let her react.

"I haven't seen my roommate since yesterday afternoon. Have you seen her?"

"No, but Bobby was here yesterday. He got sick last night at supper and is still in the apartment. I'll check with him." Sidney invited Paula into unit "A" to speak with Bobby, but warned her she might catch his bug. She stayed in the office. When Sidney returned, he told Paula that Bobby hadn't seen Donna or her car since yesterday afternoon.

"Didn't she tell you where she was going?" Sidney asked.

"No, not a word, but I'm sure she'll be home soon."

Sidney nodded, thinking this good news. "Of course, she will."

Donna's car was towed from a commercial lot the next week. By the time the authorities found the decomposed body, there were no suspects or useful evidence. Paula seemed to grieve for a while, but she was soon engaged to be married and gave notice to move out of the apartment.

With Sidney by his side, Bobby watched as she, for the last time, walked from the office to her fiancé's car. Her hips swayed gently. Sidney could hear Bobby's erratic breathing increasing with each step until Bobby's voice cracked.

"That's one hell of a good-looking woman."

Sidney reached high and patted Bobby on the head. Bobby needed guidance. Lately, he had been a lot of effort with no profits to show for it. *I've got to get my life back on track. Fun is nothing but a distraction for me. It won't happen again.*

Sidney laced up his sneakers and headed out to run his routine ten-mile loop around Vulcan Hill. He felt more in control.

CHAPTER SIX

Birmingham
1959

Christopher's best friend lived near the Gulf Coast in Mobile, Alabama. Jonathan Biggerstaff grew up in Birmingham, and he lived there until age sixteen, when his mother lost her job. She relocated the family to Mobile. Jonathan lost his father at an early age and was raised with four older sisters. Along with their mother, they treated him royally but firmly controlled him. Christopher was Jonathan's escape.

The move caused a tough parting between Christopher and Jonathan. They met in the first grade and became inseparable. Living a block away from each other, they spent almost every day together after school and on weekends exploring life together. They performed in school plays, fished at local ponds, stole cigarettes, and climbed through the challenges of puberty.

Christopher, at the age of twenty-one, weighed less than one-hundred thirty pounds. Jonathan, muscular and dominating, stood six inches taller than Christopher. Jonathan's voice was deep, methodical, and quite persuasive. They called each other weekly and visited when funds allowed. Christopher shared his intense admiration of Sidney with Jonathan.

"Well, then bring Mr. Remarkable on down to the coast."

They made the drive in Sidney's new Cadillac. Christopher's relentless insistence that Sidney meet Jonathan had worn on Sidney's patience. Sidney figured he needed a diversion and could finally satisfy Christopher.

The three dined at a locally owned seafood house recommended by Jonathan. Sidney took a seat facing the crowd. Christopher and Jonathan pulled their chairs close together looking at Sidney. Jonathan's profile, warm brown eyes and wavy dark hair reminded Sidney of a younger version of the television character Perry Mason but with slightly more emotional flair. Jonathan's personality intrigued Sidney. "So what do you do for a living?"

Jonathan chuckled and appeared taken off guard. "You would ask that today, I got my extra fifty bucks."

"For what?"

Jonathan nervously explained for the past eleven months he worked for the Hinson family, who owned and operated a property management business. "This family does very well. The father accumulated over two hundred rental houses and, over the years, they've generated enough money to pay off all of the mortgages. His two sons now pretty much run the business. The father comes in to look at the books once a week. One brother is stealing the family blind, but there's nothing I can do about it."

"What are their names?" asked Sidney.

"Rick Hinson runs the inside office, and his brother Laney does all the outside work."

"So who's the bad guy?"

"It's Rick, my boss."

"How does he do it?"

"Oh, he's a smart guy. I like to think of him as Mr. Carbon Paper."

"So spell it out," Sidney instructed as he leaned back in his chair and watched the two.

Jonathan looked over at Christopher with an unspoken question in his eyes.

How much can I trust this guy?

Christopher nodded his head to Jonathan. Sidney knew he was about to hear an obvious source of stress for Jonathan.

"Okay, Sidney, this is the deal. Rick handles all the lease agreements, takes in rent, and writes receipts. He also does the books. That's what I help him with. He skims ten dollars per unit per month, and this is how he does it. When the lease is signed or receipt is written, he does it with a piece of cardboard behind the carbon. After the tenant leaves, he removes the cardboard and rewrites the amount over the carbon with another sheet of paper in the amount of ten dollars less. The company's copies of leases and receipts all show an amount of ten dollars less than what we actually collect. Almost everybody pays in cash, so Rick slips it into his pocket. Ten bucks doesn't sound like a lot, but with over two hundred units, it adds up to nearly two thousand dollars a month. That's twenty-four thousand a year. That tight bastard figures I know, so he slips me an extra fifty bucks a month over my salary to keep me quiet. It works."

Sidney liked Jonathan. He also liked his employment situation. In the following months, Christopher and Sidney made several trips to Mobile.

A new face entered the downtown storefront of Hinson Properties. The professionally dressed gentleman carried an air of arrogance around him. He walked two steps into the reception area and stopped, while closing the door behind him. Then he pivoted back towards the door and pulled the door-length shade closed.

"Sir, may we help you?" Rick Hinson sounded slightly irritated as the gentleman approached. He stopped at the laminated counter between Rick and him, reached into his back pocket, and laid his identification out for Rick to see.

"Okay... you are the I.R.S.... are you in the market to rent something?"

"No, the I.R.S. is in the market to right a serious wrong."

"What are you talking about?"

"For starters, why don't you show me your carbon of this receipt?" He handed Rick a duplication of the original.

"Listen, you GI, or whatever you call yourself. This is a reputable business owned by a respectable family, and I don't appreciate your blasting in here, pulling down the door shade like we're closed, and demanding a review of our books. My family has connections, and we'll see if your ballistic methods will fly in this town. You think people like the I.R.S.?"

The purported agent watched sweat beading up on the brow of Jonathan Biggerstaff, seated at a desk behind Rick. Jonathan appeared shaken that the I.R.S. agent's position was being neutralized by Rick's politically charged argument.

The agent put his left hand on the counter and confidently leaned his head towards Rick. "You might want to save those words for the judge. Do you remember the new maintenance man your brother Laney hired?"

"So what?"

The agent waited patiently giving Rick time to consider Otis. He knew Rick would recall the new maintenance man leafing through the receipt book for no apparent reason. Since Rick's father looked at it every week, and the receipts matched perfectly with every entry in the balance sheets, Rick would figure Otis harmless.

"Yeah, we know Otis. What of it?"

"It seems that Otis is a little smarter than one would have thought," announced the I.R.S. representative. "He's out in the field with your tenants. Apparently your book work is ten dollars short for every unit you collect."

Sidney Wright was four inches from the eyes of Rick and wasn't blinking. "I am about this far... " holding his thumb and forefinger an inch apart, "...from throwing your sorry ass in jail for about fifteen years." Turning his eyes towards Jonathan, he added, "... and yours for about five."

Jonathan looked guilty, as if he were not a part of the effort. It gave Sidney confidence that he had put fear in the eyes of his own man, and he raised his eyebrows slightly to let Jonathan know he was witnessing a master at work.

"I'll say it once and won't say it again, if you want to screw your family out of twenty-four thousand a year, I don't really care. What I do care about are the taxes, the interest, and the penalties you owe for the last five years. You add it up, and it's about half of what you have swindled your family out of. That makes for a total of sixty thousand dollars. Old Otis gets six thousand. There is this little not well-known provision under federal law that the person who reports a tax fraud gets ten percent. So you can see that Otis is anxious to testify in court if you don't come clean with the money." Sidney strolled his accusatory eyes in a panoramic manner around the scene of the crime waiting for his words to sink in.

"I've checked the courthouse records downtown. You own a townhouse, a beach house and several cars. There are no liens on any of them. Imagine that.

"Come to think of it we can probably march two hundred of your renters into court to testify what they pay you. I suspect they'll keep about a month's rent as their fair share for putting you away. Bet that'll do wonders for your balance sheets."

Sidney watched Rick ponder his predicament, stir his feet on the floor, and rub his neck.

"Surely there are options?" Rick asked.

"You can pay it anyway you like, certified check or cash. The check will be a paper trail for the rest of your family to follow. It makes no difference to the I.R.S. Bottom line is I'll be back in two days. Pay it in cash or check. If I walk out of here in two days empty handed, I'll be headed straight to the F.B.I. and, I can assure you, there won't be any deals. That's your option. Your family can visit you in the pen. That is, if they care to visit you under the circumstances. See you in two days."

The room went quiet as Sidney Wright walked out of the front door after raising the shade he had lowered minutes earlier. After a moment of silence, as directed by Sidney, Jonathan blurted out, "My God, what are we going to do?"

"I'm not going to let that guy intimidate me. Listen, Jonathan, we've got to stick together on this."

"Stick together nothing. That guy scares the hell out of me. I'm not going down on this with you for a lousy fifty a month."

"Where am I going to get sixty thousand?"

"You and I both know you've got it and more. Sounds like a pretty good deal to me. You keep half of what you stole from your family and don't go to jail. What's to think about?"

S idney picked up the cash on the second day. He watched his friends grinning broadly when he divided the money dollars three ways between himself, Jonathan, and the recently resigned "Otis The Maintenance Man," Christopher Bonn.

"Damn, Sidney, I 'bout had a heart attack when you said I was goin' down for five," Jonathan announced in his deep booming voice. Christopher and Jonathan looked at each other with an affection for everyone around the table. Sidney smiled warmly, returning their appreciation, looked at the piles of money among his successful cast, and felt satisfied.

"With your appearance and demeanor, you could easily do the same. The key is confidence and control. We'll work on that," Sidney explained.

In the summer of 1960, Sidney found a buyer for the apartments. After paying off the note, he netted thirteen thousand, five hundred dollars. Since real estate is a matter of public record, he had to pay capital gains. *The Federal Government has done nothing for me to justify these taxes,* he thought, but then smiled, *except maybe the Department of Defense and the I.R.S. Sometimes the willingness to pay taxes is nothing more than a state of mind.*

Sidney convinced the new apartment owners to keep Bobby on to run the place. Bobby got a salary, unit "A" to stay in, and didn't have to work too hard. Sidney would keep close tabs on Bobby.

Between occasional poker games and prudent investments, by the fall of 1960, Sidney Wright had a net worth of over fifty-three thousand dollars. He wanted more.

CHAPTER SEVEN

New Orleans
1960

Jonathan Biggerstaff quickly worked his way up the ranks at New Orleans' premier auction house, Moet-Danielle. It was becoming well known for its international offerings of art. Moet-Danielle's New Orleans' location was in the warehouse district down by the river. Items submitted for auction came from all corners of the world.

By October, Jonathan's dedication to this French company landed him the position of Assistant Storage Manager. Every piece of art delivered to the auction house was required to be accompanied by its owner or a designated agent. Each piece was inspected by the storage manager or his assistant and assigned a check-in number, which was posted at a non-compromising place on the item. It was then assigned to an individual security locker and locked by the storage manager while in the presence of the owner or agent.

The three hours before the start of the auction were known as the inspection period. All potential buyers were afforded an opportunity to view each item and read its credentials. Depending upon the overall size of the auction, some fifteen to thirty security guards were used during the transport, inspection, and actual auction processes.

The last Monday in October 1960 developed into a seventy-five-lot event, comprised mostly of original oils from Europe. The pre-auction estimates averaged $93,000 per submitted item. The premier piece was a van Gogh self-portrait, which had a pre-auction estimate of between two and three million dollars. Every item was afforded the established security measures. However, two security guards accompanied the van Gogh. Jean Moet, head of the New Orleans house, personally locked the van Gogh in its storage cell in the presence of the owner's representatives with Jonathan watching at a distance. It was the finest piece ever offered by Moet-Danielle at its American venue.

Jonathan arrived at twelve noon the day of the October auction. He had become friends with the Head Storage Manager, Mick Shaw, who was the only person other than Jean with a master key to the secured lockers. Mick took a real liking to Jonathan. The day before the auction, Jonathan treated him to lunch at one of Mick's favorite restaurants in the French Quarter.

Security was tight for employees going in and out of the auction house. Every person, without exception, was searched upon leaving the complex. Employees were also subject to search on arrival. Most new or unfamiliar faces were routinely searched going in. Usually, the regulars were waved through. Jonathan had become a familiar face.

As Jonathan arrived at the transport area, he was instructed to report to Mr. Moet's office. He quickly strolled to his own small office, removed his jacket and its contents, and placed them carefully out of sight behind his desk. Jonathan then left for Jean's office. As he approached, he saw Jean motioning him with his arms. "Jonathan, I just got a call from Mick. He's sick. There couldn't have been a worse day for this to happen."

"What's wrong with Mick?" Jonathan asked.

"Some kind of stomach virus. He can't get out of bed. The situation looks like this... you're in charge of transport. I'm up to my eyeballs, catering to these high rollers interested in the van Gogh. I can't tell you how big this auction is to our house. We stand to earn a considerable commission. We may be looking at fifteen percent of over ten million. This has to go without a hitch. Can you handle this?"

Jonathan looked sincerely at Jean. "Mick's trained me well. I'll be on my toes, and you don't need to worry about a thing." Jean looked relieved as Jonathan took the master security key and resumed his duties. Jonathan felt a warm growing sense of control.

The auction house regularly used the Smith Security Agency for its guards. Although proper I.D. was required and background checks were done, the criteria for employment was not that high since Smith didn't pay much. This was the perfect situation for Bobby Depew. Bobby lived just off Julia Street, right outside the warehouse district in a lower to middle class neighborhood. When he applied with the Smith Agency, they assigned him to the auction house. He could walk to work since he had no transportation. Bobby worked various hours as needed. Everybody was needed at the October auction. Bobby arrived that afternoon at 1:30. He was searched going in and would certainly be searched coming out.

Jonathan stayed busy tending to every detail of the transport that afternoon. The auction would start at 7:00, the inspection period would open at 4:00 and the transport would take place between 3:15 and 3:55. The route between the storage facility and the auction floor was a tunnel with several turns.

One of the difficult pieces, expected to bring less than ten thousand dollars, was a six-foot ornate Japanese vase with no handles, light in weight, but extremely awkward to carry. Jonathan assigned two workers to move the vase. "A dolly might cause too much vibration," he explained to the workers. One security guard would accompany the two men. Bobby Depew was chosen by Jonathan to secure the move.

At 3:15, Jonathan announced that transport would begin. There was a distance of about a hundred yards to travel between the security lockers and the auction house floor. Initially, a few paintings were unlocked from their lockers and transported according to plan. The vase was next. Jonathan stood with his arms crossed and watched as the two men held it gingerly, and Bobby Depew followed behind, almost at their heels.

At the first turn, Bobby's toes clipped at the back of the carriers' shoes. Bobby shouted, "what the hell you doin'?" as the vase slipped from their hands. Bobby made a feeble attempt to catch it, intertwining his arms with the others', but the vase hit the smooth concrete floor, shattering the piece into a multitude of worthlessness.

Bobby grabbed his walkie-talkie. "We've got a security 'mergency at turn "A" in transport. Get over here. We need help right now." Most guards and auction house staff heard the announcement. An argument was occurring between Bobby and the rear holder of the vase.

"You tripped me, you son of a bitch."

"No way, I was three feet behind you."

A melee was occurring at turn "A." Before it was over, Jean himself was at the scene of the breakage, trying to inject calmness in the chaos. Explaining the broken vase to the owner and those who came to bid on it would be difficult. Things were not going well.

From the initial sound of broken glass, Jonathan had to work quickly. He unlocked the original van Gogh, removed it, and relocked the locker. Returning to his office, he closed the door and slipped the reproduction van Gogh out of the lining of his jacket. From the top of his desk, he performed the operation he'd practiced over fifty times in his apartment. With a razorblade, he carefully cut the backing out and removed the original van Gogh. The reproduction, which had cost Sidney Wright $8,000, was precisely placed by Jonathan into the frame. An identical backing was installed, and a forged check-in seal was set in place. The newly altered van Gogh was returned to its secure storage unit. The vase episode was still unfolding. No one had noticed what Jonathan had done.

Jonathan was waiting by the time Jean made his appearance and he followed Jean around until the management proclamation that order had been restored. Jonathan assured him that everything was under control and apologized about the vase.

"Not a problem, ole buddy, just a bump in the road of an auction house."

Jonathan knew he would be dealt with later on the strange manner he used to transport the vase. He stood back submissively as Jean himself, with six guards, unlocked, removed, and carried the van Gogh through transport.

Jonathan continued to move items, and by the end of the process, most of the security force was on the floor with the van Gogh. Jonathan pulled an insignificant painting by a relatively unknown Spanish painter named Batiste. The painting was one inch wider and an inch and a half longer than the van Gogh. Back in his office, Jonathan laid the original van Gogh over the back of the Batiste. He reapplied an additional backing and performed the same procedure with the check in seal.

By 3:55, Jonathan had seen that all items were on the floor, with the exception of the vase, and ready for the 4:00 inspection. By 7:00, most guests were registered and ready for bidding. The auction lasted until 10:45. As advertised, the van Gogh was sold at 8:00. The bidding was furious between a dozen collectors. Finally, a Swiss investment group prevailed at 2.75 million American dollars.

Security was particularly tight that evening as employees left the auction house.

"Sorry, Jonathan, everybody gets the pat-down. Moet's orders," the guard said as Jonathan raised his hands to be searched.

"Yep, you boys be careful. Check everybody. This has been one hell of a night," Jonathan said as he sighed.

"Okay, you're clean. Have a good night."

Jonathan smiled as he walked off the property. His part of the plan had gone perfectly. The following day the newspapers in Paris called the van Gogh price a bargain, and Jonathan's sides ached with laughter as he read them.

Sidney Wright had been seated near the middle of the bidding crowd. He knew the approximate value of every item being offered. He made several bids to keep up appearances. His bids came early in the process, and he'd back off to let other bidders take the gavel. He never intended to be the winning bidder, except on the Batiste.

Sidney knew of only one other bidder in attendance that had an interest in the piece. The pre-auction estimate was fifty-two hundred dollars. Sidney would prevail on that item. The opening bid was for a thousand dollars by the other interested party. The auctioneer took increasing bids in five hundred dollar increments. Sidney did not want to appear too aggressive and hesitated before each raising bid. The competition bailed out at forty-five hundred dollars, and Sidney took the prize for an even five thousand.

Sidney knew well the problem with art theft is that the market involves only a handful of players. Quickly converting a piece with the profile and caliber of the van Gogh would be nearly impossible. He was surprised that it took six months before the Swiss group discovered the painting was a reproduction. It was actually a visiting art student who proclaimed that it was not the original. The investment group was not only outraged, but embarrassed as well. It became public knowledge that the Swiss group would pursue a claim against Moet-Danielle.

Sidney followed the headlines daily. Litigation was filed and the House issued denials. "It was authentic when it left our auction premises," a press release maintained. Three years later, after a heated legal battle, a jury returned a verdict of 1.35 million to the disgruntled buyers.

As Sidney predicted, Jonathan was discharged over the vase incident. Somebody had to be the scapegoat, and it wasn't likely to be a Moet.

The week following the theft, Sidney greeted Jonathan on a Caribbean Island and paid him fifteen thousand dollars for his fine efforts. To Sidney's surprise, Christopher arrived unannounced to celebrate the success. Sidney couldn't help but laugh as Bobby

Depew's large frame awkwardly exited the small opening of the crop-dusting plane that brought Bobby to the island.

"Well, Bobby, did you get fired by the Smith Agency?"

"Hell, no. They're so hard up for people they wanted me to stay, so I just quit... told 'em I was afraid they wanted me to pay for the vase."

Sidney placed a stack of one-hundred-dollar bills in Bobby's hand, and Bobby looked around for an open bar.

Sidney Wright's liquid assets in November of 1960 were forty-five thousand dollars. The art project had involved the highest overhead of any prior effort. His non-liquid asset was another story. Sidney knew he had to exercise extreme caution. Between the disappointed buyers, the auction house, and its insurer, the heat would be turned up high and long. After all, as a reporter in the south of France queried, "where the hell is the original?"

It was no time to be engaged in a new project, nor a time to test the waters for potential purchasers of the van Gogh. It was time for Sidney to reflect.

Until the next project, Sidney decided that Bobby would return to Birmingham and resume his Vulcan Apartment manager position. The new owners had agreed to hold it for him while he was on extended leave. Sidney felt he knew the work and should be able to stay out of trouble.

Jonathan was instructed to secure a position at a competing auction house. Mick had promised him a good recommendation. That way, Jonathan would be near the trade and could pass on information to Sidney as needed.

In the weeks before he sent his comrades on their ways, Sidney took the time to create a special bond between them all. He treated them to a lifestyle unknown to any of them before. They ate, drank, and played.

The interaction gave Sidney an opportunity to analyze each man's strengths and weaknesses. It concerned him that Bobby tended to drink excessively when money was no object. But Bobby's entire life had been a collection of excesses.

Christopher and Jonathan were different. He couldn't quite put his finger on it, but the two interacted almost with perfect precision, as if they were actors in a well-scripted play.

He deeply believed that the dedication of his group would continue because he would make them all rich. *Much money commands much loyalty.* That loyalty prevailed as the years marched on, adding to Sidney's wealth. He looked forward to the day when he would have enough.

CHAPTER EIGHT

New York
1973

S idney Wright carefully cradled a plain grocery bag in his left arm entering the Wall Street offices of Corey Baker. He could see Corey standing stoically at the end of the hall as if he'd been waiting all day. Sidney grinned and nodded confidently at his partner in crime as the receptionist lead him down the elegant corridor.

"Let's take a drive." Corey nervously shifted his eyes around the office in a way Sidney knew Corey's credibility was thinning among the staff.

Corey drove the Ford Galaxy southward along Broadway, and Sidney slowly pulled out rolled-up scraps of newspaper from the top of the bag exposing piles of hundred dollar bills.

Corey chuckled. "Sidney, what a marvelous analysis you wrote on Picket Medical. I never made so much money for just signing my name. If you ever need a job... what am I saying? As much money as you'll make off Picket, you can buy your own Wall Street firm."

"You sound skeptical of the accuracy of our little article."

"It was the most brilliant bunch of bullshit I ever read. Sure Picket is losing money, sure they have management problems, and sure their books are in a mess. But that's all you talked about in the company review. You didn't bother to mention that their hard assets are worth twice the total of every share of stock. After that article, how many shares did you pick up?"

"Enough."

"Enough for what?"

"To call it my own."

"Do you know that the contingent assets in the form of unpaid hospital bills go in the hundreds of million?"

Sidney acted surprised that Corey asked the question. "A hundred and seventy three million to be exact. Twenty-six percent of it is collectible."

"It's mind boggling, you can't lose."

"It's best not to talk like that. You can always lose. Remember the horses, Corey?"

"You're right, and I'd never have signed that review of Picket Medical if I hadn't been up to my eyeballs in losses from playing those four-legged bandits. My financial analysis career will take some hits over this. I'll recover, but remember this, never again."

"There's enough in this bag to smooth out your ruffled feathers."

Sidney pushed over the cash as he stepped from the car parked by the waterfront.

"Sidney."

Sidney turned slowly, knowing what was next. Corey caressed the green between his fingers.

"This money isn't all about me. My staff's going to get a really nice bonus out of this bag."

"That's nice, Corey. I'm sure it'll make all of you feel better."

The corporate headquarters of Picket Medical was located three blocks west of the financial district. Sidney purposely waited two days after acquiring the controlling interest of the company before confronting the management.

"Mr. Wright, what a pleasure to see you. You've created quite a stir coming into our little family on such short notice. How can I help you?"

"By showing me central files and leaving."

"Leaving what?"

"This building."

"Surely you're kidding?"

"Look at my eyes. Do you see any humor in them?"

"But sir, I've been running this company for twelve years. You'll need me; we're on the verge of a huge turnaround. The investing community's got us pegged wrong. We've got a good management team here. In fact, we were about to meet. Will you please join us?"

"You can meet on the street, because they'll be right behind you. Your last item of business is to clear entry for the three gentlemen in the lobby. That's my management team or, in this case, disassembly team. I'm going to sell it off piece by piece."

"Sir, you don't have a clue what that would do to this company. There are loyal employees with families, long-term patients, people who depend on me, depend on this company. You won't be able to look yourself in the mirror."

"This is the last thing I'll say to you, my friend. You had twelve years to get it right. If you had, you wouldn't be in this mess. Quit depending on this company and learn to depend on yourself. I don't waste time looking in the mirror. I look in my checkbook. Now hit the road."

Sidney's team worked with the precision of a surgeon, harvesting everything of value to the highest bidder. Accounts receivables were marketed to financial institutions. Machinery and equipment went to competitors.

Nursing home patients soon discovered their agreements were assignable. Patients in facilities all over the country were sold like cattle with no legal recourse but to go along to the facility that bought their papers.

Many stepped up to rescue the victims of Sidney Wright. Social workers and politicians called for revisions of the laws.

But the outcry could only affect the future. On paper, his actions were perfectly legal.

Millions upon millions were siphoned from the company. The plan clicked along like a fine pocket-watch, until nothing was left of the company but what couldn't be sold, what nobody wanted.

"Why can't we get rid of this Evergreen facility and who the hell named it that?" Sidney shouted angrily as Christopher and Jonathan haggled with the accountants.

Christopher answered, "It's because Picket was being neighborly, a benevolence. They opened a nursing home for indigents. They have the same contractual rights as the paying patients."

"You think? Even I know it takes consideration in the form of money to bind us to any future care."

"We know, Sidney, the lawyers said the same thing, but even the sleaziest said we'd be damned fools to put these patients on the street. We can't be totally without a conscience."

"Then watch me. Where the hell is Evergreen?"

"Chicago."

Sidney jogged up the dingy steps leading to the third floor office of lawyer Roy Ergle. The opaque glass in the entry door rattled as Sidney walked in.

Two children rolled around on the dirty vinyl floor pretending to be some version of a salesman and customer. From a back room an irritated voice vibrated through the offices.

"I was broke and stole the brooch from my mother-in-law. Less than three days later, I had the damn thirty bucks back to the pawn shop."

"Did you read what you signed?"

"Hell, no. Aren't there some laws? My mother-in-law says the piece is worth eight thousand."

"Does she live with you?"

"No, we live with her."

"That doesn't sound stolen. Sounds like you had what the law says is constructive possession."

"So why does the pawn shop make me talk to you?"

"Because I know the law, and the pawn shop thinks you should too before you make a mistake."

"So how about the brooch?"

"Contract says $795 as long as you pay it back in the first year."

"$795 on a thirty dollar loan?"

"You're high risk, maybe a thief by your own admission. Maybe you should hold on to your money for the rest of the year and pick up the jewelry then."

"I can't. My ass is boiling in hot water, and I need it back now."

"So why are you quibbling over a few hundred bucks if the piece is worth eight thousand?"

"This is highway robbery, but I've got the money in my pocket."

"Good. Go back to the pawn shop. I'll make the phone call, and they'll have it out before you get there."

Sidney knew he was where he needed to be as the flustered father gathered his children and left the law office.

"Who's next?" shouted the lawyer.

Sidney strolled in and sat in the shabby chair in front of the lawyer's desk. He laid his three-ring binder checkbook on top of the desk and started writing.

"We don't usually see the dressed-up type like you. What did you pawn?"

"Actually, Mr. Lawyer, I think you pawned your soul years ago and the price has gotten so high that even you can't afford to redeem it."

"Then what are you doing here, and why are you writing a check?"

"Because, even though you don't know it, you're now working for me."

"Is that what you think? I pick my own clients, and I'm damn good at what I do."

"You're good at trashing people's lives without batting an eye, and that is exactly why you're going to work for me." Sidney handed the lawyer the check.

Sidney waited while the lawyer looked down at the check, and his Adam's apple started bouncing up and down.

"So, when do I start?"

Sidney sat in his West Indies mansion surrounded by newspapers covering the eviction of patients at Evergreen. Palm tree branches rattled in the wind as he turned pages and pondered Lawyer Ergle's progress.

Sidney's position was solid, the only way his new lawyer was getting away with the daily rolling out of patients into the streets of Chicago with no family to claim them. All were being picked up as wards of the State of Illinois.

The press announced there was no more room in any state facilities due to the huge supply of indigent patients exiting Evergreen, and he relished the idea of no one being able to legally touch him. But he questioned Ergle's stability, and he decided to go to Chicago to watch the last of the evictions.

Sidney donned a black cashmere overcoat as he walked up the steps of the nearly vacated Evergreen building. He already had a fifteen million dollar offer for it.

He watched his lawyer smiling broadly, hurriedly bounding down the steps to meet him.

"The very last one is coming out now. You got what you wanted, an empty building".

A stretcher with rollers, pushed by a nun, slowly descended on the concrete ramp running along the steps. Sidney noticed the figure stretched across the bed was crying. He couldn't tell if it was pain or sadness, but he felt strangely drawn towards them.

The crying woman was layered with horrible scarring.

"Do I know you?" the lady asked, looking up at him through her tear-laden eyes.

"You've probably seen my face in the newspaper, but you don't know me."

"I don't read newspapers. I knew you long ago. I don't forget a person's eyes."

"I don't live around here, you're mistaken."

"I'm sure this man is too busy to waste his time with us, Aunt Mary," the nun said with a layer of skepticism.

"Where are you taking this patient?" Sidney asked.

"There's nowhere. She'll go to the public shelter and probably die. I would take her with me, but there's no room with the other nuns."

Sidney looked at the patient's burn-scarred skin and felt a sharp pain of recognition. He glanced at the plastic armband around the lady's arm. "Mary Hughes."

"How long has she been here?" Sidney asked the nun.

"Since her accident. She was a nun too, my father's sister."

"What happened to her?"

"She worked helping young people around the streets of the mission down on W. Armitage Street after the Second World War. She did that until this happened."

"What happened?"

"The fire. She talks of it like yesterday. A terrible fire in a building a couple of doors down from the mission. She tells me she got up in the middle of the night to sounds of firemen and screams and smoke."

"What else did she tell you?" Sidney asked, feeling empty.

The lady on the stretcher took over the conversation, speaking in a shaking, broken voice.

"There was this boy... this precious child living in that brothel. He needed me."

"What boy?" Sidney asked the question but wasn't sure he wanted the answer.

"A child with a good heart, full of love. I couldn't let him die in that fire, so I went in after him."

Sidney looked back up at the niece. "How bad was it?"

"She hasn't been able to walk since. She lies in bed all day. It's a pity. She had so much to give."

"Can I see your eyes again?" the lady on the stretcher asked.

Leaning his head forward, Sidney felt warmth beaming from Sister Mary's face. "You did get out, didn't you? I didn't fail God."

Sidney nodded. Sister Mary was his nun. *The only one who cared.*

He watched Sister Mary's contented eyes roll back as she passed into her eternity. He closed his own eyes as the niece cried.

Sidney's reflection was broken as the lawyer came from behind, gloating over his success.

Sidney gently grabbed the niece's arm. "Your aunt was right; she did once know me. She gave me hope at a time when I thought I needed hope, and I owe her."

"Why would you, of all people, owe my aunt?"

"It's not why; it's what, a debt." Sidney grabbed Roy Ergle from behind his shoulder, sharply, almost rudely, and pulled him to the niece. "This lawyer is going to write you a check for a million dollars. It's yours to do whatever you think your aunt would want. The debt is settled. Sorry for your loss. Good day."

In the year 1975 a simple brown paper package arrived in Detroit at the residence of Mrs. Harold Brown. It contained $1,378.42 in cash, plus interest, and one man's gold wedding ring. There was no return address. The package arrived several days after the funeral of Mrs. Brown and sat unclaimed as a memorial to emotions unexpressed.

Raindrops splattered on the stone steps sending a spray upon the aging paper as a young thief eyed the obviously abandoned package. The contents he would find wouldn't tell the story of a couple that became heartbroken with the loss of what they considered a son and how their misjudgment of his character caused them to abandon retirement. The original wearer of the ring had continued to run the grocery until he died nineteen years later from a heart attack while lifting a case of frozen chicken.

The package would not reveal the secret that died with Mrs. Brown years after losing her husband. A day never went by at the grocery that Harold didn't gaze up Elizabeth Street, hoping for the return of a remorseful Sidney Wright. His wife stood close behind him.

The few dollars that a pawnshop would yield for the circle of gold wouldn't reflect that the mailing was not of remorse, but rather of a due debt. At least, that's how Sidney Wright justified it.

Sidney figured it would take many years to liquidate the van Gogh for anywhere near its value. He had no idea that nineteen years would pass before he would sell the painting. There were times when Sidney wanted to break from his carefully developed theories on proper handling of the piece. He didn't. In the final analysis, in 1979, Sidney Wright sold the van Gogh to an independently wealthy collector who had no desire for outsiders to know he was the owner. The buyer had the resources and the personal love of van Gogh's work to pay the quietly marketed price of twelve and a half million. The price was paid in certified funds as Sidney Wright directed. The van Gogh self-portrait had surely appreciated over those nineteen years.

He matured both intellectually and physically over the time frame leading to the liquidation and felt a great pride in being patient and methodical. His only obsession was exercise. He demanded of himself the daily pushing of his body beyond what most could tolerate. The forests and beaches of the West Indies' Island he called home were his gym, spa, and physical playground. He mirrored strength with no gray hairs and no excess fat.

He traveled only when necessary and conducted, in varying combinations, operations involving Jonathan, Bobby, and Christopher. Occasionally, other operatives were used, but their inside information was limited to a need-to-know basis.

He recruited each new operative carefully, a honed skill he first learned back at the Starlight. By merely watching people over a period of time, he could tell if they were for sale.

Balance, a word and concept, became Sidney's friend and vocation. *It's an island from which to strike against most who are polarized towards their emotions,* he told himself. Balance gave him stability. Only once did he feel he strayed.

"Who's Rosie?" the Caribbean-tanned servant, trusted for many years, asked.

Sidney looked up from the luscious native fruit luncheon plate. "Ask your question once again."

"Boss mon, you be sayin' it all the time when you sleep. I worry. You seem troubled."

Sidney rose from his untouched plate and excused his faithful help. The comment finally explained the sweaty scalp he felt most mornings upon awakening. *Why do I still think of my mother? What possible reason? There is none. It's not balanced. She's not in the equation.* He fell upon the bed, contemplating his life and, subconsciously, reached for a pillow that was not there.

Before receiving the proceeds of the van Gogh, Sidney had amassed millions. Even without the painting, he could have lived comfortably on his well-invested money. For the past nineteen years, he had plenty of time to research and reflect. He subscribed to all notable publications and was well read in most areas. He also studied international law, advanced business theory, and personal behavioral sciences. Behavioral sciences interested him the most.

He meticulously developed dozens of project conceptions. He kept coming back to one of them. Sidney certainly didn't need to work. He thought, *more than I can ever spend. Maybe it's time to retire.*

CHAPTER NINE

Greenville, South Carolina
September 4, 1980
9:15 a.m.

Josh Rankin walked up the granite steps of the Commerce Building in downtown Greenville. He exited the elevator on the third floor which was entirely occupied by the law firm of Roberts, Justin, and Tower. The bluish hue of the Italian marble floor and highly polished walnut paneled walls caught Josh's eye. The rubber soles of his deck shoes squeaked as he approached the reception desk. With a polite smile, a middle-aged lady pivoted towards him in her rotating chair.

"My name is Josh Rankin. I'm here to see Jordan Tower."

"Yes, Mr. Rankin, we're expecting you. Have a seat. His legal assistant will join you shortly."

His trim, muscular body fell backwards into an overstuffed chair, and he exhaled a deep breath. Less than twelve hours ago his wife gave him the ultimatum. He started the morning driving aimlessly in his car. Not knowing what to do, he called his best friend Austin Clemmons and explained his family problems.

"Look, man, I'm feeling for you, but you don't need me... you need real help... real good help. I've got a name for you. Tower. The guy's got a major reputation for working miracles, and it sounds like you need one."

Josh took the phone number from Austin over the car phone and was surprised to secure an appointment within the hour.

A pleasant lady approached Josh, led him into a private office, and brought him coffee. She handed him a lengthy information form. He pulled a chair up to a small desk with a dozen or more pens sticking out of a leaded-glass container. The paper shook slightly in his hands as he began to read.

The questionnaire requested usual information such as name, address, and phone number but went into areas Josh found strange. He filled out the form anyway, because it was stamped "confidential" on the top of every page, and remembered something in a seminar about a lawyer's ethical duty to a client. He wrote down he worked as an independent sales representative of chemical products, gave his marital status, listed all the names and addresses of extended family members, along with who referred him to the law firm. He fumbled through his wallet as he listed numbers for all personal and business phones, credit cards, bank accounts, and social security. He felt exhausted by the time he finish and reached for the small china coffee cup sitting on a hand-painted oriental tray. The door opened from behind and he jolted, splattering cold coffee on the white paper. The lady gathered the papers and escorted him into Mr. Tower's office.

Jordan Tower sat behind a magnificent mahogany desk with maple inlay. The desk, elevated above Josh's chair, put Tower in a superior position looking downward, and Josh felt his authority.

"How may I help you?"

"I've got a problem with my marriage."

Tower chuckled. "Don't we all?"

Josh didn't appreciate the sarcasm, but he went on to explain that his wife Terri was eight months pregnant with their first child. Josh related the events of last night. "Terri found a condom in my pocket and jumped me about it. I had no answer... she knew... I knew she knew. "

"Knew what?"

"I was cheating."

"...and you told her?"

"One woman, for only six months. It was the truth." Josh sighed in frustration. "The problem's my own stupid-ass fault. We shared an intimate secret, and Angie would never have told anybody. I blew it by leaving a condom in my pocket. Funny thing is, I don't even remember putting it there."

"What did Terri say?"

"Very little. This upset her more than I'd ever expected."

"You didn't answer my question. What did she say?"

"She sat for an hour and a half in the study. She's crazy that way... closes herself up somewhere until she reaches some off-the-wall decision and never changes her mind. Then she told me I had two days to make up my mind. If I'd walk away, just chunk her and our child, I could have all of our money, the house, the boat, furniture... all of it."

"What's the value of all that?"

"Probably a couple million."

"What possible reason would she have to give you money and assets for breaking up the marriage?"

"She wants me out. Totally."

"How would she live?"

"Sorry. I'm getting way ahead of myself."

Josh caught his breath and began detailing the facts. Terri's maiden name was Lippard, as in Lippard Industries. Tower mentioned that Lippard had reportedly been bought out by International Textiles. Josh nodded his head and went on to explain Terri's father, Charlie, was the owner and the second generation to head the company.

"Her father's dying, has probably six months to live, some bad heart disease. Terri's mother died last year, real sad."

"Does Terri have any siblings?"

"She has one brother, a couple of years older, who worked in the company and never amounted to much. His father made up a job for him. People know him as Chip, but his name is actually Charles, after his father. But he couldn't run the company or anything else for that matter. He's been an embarrassment to the family. But he's still a pretty nice guy, the only one who shows me any respect."

"So how much was the sales price of Lippard Industries?" Tower asked loudly as if it was of paramount importance.

"I don't know the details, but it must have been a bunch."

Josh watched as Tower pushed a button on his desk, and a lady appeared to freshen Josh's coffee and to lay a tray of Danish before him.

"I'll be back in a minute. I want to check something."

As he left, Josh noticed the lawyer was impeccably dressed and would probably be very expensive to hire.

After ten minutes, he returned. "I've just spoken to a financial source. Mr. Rankin, your wife stands to inherit fifty percent of eight billion dollars."

"Man... those numbers are way bigger than even I'd have guessed."

Josh sat up straight as Tower began asking specific questions about the forty-eight-hour deadline Terri had set and noted twenty-five percent of it was gone.

"Don't you suppose your wife shared your little secret with friends or maybe her father?"

"Nope. Not a chance."

"How do you know? Why do you say that with such confidence?"

"I know her better than... listen, she has this stubborn streak... if she says forty-eight hours, count on it. She won't say anything until I make a decision. If I take her offer, she'll probably never repeat any of this. But, I'll be history."

"You want to be history?"

"No, but I like the idea of our marriage being private."

"Except Angie," said Tower.

Josh groaned a little. "Well, I guess so."

"What makes you think that this will not all pass? She'll forgive you, and you'll get on with your happy lives."

"I tried to talk to her, to apologize, to put this behind us and, well, she wouldn't listen. I watched her sit in the study. Her face was stern and determined, clay-like. She never cut her eyes or took a break. Her mind is made up, trust me. I'll either take her offer, or she'll fight me."

"Unfortunately, Mr. Rankin, between four billion and maybe a couple of million, it won't be a fair fight. However, there may be a better way."

"How's that?"

"How serious are you about keeping your child?"

"Very serious," Josh said. *Now we're going to find out how good Austin Clemmons' lawyer is.* Josh smugly thought to himself as he leaned back and crossed his legs.

"There may be some alternatives to your problem."

"What do you mean by alternatives, and how much does it cost? You need to understand that I've got very little in cold cash."

"There is help for your situation. It's called Family Intervention." Tower repeated the name like he was announcing the President to Congress.

"Family Intervention, what kind of help is that? It sounds like an adoption center or something."

"Don't read too much into the name. Just trust that it is completely adequate to address your problems. Are you interested in exploring this, Mr. Rankin?"

Josh hesitated, rubbed his chin, and felt puzzled as he answered. "Yeah, I guess."

"Family Intervention is a specialty firm. It helps a select few. If you are lucky enough to become a client, you'll be amazed at its resources and innovation. I've now told you all that I'm permitted to say about what may be the most unique opportunity in the international community, an opportunity that now sits in your lap."

Josh uncrossed his legs and leaned forward. "Well, I must say this all sounds intriguing. I like the idea of making the problem go away."

Tower nodded, stood and began to bark orders rapidly. "Here are your instructions. First of all, you owe me no fee. In fact, you are not now and never will be a client of this firm. All records of this visit will simply not exist. You need to leave this building. Go out the front door. You'll be on Jefferson Avenue. Forget about your car. Give me the keys, and the vehicle will be delivered to you later. Go right a quarter of a mile until you see Brownlee's Deli on the right. Outside there are two patio tables. At one of the tables, a gentleman with a navy blazer and a pink handkerchief in the front coat pocket will be seated. Have a seat at his table, and he will introduce himself as Paul. Paul will take very good care of you from there."

"Whoa. Why is there such a rush that I can't get my car and make arrangements? I'm a businessman. I don't rush into any decision."

"Mr. Rankin, the deadline was not set by me, but rather between you and your wife. I take you at your word that in less than thirty-six hours your life could be materially changed. If you are not serious about this, then go home and best of luck to you. Quite frankly, I have a dozen jilted spouses to tend to. If you question my experience or advice, you won't hurt my feelings. Good day, Mr. Rankin."

The look on Tower's face, before he turned his back, rattled Josh, throwing him off balance. The dejection caused him to think quickly.

"No, no," Josh interjected, "Austin Clemmons sent me here. He said you're the best; push me in the right direction. I guess I should be grateful. Take my keys; I'm on my way to Brownlee Deli."

Josh promptly left the building, dragging his emotions onto Jefferson Avenue. He quickly strolled his solid one hundred sixty-pound frame along the sidewalk. His long, but well-groomed, golden hair flowed gently in the breeze behind the collar of his yellow, starched, button-down Oxford shirt. The color complemented his smooth tanned skin, and he caught several ladies stealing a casual glance as he walked.

Josh's excitement rose with each step. Thoughts of letting some company fix his marital problems troubled him. But after hearing about all the money and how it would clobber him in court, his thoughts shifted and his steps quickened. *Billions of dollars, and all I get are some scraps and don't get to see my own child.* He wrestled with the injustice. He hadn't realized the vastness of her wealth. *All over a stupid rubber.*

He flashed his soft blue eyes around the front, outdoor patio of the Brownlee Deli, and found the first table empty. A man reading a newspaper occupied the second table. As Josh approached, the man lowered the paper, exposing the pink handkerchief. He took a seat and watched the gentleman slowly fold the newspaper, set it on the table, and extend his hand. "Hello, I'm Paul. I'd offer you lunch, but we need to be on our way. There are sandwiches and beverages in the car. We'll take a short drive. I'll explain more in the car."

Josh awkwardly followed him to the dark-blue Ford Crown Victoria parked on the street at a two-hour parking meter and noticed that the meter was showing fifteen minutes left, before it would expire. It had been less than an hour and a half since he'd walked into Mr. Tower's law office.

Paul quickly opened the rear passenger door on the curbside as if expecting Josh to jump right in. Facing Paul, Josh stopped with his back to the opening of the door.

"Where are you taking me?"

Paul spoke slowly and clearly. "My instructions are to get you safely to our headquarters as soon as possible. It'll take about an hour and a half and is out in the west countryside. Try to relax, and all your questions will be answered in the next few hours."

Josh sat slowly into the seat, pivoted his legs in, and Paul clicked the door closed.

CHAPTER TEN

Terri Rankin never thought of herself as pretty, but carried herself gracefully. Faithfulness burned in her soul, and she was intensely committed to her friends. She always had money, but friendship started and ended in trust. Terri understood what she was born to, but maturity brought her to believe the value of one's conception shouldn't deliver standing to succeed.

Amanda Loring was Terri's best friend. After high school in Greenville, they both attended a private women's college in Georgia. Early in the first semester Amanda drank herself into bed with a guy and got knocked-up. Terri's heart went out to Amanda when she confessed her pregnancy.

"I'm here for you. We'll get through this together".

"I'm trash."

"You're beautiful; you'll be a beautiful mother."

Terri juggled her studies and gave her constant support. Amanda said her skin crawled every time she saw the father, and Terri couldn't help thinking how foolish Amanda had been. But Terri was not judgmental and guarded Amanda's every step, until she announced she'd abort the baby.

Terri wouldn't talk to her for two days. She harbored disappointment and sadness and couldn't sleep. After her anger subsided, Terri took charge.

"That's okay, if that's what you want. It'll be like flushing the baby down the toilet... problem solved," Terri said, rolling her eyes.

"But what if it looks like him?"

"What if it looks like you and you never knew it?"

"I can live with that."

"What makes you better than what's inside you?"

Fearfully, Terri realized pressing Amanda was backfiring and eased off. She gently came back to the subject of the baby.

They talked about life and chances and adoption. Terri held Amanda in her arms, wanting everything to be as it was. But it couldn't. The baby's life engulfed Terri.

"Will another person love your baby the way you would?"

She watched Amanda shake, rub her hands across her face, and cry.

Amanda became a wonderful mother and finished school while raising her daughter. Terri loved being her cheerleader. Every visit they shared caused an unspoken appreciation of the decision they had reached together. Amanda eventually located along the coast of North Carolina. They remained close friends, and Amanda was the maid of honor at Terri's wedding.

Terri met Josh on Spring Break during her senior year. Josh flunked out of college during his junior year and took a job as a waiter in an upscale restaurant at Myrtle Beach.

"Whoa, baby, are you on the menu?"

As Josh smiled at the group of girls from Terri's college, Terri's stomach shifted like never before, and she felt magic.

"I don't think management wants me on the menu, but we do have some great catch of the day specials. May I tell you about 'em?"

"You can sit right here on my lap and tell me anything your heart desires," said one of the half-intoxicated gals in Terri's dining group.

"You'd think these girls never get off campus. Hi, I'm Terri." She extended her hand and felt the gentleness of Josh's manner as he shook it.

"Well, hello, Terri, I'm Josh."

"I'd like Josh to shake something of mine," another rowdy member at the table said.

Terri smiled slightly as Josh blushed. It complemented his tanned skin and sun bleached hair. In her controlled way, she melted inside.

"Josh, I'd better order for all of us before these friends of mine get us thrown out of this place."

"Don't worry about it. I love fun groups."

Terri shook her head at her friends to stop their next comment.

"Would you bring us some white wine?" Terri focused on Josh's deep blue eyes.

"Sure, I'll pick out something you'll like."

As he left, Terri watched the girls go hysterical.

"I think Pretty Boy likes you, Terri."

"When he brings back what he thinks we'll like, I'm gonna give him something he'll like," replied another.

"Knock it off," said Terri through her giggles. "He *is* cute."

Dinner lasted two hours, and Terri's infatuation with Josh grew.

Her heart reached out as she absorbed everything about him. It beat harder and harder as he seemed to open up like a puppy to warm milk.

"Josh, I've got this feeling you have a gift."

"Right. That's why I'm waiting tables."

"Exactly, and you're good at it. Maybe you just need a break. You'll grow your gift."

The girls laughed, but Terri ignored it, and Josh didn't seem to hear it.

"I don't know, I dropped out of college... didn't know where life was leading me. I suspect I still don't. I'm treading water at this place till I figure it out. Hope I don't drown in the process."

Terri soaked in his innocent attractiveness. She paddled emotionally not to drown herself. He lifted her spirits and tugged at her heart.

The girls hired a limo to take them to the restaurant. As they exited for the ride back, Josh appeared in the parking lot. Pleasantly surprised, Terri said, "What are you doing out here? Don't you have to finish your shift?"

"With the tip you girls gave me tonight, I won't need to work the rest of the week. Actually, I wanted to say, well, thanks for coming in. You kinda made my night, maybe my whole summer."

The episode felt like an unfolding dream to Terri. Uncharacteristically, she abandoned her cautious manner. "I live in Greenville. Would you like to call me sometime?"

"I'd like it a lot."

She watched the phone for two days, and then he called.

"You might not remember me..."

"I suspect I do, Josh Rankin. I guess the proper thing to say is I've been too busy to notice you haven't called, but hoping you would is all I've thought about."

"Oops, sounds like I should've called earlier."

"Sounds like I'm going to scare you away."

"Not a chance, I love your honesty."

Terri knew she often came across a bit corny and too principled. She couldn't help how she was raised and chose to act. It had cost her more than a few dates with no call-back. It depressed her to think that her family money was the driving force behind most of her social connections. But Josh was different, and she had this warm, nearly burning feeling, he could fulfill her needs. He saw her beyond her money. She was unique and would capture this gorgeous man.

Josh called nightly sharing doubts about his life. It thrilled her to have answers to questions bothering Josh, and she felt him becoming more dependent on her with each conversation.

"Quit worrying about saving the world, Josh. Save yourself, and in the process do something that'll make the world better."

Terri's long, wavy, brown hair fell gently across her broad shoulders. Mesmerizing green eyes and a smooth light complexion highlighted her lovely face. Her slightly heavy frame didn't detract from her prettiness. But to Terri, her strong commitment to values meant more than good looks. She thought of Josh, not as a trophy, but one growing in-step with her beliefs.

Terri arranged a job for Josh in Greenville in a restaurant owned by a good friend of the Lippard family. After work he'd come by her apartment.

"Wouldn't it be fun to unwrap each other on our wedding night?" she asked one evening in her frequent effort to control his unbuttoning her clothes. She convinced him moral compassion beat some flash-in-the-pan tumble with no vows behind it. Their love for one another blossomed, and they became engaged. Terri's announcement to her parents was not as smooth.

"I don't doubt he's an honorable man, and I don't doubt he loves you. But look at the guy. He's a waiter, for God's sake. He's got no education and no future."

"Daddy, I've watched you all my life. Everybody around you seems to need you in one way or another. You thrive on it. Now, for once in my life, there's someone who needs me. Just like you would do, I'm standing strong on this."

Terri felt she had made her point when her mother looked at him with a contained grin and said, "Okay, what have you got to say about that, Charlie Lippard?" He said nothing.

Terri was filled with joy as Josh treated her as a life-line. She loved sharing her views on how the world should be.

"Listen, Josh, I know I don't need to work, but this is why I'll stick by this children's home. I see no social injustice in saying no to any adult who has already had a fair chance and refused it. But the children in this place have started life in a hole. Their parents have abandoned them, and I'm going to fill that hole. My fingers might bleed by the end of the day, but I'll work so they get a chance... some hope."

Terri knew those close to the Lippard family gossiped about Josh marrying for the money. His looks were magazine material compared to Terri's. But Terri's faith in Josh flowed from her heart.

In the year and a half of marriage, Terri helped Josh open a sales-rep business with fifteen employees. He struggled and could hardly meet payroll. Terri wiped away his tears after difficult days and found ways for Josh to get through the doors of financial institutions to secure needed business loans. When the operation went under, the banks all forgave the debt in exchange for the meager remaining assets. Terri, quietly behind the bailout, never mentioned her help to Josh. *I don't want him to feel like a failure,* she told herself.

The last business endeavor highlighted his only proven skill, selling. She helped him set up a small office with a phone and answering machine to market chemical products. Josh pleased Terri by working very hard.

As Terri kissed him passionately, she said, "I'm so proud of you." She was relieved he was now working by himself.

Being a part of the Lippard family gave them extensive opportunities for social engagement. Terri tended to shy away from most, and felt repulsed having friends bought by her money.

Devoted love and attention by Josh dominated the first year of their marriage. When Terri told him she was pregnant, he sobbed, the most special moment in Terri's life. Josh Rankin loved her, and she knew it.

Josh met a fellow at the gym, shortly after she became pregnant, named Austin Clemmons. Terri liked Austin because he came to Josh in an honest way, racquetball. Although Josh and Austin did a lot of guy things, Terri frequently joined in. In a short time, Terri felt Austin was both fun and good for Josh.

Terri and Josh agreed Amanda and Austin could be a splendid couple. Athletically built, Austin's handsome face was blemished only by a jagged scar on his forehead. He claimed the wound was inflicted by a speeding baseball as a child.

"I don't know, Amanda, he's got you written all over him, strong, handsome, and sensitive. He's what you've been looking for. You think about it," Terri whispered to Amanda over the phone one night before bed.

CHAPTER ELEVEN

Greenville
September 4, 1980
10:55 a.m.

The last six months had been different. Those were the Angie months. While Paul drove skillfully through the traffic, Josh recalled how they met at the Green Grass Old Irish Pub. He and Austin had been playing in a racquetball tournament. Josh had lost in the quarterfinal round, and Austin was advancing to the semi-finals. Austin had said, "Josh, I'll probably lose this next round, so I reckon I'll be less than thirty minutes behind you. Why don't you meet me at the usual spot across the street?"

Josh had taken his time, showered, dressed, and went into the pub. He took a table near the rear and ordered a draft beer. Straight ahead, he spotted a lushness, an overwhelming, a woman huddled over a pile of paperwork. Her preoccupation gave him a perfect opportunity to watch her without being noticed. He sipped his beer and became mesmerized by her smooth tan skin, lovely shaped face, and tasteful clothes layered around her petit body. The hidden forms beneath her clothing were almost too perfect as they would come and go with the movement caused by her handwriting.

Finally, butterflies erupted in Josh's stomach as she broke from her reading. Her eyes rose and turned in his direction. She appeared to look straight past him and then around the noisy pub.

Her line of vision returned in his direction and then dropped to the level of his face. Her brown eyes were pure, and then she smiled the smile that melted Josh's heart. He rose slowly and stepped towards her as if he had no choice.

"You seem very busy with your work. I didn't mean to interrupt you."

"Oh, thanks, I needed a break. Hi, I'm Angie."

He took her extended hand which felt like pure silk, and Josh's knees buckled as he fell into the chair beside her.

"Could I have one of those that he's drinking?" Angie asked the waiter. As she began speaking, Josh soaked up every movement of her face. Every statement that she made or question that she asked was like a new strand in a web of wonderfulness. Angie seemed intrigued and delighted about everything he said. Josh had truly dismissed any desire to be with another woman since he met Terri, but he'd never met anyone like Angie.

She began to pack up her things in her canvass backpack and Josh felt dismayed, empty. But she softly suggested she'd be back tomorrow, about the same time, and would really enjoy talking with him again. Before Josh could collect his thoughts, she turned and walked toward the door. Her figure from behind took Josh's breath away.

Five minutes later Austin joined him. They drank a couple of beers and spoke mostly of racquetball. Josh said nothing of his earlier encounter, and felt distracted, nearly unable to breathe. He hoped Austin hadn't notice.

For the next twenty-four hours, Josh couldn't get her out of his mind. Thoughts of Angie distracted him constantly at home and work the next day. Several times he nearly came to his senses and almost let go of the temptation to see Angie again. He really loved his wife and was elated about the prospects of becoming a father. But Terri had been distant since her mother died several months ago. Josh once mentioned they needed to get on with their lives, and she blew up in anger.

He figured he needed to get Angie out of his mind and convinced himself he had mentally expanded Angie's beauty over the past twenty-four hours and, if he saw her again, he would come down to reality. But he found himself back at the pub, her sitting at the same table, her beauty as intense as he had recalled. Her smile beckoned him to take the chair next to her. Angie's gifted personality made him feel yesterday's conversation had never ended. As Angie reached down to pick up a pen she had inadvertently dropped, Josh reacted. Their heads raised evenly only inches apart, and he noticed her long dark-brown hair slightly out of place. Josh took his hand and brushed it back to the side. Angie's loving eyes met his.

"You have the most beautiful eyes," whispered Josh.

"You can't imagine how good it feels to be here with you," she said as Josh watched her blush slightly.

"Oh, but I can imagine."

He slipped his hand over hers and felt her ease her other hand over the top of his, rubbing gently and sensuously. The softness of her flesh merely touching his hand sent blood rushing to his extremities. The intensity of the moment grew as their legs met under the table.

"Should I be asking if you have a girlfriend or something?"

The question frightened Josh. He had intentionally left off his wedding band. *I'm going to spoil this perfect moment,* he feared silently. But as she wrapped her left calf behind his right leg, the question nearly vanished.

"This feels special, and I don't need to know anything more," she said. Her smooth and luscious lips neutralized Josh's guilt as she spoke.

The fire between them grew by the second, like a delicious dream. He felt mentally vacant, spell bound, and didn't know what to say next.

"Can I take you somewhere?" he finally asked, wondering where his assuming question came from. He tried to suppress his emotion, uncertain of her reaction.

"I live alone and would consider it an honor if you could get me home safely."

Relief came over Josh as she rescued him from his clumsy words. He followed her home and entered her apartment through the door she left ajar seconds earlier.

There was no aggression by either. Josh stared in awe at Angie's beauty. *My God, this is too good to be true*, lingered in his mind. The fundamental faithfulness he had for his wife evaporated in his infatuation.

As Angie slipped her sensuous frame slowly down the sofa beside him, their fingers intertwined gingerly, and his temperature rose. He pulled her gently towards him. In what seemed like slow motion, their lips touched. She tasted like honeysuckle, which meshed wonderfully with her light perfume scent. Her lips parted as she took his tongue in rhythmic fashion into the wet warmth of her mouth, causing his heart to pound violently. Time seemed to slow as he fell into a near trance in her arms. Her lips moved around his ears and neck, bringing new life to each place.

Her tanned skin, flawlessly smooth under his hands, brought life below his clothes, and almost as if she sensed his need for freedom eased the fabric from his confines. She rose from her seat, glided two steps backward, unbuttoned her blouse and paralyzed him.

Frozen, his eyes feasted on her delicate frame showing well-toned muscles and breasts, not so large, pink, perfectly balanced. Feeling undeserving, he gazed at her shapely legs leading to her heavenly gift. His rising eyes finally settled on her face, her precious smile, her beckoning loveliness.

"Let me undress you." She reached for his shirt collar.

Josh stood. Suddenly the magic grew as she released him from his clothing. He gently shook as she gracefully caressed him. Joy came over him as she eased him back on the sofa, nestled on top and controlled a steady stroke inside her soft wetness. He captured her in his hands and couldn't control his moaning as she worked in a circular motion. A blessing was all he could think of as she seemed to climax in harmony with him.

"This has to be a dream," he said, their legs entangled across the sofa.

"Yes, my prince, a dream. Don't awaken me."

The dream continued for months. She became his trusted confidant in passion.

CHAPTER TWELVE

Foothills Smokey Mountains
September 4, 1980
11:15 a.m.

The drive with Paul involved many turns, and soon they were out of the city and into the foothills of the mountains. Josh closed his eyes. The whole thing seemed like a nightmare. He couldn't make sense out of the situation. Why would Towers try to help him, not charge a fee and then act like Josh Rankin didn't exist? Who is Paul, last name unknown, who is acting like a guardian angel? *Where the hell am I going, and where's my car?* Josh pondered. His mind raced faster than the car. Over an hour had passed.

"Paul, I appreciate everything, but maybe I should head back to Greenville to sort things out."

"This is a natural reaction in face of much uncertainty. But in a few minutes we'll arrive, and Mr. Sid Richardson will answer all of your questions."

Josh started to demand the driver conform with his instructions but recalled Austin Clemmons' advice. "You've got to be willing to let professional people do their thing. From what you're telling me, Terri is throwing you out. Don't get me wrong, I like Terri. But this lawyer fixes things. Trust him."

In three minutes, the car pulled into an open gate. The manicured hedges, the neat rows of pansies, and the tall backdrop of hemlocks created a private and professional atmosphere. The facility was huge with lots of parking spaces, but there were very few cars. Josh looked rapidly, back and forth, as Paul pulled the car all the way around the building and into a covered drive. A gentleman with a generous smile opened his car door. He was about six feet tall and wore a soft tweed jacket, sable tie, and brown slacks. He appeared to be in his mid to late thirties.

"My name is Sid Richardson. Welcome to Family Intervention."

Josh followed Sid's slow pace into the building. As they passed a restroom, Josh excused himself. He washed his hands and face and looked at himself in the mirror. *What the hell am I doing?*

As he walked out, he noticed the immaculately clean white walls and vinyl-tiled floors. The halls smelled like a medicine cabinet, and soothing music of piano and violins flooded his ears.

A lady in a starched lab coat took him to a small office with comfortable furniture. Calmness came over Josh as he nestled into the chair and soaked up the pastel colors and soft music. He hardly noticed the interruption when Sid entered the room from the opposite side and sat next to him. The warm, pleasant, and trusting air of Sid's personality settled around Josh.

"Josh, we're in the business of helping people. I know you're probably feeling apprehensive and uncertain about this hurried meeting. If you like, we can take you back to Greenville right now. You're under no obligation, no pressure. We're only here to help if you feel good about us and what we're prepared to offer."

"I'm listening."

"We deal with family problems the way no other agency can. Our clients are extremely few, and the mere fact that you're here is a credit to your situation. If you decide to let us help you, we'll be in your life only for a brief time. Do you by chance read the *New England Journal of Medicine*?"

"No, why should I?"

"The current issue features Dr. Chris Sinclair, who has developed a non-invasive technique altering a minuscule portion of the brain. The cerebral cortex is the part of the brain controlling memory. The technique deals with a concept closely tied to the phenomenon of amnesia. I'm certain you've heard of people who've been in some type of accident and can't remember the event which triggered the injury. This process Dr. Sinclair has developed uses those same principles, but there's no accident involved. Merely by making a very small alteration, it creates the same forgetfulness over a brief recent time frame."

"So what does this have to do with me?"

"Wouldn't it be good family intervention for your wife to remember nothing of the past twenty-four hours, deliver your beautiful baby, and your marriage proceed as if your little indiscretion had not occurred?"

"This is nuts. You're proposing doing a lobotomy on my wife?"

"This is nothing remotely like a lobotomy. That procedure is high-risk, involving cutting into the skull and destroying portions of the frontal lobes in order to change the personality of the patient. Our procedure will not change anything whatsoever about Terri except her memory of the last twenty-four hours. The process is much like an x-ray. It doesn't hurt, and the patient doesn't even feel it. The x-ray device is called a Gamma-knife. It's not really a knife. It's only a helpful machine that produces a radiation beam. The beam will merely alter a tiny part of the temporal lobes to achieve the result you desire. Dr. Sinclair has developed this procedure to a fine art. He works for us. I want you to watch this video."

With the ease of a button, a production narrated by Dr. Sinclair appeared on the screen. The video carefully explained how the temporal lobes control many mental functions, including the ability to remember. The video offered several examples of how traumatic events make people forget recent history. Dr. Sinclair stated the procedure happens quickly, involved no incisions, no holes, and is predictably accurate to within 99.5 percent. The results so far had been 100 percent, and this routine procedure could be available to anyone who could benefit from a selected memory loss.

Dr. Sinclair gave an example of a mother who witnessed the tragic, bloodletting death of her child. For months after the child's death, she was unable to function and had no quality of life. This simple procedure gave her the freedom of not remembering the gruesome event and afforded her the opportunity to recall the many wonderful times she'd had with her child.

This case, as with all the other cases, had been totally successful without any medical complications. Dr. Sinclair modestly claimed credit for the cutting edge use of the Gamma-knife. He predicted by the next decade it would be commonplace to use it to cure depression, anxiety, and other emotional problems.

The video concluded with a quote from Dr. Sinclair that sounded to Josh like he was witnessing the future of science.

"A year or two from now, people will look at this revolutionary process as simply as curing a headache. The use of the Gamma-knife with its enormous benefits will seem like nothing more than taking an aspirin."

The doctor's eye contact, his absolute confidence, his conviction, grabbed Josh somewhere between his heart and his wallet. But it felt right.

As the video ended, Dr. Sinclair himself appeared. Two nurses stood behind him. As the doctor began to speak, knowledge and confidence filled the room, leaving Josh nearly overwhelmed. He thought he ought to ask a question but struggled coming up with one. Then Dr. Sinclair began again.

"I know this procedure sounds new. It is. But the technique is exciting because your wife will have no side effects. The fetus will be preciously shielded during the short process, just as any doctor does when taking an x-ray. If we act quickly, your wife will wake up in her own bed at home late tomorrow morning. She'll be rested and will remember you just the way she remembered you two days ago."

"Don't take this the wrong way, Doctor, but, if you're so good, why are you here?"

"Not a bad question, young man. In fact, it's quite a good one. My research takes a lot of money. Quite frankly, I don't have time to sit back and wait for our good government or some foundation to fund this project. It's too important. I'm here because I can fulfill a need... your need, and Mr. Richardson will see that I'm properly funded, simple as that."

As Josh pondered the comments, the doctor added in a comforting tone, "If you agree to this, you'll go to sleep tonight, and tomorrow this problem will have gone away."

Josh turned to Sid Richardson. "How much will this cost?"

"We don't want you to pay anything now. In fact only if, and until, you come into control of certain monies, we don't expect any payment."

"What is that supposed to mean... control of what money? Do you expect me to pay you or not?"

Josh felt the urge to regroup. Being a salesman himself, this started to sound like a sales pitch. It was like he needed to walk away, but the air of authority and total confidence around the doctor and Sid held him in place. Dr. Sinclair and the nurses eased out of the room as Sid adjusted his chair back in Josh's direction.

"Under the best case scenario there's a possibility that one day, Josh, you'll come into control of approximately a billion dollars. This math is based on eight billion which, after estate taxes, is divided by two siblings of which you might ultimately become the owner of fifty percent of the marital estate. The fee is twenty-five percent of what you receive, two hundred and fifty million."

Josh was astounded. "How do you know about my wife's family and its money?"

"All of the information you gave to Attorney Tower is in our possession. The minute he saw fit to put you in our care, our wheels began to turn for you non-stop. We know what you're up against, what's at stake, and how to help you."

"I don't know if I'll ever see any money or, if I do, when that will happen. Even if I did, that's too much."

Sid placed his hand on Josh's arm. "Josh, let me explain the incredible sum of money we are advancing to help you. Consider we've hired for your needs the best neurosurgeon in the country, perhaps the world. He has a highly trained medical staff. All of this talent is on standby should you decide to enlist our help. This is just the tip of the iceberg of our costs. We have untold millions in technical staff and equipment dedicated to your situation as we speak. We run the risks and take the chances of everything. If you don't eventually come into the money, you owe us nothing. The reason we take these calculated risks is we're good at what we do. Also, we're confident this family plan for you will succeed. You'll become a very rich man, and we'll receive a very legitimate fee.

"Now, I could offer you a fee arrangement not tied to our success, but you'd need ten million up-front, if you want to go that way."

Josh thought of the difficulty of scraping up even ten thousand in cash.

Sid continued, "The problem existing at this moment is you need to decide if you wish or don't wish to become part of our program. If you're in, there are several questions I need answers to before we can commit our program to you."

"The answer is no. Maybe I screwed up. Maybe I've got some... what do you call it... domestic problems. But this sounds criminal. I'm ready to go back to Greenville."

"I understand and respect your decision. We'll bring the car around."

Josh watched as Sid softly summoned for the car. But as Sid was leaving, he slowly turned and squared his shoulders firmly towards Josh. Josh felt the penetrating eyes of Sid disarming him.

"What will become of you?"

Josh paused. "I guess my wife will divorce me, and the chips will fall as they may."

"And what role will Charlie Lippard have in the falling of these chips?"

Josh felt helpless. "Terri has always said, though she hated him for it, her father crushes everybody who crosses him."

"So who'd be crossing him this time?"

Josh focused his eyes on the floor, stirred his feet, and exhaled loudly. "Me."

"Meaning you'll lose your child?"

"Attorney Tower said, with the Lippard money, it won't be a fair fight."

"Josh, is there something terribly wrong with erasing a small mistake? Why should this be a Charlie Lippard matter? Do you think you could make good on your marital vows if given another chance? Do you think if Terri mentally dismissed your one and only act of unfaithfulness you could spend the rest of your life making it up to her? Does our fee make you want to spit into the winds of Charlie Lippard, or could you better live with yourself knowing you spared Terri the pain of your infidelity?"

Josh's head rattled with indecision as Sid left the room. *These folks might be my only chance to stand toe to toe with the Lippards. What's a few million compared to billions... especially if they're that good?*

After a moment, Josh pulled open the door he had entered and found Sid waiting.

"Your car's ready. Greenville awaits you."

"Austin Clemmons said I should trust the professionals. I want you to know I'm uncomfortable with my decision, but do you understand if I go along with you, it's got to be for the right reasons? If Terri can forget my mistake, I'll spend the rest of my life making it up to her. If I do this, will I have your absolute promise Terri will not be hurt and our child will be protected in every way possible?"

"Yes. It's not only my promise, but also my commitment. I'm certain you will soon look back and know this was the best decision you ever made."

Josh took a deep breath. It weighed heavily in his mind Terri never gave him a chance to explain. *She has a right to be mad, but why not give me a second chance? Why buy me off? Because I'm not a Lippard? He* contemplated as Sid waited patiently.

"Okay, I'm in. What's next?"

"Let's sit back down and review the time frame since last night."

Josh felt the burden of the world had been lifted as he returned to the office and fell back into the chair.

"I have all the information you provided to Attorney Tower, but we need to be sure of a couple of things. It appears approximately 7:15 p.m. yesterday you arrived at home. At 8:45 your wife found your protection in your pocket. By 9:00 you confessed your indiscretion. Did you at any time mention the name of your mistress?"

"Nope, and she didn't ask."

"Okay, from 9:00 until approximately 10:30 she sat alone in the study. Is that right?" Josh nodded his head. "Did she call anybody?"

"No, I would've heard her."

"What time did she give you the ultimatum?"

"Oh yeah... the ultimatum. About 10:45."

"So what happened then?"

"She slept in our bed, and I slept on the day bed in the adjoining sitting room."

"What happened the next morning?"

"I fixed coffee, and nobody talked. Terri hasn't worked in two months and stays at home. I left at 8:45 this morning and called Mr. Tower's office on the way to work. Surprisingly, he could see me right away, and I was in his office by 9:15."

"Are you sure your wife made no phone calls before you left?"

"Yep, our house is not big, and I was listening."

"Other than your usual home phone and her car phone, are there any phones available to her?"

"That's it."

"Josh, we've verified she has made no calls since 10:00 a.m. All incoming calls have, since then, received a busy signal. You seem quite confident your wife wouldn't discuss your little problem with anyone until you made your decision."

"Right. When you live with someone for a year and a half, you understand what the other means, and she definitely meant to keep this to herself until I decided. You'll have to trust me."

"Then I will, Josh. Family Intervention will accept your case. There are fifteen documents you need to sign. There are fee agreements, medical authorizations, powers of attorney, plus other written instruments necessary to complete our services to you. Take your time."

Josh took the stack and started to read the first document under the watchful eye of Sid Richardson. He didn't half understand it. As he asked questions, Sid gave very logical explanations for all of the lingo. By the time he finished the first document, he felt it was in order and signed it. He proceeded to the second one. Sid again answered his questions satisfactorily, and he signed the second document. As the process continued, it became so routine Josh promptly signed all fifteen documents, trusting he was doing the right thing.

Upon signing, Josh felt he had washed his hands of the problem until Sid explained they needed assistance on one matter.

"Do you have a place away from your home that you and Terri frequent?"

"Well, we have several favorite restaurants... " Josh began, but he was interrupted.

"No, that's not the setting we need. Do you ever go to zoos, or hiking trails, or maybe parks?"

"Oh, well, of course, we go to Cedar Grove Park several times a week. It's our special place and is only a quarter of a mile from the house. We take walks, have picnics, eat ice cream, that sort of thing."

Sid asked to be excused for a moment, and Josh waited until he returned several minutes later. "Josh, of course, you are familiar with the layout of Cedar Grove Park."

"Right."

"You know the lake and the layout of the trails. One trail goes around the lake, and, on the wooded side, another trail goes into the trees where there's a picnic table."

"Well, yes, I know it like the back of my hand, but how do you?"

Josh watched Sid lift his chin with a subtle degree of authority. "You're now starting to understand how thorough and detailed this program is. You're in good hands. This is what you need to do. Your car is waiting outside."

"How could my car be outside? I didn't drive it here."

"Of course you didn't, but we're not going to let you be without your car. We handle these details. Now head back to Greenville. Take a right out of our parking lot onto Highway 221. As soon as you're on the road, call Terri on your car phone. Your home phone won't be busy this time. Tell her you're ready to talk, and ask her to meet you by the lake at four o'clock this afternoon."

"What if she doesn't want to come to the park?"

"Josh, it's not hard. Tell her you're going to do it her way and would rather talk in your special place. Can you handle this small detail?"

"Yeah, I guess. But I thought somebody said I'd go to bed tonight and tomorrow will be hunky-dory."

"Exactly, Josh, but let us get our foot in the door."

As Josh thought of it, he would logically need to point them in the right direction, so he nodded his head in agreement.

"Go straight to the park. When you arrive, go through the front gate. The ice cream stand is to your left. Buy two cups of chocolate ice cream. One will have a white napkin and one will have a yellow napkin. Find your wife and give her the one with the white napkin. Think to yourself, 'my motives are as white as snow'. Walk with her, and take the path leading to the picnic table in the woods. When you arrive, ask her to sit. The ice cream she'll have has a mild sedative to relax her. Be calm and tell her you'll do anything she wants. Listen to her, agree with what she says, but she needs to finish the ice cream. She'll get a little tired, and we'll gently take care of her. Do you understand?"

Josh began to feel reluctant and confused again, still stuck knee deep in what Sid Richardson had promised to fix.

"Listen Josh, all you're doing is allowing us to get traction. Then you can stop worrying. Two hours from now your part will be done."

Josh scratched his head in frustration. "So what's next after the park?"

"After Terri is in our control, go back to your car. This key is to Room 208 at the Pinkney Hotel in Spartanburg which is only twenty-five minutes from the park. Do you know it?"

Josh took the key. "That's funny. We used to go there for brunch after church services with the Lippards. It's a grand old hotel in downtown Spartanburg. The whole group would ride over in two separate limos with security in front and rear, a real spectacle."

Sid laughed. "I can hardly imagine. You'll be very comfortable there and our associate, Bob Chambers, will come by your room after you arrive. You'll spend the night, and tomorrow morning you'll have your life back the way it should be. Is this okay with you?"

"How do I know? Could something go wrong? Why am I trusting you to give me my life back?"

"Nothing's going to go wrong. We're professionals. When I told you we're in the business of helping people, I meant it. It's a promise to you, and it's a promise which will be kept. Have a good trip back to Greenville and we'll talk soon." Sid Richardson handed him the car keys.

CHAPTER THIRTEEN

September 4, 1980
2:15 p.m.

Josh walked out of the same door he had entered at Family Intervention and found his car immediately in front of him. He fumbled for the key, got in, cranked it and noticed it registered a full tank of gas. He drove out of the facility, trying to hold on to his fill of courage. Setting his bearings on Highway 221 South, he grabbed his car phone and called Terri.

"I'm ready to do it your way. Can you meet me at the park in about an hour?"

"Why can't you come to the house and talk?" Terri asked.

"I'd feel better if we could do it at the park, if that's okay with you. Maybe some fresh air will help."

"Sure, why not? I'll see you by the lake."

The conversation ended tensely.

A few minutes before four, Josh found a parking place right outside the park. He locked his car and walked into the gate he'd entered so many times before. Without looking he knew the location of the ice cream man. But the usual jovial overweight man had been replaced with an unfamiliar lady wearing a candy cane jacket. He walked up to her and ordered two single scoops of chocolate in cups. She nodded and pushed the cups, already prepared, across the stainless steel counter. They sat on two napkins. He dug into his pocket for payment and she waived him off. Knowing Terri got the white one, the yellow color of the other fit his mood.

As he strolled toward the lake, he saw Terri. Chimes were ringing the four o'clock hour from the old Baptist church a block away. The sun was shining just above the tree line on the opposite side of the lake. Its rays bounced across the ripples on the water and seem to highlight Terri's profile in her tan maternity dress. He smiled, awkwardly. Handing Terri her ice cream, Josh asked, "Can we walk?"

Silently they strolled side by side around the lake. Josh's heart beat excessively for the slow pace. Terri didn't touch her ice cream. When they reached the tree line, Josh asked, "Mind if we sit?" They walked the path into the trees up to the solitary picnic table. Nothing moved except the pin oak leaves rustling in a gentle wind. She awkwardly climbed and sat on top of the table with her feet on the bench. Josh noticed her belly had really extended over the past month. He sat on the other end of the bench. As her ice cream started to melt, so did his resolve.

"So what's your decision?" she asked.

"Terri, I'm going to do whatever you want me to do."

Josh watched her take a deep breath and then a bite of her ice cream. "This is hard for both of us, but I didn't ask for this."

"I know, Terri. It's my fault."

"You haven't been happy with me over the last six months and have obviously found someone better."

"Not true. There's no one better, Terri. I still love you very..."

Terri interrupted him as she turned her head away, shaking it with disapproval as if to say, "don't bother." Josh couldn't see deep inside Terri wrestling with her emotions. Her exterior didn't show her love for her husband would probably prevail in this difficult situation. Josh saw only her extremely head strong nature. She got it from her father.

Josh sat clueless on the concrete surface looking at the leaves starting to change colors. Only the distance of eight feet stood between their separate thought processes. He couldn't see

Terri, in time, wanted Josh to be a part of their child's life and her forgiveness was necessary for both her and the baby's well-being.

Silence prevailed as they ate their ice cream. Josh avoided her eyes until Terri yawned.

"I guess I didn't sleep well last night."

"Me, either."

He watched Terri slide from the top of the table to the bench. She rested her back on the edge of the table. Her belly pressed against the top of her legs. She leaned her head backward and seemed to go limp. Suddenly a nicely dressed lady in her early thirties came from behind and held Terri's head and arm. It all startled Josh. The lady looked familiar.

"We have her now. Don't worry about a thing. You need to leave."

Josh suddenly figured out the lady was the same person who had served the ice cream. She had changed clothes.

He walked toward the lake and looked back only to see a syringe in the lady's hand, giving Terri some type of injection. Josh sighed. *Oh, God, what have I done?* He felt sickened as he walked back to the car. His steps were uncertain and seemed to fight against his planned destination.

As he began the drive to Spartanburg, his heart beat erratically and his gut burned. Three miles out, he slammed on the brakes, nearly causing the car behind him to collide. Horns were blowing as he abruptly made a U-turn on the street filled with motorists leaving work. He ignored them and sped back to the park. Pulling into a "no parking" zone, he jumped from the car and sprinted back to the secluded picnic table. Vacant, empty, horribly quiet. He stumbled through the surrounding woods out of control. "TERRI!" Her name echoed through the trees, across the lake, and through his mind. But she was gone.

Back in the car, he gained control. He rationalized, had he found her, he could never explain to Terri why she was drugged at the park. He thought to himself, *Family Intervention better be very good and very quick.*

By 5:45, he walked into the front entrance of the two-story lobby of the Pinkney Hotel. He weaved around the antique furnishings and made his way to the registration area. The smells brought back the sensations of Sundays past. He almost expected to see the tall white hats of the chefs highlighting the carving of huge sides of beef in the dining hall. Those Sunday lunches always felt like a celebration of enduring the Presbyterian sermon. But the dining hall was as empty as his reservoir of confidence Sid Richardson had filled.

As he approached the attendant behind the counter, he remembered the room key in his pocket. He turned and climbed the hand-carved, ornate staircase to the second floor and found his room.

He collapsed onto the bed. He closed his eyes momentarily and sat back up, still talking to himself. *Relax, quit worrying, by morning this will all be fine. The best decision... right?* He bounced up and down on the foot of the bed like an impatient child.

After a few moments he got up and looked around the room. He smelled the same pleasant smell of cedar he had encountered in the lobby, but sensed a competing odor resembling a cattle barn. Hanging in the shallow closet were three outfits, all his size. In some drawers, he found shoes, belts, socks, underwear, and even a swimsuit. The bathroom, stocked with toiletries, gave Josh an eerie feeling.

He paced the room until a knock sounded on the door. Josh opened it. He discovered a big man appearing strangely dressed in a dark polyester suit a size too small. A black clip-on tie hung from the tightly buttoned white shirt. After an awkward moment of silence, Josh spoke.

"I'm Josh. I guess you're the guy Sid Richardson said would come by. Do you want to come in or something?"

After stumbling through an introduction, Bob Chambers seemed uncomfortable as he entered the room and began his attempt at being hospitable.

"Are you doin' all right?" Bob asked.

"Yeah, I'm okay," replied Josh. "Are these clothes supposed to be for me?"

"Yes, hopefully they will be the right size. Our staff picks out these things."

"Why do you think I'll need clothes? Remember, I'm headed home first thing in the morning."

"The clothes are there in case you need them. Don't worry about it."

"So what time do I get out of here?"

"Josh, the only thing you need to do is relax and enjoy. We don't know if you might want to take a swim or somethin'."

"I didn't ask you about a swim. I want to know what time I'll see my wife at home. Do you have an answer?"

Bob looked frustrated as he considered the question and took several slow deep breaths. "Dinner will be delivered in about forty-five minutes. There's a phone on the table. I'm thinkin' you might want to call your friend... I believe you told the 'turney her name is Angie. Tomorrow you and your wife can be reconciled. Be smart; don't see your mistress again. I'll give you some privacy."

Josh looked at Bob, wondering why Family Intervention sent this clown. His appearance in the room had solved the unidentified odor. His words seemed practiced and programmed. But the Angie suggestion took his mind off Bob Chambers. He picked up the phone. Over the last six months Angie's phone number had become committed to memory. On the second ring, Angie answered.

"Hi, it's Josh. How have you been?"

Angie's soft, silky voice brought back what made the back of his neck tingle. "I'm fine but worried because you haven't called. I've missed you. I've missed you a lot."

"Angie, the last six months have been great, more than great, but I guess I can't do this anymore. I'm under a lot of pressure at home. With the baby coming it sort of complicates things. Am I making sense?"

"Look, Josh, we both went into this with the understanding

there were no promises and no commitments. I want you to know our special times stay with me. It's been fun."

"Oh, baby, I appreciate your being so understanding," he said. But before he finished the sentence, he heard the phone hanging up.

Josh thought, *six months and it's over? Maybe she's upset with me, the first time she ever hung up. Ever.* He re-thought the conversation. Angie's passion continued to burn in his subconsciousness. Her intense beauty and the way she did things to him rattled in his confused head.

Josh looked into the bar, built into an old chiffonier. He found several minibottles of Jack Daniels and poured two of them into a glass of ice. He took a long drink. His emotions were running rampantly throughout his body. *I must be losing my mind.*

Another knock came to the door an hour later, and he found dinner set out on an elegant tray in the hall. He carried the tray and placed it on the foot of his bed. A thick filet mignon, medium rare, covered with all his favorite garnishing covered the plate. He couldn't understand how a meal he never ordered could be so near perfect. After taking a few bites, he downed the Jack Daniels and had another. Before he finished dinner, he fell soundly asleep.

Morning sun light on his face awakened Josh. He opened his eyes to see Bob Chambers.

"Good morning, Mr. Rankin. Breakfast is in the corner by the chair. Grab a cup of coffee. I'll be in the 'joining room and will leave the door open in case you need anything. Sid needs to talk at you. He'll call you shortly."

As Bob left for the other room, Josh looked at the phone by the chair and then at his watch. *8:30, boy, I slept hard.*

Josh got up, went to the restroom, and brushed his teeth. He was wearing the same clothes from yesterday. He got a cup of coffee and gently sat down in the chair behind the food tray. The phone rang.

"Good morning, Josh, Sid Richardson here. Were you comfortable last night?"

The slow meticulous way Sid spoke brought back a confidence to Josh.

"Pretty relaxed."

After a brief pause in the conversation, Josh asked, "So how is Terri? Is she at home waiting for me?"

"Josh, we're having a little problem with Terri."

"What do you mean, a problem?" Josh asked as he stood up from the chair.

"The erasing procedure went well, but she is not coming around quite the way she should. Mission is accomplished as far as your problem. We are monitoring her carefully and, hopefully, she will come around nicely in a short time. Your baby is doing perfectly. Everything is completely normal."

Josh abruptly slammed the base of the phone down on the front of the breakfast tray, flipping it over and spilling buttered grits on the front of his pants.

"What the hell is it?" Bob yelled.

Bob's presence aggravated Josh to no end, and he turned to him angrily and handed him the receiver dangling from the phone cord, covered with food. "You can talk to him. This is not my deal."

Josh stared intently as Bob put the piece to his ear and excitedly said, "I-munna call ya on "J" line in a few minutes." Then he hung up the phone and wiped grits off his ear.

Josh walked outside on the balcony and stewed in a white wicker chair while he waited for Bob.

"Try to be relaxed," Bob said as he stumbled over the matching wicker table.

Josh jumped from his seat. "I don't want to relax. I don't want to be around you. I don't want anything to do with you people. I can't even figure out why I'm here."

Josh watched Bob, wearing the same suit of clothes, pulling aggressively at his shirt collar while sweat beaded on his upper lip.

"Josh, I understand your frustrations. But you are in the hands of a very capable group, extremely professionally, completely dedicated." Bob sounded as if he was reciting lines, not pronouncing the words entirely correctly.

"So what? Look what your group has done to my wife. You're anything but professional. So, what's next, Mr. Bob?"

Josh watched Bob's face turned red as if about to explode. And then Bob's fiery blue eyes focused on him and then on the parking lot below. Josh felt threatened and vulnerable. He sighed relief as Bob quickly exited the balcony and returned to the adjoining room.

Over the next ten minutes, Josh considered what the "J" line could be. Then Bob reappeared, looking much more collected and relaxed, his tie hanging from his pants pocket.

"What's next is you're going to be informationed on every detail and know we are going to do good for you. You will partic... I mean join in on all talks, and all this will turn out fine for you. If you will shower, shave, and dress, I'll drive you to the medical facility."

Josh entered the bathroom and rinsed cold water over his face. He raised his head to the mirror and thought; *you're a coward and a disgrace.*

Twenty minutes later, cleaned, dressed in clothes not his own, he stood under the canopy in front of the Pinkney. Bob pulled up in his dark grey Crown Victoria, got out, and opened the front passenger door. Josh looked at Bob, opened the back door, and slammed it as he got in.

Soon they were headed north on I-85 and traveled for several minutes, departed and drove west toward the mountains on Highway 221. Small towns came and went on the route, Mayo, Chesnee, Spindale, and Thermal City. No conversation took place between the two. After about an hour, they were deep into the mountains south of Linville Caverns, and they turned left at the entrance.

Josh suddenly noticed no sign, banner, or marker, announced the name of the place. They took the same route around to the back of the complex and pulled beside the building entrance Josh had used before. When the car stopped, Josh hurriedly pushed open the door, got out, and nearly ran into a nurse wearing a highly starched white uniform.

"Thank you for coming, Mr. Rankin. I'll take you to your wife."

As he followed her, hospital smells invaded his senses. He took several turns through a series of halls. Josh felt turned around as he stepped into an opening and saw a man in a white lab coat coming towards him. He recognized the man immediately, Dr. Chris Sinclair. Josh jerked away as Dr. Sinclair attempted to place his hand on his shoulder.

"Where's Terri?"

"Relax, Josh, your wife is resting nicely, and the baby is doing remarkably well. Why don't we have a visit?"

Josh glared at the doctor as they strolled toward a mahogany stained door. Josh walked in and saw Terri for the first time since the park. In her arm, there was a needle connected to a tube running up to a transparent bag with a clear fluid. From under the bed sheet, another tube extended downward to a bag containing Terri's urine. Other equipment, all unfamiliar to Josh, surrounded her bed.

She looked neatly groomed, wearing a beige flannel gown he didn't recognize. Her eyes were open, and Josh leaned toward her face and touched her cheek. The cadence of her breathing and warmth of her smooth skin seemed the same. But her expressionless eyes, like Terri had left her body, grabbed Josh with the intensity of a death grip.

From the corner of his eye, he spotted Dr. Sinclair stepping forward toward the bed, and a nurse handed the doctor a clipboard. Josh watched him leaf attentively through the sheets of paper.

"Her pulse is regular, blood pressure excellent, and temperature normal. Terri is fine in every way, except normal cognitive functioning has not returned. This should improve within the next twenty-four hours. All functions related to the needs of the baby are being met. I wanted to speak to you personally, in case you had any questions."

The ease in which the doctor spoke and the confidence each word projected caused Josh to hesitate. The hysteria he had carried into the hospital mellowed only slightly.

Josh looked eyeball to eyeball with Dr. Sinclair. His face flushed with anger and guilt. "Yeah, I want to know what went wrong with your so-called ninety-nine and a half percent guarantee? I didn't want to do this and find myself extremely upset with your performance. Ya'll got some explaining to do."

"Please understand this is the first complication our medical team has ever encountered with this procedure. Actually, the problem has nothing to do with us but rather with a brain condition your wife has that no one could have predicted."

"What in the hell are you talking about?"

"When we set up Terri for the irradiation procedure, we performed some routine neurological tests, and found a tumor. Neither you nor Terri could have known of the tumor. It was located in one of her temporal lobes.

"I understand what you are going through right now. Tell me if I'm wrong, but you're having the urge to blame. That's natural. Blame my efforts, and you'll feel mad. Blame yourself, and you'll hurt deep in your heart. I suggest you do neither and listen.

"I could not, in good faith, not deal with this tumor while I had the Gamma-knife in place. Had I done nothing with this cancerous mass she's been living with, by the time Terri turned thirty-five, the tumor would have continued to grow and killed her. My diagnoses and treatment is the reason Terri has not regained complete cognizant functioning. The irradiation of the tumor had absolutely nothing to do with her slight memory. That part of her procedure went perfectly.

"As upset as you are about her current condition, you should actually be thankful. Your participation in this program, in all probability, spared her a slow and tragic death at some time in the future. I could have violated my ethics as a physician and, at this very moment, she'd appear completely normal. I sincerely hope you can appreciate my concern for the well-being of my patient.

Your interest in this procedure was a short-term goal. My interest has to be Terri's long term health... her life, if you will."

Josh saw no bright side to the story. The doctor's suggestion he spared her life seemed like Josh had done Terri a favor.

"Are you saying I should be thanking you for this?"

"No, Josh, your appreciation is not necessary. Your understanding is."

"Why do you need my understanding?"

"Because I didn't put the tumor there and neither did you."

"Okay, so what now, Dr. Sinclair?"

"We'll monitor her every minute and, hopefully, she will come around soon. If she does, and I'm confident she will, everything will have returned back to the original plan."

Josh then changed the subject. "So what about our friends and family? They must think we've both fallen off the end of the world."

"Now, Mr. Rankin, you're asking me a non-medical question," Dr. Sinclair stated.

From behind came a voice becoming all too familiar to Josh. "Hello, my friend. If you have finished with Dr. Sinclair, let's step down the hall," Sid Richardson said. Josh walked with Sid back down the hall and entered into the same office where he had signed the agreements. Appetizers and cold canned soft drinks lined the table.

"Please help yourself."

Josh opened a diet cola and nibbled on cheese sticks.

"Josh. I'm sorry for the glitch in the procedure."

"My wife is nearly comatose, and you call that a glitch."

"You're right, a poor choice of words, but it is important to stay balanced and focused. There's nothing you or I can do for Terri at this moment. Dr. Sinclair has twenty-eight professionals in this facility. Eight are medical doctors of different specialties. The rest are highly qualified RNs and nursing assistants. She could not be in better hands. The problem right now is you need to go home so all who know you and your family will think everything is normal."

Josh grunted. "Well, I suspect it's a little late. Two days have passed, and we know a lot of people."

Josh watched as Sid calmly extended his hands toward Josh pushing his palms downward. "Don't think for one minute we're not watching out for you. This is not a problem. Do you remember when you filled out your information sheet at Mr. Tower's office?" Josh nodded his head. "You stated you had been referred by Austin Clemmons."

"Right, he's a good friend."

"We used a mutual friend to contact Austin. He has been at your house since yesterday, answering the phone, taking visitors, etcetera. He told everyone he's house sitting your dog... Sam, I believe, is his name... and you and Terri had left for a private couple of days at the Lake Lure Inn for a little R&R."

"My God, I totally forgot about the puppy!" Josh said, slapping himself across the side of his head.

"Not to worry, this covers things nicely so far, but you need to get back. Here is a list of calls you need to return. The only visitor was Mrs. Ledbetter from next door, returning the dish from the casserole Terri took over last week while Mr. Ledbetter was ill. Return the phone calls. Anyone who asks about Terri, you need to tell them she decided to visit with her friend, Amanda, who lives in Beaufort, North Carolina. Inform them Terri left this morning at 11:45."

"Now you're driving me nuts. How the hell do you know about Amanda or where she lives? So what happens when Terri doesn't arrive at Beaufort? Have you bothered to think about that?"

"Yes, Josh, it's handled. Terri's trip is a surprise. Even if she were to arrive at Amanda's, Amanda wouldn't be there. She's visiting her grandmother in Maryland. Terri's Volvo won't be in your garage when you get home, since she's purportedly driving it to Beaufort. Your car is out front waiting for you. It's gassed and you should be home between 2:45 and 3:15 this afternoon."

"Sid, this is getting out of control, and I'm feeling sick to my stomach. What are you planning to do with Terri?"

"Good question. As soon as she comes around, our staff will take her straight to your house. She'll be a little groggy when she wakes, but she won't remember anything since two days ago. Telling her she slept hard, was talking in her sleep, and probably had a bad dream, will be sufficient explanation. Josh, pregnant women are prone to emotional ups and downs."

Josh cut his eyes sharply at Sid. "You'd better be right."

"I'll call you at five o'clock with an update on Terri's progress. Hopefully, there will be good news. Don't invite company over. The less you have to talk, the better. Keep the facts straight about the Beaufort trip."

Josh repeated the story as Sid nodded after each sentence.

"Very good, Josh, wait for me to call and have a safe drive home."

"Like you care if I'm safe."

"I care, trust me, I care." Sid told the truth.

A couple of nurses escorted Josh back to his car waiting outside the door. Josh sat in his car, stunned. *These people have been in my house, taken the Volvo, messed with my buddy Austin, and who the hell knows what else.* The more he thought about it, the madder he got. Suddenly, Josh got out of the car and walked angrily back toward the door. As he approached, he watched Sid Richardson step out and begin speaking in a calm and soothing voice.

"Josh, you've got a thousand questions. They'll all be answered. But right now you need to go home."

Josh left the complex at 1:05 p.m. and walked into his house an hour and forty-five minutes later. Sam nearly knocked him over. Josh cruised the house yelling for Austin, and found no sign of him. Josh looked at his clothes, not his own, and changed. He grabbed a beer from the refrigerator and settled into his leather chair in the den. Sam settled in beside him.

Josh returned the previous day's calls. They included a couple of friends, Terri's brother, Terri's father and Terri's hairdresser, who wanted to confirm next week's appointment. Josh was consistent.

"Yes, we had a great get-away to Lake Lure. On the way back Terri decided she had to see Amanda before the baby comes and decided to leave today. I couldn't go because I'm covered up at work. She's to call me when she arrives in Beaufort. I'm sure she'll call you from there or as soon as she gets back the day after tomorrow." Everyone seemed pacified over the details, and all new callers got the same routine.

"I'm out of my mind," he said looking down at Sam. "How about something to eat, puppy?" As he checked on the bowls, both the food and water containers were completely filled. Josh let Sam out in the back yard. As Sam tended to business, Josh checked the garage, no Volvo.

He slowly sat down upon the steps descending from the house to the garage floor and focused on the empty space. It seemed like weeks since this all started. He felt helpless, being totally dependent on Sid Richardson. Thinking through the details made Josh so uncomfortable he decided to get another beer.

The next hour became emotionally difficult for Josh. He didn't really understand what he had done, but he knew he loved Terri. Ridding her of the tumor gave him a sense of justification. *I saved her life, spared her the agony of a divorce, fixed things all around.*

Josh, not an overly religious man, knelt down on the garage floor and prayed God to make everything all right and take care of Terri and the baby. *Forgive my stupidity, my unfaithfulness, and my selfishness.* He felt a lick on his ear. Sam.

They both napped in the leather chair until the phone awakened Josh. He lifted the receiver as the mantle clock rang the five o'clock hour.

"Josh, this is Sid, and we need to talk. Do you know the Waffle Queen at Exit 54 on I-85?"

Groggy from the sleep, Josh sat up straight and cleared his voice. "Yep, I think I know where you're talking about, but..."

"Please meet me there. Leave Sam at home and don't come into the restaurant. There's a large parking lot to the rear. I'll be in a tan Continental. Come now, it'll take you five minutes."

As he hung up the phone, he turned to Sam. "What have I gotten us into?" He found no sympathy in the dog's eyes. He grabbed his keys and headed for the car.

Josh stepped toward the tan Continental, and the door opened. "Get in, my friend." Josh slid into the brown leather upholstery and saw Sid's sad eyes.

"What is it?"

"Your wife will get no better. The neurological defect Dr. Sinclair discussed renders her condition permanent."

"What do you mean?" screamed Josh.

"I mean she'll not recover because of the tumor. The immediate consideration at this point is the future of your child. You don't know this, but your child is a boy, your son. He's healthy and viable. Terri had a bad turn of luck and, from the bottom of my heart, I'm truly sorry."

"Mr. Richardson, I'm sick and tired of your talk and your promises and your company. This is the bottom line, listen closely. You're fired."

"Josh, get a hold of yourself. You're not thinking straight."

"The hell I'm not. It's the first time I've thought straight since I crossed your path. You're out, out of my life." Josh reached for the door, but found it locked.

"Josh, I don't blame you. Go ahead and fire Family Intervention. Do your own thing. Why don't you take control and manage this crisis? Let's say that our contract is at an end, and you owe us nothing. Your wife's body will be found wherever. It might be in alignment with Beaufort, or maybe it won't. You can explain to the authorities how her body ends up two miles in a deserted field from your house in a direction opposite from where you told everyone she was headed. You can explain why the autopsy demanded by her father found brain alterations. You can explain why the Lake Lure Inn has no record of your weekend folly. When the jury renders its verdict, look around and see if anyone in Family Intervention is in sight. They won't be. You'll be on your own."

"Why are you doing this to me?"

"We're not. We don't want you to handle your situation. We want you to stay with the program which will make you a billionaire. You can raise your son any way you wish, and money will be no object."

"You're really nothing but a bastard. I really don't have much choice here, do I?"

"You do have a choice, but there is no way you can come out of this without the help of Family Intervention. Let me explain the plan. As we speak, our engineers are staging a single vehicle automobile wreck which will occur near Morehead City, North Carolina. This is on the route from here to Beaufort. The vehicle involved is your wife's Volvo."

Josh interrupted. "Stop right there, I won't risk a wreck involving my wife and son. The answer's no."

"You don't understand, Josh. No one will be in the car when it wrecks. Immediately after the so-called accident, Terri will be placed in the vehicle in the same condition she is now. This carefully staged wreck will logistically explain her brain-damaged condition. The damaged Volvo should be spotted within ten minutes from the time Terri is placed there. The hospital is five miles away. This hospital, incidentally, has one of the best neonatal units in the South.

"The plan gels consistently with the information you've shared with your family and friends. Although Family Intervention has no ownership interest in the Morehead City Hospital, we have good contacts within. The accident will occur between 9:30 and 9:45, depending upon traffic. You need to return home now. After you arrive, go next door and thank your neighbor for returning the dish. This firms up your alibi."

"What do you mean, alibi?"

"It means you couldn't have caused it, you're clear. Remember, Family Intervention must at all costs protect you. You're the key to everything."

"I'm indispensable? Right. What exactly do you want me to tell our neighbor?"

"Mention you're sorry you weren't home when she came over. Tell the neighbor about Terri's trip to Beaufort and go back to the house and wait for the call. When the call comes, ask where, when, what and why. Call her father and ask him to help you. Do what he suggests. It'll probably be over a week before we'll need to talk to you. Be an attentive and supportive husband and father. Do you understand?"

"Yeah, I understand you're still a bastard– okay– I understand."

Josh pulled the handle of the now unlocked door. He exited the vehicle and walked towards his car. His chest ached with each breath. He stopped. Anger flooded his mind as he turned back towards Sid Richardson. He was gone.

Back in his car, Josh picked up the phone and called Austin Clemmons, receiving a busy signal. He drove home, in his growing nightmare, and stumbled into his house. After all instructions were followed, he settled into the chair with Sam at his side and waited. He felt numb and helpless.

CHAPTER FOURTEEN

Greenville
September 5, 1980

The phone rang at 10:25 p.m. jolting Josh from his sleep. A representative from Morehead City Hospital called reporting an accident involving Josh's wife. Fear swept through Josh as if the information were new. It stung raw emotions.

"Is she hurt? Is she alive? How did this happen?"

"Please, Mr. Rankin, your wife is alive, the baby seems to be fine, but you need to join us as soon as possible."

Directions and phone numbers were given, and Josh promised to get there soon. Then he called his father-in-law.

"What's wrong, son?"

Josh tried to summarize and added, "All I know is she's alive, the baby's okay, but they need me up there right away."

"Pack quickly. My driver will pick you up in ten minutes, and I'll meet you at the airport. You've got a new puppy. Leave him out back, and we'll get someone to feed him."

Josh sat in the back of the 700 Series BMW. The guard at the private gate at the Greenville Municipal Airport waived them through. Across the jet tarmac, Josh could see the frail frame of Terri's father. Beside him was Mac Carter, his capable assistant who rarely left Mr. Lippard's side.

Josh jumped from the car and walked briskly to his father-in-law. A handshake once firmly in control of multi-million dollar deals now felt closer to mush. But his mind was still sharp.

"Let's get into the jet. We can talk there," Charlie Lippard said.

At Charlie's request, Josh tried to replay all of the details received from the hospital. Charlie listened carefully for any slip-up from the first conversation, but twice Josh kept the story straight, like a well-rehearsed sales pitch

Within forty-five minutes they landed at a small airport and, without delay, were taxied by limo to the Morehead City Hospital. Josh, amazed not a wasted minute occurred in the transportation detail, followed his father-in law's slow, but purposeful steps into the hospital.

Josh introduced himself and Charlie Lippard to the same representative who made the phone call and followed her to Dr. Scott Blanton's office.

"Thank you for coming, Mr. Rankin. I'm the neurosurgeon consulting on your wife's case. It appears that her only significant injury was a sudden deceleration injury to portions of her brain."

"Slow down, Doctor, I'm just a businessman who happens to be the father of your patient. What are you saying?"

"Her car apparently left the road and struck a large oak tree at 70 miles per hour. I'm no car nut, but the authorities say she is fortunate because the Volvo is engineered so the passenger compartment didn't collapse. The impact of her seat belt itself wasn't too bad because of her thick wool overcoat. The problem is high speed deceleration injuries can be fatal."

"What do you mean?" asked Josh.

"The present condition of your wife was caused because the large oak stopped the vehicle cold. The seatbelt restrained your wife which, of course, included her head. So far as we can tell, her head had no outside trauma. But even if her head didn't strike anything, her brain continued to move forward within her skull. The brain is actually capable of taking a substantial injury because of the protective fluid between the brain and the skull. But at 70 miles per hour, the accelerating force of the brain penetrated beyond the fluid and sustained a major impact with the skull itself. Although we need to remain optimistic, it's necessary we run a series of diagnostic tests. At this time, we can't rule out injuries to the frontal lobes, temporal lobes, or even the brain stem."

"I'm confused. What's the bottom line?" Josh asked.

"As bad as this sounds, there's still a good chance she'll recover. It's quite possible, days from now, she may be as normal as before the accident. Her vital signs are very good even though she's unresponsive. We should know more about her condition over the next ten to twelve hours. The main concern now is to deliver your baby while she is still stable. Dr. Joe Taylor is with her now, and we'll let him know you're waiting."

Finally, Josh felt Terri's father elbow him out of the way. "Dr. Blanton, I want you to understand you're to do everything in your power to save her life. Money is not an issue. I sit on the Board at Greenville Regional Hospital, and I'll get you access to any doctor you wish to consult within this country. You tell Dr. Taylor Terri's own OB/GYN from Greenville will make decisions regarding birthing the child. I'm going to call Greenville now, and I'll have the Greenville Director of Medicine call you to see how we can assist you. Is this acceptable to you, Doctor?"

"Yes, it is. Terri will be out of radiology within the hour. You can see her in her room."

Josh watched Dr. Blanton walk away, obviously trying to maintain his composure. Charlie Lippard demanded a phone from a passing nurse, and Josh felt out of the loop. Being the husband would carry little weight. Josh walked out of the hospital, found a café, and ordered coffee. An hour later, Josh returned to find Terri in a private suite with medical personnel adding its numbers by the minute. He sat by Terri's bed.

Without warning, Josh felt Charlie's hand on his shoulder.

"This is a tough time for all of us. Let me handle the doctors."

Josh nodded his head, and then leaned over to Terri. She had the same expression he had seen that morning at Family Intervention.

He wanted to beg her forgiveness. As tears rolled down his face, he realized he'd failed her. "I should be in this bed," he whispered under his breath.

"Would you like to hear the baby?" asked a nurse, startling Josh from behind. He took the stethoscope.

"Go ahead... right here."

With help from the nurse, he guided the instrument over Terri's abdomen. The heartbeat of the child sounded clear. His remorse overwhelmed him.

As Josh sat in a chair by the bed, listening to the sounds of his son, he fell asleep with his head on the edge of the bed. After about three hours, he awoke to loud activity of doctors and nurses. He jumped as Charlie Lippard took him by the arm and told him to come out into the hall.

"We now have four independent opinions as to what to do about delivery. The consensus is to perform a C-section now. This will relieve Terri of a lot of physical stress, and we can then focus on her recovery."

The C-section surgery started at 7:30. Josh dressed in surgical scrubs and washed his hands and arms as instructed. He stood by Terri among the various medical personnel. Josh nodded his greeting to Dr. Fisher as he saw the doctor enter the delivery room. He and Josh had met at one of Terri's routine appointments after she had become pregnant.

Within twenty minutes, Josh held his son. The staff, noticeably quiet, gave him space. He surrendered the child gently to a nurse to make the routine measurements. From an anterior room came a question.

"What's the child's name?"

Josh, taken by surprise, paused and remembered Terri wanted to name the child after him if it was a boy. But what he cuddled in his arms less than a minute ago crushed every selfish thought he ever had. *I can't name this precious child after a worthless, selfish jerk.*

"His name will be Terry, T-E-R-R-Y. Terry Charles Rankin." For the first time in three days something felt slightly right. Josh leaned down to Terri's ear. "I'm so... so sorry."

For the next few days Josh stayed in a modest motel across from the hospital. Charlie Lippard seemed to fly in and out several times a day. Little Terry continued to gain weight and was doing well to be a month premature. Josh visited Terri twice a day but spent most of the time in the neonatal ward watching, holding, and feeding Terry.

One morning before leaving the motel room for the hospital, the phone rang.

"Josh, this is Charlie Lippard, and I think we need to move Terri to a Greenville facility. They'll fly her out this afternoon, and I'll go with her. Since little Terry is doing well, my driver will take the two of you home. Janelle Barr is a private nurse who will assist you when you arrive. I'll call you soon."

Josh never got in a word during the call and, six and one-half hours later, he arrived home with Terry bundled beside him. Josh noticed Janelle, sitting patiently in her car, when they pulled into the drive. She began unpacking formula, diapers, lotions and a huge array of miniature outfits. Once in the house, Josh handed her the baby.

There was little for Josh to do, but he felt obligated to cancel his sales appointments. Soon he would need to work since sales had been a bit slow lately. Being an in-law of the Lippards had its advantages in a collateral sort of way, but it seemed he was on his own when it came to paying personal debts.

Soon Janelle had things nicely organized, and Terry was quietly resting.

"This is a big help. I apologize, but tell me what I need to pay you and what hours you'll work."

Janelle smiled professionally. "Thank you for asking, Mr. Rankin, but you don't need to pay me anything. It's all been arranged, and I'll work whenever you want. Even if I need time off, I've got friends, all nurses, which can substitute."

Josh sat silently for a minute feeling inadequate. He rubbed Sam's fur trying to come up with something important to tell Janelle.

"We're here to help you, and you need to trust us," said Janelle.

Josh thought about how familiar that sounded. Not only did he not trust anyone but, with Charlie Lippard, his choices were as few as with Family Intervention. His life lacked any self-control.

"Could you come back in the morning at eight, and we'll see how it goes?"

"Yes, sir, good idea."

The phone rang, and Josh started to answer, but he hesitated, fearing more from Family Intervention. Before he could decide, Janelle answered.

"Rankin residence. One moment. It's Mr. Mac Carter for you." Josh took the phone from Janelle and wrote down Terri's room number at the neurology wing at Greenville Regional. He promised Mac to visit her soon and often.

Mac Carter was born and raised in the small town of Travelers Rest, close to Greenville. His father had died at an early age, and his mother raised three children while working twelve-hour days at a local mill, owned by the Lippard family. Mac, the youngest of the children, would often walk from the house to the mill's front entrance to wait on his mother to leave work. In the early 1950s, at the age of ten, a man walking into the front gate, Charlie Lippard, the 50-year-old president of the company, confronted Mac.

Mac's mother appeared to be having a stroke when Mac, her sandy-hair child, walked hand in hand with Charlie Lippard toward her machine. Mac watched his mother shake as Mr. Lippard explained he was giving Mac a tour of the plant.

"Why do some people seem to be working harder than others?" Mac asked.

"That's a question I've asked myself about every day I've been at this place, son."

"So, why is it so?"

"My lad, if I had an answer, I'd have the combination to the safe."

"Sir, I don't have a safe, but I think I know the answer."

"And?"

"It's because they want to work harder."

Mac endeared himself to Charlie Lippard and, by the time the inquisitive child finished the tour, he had received clearance to go by the President's office any time.

Mac became a quick study. It gave him a sense of pride when Charlie commented Mac asked better questions than many of Lippard's managers. By the age of fifteen, Mac, doing exceptionally well at school, started working summers at Lippard Industries. He learned to work virtually every machine in the mill, and he got first hand lessons on what makes people work hard. At age sixteen, Mac wanted to quit school and work full time in the mill. Fortunately Charlie Lippard forbade it, and Mac finished high school near the top of his class.

Through the "Lippard Scholarship Foundation," Mac attended Clemson University and earned degrees in both engineering and business. Mac, who graduated summa cum laude, felt delighted to see Charlie Lippard himself at the ceremony. Charlie personally offered him a position at Lippard Industries.

Mac, too young for Korea, avoided the war in Vietnam because of his excellent academic standing at Clemson. However, he was extremely patriotic. The flat top hairstyle he wore in the fifties grew a bit longer in the sixties. But as he began his career at Lippard, he went back to the flat top and conveyed the impression of a polished drill sergeant.

Mac, only five feet, four inches tall, overcame his short stature by a tenacious positive attitude and meticulous talent for tending to details. But beneath his hard exterior was a compassionate and loyal man. The only vice he never corrected was chewing tobacco which he learned at the mill as a kid.

Mac always had his grayish-blue eyes on the future, but he never failed to look back at his mom. Deep inside, she inspired him. He knew Charlie Lippard wanted results... a big bottom line. But his single mom, scratching out a living, gave Mac an understanding of what is important to the folks making what is being sold.

He learned to motivate, not by being a great speaker or dictating work theory to the mill workers, but rather creating an atmosphere where workers knew management cared about them. Mac never forgot his mother's dreams, small as they were. A ten-cent-an-hour raise, a pat on the back, some time off to tend to a sick child became the fabric of Mac's approach to help those workers work harder. And it worked.

An unspoken friction existed between Mac and Charlie Lippard's son Chip. Mac, three years older than Chip, worked tirelessly for the company. He quickly advanced through management positions. As individual mills would develop internal problems, Mac became the point man sent in to bring order and productivity, a problem solver.

Chip graduated from College of the Piedmont, not by meeting minimum requirements, but rather by virtue of a generous donation by the family. Chip partied as hard as Mac worked. But Mac admired his flare and personality, which caused almost everyone to like Chip.

During the mid to late 70s, Charlie Lippard tried to bring Chip into leadership positions in the company. More often than not, Mac cleaned up Chip's mistakes. In 1979, the workers at one mill staged a walkout in protest of their non-union wages. Chip reportedly walked out of the mill at the same time as the workers and into the nearest bar. When Mac told Charlie about it, he fired Chip entirely from the company. Mac had restored order within two and a half days at the plant.

Mac watched Charlie cool down after a couple of months and let Chip back into the company in a controlled environment. "Media Liaison" was his title. The job description meant if any television or newspaper reporter called, he had authority to accept the call and transfer it to his father or Mac. In the meantime, Mac became Charlie Lippard's right-hand man. By 1980, Charlie

Lippard rarely made a decision without Mac's approval. Mac dedicated his life to the company, never forgetting what Charlie Lippard had done for him. Loyalty was as important to Mac as family. Mac had several girlfriends over the years but dated only when work permitted.

The next morning Josh slept until eleven. Being up every three hours to feed Terry exhausted him. When he got out of bed, Janelle had coffee ready, and Terry was looking comfortable in his cradle.

"I think I'll get cleaned up and go over to the hospital to check on Terri. Call her room if you need me."

Josh entered Room 200 which, by hospital standards, rated as a royal palace. Two attendants were in place, apparently monitoring every bodily function of his wife. Her facial expression had not changed. She seemed no better or worse.

Josh's twisted thinking became more than he could handle. He vacillated between trying to justify his decisions or block them out. But as stupid as he felt, he cared for Terri and wished deeply to make things right. He didn't know how.

He sat with her for a couple of hours until he felt hungry and went to the cafeteria. The lunch crowd had thinned. After a short wait in line, he picked up a corn beef on rye, an apple, and a soda. He searched through his thinning wallet and found six one-dollar bills for a $5.75 tab. He located an isolated table in the corner, took a seat, and looked across the room at mostly sad faces. Slowly, Josh watched a gentleman from two tables over rise, walk over, and hand him a large envelope. Josh waited for an explanation, but the man disappeared without speaking. He reached into the envelope and pulled out a phone with no wires attached. Josh had never seen such a phone. Then he saw a smaller envelope, but he was startled as the phone rang. Scanning the face of the phone, he spotted a button labeled "talk" and pushed it.

"Hello, Josh, it's Sid. How are you holding up?"

"I guess I'm getting along, considering the circumstances."

"In the envelope you'll find three thousand dollars in twenty dollar bills. You haven't worked much lately, and we'll need to see you through your financial needs."

"I don't want your money."

"Understand, we're in this together. It's important to us and to you not to have any more problems right now. When we finish this conversation, throw the phone you're holding away with the trash from your lunch."

Josh smirked. "That's not all I'd like to throw in the trash."

Sid seemed to disregard the comment. "When do you plan to start making sales calls again?"

"I thought on Friday I'd go to Columbia Salvage. It's a good, long term customer of mine."

"Good idea," said Sid. "On the way to Columbia, pull off at the rest stop right before you get to I-26. It's that funny one located in the middle of the road. Do you know it?"

"Yeah, I know it."

"Could you meet me at 11:00 a.m.?"

"Do I have a choice?"

"You always have a choice. See you Friday at eleven."

The conversation ended, and Josh dropped the phone in the hospital trash as if it were contaminated with an incurable virus.

A perfectly good phone wasted... Family Intervention seems to waste a lot of things, he thought.

CHAPTER FIFTEEN

Greenville
September 12, 1980

Josh held Terry gently in his cupped hands. He relished evenings alone with his son and talked of tennis and baseball by the fireplace until Terry fell asleep. Josh preferred making funny faces until he thought Terry smiled, rather than thinking about the past.

"We might have to get you a tiny bat, you big boy. Maybe Mommie can pick one out next week." Josh fought back tears as Terry started to cry and felt inadequate and guilty while he waited for Janelle to come off her break. She could handle Terry much better.

The next morning Josh left for his hardly-used downtown office. As he walked in, he noticed the light on the answering machine showed no messages. With no work to do, Josh spent the day behind his old oak "partners" desk, leaning backwards in the swivel chair, trying to figure out how he'd gotten into such a mess, how so many strangers invaded his life. A lawyer, driver, corporate executive, doctor, and many more had created a situation far worse than being a cheating husband.

"Did they create this situation, or did I?" he said out loud in his empty office. The question echoed back at him. Either way, it was devastating. But who could he turn to?

Austin Clemmons, who had stayed at his house and answered his phone, had not bothered to stop by or call in weeks. Josh couldn't understand why he hadn't heard from his friend. He picked up the phone and dialed. The phone rang once, and he received a recording the number had been disconnected. He tried again with the same result.

Josh leaped from his chair and walked rapidly out of the dusty office. The transom glass rattled as Josh slammed the door, and realized, as he jogged down the hall, he'd not locked it. *Who would want in?* He jumped into his car and headed over to Austin's apartment.

Looking through the front window, the vacant apartment left Josh with an empty feeling. Austin had been his anchor and the rope was now untied. *We were best friends.*

They had met at the Greenville Athletic Club in a round- robin racquetball tournament. Although Josh recalled Austin being more aggressive in befriending him, it was a perfect fit. About the same size, they were a close match in racquetball and both played tennis, but not golf. Both loved the Atlanta Braves, and they bought season tickets together. Seemed like they had been friends for years but, as he thought of it, less than ten months.

Where is he? He strolled to the apartment office puzzling the question. The manager looked angry as he informed Josh Austin had moved out three days ago and gave no notice.

"I'll be keeping his security deposit. He should consider himself lucky I don't sue him for the two months left on his lease. You tell him that."

Josh digested this new information and thought through the events of the past two weeks. *Why have I been so distracted I waited this long to touch base with Austin? What possible reason would Austin disappear?* Josh worried about his pal and paced around the parking lot before leaving.

He traveled east on I-385. Questions came to him as fast as the mile markers. He pulled off to the left into the rest area and parked in the first space braking hard to an abrupt stop. He stepped out of the car into the mild, crisp late-morning air. A rented Chevrolet pulled in beside him, and Josh saw Sid sitting alone in the driver's seat with the window rolled down.

"Hello, my friend, join me?" Sid asked cheerfully, leaning his head out toward Josh.

"Why don't we stand outside," Josh said, tiring of doing things Sid's way.

"Sounds like a good idea. What a marvelous day this turned out to be, blue sky, full of promise."

Sid's soft-spoken persuasion relaxed Josh in spite of the bitterness inside of him. "So what's this meeting about," Josh asked, as they both stood on the grass in front of the cars. Sid handed him another envelope containing three thousand dollars.

"Charlie Lippard."

"Why him?"

"The plan is working as well as it can, but behind the scenes, he's asking questions. He tries to conjure up medical issues Terri's own doctors can't see. Every day he has a different doctor reviewing various diagnostic tests and pictures of the accident scene, trying to prove the wreck couldn't have caused these injuries."

"It didn't," Josh said lividly.

"Your father-in-law will not come up with anything, but it's costing us millions of dollars to contain and control information. This isn't your problem, Josh, but we need to revisit Family Intervention's fee for managing the complexities of your situation."

"I thought you were getting two hundred and fifty million."

"We want to share on a fifty/fifty basis."

"A billion dollars?" Josh said, pulling at his blond locks of hair.

"No, no. We share in your net. Don't forget there are Federal estate taxes and state inheritance taxes. Whatever you come up with, for better or worse, our fee is one-half."

"What if I say no?" Josh asked, kicking at a tire on Sid's car.

"Josh, the fee isn't negotiable. Your only option is to deal with your father-in-law alone. You'll lose. You'll be criminally charged.

You'll inherit nothing and have custody of your son jerked out from under you."

"Why do you keep bringing my son into this?" Josh dug his hands deep into his pockets to fight off his need to strike Sid.

"Think of it this way, Family Intervention will have the exact same thing at stake as you do. We'll not fail. We'll handle everything."

"So I guess you want me to sign something?"

"No, we have every document we need. I just want to see your eyes and hear your agreement to the terms."

Josh caught an intensive stare from Sid, as if life or death was at stake. "Well, I guess you got your deal." He stared back at Sid with all the hatred he could muster.

Josh swallowed hard as he struggled to seek an answer to what had nagged him over the past couple of days. "Mind if I ask you a question? Where's my friend Austin Clemmons?"

"Sometimes friendships and good memories should be left in the past. Go make your sale in Columbia."

An hour later, Josh got his usual sales order of four fifty-gallon drums of cleaning solvent, netting a 15% commission of the $2,500 charge. He arrived home at seven, crashed into his leather chair, and Janelle brought Terry to him, the only decent and innocent thing in his life.

"Can I get you a beer, Mr. Rankin?"

"Yes, and it's about time you started calling me Josh."

He took a long chug of the beer, exhaled deeply, and sighed. "Been a long day, Janelle."

"Well, you've got a lot on your mind, I'm sure."

"Maybe I do, but mostly I feel like I don't have a mind, or at least don't bother to use it."

"Don't beat yourself up. You're doing the best you can."

The beer and Janelle's kind words relaxed Josh, and he stepped closer. He sensed an abrupt tenseness in Janelle and excused her forty-five minutes early.

Little Terry and Josh drifted slowly asleep on the leather chair as Sam pushed his nose against the glass in the back door, looking like he was wondering where all the attention had gone. Josh soon fell into a deep, dreamless sleep until he awoke Saturday morning to a wet diaper leaking at the seams.

"My gosh, little fellow, we slept through the whole night."

Terry cried while Josh warmed a bottle, gave him a sponge bath, and put on a fresh diaper. A new sense of guilt pulled in Josh's gut as he reflected on the events of yesterday. He changed his own damp clothes.

"Let's go see your mother," he said. It took Josh an hour and a half to assemble and install the infant car seat he had purchased, at Janelle's suggestion. He drove carefully to the hospital.

His knees were weak when speaking to Terri, even knowing she didn't hear him. He felt better to snuggle blankets around her when she was cool and blow on her neck and ears when she was warm. He still adored her. His cheating tormented him. The deal unnerved him.

As Josh held their son by Terri's bed, he whispered to her softly. "Somehow I'll make this up to you." He wondered if he ever could.

That night at home, Josh pulled out all the neglected mail. This had always been Terri's job. There were bills to pay and checkbooks to balance. Since Terri stopped working at her twelve-thousand-dollar-a-year job at the children's home, they were living off Josh's salary ranging from sixty thousand on a good year to less than fifteen thousand on a slow one. There had always been more money in their checking account than the two earned. His father-in-law subsidized, Josh guessed, but never asked.

Josh wrote checks for all the bills and balanced the books. Two thousand, six hundred dollars short, and he looked to the heavens for an answer. But all he saw was a spider spinning a web between the ceiling and light fixture. He'd have to go down to the bank on Monday and make some arrangements. *There must be some equity in the house, so I can get a second mortgage loan... right?... unless Terri has to sign.* He put the checks in envelopes to be mailed, subject to available funds.

Josh was getting better at putting Terry to bed. The routine was play, feed, change, story, down and out. Josh turned on the television and watched the last four innings of the Braves game.

During the night, Terry had three wake ups, two bottles and one changing. Between tending to his son's needs, Josh slept soundly on the den sofa. At sun up, Sam's scratching on the back door caused an interruption in Josh's snoring. He rolled his face towards the new daylight shining through the windows. He silently wondered what the future held as his face soaked up the rays. "Somebody help me fix things." His voice quivered through the stillness of the morning. No one answered until Terry cried.

Once things settled around the house, Josh went out to take care of Sam. He then walked around the house to get the newspaper. A beautiful warm day with a blue hue blanketing the sky made him smile thinking this day could be his friend. He didn't seem to have any. Glancing down at the *Greenville Post,* he saw the headline — HEIR TO FORTUNE DIES IN PLANE CRASH. Josh stopped. His stomach dropped, and he fell to his knees in the grass.

The story took nearly a third of the front page, describing the family connections, the business, and recent sale. It mentioned a hospitalized daughter and reported no comment available from the family. Chip, from the preliminary investigation, had traces of heroin in his bloodstream. From news archives, the paper had dredged up dozens of colorful stories of the free-wheeling son's lifestyle. DUIs, disorderly conduct at parties, and wrecks where victims had been quickly handled by the Lippard family were summarized. As Josh continued to read, he figured it was no big pill for the public to swallow that this spoiled party boy loaded up on heroin and took a plane ride.

The only twist to the story was that the airport manager spoke with him minutes before takeoff and noticed nothing suspicious about his conduct. The manager was righteously quoted the plane would never have been permitted takeoff if he had observed anything unusual. There were no details about visitation or services.

After finishing the story, Josh fell on his back, seeing nothing but grey above him. He crawled to his feet, went inside, and called the Lippard house.

"Mac, what's happened?"

"Sorry you had to read it in the paper. I've been up since midnight, a tragic mess."

Mac told Josh to come to the Lippard's home and bring Terry. At 2:55, he drove through the guarded gate at No. 2 Chanticleer Drive. Once a year, the same paper reporting Chip's death listed the top ten highest residential county tax assessments in Greenville County. The Lippard mansion was always number one on the list with a value of twenty-eight million dollars. Josh heard Charlie Lippard chuckle the county had it wrong by about seventy percent, but decided not to complain. There would be no humor in this visit.

Chip's death added another layer to Josh's depression. He always liked Chip and felt an unspoken bond under-achievement was okay.

A long time servant of the Lippards appeared, and Josh followed his slow methodical steps into the main entrance. Josh saw a new face in a white uniform waiting stoically by the wall. He turned Terry over to her as Mac appeared.

"Mr. Lippard will see you in the study."

He followed Mac to the elaborate room featured in the most recent issue of *Traditional Southern Homes*. Josh couldn't help but notice his father-in-law appeared ten years older than during the plane trip to Morehead City. His eyes were swollen, and he appeared to be shaking slightly. Yet, emotionally, he seemed to be in control.

Josh looked into Charlie Lippard's tired eyes. Determination seemed replaced with defeat.

"Josh, I'm an old man, and my money has lost my interest. All a man really has in this world is his family. When Elizabeth left this world, I didn't think I could carry on, but I did. Still, a part of me went into the ground with her. Part of me lies in the hospital with Terri. Now I'm told Chip's dead."

Josh watched his father-in-law fall limply against the padded, rounded arm of the Chippendale sofa but then stiffen his back as he continued speaking.

"Countless times I've saved his hide. So many times he has squandered opportunities and disappointed me. But he was always full of life, a decent person. He loved me, and I loved him. The way the media is playing this up, Chip nearly committed suicide. I am quite certain he would never take his own life. I should conduct my own investigation and disprove these allegations, but I'm too tired. What damn good would it do? I've had a bountiful life, but between Terri and now Chip, it's just draining out of me."

Not knowing what to say, Josh merely nodded and listened.

"Josh, I know you and I have never been close but, as I said at your wedding, I believe you to be a man of integrity and honesty. I'm running out of family. I can hire people to handle the details of Chip's funeral, but I want you to do it. Mac will take care of all the financial details. Thousands of people will want to share their sympathies. I really don't have the strength. My brother from Texas and sister from Raleigh will be here shortly. They'll receive visitors with you. Can you do this for me?"

Josh's confusion and weakness made him hesitate in answering the question. Somehow, in the back of his mind, he was to blame for all of this.

"Yes, sir," Josh replied with as much confidence as he could project. Josh vacillated between a hug and a handshake, and the two resolved it with an arm embrace.

"Now, bring me my grandson," Charlie said with renewed gleam in his eyes.

The visitation, set for Monday evening, took place in the Lippard grand hall. Other than a select few, no one had access to the former owner and CEO of Lippard Industries. Josh managed the crowd well, and Mac stood near with useful information as the line progressed. Josh actually became quite proficient in covering his father-in-law's absence.

"Your sentiment means a great deal to Charlie. He appreciates your coming."

The line subsided after 10:00. Security had been tight. Terry stayed at home with Janelle. As Josh drove home, he remembered he had forgotten to go by the bank. *I'll deal with it in the morning.*

At 10:45, he entered Southern Regional Bank. He stopped by the teller to confirm the balance. The teller confidentially slid a piece of paper with the figure. It was six thousand dollars more than his calculation.

"When was the last deposit made?" asked Josh, feeling a bit of relief.

"Yesterday in the amount of three thousand dollars, and the previous deposit was a week ago Monday for the same amount. These appear to be direct deposits into your account."

He first thought Lippard was helping him out, but quickly dismissed it based on the two prior donations courtesy of Family Intervention. "Guess I don't need to see the loan officer," Josh said as he walked out the door. He thought, *honesty and integrity... Charlie Lippard doesn't have a clue.*

"The funeral's at noon, and I need a drink," he chimed out loud as he pulled into *Sam's*. *Sam's* was Josh and Terri's favorite bar. They bought a puppy one afternoon and stopped in to celebrate. On the way out, they giggled they'd found a name for the dog.

"Sorry, sir, but we are not quite open for lunch."

"How about the bar?" "Sorry, sir."

Josh saw Preston, who'd been a bartender there for years, and waved.

"Come on back. Don't pay any attention to these new guys. They come and go. What'll you have?"

"Jack and Jack," Josh said, pulling up a barstool.

"We can handle that. What brings you in at an hour like this?"

"Preston, sometimes life stinks."

"Tell me about it. I am thirty-four, and I can't afford not to be a bartender. I tried my hand at honest work and took a pay cut of fifty percent. I'm good with a bottle and customers are good with tips. I'm stuck."

"I thought you were supposed to listen to my problems."

They both laughed while Josh downed the double Jack Daniels.

"Just what the doctor ordered." Josh laid down a ten-dollar bill and strolled unsteadily out the door.

Two miles, two mints, and two minutes later, he rushed into the house and took Terry from Janelle's arms. "Thank you, Janelle. I can handle the balance of the day. See you tomorrow."

He felt the warm glow of the drink as he chewed a third mint to mask his breath. The curvy gravel trail leading from the busy downtown street to the side of the church was almost like a country road among the vast trees, and Josh spotted Mac with both hands in his pocket, eyeing him like he should have been there much earlier.

As Mac instructed, Josh held Terry and sat beside Charlie Lippard and reverently watched the funeral. The entire staff of ministers from Live Oak Presbyterian Church participated.

Josh remembered Terri, in her frequent efforts to explain her family roots, explaining the history of her church. The original congregation, organized before the Revolutionary War, erected its chapel on the top of a hill which is now in the center of Greenville. An oak brought from Charleston was planted on the "sunset" side of the church to commemorate the occasion. The church adopted its name from the tree because it remained green all year long.

The British burned the chapel prior to the Battle of Cowpens. The congregation buried its losses by the oak. The rebuilt church partially burned again during the Civil War.

The front of the surviving church pointed west, overlooking the gravesites. The engraved side of the headstones looked back at the church to observe the rising sun over the steeple. The live oak continued to grow, as did the casualties buried around it. Many generations of Lippards were identified by worn granite rising up under the ever-expanding limbs.

The service was traditionally Presbyterian. Josh noticed there were no real opportunities for tears. The comments were focused on Chip's relative successes. He had been Chairman of the

Chanticleer Society Ball and headed up Homes for the Homeless in Greenville. It caught Josh's attention flying accomplishments seemed purposely omitted. After a final hymn, the pallbearers, many of who were Chip's party buddies, carried the casket from in front of the pulpit, out of the front of the church and down the long steps leading to a cobblestone parking lot. This area once served to drop off carriage passengers and tie up horses a century earlier and wasn't fifty yards from bustling downtown commerce. Josh remembered Mac saying the crowd would walk behind the casket straight to the newly dug grave.

Charlie Lippard followed the casket, and Josh walked several steps behind him, still holding Terry in his arms. Charlie nodded to the many well-wishers, straining their necks, trying to show concern and respect in their eyes. The procession circled the church and slowly descended to the huge tree where fresh dirt was piled. To the side, bagpipers played an old Irish hymn.

The graveside service was short. With the funeral over, the crowd went into an almost chaotic, but slow moving, ritual of greeting the family. Josh couldn't figure out how it would all end. But after about an hour it did.

Josh accepted Charlie Lippard's thanks for the fine effort he had made with the arrangements knowing it was all Mac's doing. He agreed to visit Charlie on Saturday evening.

Josh, preparing to leave, adjusted the straps of the infant car seat around Terry. He cranked the car, ready to pull off, when Mac appeared at his window.

"I enjoyed working with you, but alcohol and funerals don't mix well. Let's not let that happen again. Come at seven o'clock Saturday."

The week following the funeral moved slowly. He visited Terri daily, but the realization of no improvement had become the norm. Surgeon after surgeon reviewed her case. Josh always got the same conclusion. The brain damage was not reversible.

Josh, being pulled in two directions, mentally fought the battle between Charlie Lippard's insistence his daughter will recover and his knowing she wouldn't. His sanity stretched to its limits.

Saturday was clear and comfortable. Josh thought a long stroll would be great for Terry. When the most likely destination came to mind, Cedar Grove Park, he erased the plan and opted for a nice drive toward the mountains. The mountains were beautiful with the fall leaves bursting with a kaleidoscope of red, yellow, and orange. The sun shined through the colorful foliage, causing Josh to relax in a way escaping him for some time. He drove up to Caesar's Head and took a little walk with Terry warmly bundled in his arms. By sunset, they were back in Greenville and turning into the Lippard complex.

After turning Terry over to the same nanny, Josh followed Mac into the parlor. As Mac began to speak, he saw a look of distrust.

"I've worked for Charlie Lippard for many years. I'm not family. I'm a paid employee. But there is no one more dedicated to your father-in-law. I'm his closest friend and confidant. There's very little I don't know about his affairs. To be quite blunt, I have my concerns about you."

Josh adjusted the collar of his shirt. He couldn't figure what this was about, but it didn't sound good. He couldn't help but squirm in his seat.

"Why are you so concerned about me?"

"Give me a minute, and you'll understand."

"Okay, so I'm listening."

"Charlie has decided to trust you, but I have some reservations. Things happen around you that don't add up. Terri's not one to go to Amanda Loring's house unannounced. The temperature on the day of her accident in September was approximately sixty-five degrees. It makes no sense she would be wearing a thick overcoat. Your father-in-law and I see Terri on a fairly routine basis and never remembered seeing that overcoat or observing her being particularly cold natured."

Josh brushed his hair behind his ears with his hand as he watched Mac dissecting him with his eyes. Tobacco juice pooled slightly at the corner of Mac's mouth.

"Another thing is she called her father one morning a few days before the wreck. She sounded miserable and upset but wouldn't tell him the problem. I'm feeling a little guilty about that call because your father-in-law asked me what I thought. I told him to stay out of it. If Terri wanted to share her feelings with him, she'd do it her own way and in her own time."

As Josh continued to listen, he felt sweat beading lightly above his hairline. He said nothing as he glanced between the floor and Mac's face, trying to keep a controlled expression.

"As I hope you know, Charlie Lippard has had numerous doctors review her case. Most everyone who has considered the accident and her injuries can't quite fit the pieces of the puzzle together. But no one has been willing to totally rule out the car accident caused her injuries. Charlie has finally decided there's no real proof of any wrongdoing and wants to drop it right now."

Josh finally interjected. "What are you talking about? Terri's my wife, and I love her. What do you expect me to say?"

"You don't owe me an excuse, but you need to know I always speak my mind. My instructions have been to drop it. So it's dropped, but I don't have to like it."

Josh felt powerless hearing Mac's words, but slowly exhaled a long breath on the hope it was over. A moment passed as Josh struggled to show some righteous indignation. It wouldn't come.

"Now, we need to talk about your father-in-law's health. We're losing him. Terri's accident and Chip's death have taken a hell of a toll on him. His doctor gives him less than a month. This may be optimistic. His body and mind are fading, and I see the end getting close.

"I don't know why I am telling you this, maybe I shouldn't, but four months ago, when Chip wrecked his new Jaguar, Charlie went into a fit of rage. He tore up his last will and testament. I stood there and watched him do it. The will not only took care of Chip, but also set up trusts for present and future grandchildren for generations to come. Dozens of charities, some founded by your father-in-law himself, stood to benefit from that will. The virtual life of these wonderful institutions, helping folks far more worthy and needy than you, depended on the money. He said he'd redo the will later, but he never did. I'm not sure his mind is sound enough now to even be legal. Bottom line is he has no will. Present circumstances leave Charlie Lippard with one child."

Josh nearly fainted as Mac leaned toward him with a penetrating look that could have belonged to the devil himself.

"Does Terri have a will?"

Josh's face turned white. "A will? I haven't thought about it." He paused. "Come to think of it, we had an attorney friend in our wedding. He prepared them as a wedding gift. We signed the wills after we returned from the honeymoon."

"So how does Terri's will read, Josh?" The question came to Josh in a slow monotone voice.

"Well, we had no children then, so we left everything to each other."

A small cold smirk appeared on Mac's face. "My, my, fortune has a way of smiling on you, Mr. Rankin."

It took a moment for the gravity of what Mac said to fully register with Josh. A feeling of guilt tugged at him, and the room went silent again. Josh tried to regain control of his thoughts as he wondered why Mac, only now, had decided to confront him. The thought crossed his mind Mac wanted something, but what?

"Josh, maybe I'm of line. I should apologize."

"I thought you always said what was on your mind. Why are you apologizing?"

"Okay, then, I won't. There is a concept in business I use when there doesn't seem to be a clear answer to a problem. Its called *follow the money*. Problem is, Josh, if I started running after the dollars flowing from all this tragedy, I'd collide right into your wallet."

A knock at the parlor door interrupted Josh's dilemma, and the nanny entered standing professionally upright. "Mr. Lippard would like to see Mr. Rankin and little Terry."

Josh climbed the long ornate flight of stairs leading to Charlie Lippard's bedroom. Inside sat nothing but a fragment of a once powerful businessman. Josh marveled at the detailed heavy moldings encircling the huge room. Beside Charlie's massive empire-styled bed, Josh spotted Terry in an antique crib nestled close to his grandfather's side. Less than a month old, Terry appeared to have twice the strength of the man sprawled feebly on the edge of the bed, trying to talk to his only grandchild.

"Terry, I know you can't understand me, but you're my future. As my blood flows in your veins, be true to your family."

Josh fought back his emotions as little Terry's arm reached in the direction of his grandfather. Their hands met and held together until the grandfather's arm fell from exhaustion. To Josh, his father-in-law appeared as a pile of bones only held together by evaporating courage. Josh wanted to say something, but he had neither the guts or the words. Josh's spinelessness relegated him to silence. Early the next morning, Josh learned Charles Lippard expired in his sleep.

The funeral arrangements were nearly flawless. Josh, with Mac's help, followed basically the same routine. But the full greatness of Terri's father's accomplishments had never been known nor appreciated by Josh. The lives of countless individuals had been enriched. Charities numbering in the hundreds owed their very existence to Charlie Lippard. But in all of the tribute, what Josh knew would never be mentioned were the financial deaths of entrepreneurs crushed in the name of American capitalism by the Lippard might. He remembered a conversation with Terri.

"Everybody loves Daddy and ignores those poor souls in his way."

"What poor souls?"

"Those trying to get part of Daddy's piece of the money pie."

"What's wrong with that... free enterprise?"

"Yeah, a legal way to wreck another person's family and dreams."

Josh stayed through the last comment, the last tear, waiting for the last guest to leave the graveside. He had left Terry home with Janelle. Josh stood alone under the great oak, except for Mac.

"Josh, I'd appreciate your letting me finish this thing with Charlie by myself. Under the circumstances, Charlie would want it this way, and I've got some things to say to him."

Josh nodded his head solemnly. "Mac, handle it your way and let me know what's next."

"Give yourself a couple of days to mourn. Spend some time with your son and your wife. I'll call you Thursday. You've got some decisions to make."

Josh walked up the hill to his car, amazed at Mac's calm, collected demeanor under the most difficult times. As he unlocked the driver's door, he looked back at the setting sun over the cemetery and noticed Mac on his hands and knees crying like a young child. He couldn't bear to watch.

Josh agreed to meet at the Lippard mansion for lunch on Friday. He drove up to the front steps, and there was no one to open the car door. He escorted himself through the opened front door, was greeted by Mac and followed him to a bountiful luncheon set up in the sunroom on a glass table. There, in privacy, Josh began listening to Mac's carefully worded comments.

"Charlie Lippard's estate will soon begin probate. Under the laws of intestacy, your wife Terri will inherit everything. There will be a handful of greedy relatives with the last name of Lippard, who will want to serve as Terri's conservator. They still hold a grudge for being muscled out of Lippard Industries decades ago."

"Why?"

"They can't acknowledge to themselves they sold out to their own laziness and self indulgences. You'll defeat these challenges. In other words, when the dust settles, you'll be in charge of all Lippard assets. Two years ago, these assets weren't liquid. Privately held stock, real estate holdings with long term corporate leases, and other committed assets would have really tied your hands. That all changed when Charlie sold the company to International."

"I'm not sure I'm following you."

"Six months ago Charlie Lippard's estate turned primarily into cash which, in the Lippard tradition, has been compounding nicely in market securities. Simply put, you're rich."

"What if I don't want to be rich?" Josh asked, sounding somewhat insincere, even to himself. He wished he had chosen better words, as Mac seemed to be relishing choosing a pointed response.

"Get use to it, Josh."

Josh fumbled with a butter knife, attempting to spread a port cheese over a cracker, breaking it in half. He finally put both down and decided to listen to Mac.

"Josh, the first decision you must make is what about me. I've given you every reason to dislike me. What I said, I meant. Feel free to relieve me of my duties. I have the skills to take my career elsewhere. However, I know this family, its assets, and the pitfalls better than anyone. I can cut to the chase where it'll take others months to unravel the same mess. But I'll honor whatever decision you make."

Josh thought long and hard as he swallowed his fresh tuna salad. "Why don't we take things a day at a time? Maybe we can grow to like each other and earn each other's respect."

Mac looked somewhat neutral to the idea. As Josh waited on an answer, it occurred to him, no matter how valuable Mac might be, Josh held the key to the vault.

"Okay, that sounds like a practical decision. Now, may I recommend an attorney to probate the estate?"

Josh looked up from his plate. "Like I said, let's take things slowly. I'll find an attorney."

Josh, a single child, hadn't been as close to his parents since joining the Lippard family. They'd been down for the wedding a year and a half ago and communicated infrequently by phone and cards on holidays and birthdays. Josh called them about Terri's wreck but asked them not to come down. He thought it best now to fly to Ohio to patch things up and get a handle on his new situation. He certainly had plenty of money in his account with the weekly three thousand dollar direct deposits. He wanted to see his folks, and Janelle could keep Terry.

When he arrived, his parents seemed disappointed he didn't bring the baby. He promised to bring Terry next visit and then spent hours explaining his new fortune. Somehow, he believed some cash would make up for the lack of attention he had given them.

"Josh, we don't care about the money; we care about your wife. Tell us what we can do for Terri," said his mother.

The next day Josh visited an old high school buddy who now practiced law. The attorney did some checking and recommended a Greenville attorney named Herb Hall. Before leaving Akron, Josh made an appointment for Tuesday.

The sign outside of Hall's office indicated he practiced alone. Paint peeled around the entrance door of what used to be a home near the courthouse.

A smell of stale carpet and dusty furniture penetrated Josh's nose as the receptionist announced him over an old intercom. The attorney emerged before he could take a chair.

Hall explained his law practice of domestic, criminal, and probate. Josh felt uneasy this guy wasn't the caliber of a Jordan Tower. But since the contact came through his friend, Josh agreed to the ninety-five dollar an hour rate and began giving Hall the details of the Lippard estate. Josh was surprised to learn that Hall had never heard of the family name.

"Wow. This would be the largest estate I've ever handled."

Because of Hall's child-like excitement, Josh questioned in his own mind how much "checking around" his friend had done. Josh agreed, since he had only basic details about the estate, to have Mac call Hall later in the week. Josh could schedule another appointment later.

CHAPTER SIXTEEN

Greenville
Wednesday, October 2, 1980

Josh's daily visit at the bedside of his wife stirred emotions between boredom and a broken heart. He watched her always-constant stare and listened to the ebb and flow of her signs of life. There had been times when Josh had fallen asleep at the bedside, listening to the cadence of her breathing. During those times Josh felt peace in his heart, as when they had slept in each other's arms, in love, committed. In the moment when Josh awoke at her bedside, he anticipated her hand rubbing his face with the familiar touch meaning everything is okay. Whatever once caused the touch was no longer behind Terri's eyes. *Where did she go?* He repeated the question constantly to himself.

Josh heard a new voice from behind.

"Hello, Mr. Rankin. My name is Dr. Pat Davis, and I recently opened my own neurology clinic here in Greenville."

Josh felt a bit annoyed. "Really?"

"Yes sir, new in town."

"Oh? Why are you in here? She has a bunch of your types."

"I practiced in Miami for about ten years but needed a change of scenery. It sure beats the heat."

"Well, I guess I should say welcome to town, but I'm trying to visit with my wife right now if it's alright with you."

"Of course, I didn't mean to interfere. I thought you ought to know something."

Josh, tired of the interruption, cut his head sharply toward the doctor. "Know what?"

"From a clinical standpoint your wife's condition is very interesting. May I speak confidentially?"

Josh looked at him suspiciously. "Go on."

"Rolling Hills Neurology Group seems to have no desire to resolve this case. Word around here is her father said money was no object, so they keep her alive. You know... it's sort of a cash cow for both the doctor group and the hospital. You may have noticed this hospital has plenty of empty beds."

Josh felt confused. "So why are you telling me this?"

"No reason in particular. I feel folks ought to get a fair shake, no matter how much money they have. It's good to know you have options. Good day, Mr. Rankin."

The balance of the week involved Josh making a few local sales calls, but nobody was buying. Actually, he felt a loss of interest in selling. Maybe in the past month he had heard one sales pitch too many.

Friday afternoon, he called Mac and got confirmation Herb Hall had the essential information. On Monday morning Josh received a call from the secretary stating Mr. Hall wanted to meet with him as soon as possible. Josh made an appointment for four o'clock that afternoon. When he arrived, no secretary greeted him. He followed Hall back to his office and noticed the attorney seemed very excited.

"Do you have any idea how much money is involved in this estate?"

Again, he felt he may have been too impulsive in his choice of an attorney. Josh tried to act casual about his new wealth. "Maybe eight billion?"

"Well, pretty darn close. Try 9.2 billion."

"Listen, Mr. Hall, I may need to get a second legal opinion on this."

He made a mental note never to consult his high school chum on any more legal questions. Josh's attention shifted when a distinguished looking gentleman emerged from an interior office. He appeared to be in his forties and was tall, broad, and well dressed.

"This is John Hamilton of the Atlanta firm of Hamilton and Hamilton. I've now been associated with the new office they're opening here in Greenville".

When Mr. Hamilton stepped forward, Josh perceived great skill and discretion. His reluctance for Hall melted as John explained in his deep methodical voice his firm specialized in nothing but probate and tax.

"I promise, Josh, the focus of our efforts will be to see the most minimal estate taxes are paid, the assets are properly accounted for and well invested to protect your principal, and give you attractive returns. Due to the size and importance of this estate, three attorneys, in addition to me, and four paralegals will work basically around the clock."

Josh turned to him. "Are you honoring Mr. Hall's ninety-five dollar per hour rate?"

"Of course, we will, and there will be no charge for our paralegals' time. Since Herb is our local counsel, he'll sign pleadings and petitions in Probate Court, along with tax documents."

John confidently answered Josh's questions and gracefully put his mind at ease. He felt very comfortable with the new attorney. *Now this guy knows his stuff,* Josh thought.

When Josh looked at his watch, John said, "It's getting late. Could I take you for dinner? I could finish answering whatever questions you might still have."

"Sure, but I need to be home by eight o'clock."

Herb Hall, noticeably left out of the invitation, appeared to fade into John's shadow, which suited Josh fine." Josh suggested dinner at the Sea and Vine restaurant. Josh had a sense of importance when the owner greeted him by name and quickly found them a table overlooking the fountains highlighted with lights. During cocktails, Josh suggested he order dinner for both.

"I spent quite a bit of time in restaurant management. You wouldn't believe what goes on in some kitchens, John. I've got a pretty good handle on what the chefs have to work with here."

"I feel like I've struck gold, Josh. With my luck in ordering, we'd both be eating rubber chicken. Please take charge."

Josh liked controlling the meal and couldn't help noticing John's eyes focused on his every motion and every word. *This is one dedicated lawyer,* he thought.

After dinner and dessert, he ordered cordials and began to relax. The conversation turned to Terri's condition. Josh explained she had not spoken or shown any signs of brain activity for nearly a month and a half. "The physicians' consensus prognosis remains no recovery.

John said nothing for a moment, leaned back in his chair, and the sad, soothing look in his eyes put Josh in a calm mood. He threw back his hazelnut liquor hoping John could give him some direction in his life.

Finally, John spoke in a compassionate voice. "Josh, I practice law, but that doesn't mean I can't care. I never met Terri, but I can tell by the passion in your voice you feel her in every heart beat."

"You're right. I love her more than you could know. But it's hard, hard because of things I can't tell you. Hard because I can't help her. Hard because I've finally decided I've lost her for good."

"Josh, what would you want for yourself if you were lying in bed, in her condition?"

"Let me go."

"Did you and Terri make wills and, if you did, did they contain a living will?"

"What's that?"

"This is a commonly used instrument to deal with situations like this. The law is called 'Death With Dignity' and makes it much easier to end unproductive suffering upon proper medical documentation."

"I don't know if we signed one of those or not. I remember storing the papers in our safety deposit box, probably haven't looked at it since.

"If it's not inconvenient," asked John, "would you mind retrieving the wills and related documents so I can review them?"

Josh agreed.

"The banks will re-open on Monday. I'll be in all day."

Josh reached for the check, but it was already in John's hand.

"Let it be an expense of the estate... it saves taxes."

Josh grinned. "See you Monday."

By eleven o'clock Monday morning, Josh had retrieved the wills and other papers and left for Herb Hall's office. Neither Hall nor his receptionist were present. Josh found John Hamilton flipping through papers in a back office.

"Good morning, Josh. You're quick. Let's see what you've got."

John read through the documents, showing no emotion and speaking not a word. After eighteen minutes, Josh watched him put down the documents and lift his eyes.

"You and Terri both signed mutual wills and respective living wills. It's good you have an opportunity to respond to her wishes."

"What are you saying?"

"Over the past few hours, I have confirmed what you have told me about Terri's condition. She'll never talk, hear, or have any level of basic human feeling. A life on machines is no life at all. There's no dignity to such a life. The estate, which you are appointed to handle, is paying eighteen thousand dollars per day to sustain this so-called existence.

"What choice do I have?"

"You can do the math over the next ten years, should you choose to prolong her suffering. But her living will provides, if the primary medical provider documents a condition such as hers, she should be removed from life support systems. Her body will then be left to its own means."

"You mean she'll die?"

When John Hamilton did not reply to his question, Josh got up.

"I'll need to think about this." He left the office with one destination in mind, his wife. As he entered her suite, the entire staff in charge snapped to attention, like a show. They began checking tubes, resetting monitors, recording data, and making things look busy. What were the words he recalled... *cash cow*?

"Hello, Mr. Rankin. She's doing fine today. Can we get you something to drink or eat? We can call the doctor if you have any questions."

The same routine, he got all the attention and Terri remained the same. After all, he was paying the bills.

"Everybody out."

"What?" a nurse asked.

"You heard me. I need time alone with my wife."

The staff looked shaken in response to his uncharacteristic behavior as they left, and it didn't bother Josh at all.

He walked to the side of the bed and held her hand. "They say you want death with dignity. I don't remember talking about that, do you? When we signed those papers after the honeymoon, did we understand it? Hell, I didn't. I wrote my name by the sticky arrows. You did too, right?"

Josh felt helpless. "Tell me what to do. You understand stuff, and you know I can't handle this. I need you right now. I've always needed you." A lump stuck in his throat.

"I'm sick of this dignity crap. I'm alive with no dignity." He cried, sobbing long and hard, hoping she'd wipe away the tears, or somehow rescue him from his misery. After an hour, the tears dried by themselves.

"You're not coming back, are you? You can't make things better."

Josh needed a friend, the tearing of his emotional fiber to share.

Where's Austin when I need him?

By default, he called Mac and found a stable friend willing to carefully listen to his dilemma.

"Josh, if you want to know what her dad would do, a Lippard doesn't pull the plug on a Lippard. He'd be inflexible on the matter. Charlie's dead. It's your call. Quite frankly, I've personally reviewed all the medical reports, and we've lost her. Terri's not coming out of this."

"I know."

"I've seen more people than you can possibly imagine milk the Lippard fortune. At times it sickens me, but Charlie always made the calls for his own reasons. Eventually you'll need to make the decision. Eighteen thousand dollars a day, if it makes you feel better, is something you certainly can afford. She's your wife and mother of your son. Do what you think best, but don't waiver. Be strong in your conviction."

As Josh thanked Mac for the talk, he thought to himself, *what a joke. Strong in my conviction? I wasn't strong enough to face up to my own failure as a husband, and now I stand to be a rich man by ending the life I caused to become non-functioning. Terri deserves better. Our son deserves a better father.*

Josh, with Mac by his side, handled the third funeral in two months. So much money and so much death. Virtually the same cast of players from Greenville made the rounds. Rumors circled around town about the coincidences. Not knowing how to deal with it, Josh again turned to Mac.

"Ignore them. These same people will be crawling back to you when they need a donation to their charity. Trust me, this will all pass."

The process for removing life support systems had come quickly and easily after Josh wrote a certified letter to Rolling Hills Neurological Group advising that Dr. Pat Davis would take over primary care of his wife. Within days, Dr. Davis honored Josh's requests and fully documented the patient's irreversible condition. The document contained the medical nomenclature meeting South Carolina's legal requirements for a "Death With

Dignity." John Hamilton stood by him in the decision, offering sympathetic counsel and support, lending confidence to Josh's difficult circumstances.

Josh dreaded his final visit. Before leaving the house for the hospital, he took Terry from his crib and they slipped under the covers of Josh and Terri's unmade bed. Josh placed his head beside Terry's on the same pillow Terri's head rested when Terry was conceived. Josh remembered the exact night and the happiness that followed when they found out they were expecting.

"I'm so lucky. I couldn't ask for more," Josh had told Terri. He somehow knew she was behind any success he had since their marriage.

"I love the idea of having your baby, and I hope I'll love it as much as I do you," he recalled her saying.

Josh's soul ached as he cuddled on the pillow beside his son. He couldn't stand thinking about the gravity of the wrong he had committed. As he cried, he tried to confess.

"I don't know why I'm the way I am. You've got a lousy dad. I've prayed, wished on stars, and begged and begged for your mama to get better. If she could talk right now, she ought to tell you how much better you are than me. But she wouldn't. She'd tell you to be patient with me. I hope your heart and mind will be like hers. You'll be better and smarter.

"But I need to ask you something," Josh said as he began to sob heavily. "It's because she can't hear me." The words failed to come to his lips, as they felt choked within his throat. They emotionally struggled to his tongue and exited slowly. "So I've got to beg you instead... please, please forgive me."

Josh stood by Terri's hospital bed. His swollen eyes met Terri's face. Her eyes looked different somehow or, perhaps, it was his imagination. Ending her life with her son in his arms crushed him. Josh watched Terry touch his mother's face, her nose, and her ears as if they communicated. Josh broke down weeping. "Why did I do this to you?"

Josh heard Dr. Davis come into the room and order a nurse to take the child. Josh jerked his head towards the nurse. "Get away from me." He quivered as the doctor put his hand on his shoulder.

"Don't blame yourself, Josh. Everything possible has been done. It's best to let nature run its course."

Josh wrestled from the doctor's touch. He put his arms around Terri's neck and hugged her for the last time.

As Josh carried Terry carefully out of the hospital, he could visualize the staff stripping Terri of her life support, vitals draining from her slowly, death sneaking up on her, all because of him.

Hours later, Josh called his family in Ohio, hoping to unload some of his guilt. His mother's soft, concerned voice brought him again to tears. "Mom, I've failed everybody."

Josh saw Herb Hall and John Hamilton at the visitation on Thursday night and Dr. Davis at the funeral on Friday. He wondered if they'd met

An early morning phone call from John Hamilton on Tuesday brought Josh back to Herb Hall's office. Again, the offices were empty except for John. Josh accepted John's explanation he had staff personnel, located in different offices in both Greenville and Atlanta, who were very busy with the estate.

"I know these last few days have been very difficult for you. Sometimes getting busy with the estate can give you some diversion and a sense of purpose. Do you think it appropriate if we got started?"

"Sure, why not."

"Because Chip died before Mr. Lippard, he's not considered a beneficiary under his father's estate. Since Terri outlived her father, she's the only heir to her father's estate which will be controlled by the laws of intestacy since he had no valid will. He apparently had a prior will, but revoked it by an act of destruction. Therefore, Terri owns everything Charlie Lippard owns. Terri had a will. You're the sole beneficiary since you outlived Terri."

"Whoa... you're talking Greek. Cut to the chase."

"Of course, Josh, subject to estate taxes, you're the sole owner of real and personal property in the neighborhood of nine and a half billion dollars."

"Man alive."

Josh's attention focused as John oddly shifted in his chair and continued, "This morning a complex package of documents arrived at my office. This, quite frankly, took me somewhat by surprise since I knew of no other interest in the estate. I have, however, reviewed the package, and it seems to be in order."

"What are you talking about?" Josh asked, as if he had innocently forgotten.

"A concern by the name of Family Intervention has presented several interesting documents, and I need for you to verify whether or not these are your signatures."

Josh took a large stack of papers from John. He slowly leafed through the pages and found his signature on frequent occasions. The documents were no strangers to him. It hadn't been long since he signed them.

Josh answered truthfully. "Those are my signatures."

"Josh, my job is, on your behalf, to administer these estates. It's not my place to question your arrangements. I'm certain your reasons are good, and you intend to honor them."

Josh looked at John with an expression of "thank you for not asking."

"Since you have verified the signatures, there's no reason to worry about the details. That's why you pay me. Let's talk about the Lippard mansion. Do you think you and your son would like to live there or sell the place?"

"Wow, you're throwing me a curve ball. The old home would be one great place for Terry to grow up, but it may be too much, too quick. I don't know."

"Maybe you should sell your house first. It'll be easier to sell your place and figure out whether to move into the mansion later."

"Not a bad idea. If I move into the big house, I could direct maintenance and operate my office out of there, save costs and rents."

"Josh, you don't really need to worry about money, but it's probably best for you to keep your mind busy over the next few weeks to get you through this emotional time."

"So how much money will I be left with?"

"A lot, but we won't know for sure until we deal with the South Carolina Department of Revenue and the I.R.S. I may try to work out some charitable donations to help you meet your obligations to Family Intervention, save you a bundle in taxes."

Josh nodded his approval on saving money, but he felt clueless about the reasoning.

"Remember, you need to leave these details for me to handle for you. If you want to do something, go list your house and make arrangements to move to Two Chanticleer Drive. I'll call you towards the end of the week."

Josh walked out of Hall's office feeling liberated. John Hamilton would handle Family Intervention. *Maybe saving me a bundle will stick it to Richardson. I'll finally wash my hands of that bastard and get a normal life.*

CHAPTER SEVENTEEN

Greenville
November 5, 1980

Josh received a letter dated October 21, 1980, from Herb Hall, two weeks since their meeting. The letter laid out details of probate, legal advertising, and something about a probate deed for the Lippard house. Josh quit reading after a couple of paragraphs out of boredom. *That's why I'm paying those guys.* But Josh did think it was strange that John Hamilton hadn't written the letter and decided to follow up first chance he got.

For some reason, his sales rep. business had gotten extremely active, and it looked like the orders would exceed his best month ever. The phone wouldn't stop ringing with new orders, taking up all his time. It made him feel good to see the answering machine full every time he walked into the office. Between constant sales calls, realtors showing the house, and weekends with Terry, time flew by. After a couple of weeks, Josh quit answering the business phone, took the day off, and arrived unannounced at Herb Hall's office for a status report.

He found the receptionist filing her nails at her desk and asked her to see John Hamilton.

"Have a seat, and Mr. Hall will be with you shortly."

After about ten minutes, Herb Hall stepped out of his office and motioned Josh back. "Where's John Hamilton?"

"I thought you knew John's law firm no longer needed a Greenville office, and they felt comfortable with my handling of the estate."

"What?"

"John said he had met with you over lunch, explained it to you, and you were fine with it. You wanted an update on progress each month. In fact, I wrote you a letter the next week. Did you get it?"

Josh felt sick to his stomach. "Yeah, I got it. So where's my money?"

"John handled the complicated part of setting up accounts, selling stocks and bonds, and wiring creditors. I've mainly worked on the real estate that, for the most part, is the Lippard mansion. John worked on the rest of this until yesterday when he left."

Josh screamed, "Left where?"

"Well, Atlanta."

Josh watched Hall begin to shake, rise from his aging padded chair and pace back and forth. The unusual behavior aggravated Josh more, and he ordered Hall to get the file, which turned out to be five large boxes.

"This one box is the real estate file. The rest are John's part that he turned over to me with, what I understood, was with your permission. I haven't had a chance to go through John's boxes yet. If you'd like, we could do that now."

"Stop," Josh shouted while getting three inches from Hall's face. "First of all, there was no luncheon. John never said anything about not handling things, and I didn't agree to let him out. Something's bad wrong here. You leave these boxes right here on this table. Don't move them, and get me a phone."

Josh called Mac Carter. "I don't know for sure if anything is wrong, but something smells rotten about this estate business."

"Slow down, Josh, what are you saying?"

Josh summarized the events since his first visit to Herb Hall.

"Damn, I'll be there within the hour."

In thirty-five minutes, a parade consisting of Mac and three of Lippards regular lawyers marched by Josh. There were no courtesies at the reception desk.

"Mr. Hall, I suggest you sit in the corner with your mouth shut before it gets worse for you," said Mac with a look that could sink the battleship Constitution.

Josh smiled a bit as the other lawyers nodded their heads at Hall while passing as a row of penguins. The receptionist left hurriedly with a fear in her eyes.

After about two hours, Josh watched Mac and his three lawyers emerge from the conference room.

"Look, this lawyer of yours has screwed up big time. We don't see any record of an Atlanta law firm of Hamilton & Hamilton as participating in this estate. It's all Hall. It'll take a lot of time to figure out what has happened, but around 4.75 billion dollars, the majority of the liquid assets coming from the sale of Lippard Industries, have been paid out to five separate charities. What were you thinking when you hired this sleazeball?"

Josh sensed the familiar failure plaguing him as long as he could remember. His freedom of Sid Richardson felt snatched from him like a house shingle in a hurricane.

"Half of the estate has gone, and taxes have yet to be paid. These so-called charitable organizations are ones nobody ever heard of. These three attorneys will work through the night on this."

Josh took a step back as Mac cut his eyes towards the legal talent, suggesting they not sleep until he says sleep.

Josh felt Mac's eyes flash back in his direction. "And the last damn thing I'll say, while your piss-ant lawyer quivers in the corner of this gutter-slime office, is he better call his malpractice insurer."

Josh watched Herb Hall melt in the stains of the carpet as Mac fumed out the entrance door, slamming it in his wake.

There was a South Carolina Supreme Court decision handed down many months after Josh Rankin retained Mr. Hall. Most grievance opinions are generally boring, ranging from neglecting a client to embezzling a client's money. The reading of these opinions is slow, tedious, and done primarily by other lawyers, judges, and mad clients.

Not so with Matter of Herbert L. Hall. Four and three-quarter billion vanished, and the Atlanta firm of Hamilton & Hamilton never existed. Television and radio talk shows had a field day with Herb Hall. "Got legal problems, watch'em grow under the careful legal analysis of Herbie Hall."

All transactions were made by virtue of Power of Attorney signed by Josh Rankin in favor of Herb Hall. Handwriting analysis proved Rankin's signature genuine, Hall signed all probate documents, and Hall's signatures on all bank accounts were remarkable forgeries.

The Court disbarred Hall, a unanimous decision with the exception of one dissenting Justice. The dissent concentrated on Josh Rankin's basic agreement of the facts and his unwillingness to divulge the reason he signed so many documents that became the tools used to transfer money out of the estate. The lone dissent found Hall to have been extremely naive but felt Rankin played a part of a conspiracy with motives known only to Rankin.

Josh couldn't care less about Herb Hall's law license or the hoopla of the decision. For weeks following the disappearance of the money, he was nauseous, unable to hold down food, and dropped to one hundred thirty-two pounds. He counted on Janelle more and more to keep Terry. He hardly went to his office and spent most of his time sleeping or stirring about, without purpose, in the sitting room.

When he finally got his head straight, he began a mission to find out what happened. He needed help, but whom could he turn to?

Josh had let the Lippard lawyers put words in his mouth. He basically said he signed the documents because Hall put him up to it. He couldn't tell the lawyers the documents had been signed many months before anyone died. Any truthful explanation to the Lippard lawyers, would land him broke and in jail. He led the lawyers to think the missing four and three-quarter billion had been embezzled from the estate, and he was the victim. He certainly couldn't complain Family Intervention took far more than the fifty/fifty split after taxes. Unable to manage the frustration, he turned again to Mac.

"Josh, this problem is too big, too strung out. Turn it over to the Feds."

The Feds were slow. Nearly twenty months passed from the time his fortune disappeared until Josh learned the trail of money led to five organizations. Each had tax-exempt status, all perfectly legal corporations, registered with the State and Federal governments. The respective Articles of Incorporation listed officers, board members, and location of corporate offices. Each proclaimed humanitarian purposes such as AIDS research, food banks for third world nations, or environmental rescue efforts. Josh fumed as he discovered every corporation had a bank account with a large national bank, and in each account nine hundred fifty million dollars was deposited. The money moved through an ingenious network of deposits and withdrawals. The paper work went through reputable banks and loan institutions which had no knowledge the monies were tainted. The trails of money eventually were funneled into poorly regulated third-world banks. Individuals operating under fictitious names made withdrawals. The trail went cold. The money was gone.

Josh repeatedly asked government agencies to investigate these charitable corporations. All application and charter documents were in order, but the names turned out to be fictitious. The only break in the investigation involved a man by the name of Wilbur Brewer. He presented his driver's license and became the authorized signature on all of the original five bank accounts.

The FBI and Federal Reserve officers investigated Brewer. Josh found out that he was given a thousand dollars a week to go to various banks to open accounts and later sign checks or withdrawal slips. He identified the man providing the money as James Sexton.

"He bought me a nice suit and took me to all of the banks. He always told me what to say. Strange, I know, but a thousand dollars cash a week was more than I could turn down. Since losing my last job, I was behind on my car and mobile home payments, and my wife was giving me a fit."

Josh considered the official recommendation of charging Brewer but ultimately agreed to the unofficial comment, "Why bother?

CHAPTER EIGHTEEN

Greenville
June 10, 1982

Josh decided to help himself and make some visits. He started with the law office of Roberts, Justin, and Tower. "I'm here to see Jordan Tower."

"Your name?"

"Josh Rankin."

"Do you have an appointment?"

"No, but he'll remember me, and it's urgent."

"One moment, please." He watched her disappear into the inner sanctum of the law firm where he was a catered client less than two years ago.

"I'm sorry. Mr. Tower sees clients only by appointment and doesn't recall you," the receptionist said returning to her chair.

Josh got agitated. "You look at your computer. On September 4, 1980, I saw him right here in this building."

He watched the receptionist type and then look up at him. "Are you certain you have the right law office? There's no record of you."

Josh was bitter. "Now you listen, I'm staying right here until Jordan Tower sees me. Got it?"

A gentleman appeared, startling Josh. "What's going on here?"

"He has no appointment, and he won't leave."

"Sir, my name is Landon Justin. If you don't leave, we'll simply call security and have you arrested. Is that what you want?"

"Okay, okay. I'll handle it my own way."

Josh left, stumbling across Jefferson Avenue and collapsing on a park bench. His plan was falling apart, and he needed to collect his thoughts. Returning to his office, he spotted the City Directory. It had both office and home addresses. As he went through the "Ts," he found Jordan Tower, 1843 River Road. He knew this street and left to stake it out.

Late that evening, with no headlights, he pulled in behind Jordan Tower and followed him a quarter of a mile down Tower's driveway. Turning on his headlights, Josh jumped from his vehicle and confronted Tower. "Hello, Mr. Lawyer, remember me? Remember Family Intervention? Remember my billions?"

Tower appeared shaken. "I don't know you. If I ever did, I have forgotten you. Get off of my property."

"It's not that easy. I'm ready to go down and take you with me if I don't get my money back."

"As sure as I know we've never met, I'm as sure you're in way over your head. Whatever record you think exists, doesn't. Whoever you think can corroborate your paranoia, you won't find. Good day, Mr. Rankin."

"You think this thing's over? Not by a long shot... you wait," Josh threatened as Tower disappeared through the huge wooden door of his home.

Josh, tired and frustrated, needed to figure out his next move. He decided to have a drink and regroup. *Maybe my next stop will be the Family Intervention complex.*

He found Janelle and Terry patiently waiting for him at home. He grabbed Terry, now twenty pounds and the joy of Josh's life. Josh took a Jack Daniel and water from Janelle and sat down in his leather chair.

"Realtors are calling every hour, a bunch of hot prospects," Janelle said.

Josh took a long sip of the drink. "You know I'm losing interest in selling this place, take the receiver off the hook, please."

"Sure, I'll take care of it. It's only seven o'clock. Can I fix you some dinner?"

"No, but you could have a drink with me."

Janelle appeared to hesitate. "Maybe a short one after I change." Then she laughed. "It's not like someone's waiting for me at home."

Janelle Barr, divorced and childless, escaped a short and abusive marriage. She physically looked a few years older than her twenty-eight after years of working in an emergency room and handling severe trauma cases over long shifts. Between her job and an unreasonably demanding husband, she simply burned out. After the divorce, she quit the emergency room job and began working part time in various nursing positions.

The Rankin child position, quickly posted in a nursing trade publication, received more than usual attention because of the generous hourly rate. The interview process took place at the old corporate offices of Lippard Industries. She, along with a dozen other applicants waited her turn for an interview with Mac Carter. Janelle thought they needed a babysitter, not nurse, but a big paycheck with no stress sounded appealing, a welcome break.

Janelle liked living her life quietly, safely, uncomplicated. She looked very pretty and shapely, but wore little makeup or jewelry. Her auburn hair, cut into a neat Dorothy Hamill style, contrasted radiantly above her white uniform. Protective and apprehensive, she hadn't had a date since the divorce, in spite of several friends actively trying to line her up.

Men scared her. Her father had touched her inappropriately, starting with her thirteenth birthday. She became victim to her mother who feared losing a husband with a good job. Janelle heard through the walls her mother's half-hearted lectures to her father which apparently fell on deaf ears. After high school, she went into nursing school and never returned home.

Josh, never seeing Janelle out of a white uniform, was caught off guard when she returned wearing a lavender silk top with black slacks. Josh, on his third glass, glanced over her nicely curved body. She took a seat half way down the sofa, and faced Josh seated on the end. He admired her hazel eyes and handed her a drink.

"I don't know what I'd do without you."

She looked appreciative. "Keeping Terry is rewarding enough, and you pay me well."

"How well do I pay you?" Josh asked, knowing Mac took care of her arrangements out of the Lippard Transition Account.

"Forty-five dollars an hour."

"You're worth it."

Her smile and the warmth of the alcohol pleased Josh as their eyes joined while she finished the drink.

"Well, I guess I should be going."

Josh gazed at her as she began picking up the empty glasses. "I really wish you wouldn't." He stood, stepped forward and gently touched her arm.

"Look, you've lost your wife. You're working through things, and I need this job." Her hand felt soft on his as she patted him and said goodbye.

Josh's face, flush from the brief moment with Janelle, realized over a year had past with no affection. His thoughts reflected on Angie. Six months of unbelievable passion ended with one phone call.

Josh heard Terry crying, changed his dirty diaper and gave him a bottle. They both fell asleep, moving back and forth in the big wooden rocker Janelle ordered.

After a few hours, Josh awoke. "Sinclair," he screamed. He put Terry in his crib, walked to a computer a technology salesman in his office building sold him and installed and entered a relatively new world, the Internet. Remembering the instructions, he typed *New England Journal of Medicine.* He found a web-site but no article of a Dr. Sinclair. Josh retried a dozen times in various word combinations, but he only pulled up a Connie Sinclair who contributed to an article on orthopedics.

Josh lay awake until Janelle arrived at 8:00.

"You look exhausted," she said.

"I am."

Within an hour, Josh showered, shaved, and dressed. He told Janelle he had to go, and by 10:15 he nervously approached the intersection of Hwy. 221 and the Family Intervention entrance way.

His tires slid on the gravel upon the pavement as he braked to a stop before striking a welded pipe gate. Upon it hung a sign, "For Sale or Lease."

He sat for a moment, looking past the gate into the empty parking lot. Slowly he got out of the car and found the waist-high gate padlocked. He slipped around the galvanized pole at the end of the gate and into the vacant lot.

Neglected landscaping, cracked asphalt, and peeling paint reminded Josh of a ghost-town as he pulled on dead-bolted doors around the building. He returned to the car and called Mountain Ridge Realty, the listing agent advertised on the sign.

"Hello. I'm calling about the block building facility off Highway 221."

"Oh, you mean the Sun-Grill Plant."

"Well, there're no signs other than yours."

"Let me let you speak to Conrad Reed. He handles our commercial property."

"May I help you?" Reed asked.

"Yes, my name is Josh Rankin, and I wanted to inquire about the... I believe you call it the Sun-Grill Plant?"

"Yes, sir, may I ask what type of business or industry you represent?"

"Well, I'm actually an individual."

"Mr. Rankin, I'll be glad to show you the property, but the price is three and one-half million, and the facility has fifty thousand square feet and is suitable only for an industrial use."

"I'm the executor of the Leopard Estate in Greenville. Have you heard of the family?"

"Of course," replied Reed. "Tell me where you are."

"Just outside the plant."

"I can be there in less than an hour."

"I'm waiting."

Twenty-nine minutes later, Josh saw Conrad Reed turning off of 221 nearly on two tires, unlock the gate, and drive towards him.

"I'm sorry about my hesitation, but we get so many entrepreneurial hustlers up here."

Josh interrupted. "Say no more, I understand."

Josh requested a tour of the place and followed Reed through the front door, which faced the gate, the opposite side from where both Paul and Bob Chambers chauffeured him to the building. Dirt, cardboard boxes, and abandoned shelving covered the massive concrete floor.

"Who used this place?"

"Sun-Grill once owned it and employed some twenty-five hundred people at its peak, making outdoor grills. The company got into financial trouble about four years ago and went into some type of bankruptcy. A trustee shut it down, a hell of a blow to the economy in this part of the State, causing a bunch of unemployed families."

"So what happened then?"

"It's been on the market for the past four years. We're actually the third realty firm to try and market it. They stripped out furniture and any machinery of value. To be perfectly honest, it's a tough property to sell, and your timing is magical. You might get the buy of the year."

"Are you telling me no one has occupied this facility in four years?" Josh looked at him skeptically.

"Right. Well, except for the 'Rising High' people."

"Rising what?"

"Oh, a while back this group of sales people, some would call it a pyramid scheme, needed a huge facility with no frills to conduct its annual convention. I met a guy named James Sexton, the convention chair. I flat told him this place wasn't going to work, no furniture, dirty, and the utilities had to be changed into their name."

"Sounds like they needed a resort hotel."

"Yeah, that's what I thought, but he wanted it anyway, said they'd only use it for about two weeks and would pay a month's rent. I called the trustee who set the price at $42,000. Seemed ridiculous for two weeks, but we cut the deal. The utilities stayed in the trustee's name, and they were assured privacy. We installed the front gate, gave 'em the only key, and Sexton wrote a check. Anyway, you don't want to hear about that. Let's tour the plant."

As they walked across what seemed like an acre of concrete toward the rear of the building, Josh noticed Reed's expression change.

"This is all very strange. I don't remember this maze of walls, like someone arranged a series of offices with the back door as the entrance."

Finding no entrance into the conglomeration of walls, they walked back out of the front door. Reed breathing hard getting around the exterior of the building reached into his pockets. His hands shook getting out the right key, and Josh paced around, not liking the delay.

Although the furniture was gone, Josh stepped in as if revisiting a murder scene. Strolling the familiar halls and rooms sickened him. The state-of-the-art medical facility, nothing more than a make shift illusion, was a hoax. The memory of Terri lying there grinded in his head.

He turned to Reed. "You don't have any explanation for the mess in the back of this place?"

Reed laughed. "Well, the furniture's gone, but the wall and flooring are nice. Maybe you get some upfitting for free. We won't raise the price."

Josh fumed. "Who wrote the damn check?"

"What check?"

"The Rising High people."

"I can't remember. All I know is the check cleared the bank."

"Did you, by chance, keep a copy of it?"

"Probably, but I don't know what that has to do with your interest in this building."

"I'm interested, but I need some information on what you call the 'upfitting'."

Josh handed him a card with his office phone and fax number and requested Reed get a copy of the check and fax it to him along with other purchase information. When Josh detected some skepticism in Reed's gaze, he added, "You know Lippards don't waste time unless there's an interest."

"Fair enough," said Reed.

Josh received the faxed check and started getting daily answering machine messages from Reed which he never returned. He hadn't ruled Reed out as being a part of it.

Josh held the check, drawn on an account called "The Children's Relief Fund" and signed by Wilbur Brewer. *Damn... billions gone and only a guy with a mobile home to show for it,* thought Josh. He started to feel inspired and spent the next two days sorting out the details. He drew graphs and time frames for all that transpired between the meeting with Tower and the last meeting with Attorney Hall.

As he digested all the information, suddenly an explosion of fear and devastation with the intensity of a death grip seized his body. *Family Intervention intentionally killed my wife. No brain surgery went wrong, they always meant for Terri to die. That's the only way the plan would work. And what in Hell's name can I do about it now?*

CHAPTER NINETEEN

Greenville
August 25, 1982

His realization turned to guilt, then depression. Alone and sad, he returned to his only ally, Jack Daniels. Jack eased his guilt, dimmed his senses, and gave relief to his agony. Josh's business and the volume of calls that preoccupied his time before John Hamilton left town, dried up. Josh couldn't understand how the orders, making up his best month ever, fizzled out. He dealt with the failure by closing his office. Since the interest in his house had fallen off, Josh tried to deal with the maintenance of the Lippard home.

Thinking a hands-on role in the house might give him some satisfaction, he bought tools, ladders, and paint. But after overturning a gallon of "Parisian Pink" in the grand hall, he threw his hands up and left.

"I can't manage my own stupid house. How do you expect me to run this monstrosity?" Josh said to Mac on the phone after several glasses of sour mash. Mac, his only salvation, seemed to take care of everything. Josh, sensing Mac's disappointment, didn't care. His cared only about alcohol and ate and slept when necessary.

Josh felt as dependent on Janelle as Terry. He heard her lock-up the house behind her at midnight and arrive at eight o'clock the next morning to start all over again. He heard her talking on the phone one day.

"Mac, I can handle the overtime and the money's nice, but I'm not sure it's worth watching a man deteriorate in front of my own eyes."

The next day, Josh awoke to Mac sitting by his bed. The swelling in Josh's eyes and the yellowish tone of his skin made him look and feel ten years beyond his age. His usual well-groomed golden hair had turned brownish and unmanageable due to neglect.

"Josh, we've had an unsolicited offer for the Lippard mansion, seventy million, a fair price. The way I figure it, after all the estates are closed and the taxes are paid, you'll be left with mostly liquid assets of around eight hundred and eight-five million dollars. These bogus charitable donations have not impressed the I.R.S. Their last letter said, 'your remedy is with the charities you chose to support, not us.' I think the last semblance of taxation compassion died with F.D.R. As much as I hate it, our lawyers want to cut a deal and settle this thing."

"Mac, what are you talking about... F.D.R.... what deal... I don't need a deal, I need a drink."

"I'm concerned about you, Josh. You're not stable. Your business sense isn't good. Your son's got a future, and you need to put this money in an irrevocable trust for Terry.

"You can maintain a more than sufficient lifestyle on the weekly support payments the trust will be mandated to pay you for life. Financially you'll be fine, and Terry will have a fighting chance to restore business integrity to the Lippard name."

Josh rolled off the bed, hit the floor, and looked up at Mac. "What do you want me to say?"

"Before you make any decisions, you need to check into a private rehab facility. I've made arrangements, and they are expecting you this afternoon. Get dressed, Janelle will fix some breakfast, and I'll drive you myself. Janelle has agreed to stay here around the clock to tend to Terry."

Josh looked sadly at Mac and spoke with a slurred speech controlled by the previous night's alcohol consumption. "How did I get myself into this mess?"

As they drove to Brevard Garden Rehabilitation Center, Josh listened to Mac.

"Money is a difficult thing. People think it solves problems. It doesn't. If you're not prepared to handle money, it becomes a burden. A burden, I'm afraid, brought you to this point."

On Friday, August 26, 1982, Josh checked into the facility with Mac's promise to visit soon. The next week Josh saw a big smile on Mac's face.

"Josh, you look great."

"Thanks, I gained seven pounds, have been eating healthy and living right." Josh, for a change, felt good about himself. "How's Terry?"

"He is growing like milkweed, and he needs his father."

"Listen, Mac, I've been thinking about what you suggested about the Lippard place and the trust. It makes good sense. I'm doing great right now, but I tend to make mistakes on the outside. I want you to be the trustee."

Josh felt Mac's hands on his shoulders. "That's not necessary."

"No, I think it is. For some strange reason, you're the only person who seems to care about us."

"Not true, Josh, I'm a friend, not family."

"You're more loyal than family. I checked with our accountant about what you were charging for your services, and I found out it wasn't much. You've never kept any of the estate money for yourself." Josh watched Mac starting to laugh loudly.

"Yes, Charlie Lippard always set my salary. He's not around to give me a raise."

"I trust you, Mac, and I thank you."

Ten days later, Josh walked out a clean man and jumped into the car with Terry and Janelle. They took the scenic route home and had a picnic beside the Davidson River. The sun shone on his face. He felt relaxed and happy.

Back in Greenville, Josh decided the home he and Terri built had everything he and his son needed, no reason to sell or leave it. After several weeks of no alcohol and getting the household details back into order, Josh realized how much he longed for a woman's touch.

CHAPTER TWENTY

Greenville
October 9, 1982

Barbara Simmons spent the past two years in a state of boredom, never away from the apartment for more than an hour. After the first month, she requested to be relieved, bitterly disappointed when Sid Richardson, known to her as Sidney Wright, declined.

"We're dealing with a loose cannon, and you may be needed."

Barbara missed her husband and child more than she had counted on, not seeing them for over two years. She justified her job description by the money, $15,000 a month, plus all expenses, a nice nest egg. *An egg my husband certainly can't deliver.*

It seemed like an eternity since the last phone call from Josh. Barbara thought, *well, it's his money,* as she watched the "Dallas" episode for the fourth time on television.

But on Friday night, October 9, 1982, the kitchen phone rang. No one used that number except Josh Rankin. A chill went up her spine. She cleared her throat. "Hello."

"Angie, remember me... Josh?"

"Wow. It's been a long time. How have you been?"

"Not too bad, I guess."

"I read some sad things about your family in the paper, didn't feel my place to call, but I couldn't help but hurt for you."

"Thanks, that helps. It's been tough."

Angie heard Josh take a deep breath. "Is there any chance we could go to dinner?"

Not wanting to appear anxious, she hesitated. She needed to collect her thoughts and ease seamlessly back into his world.

"Why don't you come here tomorrow night, and I'll fix dinner. Is salmon still your favorite?"

"You remembered."

"Why don't you bring some wine?"

"I'd prefer to pass on the wine. Actually I've stopped drinking, but dinner at your place sounds super."

"Okay, then I'll see you here about seven thirty."

Barbara thought, *Well, I guess it's back to work. Notify Sidney, go to the grocery, and put the adultery stage back together. Angie Jenkins, alive and well!*

At 7:30 she heard Josh's familiar cadence of knocking on the door. The smell around the apartment, the fish, and his cologne brought back mixed memories. She danced into his arms as if their music never stopped.

"Hi, sweetheart, I've missed you," he said.

"Me, too."

"I brought a bottle of wine."

"You said you quit."

"It's for you. The wine shop guy asked me a dozen questions about your taste, and I knew all the answers, I never got you out of my mind, I guess."

"Oh baby, my heart has ached for over two years and a month since you last called."

"I'm sorry, Angie."

"You're here, all that matters. Dinner should be ready in about forty minutes." Angie leaned towards Josh and their eyes locked together. Her lips parted as he tenderly kissed her.

He tasted like she remembered, a favorite candy, nearly forgotten. She slipped her tongue under his and pulled it gracefully into her mouth, sucking it as a delicious popsicle.

She felt him pressing through his silk pants against her uncovered leg below the high hemline of her denim skirt. Slowly she unbuttoned his wide-collared shirt and eased her hand against his muscular chest while lifting her knee and, in a circular motion, caressed the near exploding hardened flesh straining at his pants for freedom.

She watched his eyes as she unbuttoned her skirt and felt it drop softly to her ankles. Hearing Josh breathing erratically, she stepped back and unbuttoned her blouse, her bra, and let them fall to the floor. She could see his eyes fixated on her chest.

"You're a goddess," Josh said, dropping to his knees before she could reply. His tongue, like an old and trusted friend, came to her. Uncontrollably, she fell backwards on the floor. His clothes started to fly away like butterflies in all directions.

Pleasure pounded everywhere as they fell into each other's rhythm, smoothly and then jerking, like a roller coaster, and a thunderstorm, and a skyrocket bursting at the top of flight and trailing off in a color of calmness in her mind.

She sighed. "Oh, I did miss that." The comment came from her heart.

Objectivity had been engraved in her training. She went into the relationship with great skill and professionalism, keeping all emotions at bay. But Josh's underlying attraction, a child-like innocence, caused Barbara to develop a sense of care and nurture for him, even though these feelings had no place in her job description.

She was certain Josh would have remained committed and faithful to his wife but for her command performance. She suppressed the guilt attempting to torment her for the destruction of his marriage. *It goes with the work, and why I'm paid so well,* she told herself.

But she refused to suppress the feelings she developed for Josh when in his arms, the joy of her crime. After two years, she had again exploded with renewed lust.

As always, they showered and had their funny ritual with bathing oils.

"Dinner is served."

"Oh, the low point of the evening."

"Horrible cook?"

"Nope, horribly wonderful lover."

Dinner and wine brought magic in the air. The shower, food, and smell of coffee freshly brewing caused her to relax. She took her wine as they retired to the den.

She expressed her heartfelt sympathy as Josh talked about the death of Terri. "So how are you dealing with all this pain?"

"I'm okay. It's day to day. I've got a lot of money, but things happened to Terri I could have... I should have stopped. It's very difficult living with myself."

"Like to tell me about it?"

"Not really. It's a crazy story and something I keep to myself. I sometimes wish I'd never met Sid Richardson."

"Who is he?" asked Angie, as she snuggled close to Josh, and tasted the luscious wine. She felt mellow and soft.

"A problem maker. Let's just say he was the source of the problem. Unfortunately, he's smarter and greedier than me."

"Where is this Sidney Wright?" rolled from her lips.

A long pause began, and she realized Josh might never have noticed her slip of the tongue except for her expression. Her face felt hot, blood-red, and Barbara feared she'd blown it.

"I didn't say anything about a Sidney Wright," Josh said.

Her muscles went limp as she considered her error. She knocked over her glass of wine and began running toward the kitchen to grab a towel until she felt Josh grab her by the arm.

"Why did you say Sidney Wright?"

She tried to be calm. "I thought that was who you said."

"No, I didn't."

"So what's the big deal?" she finally asked.

The evening ended shortly thereafter. She had little else to say, felt cold and rigid, and knew Josh noticed it. She recovered the best she could and asked Josh to call again. As Josh kissed her cheek and left, she wondered how she could have gotten so sloppy.

From the window, Barbara watched Josh drive out of the parking lot and called Sidney.

"You said what?"

Barbara tried to play down the significance.

"I'll decide what the importance of this mistake is. Go over the conversation verbatim," Sidney demanded.

With the obedience of a conditioned soldier to a commander, she carefully reviewed most of the details.

"Unfortunately, you've now connected my name. You may be right. Mr. Rankin will probably let it pass, but it's a chance this operation can't take. You're going to get your wish, Barbara. You're going home. You should implement Plan E, and be out of there before the end of tomorrow."

Barbara, with some discomfort, collected her thoughts. *In twenty-four hours I'll be in Montreal, even a professional occasionally stumbles... no big problem.* She would follow her orders and maybe take a stab at being a decent mother. *Good news.*

Josh returned home, thanked Janelle as she left, and reflected on the evening. What started so dramatically had ended somewhat flat. *I guess life is like a novel, and some parts aren't that great,* Josh pondered. He went to bed. Before he fell asleep, he got up, pulled out his box of investigative charts, and wrote down in bold letters, "**Sidney Wright**." He was not sure why.

CHAPTER TWENTY-ONE

Bermuda
October 10, 1982
11:15 p.m.

Sidney reflected upon the recent information. He contemplated the operation had been virtually flawless until now. Hard decisions would have to be made.

Project "B," originally named as the abbreviation of the sum of money it potentially could net, produced over four hundred percent of the original estimate. Project "B", the brainchild of Sidney Wright.

The project involved less than two dozen people, designated in four levels. Level I persons had little inside information and only received a sum of money for a limited task. They had no direct knowledge of the real name of anyone on a higher level and only understood the objective for which they were hired.

Level II involved persons who generally understood certain objectives and had direct contact with higher level personnel but did not know real identities. Their fee was fixed and not contingent upon the success of the operation.

Level III persons were at a higher security level. They knew, by proper identity, one or more Level IV persons. They had proven themselves to be dependable and loyal in some earlier project. However, their fees were set and not contingent upon the success of the project.

Finally, Level IV involved close relationships and higher levels of trust and security. Level IV persons were paid only upon a successful "take" in the project.

Level I people were no threat. They knew little and could not identify anyone on a higher level by the correct name. Level II were generally well paid. They were researched thoroughly for past deeds and the need of money. Level IV, due to in-depth incriminating information, could easily control Level II, if necessary. Anyone could be ruined on Level II by a simple tip of misconduct, and they knew it. Level III had a history of loyalty with Level IV. The degree of trust, along with their attractive wages, was a good fit. Level IV was by design. Percentages were based on development of the project, monies advanced to fund the project, and the degree of involvement.

Sidney Wright, as he had so often done, pondered the "List." By now, the project should be over and closed out. He agonized realizing Barbara should have been pulled after Josh Rankin made the phone call ending the relationship. But Sidney feared Barbara's disappearance might raise too much suspicion in Josh at a critical point in the project. He miscalculated the time it would take Josh to want to reconcile with his passionate lover and considered "Angie" to be useful if they needed to explore his intentions.

Sitting on an upper balcony outside his Bermuda home, Sidney angrily crumpled the list in his hardened fist and flung it over the porch rail, sending it rolling across the shining white roof.

Personnel List:

Level I	Fee	Code Name
Herb Hall	30,000	Same
Jessie Frank	1,000 day	Nurse I
Donna Kimbrook	1,000 day	Nurse II
Sally Douglas	1,000 day	Nurse III
Wreck Stage Team		45,000

Level II		
Jordan Tower	200,000	Same
Pat Davis	150,000	Same
Wilbur Brewer	1,000 week	Same
Jane Bowdre	18,000	Nurse at Park/ Ice Cream Lady
Briton Peebles	125,000	Same

Level III		
Barbara Simmons	15,000 month	Angie Jenkins
Rex Wilkerson	12,000 month	Austin Clemmons
Tim Worthy	3,500Paul	(last name Neal if asked)

Level IV		
Sidney Wright	79%	Sid Richardson
Christopher Bonn	10%	Dr.Chris Sinclair
Jonathan Biggerstaff	10%	John Hamilton and James Sexton
Robert Depew	1%	Bob Chambers

Retrieving the ball of paper with the agility of a monkey, Sidney screamed at himself. "Now Josh Rankin knows my name."

Returning to his hammock, Sidney continued to fume as he considered the circumstances. Barbara had always done exceptionally well in prior projects. He was certain she had never given her husband any details about her work, other than it involved Canadian National Security. The exceptionally large pay deposit in their account kept her husband's curiosity at bay, and Sidney monitored him routinely.

That lard ass, hammer-toting, gutless construction worker won't question a thing, as long as his wife's gravy train marches across his table. His greed is predictable as gravity.

Barbara, however, had never worked a project this long, showing both emotion and weakness to Sidney. She contacted him more than necessary, and he worried about her stability. Sidney liked her, but the name slip wasn't tolerable.

As Sidney uncrumpled the list, a big smile came to his face. The true bargain had been Briton Peebles. Sidney had thought, during project development, finding a skilled surgeon to virtually murder Terri Rankin difficult. He monitored the good Dr. Briton Peebles for months. This surgeon, a brilliant academic career during both graduate and undergraduate studies at Stanford University, became the premier member of his residency team.

This promising career took a nosedive when crack cocaine took over his life. Practicing with an upscale neurosurgical group in New Mexico, he had a large and continuous source of the substance coming to him every day. Eventually fired from the group, he continued a practice south of the border where, although the pay cheap, the drugs were also. Sidney confronted him one morning on a mattress lying beside a trash dump outside "Bar Tijuana." Dr. Peebles rapidly agreed to help in the project.

Once Sidney located the doctor at Family Intervention, he'd been sober for two days. Sidney soothed his conscience with a manufactured history of Terry Rankin. Sidney explained Terri had advanced and terminal cancer and was in continuous excruciating pain. The family had requested Family Intervention end her suffering by brain manipulation, but it must not be detectable. Sidney Wright said to him, "We're in the middle of the Southern Bible Belt. People don't understand mercy killing around here. This is the family's request, and here is her husband's signature. You'd be doing Terri and her family a great service to perform this operation."

Sidney had spent countless hours considering the procedure which would best render Josh Rankin's wife's condition irreversible. After researching the matter in much medical literature, Sidney believed it would be most expedient to drill a precision surgical burr hole into the upper brain stem. He discussed this proposed procedure with Dr. Peebles.

"Why the hell would you want to do that? Use the Gamma-knife. I can take out what we need, and there won't be a scratch on her."

Sidney had never heard of the "Gamma-knife," only available in a prototype and without regulatory approval. It was extremely expensive to procure use of the device from an unlawful source. He learned a radiation oncologist would generally be the professional to operate the device, usually used with cancer patients. Sidney mentioned this to Dr. Peebles and got a livid reaction.

"If you think you're getting your money back, you're wrong. I know how to run the damn machine, so that's up to you."

Sidney made the decision to let Dr. Peebles take aim at the patient and brought the Gamma-knife to the Family Intervention complex. He watched the sober Doctor Peebles promptly set up the cage on the skull. Gamma ray manipulation was by degree. She couldn't die, but she had to be comatose. With a surgical marker, he outlined the points of orientation on her skull, highlighting the essential structure, the brain stem. After the set-up, he directed the beam of gamma radiation, destroying significant portions of the upper brain stem.

During the process, Sidney wrestled with some feelings of guilt. After all, Terri was innocent in these matters. But he dealt with his emotions reflecting how comforting it would have been to erase everything that happened to him as a child within the walls of the Starlight.

The procedure went perfectly. All of the patient's bodily functions were normal, as if this pregnant young lady had not changed in any respect. But if her body was a temple, when you knocked on the front door, nobody was at home, the blank stare of her eyes the only outward manifestation of her condition.

Dr. Peebles showed great proficiency for a cocaine addict, taking all necessary precautions to shield the fetus from the gamma rays. Terri became comatose, and Sidney returned the $125,000 richer Dr. Peebles to Mexico with proper resources to support his habit for some time.

But as Sidney accurately predicted, when the money ran out the doctor came looking for more. The night Sidney received Dr Peebles' phone call, he put the plan in motion, and the doctor bought on credit a carefully laced dose of cocaine, putting to rest any further contact from the good doctor.

Sidney leaned back in his wicker chair and chuckled. *What an investment... if all people were that easy.*

Another smile came to Sidney. After the phone tap in Ohio, when Sidney learned of Josh's appointment with Herb Hall, rapid-fire thought processes started in Sidney's mind. Somehow it was a joy quickly working with Christopher and Jonathan developing the scenes and scripting the lines for Jonathan's character, John Hamilton. The ease of watching the professional interaction between his colleagues impressed Sidney, and the sheer weakness and greed of Herb Hall greased the money shoots of the project.

CHAPTER TWENTY-TWO

Greenville
October 12, 1982

T he following day, Josh's remembrance of the raw pleasure of the previous night still lingered. By sunset the next evening, the desire for more had overwhelmed him. He phoned Angie. The recorded message indicated her phone had been disconnected. He re-dialed the number a total of six times with the same result. His anxiety increased with each call. "Janelle, I'm going to take a ride. I'll be back by eight o'clock."

Josh noticed the large green plant outside Angie's front door missing. He knocked, no answer. "Angie, you there?" He peered through the slightly opened blinds in the small windows beside the door, and he couldn't see one piece of furniture. Then he rushed around to the back of the apartment, jumping as he looked into every window. The apartment appeared to be totally vacated and cleaned.

Josh, at his wit's end, felt a familiar uneasiness coming over him. Losing control, his movement about the apartment complex resembled a deranged chicken, and he noticed neighbors peering out their windows. He stumbled into the apartment manager's office, emotionally spurting his words. "Where's Angie Jenkins?"

The lady manager, busy at her desk counting rent checks, rose from her desk and pulled her reading glasses off. "And who might you be?"

"Well, I'm a friend, here two nights ago with her."

"Sorry, but she moved out."

"Where did she go?"

"Even if I knew, Sir, I couldn't tell you."

Josh breathed heavily. "This is insane. Did she leave a message for me, Josh Rankin?"

"No, Sir. In fact, she appeared to be in a hurry to move out, and she agreed to forfeit the balance of this month's rent and her deposit. She did a good job cleaning the place, and she and I have no problem."

"Surely she left a forwarding address?" Josh crossed and uncrossed his arms as he became more and more agitated.

"No, sir, she didn't. I've already told you more than I should, and you need to leave."

"Listen, I'm Josh Rankin…"

She cut him off. "I've got a loaded pistol in this desk, want to see it?"

Josh went back to the car. A feeling of confusion came over him as it had when Austin Clemmons disappeared. Josh drove around with no sense of direction. He remembered she previously lived in Canada and now stayed in Greenville to visit an ailing grandmother in the nearby town of Due West. Angie worked out of her apartment. On the computer, she coordinated orders from "Kids Kloz" parties all over North America. He heard her claim she could live anywhere.

Nothing made sense, so he drove around a bit before heading home. He dismissed Janelle and put Terry to bed. A loud knock on the front door startled him.

"Who is it?"

"Greenville Police Department. We need to talk to you."

Josh opened the door finding a heavy-set, uniformed cop. "Are you Mr. Josh Rankin?"

"Yes, I am."

"May I ask you where you've been for the past two hours?"

"Why?"

"Sir, I'd like to be the one asking questions."

"Well, I've been to the Colonial Apartments and, after that, riding around."

"Do you know a Barbara Simmons?"

"No, sir, I don't."

"Well, that's strange, because she had your address and phone number on a pad in her car. She also had a photo of you and her, ripped in half on the floor. Why'd she be tearing up your picture?"

"I don't know a Barbara Simmons."

"Well, Mr. Rankin, we need you to come down to the station to answer some questions."

"Can't, my son's here, and there's no one to keep him."

Suddenly, another police officer appeared on Josh's front steps.

"Sergeant, come take a peek at this."

Josh checked on Terry hoping he'd not stirred. By the time Josh returned to the front door, three officers stood around his car. Josh began walking towards the car until stopped by the extended palm of the Sergeant.

"Mr. Rankin, by chance can you explain this?"

Josh took a close look at it. "Looks like something wet."

The Sergeant stood between Josh and the car. "It appears to be wet blood on the side of your car."

Josh leaned forward to examine it.

"Don't touch that. Get forensics down here right now with a photographer. Mr. Rankin, I'm going to give you ten minutes to find someone to keep your child, or he goes to the station with us."

"Janelle," Josh yelled excitedly into the phone. "Something really terrible is going on here, and it looks like I'm going to the police department. Could you possibly come back and watch Terry?"

Mac stood by Josh in disbelief as the judge read the warrant. The State of South Carolina charged Josh for the murder of Barbara Simmons. A Lippard lawyer stepped forward decrying family standing in the community and moved for bond. Mac posted the million-dollar surety with a cashier's check in a matter of hours, and started working on determining which criminal defense attorney in the area most capable of handling murder cases. Out of fifteen well placed inquiries, the name of Nathan Winslow came up thirteen times.

That'll be the one then, Mac thought as he picked up the phone.

The next morning Mac met with Attorney Winslow and instructed Josh to stay at home with Terry and Janelle. As he paid the retainer, Mac gave some insight. "Don't treat him like a criminal. Listen to him. But understand this, Josh may look and sound intelligent at times, but he's not. He's got a good heart, but you'll have to help him with strategy in this case. Don't let him go down on this."

"I can't make any promises, but I'll do my best, Mr. Carter. Thank you for your comments."

Josh began a series of many private conferences with Nathan. They always ended with the same result.

"Give me some help on this Josh. Why would her blood be on your car?"

"It makes no sense to me either. I never saw her that day."

"Well, one thing's for certain, she died between the time you left the manager's office and the time Greenville P.D. beat on your door. The autopsy report is clear. Do you want me to suggest somebody else put a bullet in her head and poured her blood on the side of your car?"

"It had to be."

"Okay, Josh, then who?"

"I wish I knew."

"Think about it. Who do you know had a motive to kill her and blame you? Simply give me the name, and I'll have a swarm of private investigators all over it by tomorrow."

"I've thought about it over and over. If I knew, I'd shout it from the tree tops."

Nathan Winslow met with the Chief Prosecutor, Lemmond Rayfield. "Listen, Lem, I've got a real shot at a not guilty on this one."

"Yeah, yeah. This guy is going crazy to find this girl. She ends up dead a couple of blocks from his house, and her blood's dripping down his car door when the cops arrive at his house."

Nathan postured confidently. "So why don't you tell me why your pure-as-snow victim is going by an alias and lies on her apartment lease. My investigators tell me her husband and child had no clue where she was and hadn't seen her for years. She has no job, but money coming from somewhere."

"So what? Maybe she's a bit strange and doesn't all add up, but no defense to murder. I'm willing to roll the dice, are you?"

"Lem, I'm going to punch holes all in your case, and you know I'll do it. Talk to me."

"What do you want to hear?"

"Give me something to take to this guy. He's got no record. He's no threat to society."

"All right Nathan, I do have a few problems with the case, but he's not going to walk. I've got a ton of cases and don't need to bang heads with you for weeks over this. Your guy did it, but hell, probably some heat of passion to the killing. The torn photo, as you and I well know, is a double edge sword swinging at both our heads."

"So what can we do?"

"Take your guy v.m., best I'll do."

"Let me talk to him. I'll get back to you soon." Nathan walked out the door, certain Josh wouldn't be an easy sale.

Josh sat in the elaborate flame stitched client chair across from his attorney for the third time that week.

"Josh, we need to talk."

"About what?"

"Voluntary manslaughter. Twenty years Josh, you'll be out in less than ten if you play your cards right."

"I didn't kill her."

"The question, unfortunately, is not what you did, but what the jury thinks you did."

"What about beyond a shadow of a doubt?"

"The law says beyond a reasonable doubt. That doesn't mean any doubt. It means what it says, a doubt for which you can give a reason. In my opinion, the jury will find doubts. In fact, I'm going to put those doubts in their heads. But chances are they'll get back in the jury room and start weighing things out. In one pile, they'll stack the evidence for you. In another pile, they'll place the evidence against you. The pile against you will look like a mountain beside an ant hill."

"I didn't do it."

"I'm trying to salvage your future. You can do ten. The other option is life, and I can't guarantee when or if you'll be paroled."

"The answer's no."

"Listen, it'll be an easy ten... minimum security... you know white collar types. But lifers do tough time."

He adjusted restlessly in his arm chair as he pondered his lawyer's advice. A familiar decision confronted him, compromise. He thought of the short-cuts he'd taken in the past couple of years, hoping for an easy fix, always falling flat on his face. He leaned forward nervously with a questionable degree of conviction. "No compromise, I guess you need to get ready for trial."

Josh's defense was simple. He didn't kill Barbara Simmons. It was all or none. Josh's theory left no room for a jury to compromise. Without evidence of some provocation, such as a violent lover's quarrel, there was no option of manslaughter.

As the trial progressed, Josh watched Nathan Winslow hammer every witness. His lawyer rounded the bases, no gun, no obvious motive, no eyewitnesses, and no fingerprints of Josh at the scene of the crime. He painted a sea of confusion with the mysteries of the deceased.

"So does the prosecution want you to proclaim my client a murderer of Angie Jenkins or is it Barbara Simmons?"

Josh felt a brief optimism as his lawyer argued strenuously to the jury Josh's right to the benefit of any reasonable doubt. As Josh watched, he saw several jurors leaning forward as if to beg, *Please give us one.* Josh realized he had not provided his attorney with one.

For the first time, it clearly occurred to him Family Intervention must be involved, and the whole story needed to come out. It was the only way to make any sense out of his predicament. He waved so frantically it interrupted Nathan Winslow's momentum in closing argument.

"May I have a moment, Your Honor?" Nathan turned to Josh, still beckoning him, and walked cautiously to the defense table.

"I need to tell you the whole truth; maybe I've figured out who killed her."

"Josh, we rested our evidence two hours ago. The case is done."

Josh hung his head as Nathan returned to conclude his comments to the jury.

Unfortunately for Josh, the apartment manager and a hand full of tenants gave pointed testimony to go along with forensics. Barbara's eight-year-old son, held by his widowed father, made a sympathetic appearance. In the end, despite Nathan's skilled oration, the evidence proved too compelling for the jury. The trial lasted three weeks, and the jury deliberated for four days.

Josh Rankin, convicted of murder and sentenced to life in prison, turned around looking for his son. Spotting Terry, held by Janelle, he painfully extended his arms. Standing with her was Mac, who, sensing a conviction, thought perhaps Terry might not see his father for a long while and decided to bring him the final day. Mac wiped away Janelle's tears, took three-year-old Terry

Rankin from her arms and walked forward towards the walnut banister separating the spectators from the accused.

Deputies whipped out handcuffs and leg chains and headed towards Josh.

"Wait, can't I see my son?"

"Not in this life," snickered the overweight officer while Josh felt the slapping on of the steel restraints.

For the first time during the entire trial, Josh lost it. He cried out in emotional pain and frustration. He begged Nathan, packing up his briefcase, for help.

"Lem, please spare this man an ounce of mercy, let him hold his kid."

Lem waved off the deputies, affording Josh a brief moment of precious touch with Terry.

"Daddy, don't be sad."

He felt Terry's little fingers wipe the tears from his eyes. Their noses met, and Josh whispered into his ear until they were forcefully pulled apart.

Non-contact visits occurred every other week through glass and phone. Josh learned who his friends were. Mac and Janelle visited regularly, his only visitors. Josh could tell they were both heartbroken. During one of the visits, Josh had a long talk with Mac about Terry.

"I can't be his father anymore. You're all he's got. Take care of him, Mac." As Mac nodded, tight lipped, with a committed look in his eyes, Josh felt a small degree of satisfaction.

After an unsuccessful appeal, Josh transferred into a maximum security prison in the "Low Country" part of South Carolina. The facility had a tarnished reputation, infamous for its brutality.

CHAPTER TWENTY-THREE

Low Country Correctional Facility
October 1983

T-Bird Jackson, named after the cheap motel where he was conceived, rotated in and out of juvenile facilities from the age of eight. In the State of South Carolina, you have to be twenty-one to drink a beer, but a seventeen-year-old is considered an adult under its criminal laws. T-Bird celebrated his seventeenth birthday with a .357 Magnum he found under the driver's seat in a car he broke into a week earlier.

His birthday party consisted of putting the pistol to the head of a convenience store clerk. This folly netted him a couple hundred bucks from the cash register along with a case of beer held under each arm, all conveniently recorded on the store's security camera. T-Bird got fifteen years and got out in five.

Two months after his release, he happened to stumble into a party in an upper scale neighborhood. Acid being dropped, nobody bothered to ask who brought the uninvited guest. T-Bird caught a line of cocaine, thought he owned the world and brutally raped a sixteen-year-old girl, whose parents found her the next morning bleeding from both ends. If T-Bird had had an ounce of intelligence, he could have slipped away quietly and never been identified. But T-Bird, remarkably smart, showed up the next night at the same place looking for more party action. He got twenty and did ten.

By the age of thirty-five, T-Bird had done more time behind bars than on the outside. He had a different outlook in prison than most inmates. It's where he lived. He didn't think of opportunities on the outside; he focused on what the inside offered.

Such was the situation of Darryl Ward. T-Bird knew his story well. Darryl had molested an eight-year-old boy in an upstairs motel room. His parents left him in their room for thirty minutes while they dined in the motel restaurant. The parents placed the boy in front of the motel room television with a videotape and locked the front door behind them. They were basically good parents who thought their few minutes of privacy harmless.

Darryl had climbed up to the second story balcony, knocked on the sliding-glass door overlooking the pool, and coaxed the boy out with a Baby Ruth candy bar. He had his way with the child, leaving grotesque teeth marks on the boy's private areas. The parents found their son, on the concrete surrounding the pool, dead from a broken neck. Somehow, in the bizarre trial that followed, the jury believed Darryl had raped the boy but had dropped him by accident. He was convicted on criminal sexual conduct but spared on the murder charge. The child's parents, feeling guilty and vindictive, went ballistic knowing their child's killer could be out before the hedges grew well on their child's grave.

T-Bird seized the opportunity. A little hint by T-Bird's cousin to the grieving parents resulted in a tidy sum of money passing into T-Bird's hand. T-Bird smiled as he approached Darryl in the isolated shower and slit his throat with a stone-sharpened automotive shop screwdriver.

The investigating authorities had some legitimate hunches, but the State of South Carolina, not all broken up over the death of Darryl Ward, figured justice has its way in spite of the system. T-Bird laid low for a while, but in time his notoriety grew, which made him happy. "Got a problem on the inside...call the T-Bird."

T-Bird, in a different security area from Josh Rankin, learned to move in and out of different areas when necessary. In the case of Mr. Rankin, it was necessary. T-Bird didn't know where the money had come from, didn't care. He knew a running mate of his cousin did the deal and laid twenty one-hundred dollar bills on T-Bird, with twenty more coming after the job.

Josh really tried to make the best out of his situation, being polite, following the rules, and staying out of people's way. He had little in common with any of the inmates he met but lent a friendly ear when one of them wanted to chat.

He took a liking to a naive nineteen-year-old kid, in for possession with intent to distribute drugs. Dealing with a lot of emotional problems, Josh learned he'd taken the fall for a couple of drug dealers that sucked him in to holding the stash in exchange for some grass for his personal use. Nineteen and no record, when he got caught, the dealers convinced him to plead guilty and not roll on them.

"Josh, they told me I wouldn't do no time. They lied."

Josh sympathetically counseled his young friend and took some comfort in helping him cope with the stress of his injustice. He could relate to making hurried decisions, costing him dearly.

He typically got into his bunk before nine o'clock each night, shortly before "lights out," controlled by a main switch at the guard's station. Security lights at the end of each hall dimly illuminated the area. Each cell had a top and bottom bunk. Josh didn't trust his cell mate, knowing he spent most of his time on the other side of the security area with a bunch of rough cons, a group Josh tried to stay clear of.

At 9:15, a dark shadow fell over his bunk bed. Josh, trying to fall asleep, heard his cell mate get down from the top bunk and exit without a word. T-Bird Jackson, six feet seven inches tall, weighing over three hundred pounds, stood over him. Startled, he rolled to the edge of the bed and sat up with his feet on the floor. He felt like a mouse under a great owl. The whites of T-Bird's teeth glared from his smile through the dim light, in Josh's direction.

T-Bird grabbed him by the arms and raised him until their eyes were even. Josh shook. The stench of T-Bird's breath invaded Josh's senses.

"What are you doing?" asked Josh.

"You're goin' to like this."

He felt a sock forced into his mouth. He tried to resist, but T-Bird's pounding fist into his gut knocked the breath out of him. He bent over gasping for air, unable to move.

With a firm grip, Josh was lifted over the cell's single writing desk face down. His prison-issued bottoms came down to his knees while Josh heard T-Bird struggling with his own clothing. Pain ripped through his entire being. He tried to scream, but T-Bird's massive hand covered his sock-filled mouth.

The penetration continued with the degree of gentleness a sewer repairman would use routing out a severely stopped-up sewer line. Josh's head, jerked backward following the butchering, tensed as T-Bird's hot breath covered his ear.

"Say a word, you're a dead man."

Two minutes later he heard his cell mate return, and say nothing. Unbridled pain roared through Josh.

The next day, he walked the prison in silence. He had no one to turn to and didn't feel like counseling his troubled young drug offender.

At 9:45 the next night, the same shadow appeared as the cell mate left. The wounds, barely starting to heal, were ripped open. Josh suffered the pounding silently.

"Now that's a startin' to feel purty good. See you tomorrow."

Josh's psychological framework, after five days of having his manhood stripped of its dignity, began to fail. He wanted to cry out for help, but reminded himself of the retribution threatened after each session.

"You'll be dead, and you know I can do it."

As days passed and the torturing continued, he pondered death as a legitimate alternative. Mac would visit in two days. Josh considered seeking his help. Mac always had the right answers when he bothered to listen. But the value of his own life had deteriorated in his mind. In a sense, the scales of justice were being leveled, and he shouldn't interfere with destiny.

At eight o'clock the next night, before lights out, Josh talked to his disturbed young friend. "I've made a lot of mistakes in my life, and they have hurt a lot of people. Looking back, it seems all my mistakes happened when I thought only of myself. Somehow, I'd always convince myself to take a short cut then and make it right later. The short cut always turned out wrong, and I never could make it right. All a person really needs in life is to follow the golden rule. But since I could never learn that lesson, maybe I can teach it to you.

"In my mind, I probably deserve everything that has come my way, but I want you to know you'll be out of here one day, and you need to trust yourself. Be true to what you know is fair, and don't trust anyone who would tell you otherwise.

"Understand, without a doubt, there's right, and there's wrong. Don't let folks ever tell you there's a fine line between the two. There's not. That kind of thinking only happens when you try to benefit yourself. The stuff you learn from good people when you're young somehow gets twisted when you get older, and it shouldn't. Those who tell you life's too complicated for you to simplify right from wrong probably aren't benefiting well enough by what's right.

"If there's anything I can tell you, it's this. When you make your way in life, stop at every crossroad and think. Instead of asking yourself, 'How will this help me?'... ask yourself, 'What will this do to other people?' Don't act until the answer comes honestly to your heart. I only wish someone had taught me this years ago because, for me, it's a little too late."

Josh watched the kid wipe his eyes and knew he had struck a good chord. He finally felt he had shared some wisdom, though he knew he would never share it again. Josh put his hand on the young man's shoulder and left.

He walked down the hall, toward his own cell, recalling his own rejection of the guilty plea, easy time, out quick. His wisdom to the kid of no short-cut, no compromise, complicated his own understanding of being innocent, but convicted. Justice. He rationalized justice has its own methods.

The next visit of T-Bird Jackson would be in less than an hour, and Josh, ready to concede T-Bird had won the battle, finally took control of his own war, his own life.

With strips of cloth he had saved, Josh manufactured a rope. Seated on the top bunk with his feet hanging towards the floor, he tied one end to a steam pipe above him near the ceiling. He tied the other end around his neck.

His decision reached, he pondered his fate. He cast his eyes towards the heavens, and let them drift slowly towards the floor. They closed. His prayer sincere, he begged forgiveness. *When will I know if it's answered?* The answer to his question would come shortly.

His backside slid off the upper bunk. He didn't struggle. As life drained from his body, he imagined the face of his bride. Terri Lippard smiled sweetly at him. He smiled back. He completed his atonement, finally at peace. His mind, now nearly not of this world, saw a light. A hope. Forgiveness.

Death surrounded him like a warm blanket, shielding him from the harsh prison, a harsh world. His right hand reached upward for Terri and his left outward to his son. His love and emotional surrender blended into a beautiful tapestry as he faded.

CHAPTER TWENTY-FOUR

Greenville, South Carolina
September 6, 1994

"I'm fourteen today, Sam, and feel sick to my stomach. I've got no mom, no dad, and people think I'm supposed to be happy cause of all this money."

Terry rolled over in the newly fallen leaves as his dog licked his face. He hugged his pet tightly as the tears welled up. But this time Terry couldn't contain them as they spilled onto the yellow fur of his pal.

Terry couldn't let Mac see the tears. For the last couple of years, he hid his agony. He felt Mac wanted him to be stronger, so he kept his feelings inside like a good businessman would do.

Cedar Grove Park, Terry and Sam's special place for after-school walks became Terry's only real outlet for his pain. Deep inside, he wondered what he'd done wrong. He struggled to understand why both would leave him. Even though he'd heard nice tales of his mom and dad, he felt the stories were told in a way to spare him. He couldn't help but believe, had he been older, somehow he could have saved them both.

The afternoon sun warmed their faces as they lay on a gentle hill above a single picnic table, as early autumn pin-oak leaves showered their resting place in the soft breeze. Terry wrestled with the guilt of his dad taking a woman's life. In spite of Mac's calm explanations, none of it made sense. Deep inside an unexplainable need to shoulder the blame haunted him. He channeled these emotions into his schoolwork which lifted him like balloons.

He loved Mac, but he felt Mac would rather see "A pluses" than share his shame and hurt over his dead parents. Even at fourteen, he shared with Sam the weight of losing his mom and dad.

Terry watched the sun creep lower in the sky and knew a party waited for him at home. He'd smile and pretend to be happy. But it wasn't a celebration to Terry.

"I think Momma died having me, took all her strength. Maybe she traded her life for mine. What do you think, Sam?"

September 6, 2001

Terry Rankin blew out twenty-one candles before his adoring birthday guests. The valedictorian of his class at Greenville High, now entering his third year at Wharton on a full scholarship, smiled broadly to the crowd. He needed the scholarship money like he needed another "A." He could afford to buy the school.

But Terry had come full circle in his soul. The defenses he erected as a teenager helped him focus but choked meaning from his life. At Wharton, he reached an emotional truce with himself and re-developed a capacity to show what was in his heart, an openness, an endearing quality.

The smoke from the candles cleared, and Terry spotted Mac standing in the corner. He now knew Mac, who adopted him at age three, had been largely responsible for his success. Until he left for Wharton, he and Mac lived in the house Terry's mother and father built. Terry understood he could live anywhere he wanted but felt comfortable living where his parents lived. He frequently rummaged among many of his parents' old things kept in the attic, sometimes imagining being with them.

Janelle hugged Terry and pulled him to the mountains of presents to be opened. Terry wondered if every friend he ever made in high school had bothered to come, and affectionately squeezed Janelle's shoulders in appreciation for the party.

Until Terry was twelve years old, Janelle stayed with him, usually seventy hours a week, while Mac ran Rankin Enterprises. Terry loved her like a mother, but he felt she'd repeat anything he told her to Mac.

Rankin Enterprises had become the largest privately-held company in the South. The Company's estimated worth, six billion dollars, had one shareholder, Terry. Mac drew a modest salary. Terry, once at Walton, insisted that his salary, by industry standards, should exceed a million a year. His generosity was met with Mac's usual chuckle.

"Son, my salary's a matter between me and your grandfather, don't interfere." Terry knew quite well that Mac, through eighteen vice presidents, fueled his financial riches. Mac's unwavering, unselfish commitment stood as an inspiration to him.

Embarrassed by the talk of almost any girl in South Carolina being his for the asking, he tried to stay focused on school. Despite his chiseled, George Clooney-like physic, he always thought his inner spirit to be the value of his character. He had his father's blue eyes and golden hair, his maternal grandfather's mind, and his mother's determination. Soon he should be running Rankin Enterprises. Mac's sixty years had obviously worn on him, and the lines in his face and droop of his eyes told Terry he needed a break. It scared Terry to think about taking over the reins. Even in the excitement of the birthday party, Mac stood in the corner looking reflective. Seeing him took Terry back to a summer when he was eleven years old.

Why did they have to leave me?

I don't mean to cry, Mac, but tonight can I call you Daddy?

Mac, thanks for coming to the camp out, all the dads are here.

Terry eased gently over to the corner and whispered, "Mac, what can I say? No son could expect..." Tears fell from Terry's eyes. ".... more from a dad. Why don't I tell you more often? Everything good in my life happened because of you, and I'm grateful."

Mac looked gratified but quickly changed the subject to the new construction. "Tomorrow you meet with the architect and finalize the plans for your new home. Don't sign any change orders, the house is spectacular enough. Hold your builder's feet to finishing by the end of the school year."

"But what if I need another closet?" Terry tickled himself messing with Mac.

"You don't, and it'll cost you the price of a garage."

Terry smiled and nodded his head to Mac.

Envied by his colleagues, Terry made a sincere effort not to be affected. He had a common touch that impressed most everyone he met, got it from Mac.

Terry dated on weekends when he took a break from studies. His easy-going personality, coupled with his pleasing appearance, caused girls on campus to label him "the catch." Some fished him, repeatedly, to the point of being a nuisance. Terry reached out to people with the softness of a cotton blanket. But behind his inviting face was a mind, perhaps, sharper than Charlie Lippard's.

He met his only regular girl, Bonnie Freeman from Greenville, in kindergarten. His first kiss, first date, and best friend. Terry witnessed the stages of Bonnie's hair color go from a cool ash blonde to a rich walnut brown as she developed from a child to mature woman. Bonnie's luscious lips kissed like a shopping spree in a sensuous candy store.

Bonnie understood his loneliness in a sea of wealth. Growing up together gave Terry the chance to slowly invest himself emotionally in Bonnie. When hormonal cravings started to change the way they looked at each other, Terry adjusted carefully. Having Bonnie in his arms was exciting, almost ecstasy, but her blossoming maturity never tainted his respect for her, layered over the years.

Terry felt awkward seeing Bonnie as the victim of the intense competition among other girls he dated. He admired her for not engaging in the competition, never feeling pressured by her. She supported him without coming across like she had a stake in his successes. When he came to town, she didn't call but seemed really happy when he did. Bonnie was pretty but not spellbinding, and Terry found the fact Bonnie had no need to chase glamour added to her charm.

Heavy course loads and a commitment to excellence enabled Terry to finish Wharton in three years. In May of 2002, as he finished writing the last word on his final exam, a thrill came over him. He might pass on graduate school and start a career.

By mid-afternoon, the after-exams-bash was well underway. Terry sat back and sipped on a cappuccino while most of his friends threw back the heavy stuff.

"Terry, you're our man... always top of the class, best looking chick on your arm. You never stumble, and there's not a person in this room I'd call a better friend."

"I stumble plenty, we all do. You calling me friend makes it all worth while."

After several similar conversations, Terry quietly slipped away and flew his private jet to the Greenville Municipal Airport. Bonnie, who he called on the way, met him with open arms.

"I'm starved," said Terry.

"Me too. Where do you want to go?"

As it came out of his mouth, she echoed, "Sam's." They both laughed. They knew each other well. Sam's Bar and Grill, a fixture in Greenville, had been in business close to forty years and held special memories for Terry.

He got their favorite table, ordered draft beer, burgers and melted into Bonnie's loveliness.

"Well, I guess tomorrow will bring mixed emotions. The new house looks great, but my heart will always be on Grady Drive, the only home I've ever known." He then leaned forward to Bonnie. "Spend my last night there with me?"

"I'd be honored."

Bonnie and Terry made love in the same room Terry was conceived. Terry, just catching his breath, smiled at Bonnie and whispered, "You're remarkable."

"Oh, no, I think it's the other way around." She collapsed in his arms.

The next morning, Terry sat in bed as Bonnie left for an early commitment at the local soup kitchen. He could hear Mac and Bonnie meeting at the door.

"Oh, man, I'm nailed," Terry mumbled to himself.

Mac's grinning face appeared at Terry's bedroom door. "Better get out of bed. Movers will be here at noon and that gives you four and a half hours to take what you don't want broken or stolen."

Terry laughed as Mac set a large Styrofoam cup on the dresser by the door.

"Here's some coffee. I'll be back at noon."

Terry had felt funny when Mac moved into a condo a block from Rankin Enterprises after Terry left for college. He always considered the house on Grady Drive to be as much Mac's as his own.

Terry took a long sip of coffee and started to rummage through drawers. He threw a few valuables into a gym bag. *They can move this furniture with the clothes in it,* Terry thought. Eventually, Terry got around to pulling down the disappearing stairway leading to the attic. *Look at all this junk,* Terry mused as he started bringing down boxes.

One container, an old Jack Daniels box caught his eye, and he opened it. At the top sat a pad with the underlined words "**Sidney Wright**." For the next couple of hours Terry leafed through charts with dates, names, and places. What really focused his attention was a map with an "X" and a notation beside it. "This is where Terri got hurt." The location stood more than two hundred miles from Morehead City, North Carolina.

Newspaper articles of his mother's accident, his uncle Chip's death, his grandfather's death, and his mother's funeral scattered the sides of the compelling box. Mac arrived ahead of the movers, and Terry looked up at him. "Who's Sidney Wright?"

Mac looked thoughtful for a moment and shrugged his shoulders. "Don't know."

"Well, since you're so much help, why don't you come over for dinner tonight and see the new house."

"I'd be delighted."

"But don't bother to come unless you bring Janelle."

"You bet."

Terry laughed as Mac barked directions to the arriving movers. Terry looked around and concluded the movers, if Mac let them, could handle the balance of the transition. Terry picked up the Jack Daniels box, the gym bag and left.

That evening after dinner, Terry asked Mac if they could talk. They sat in the study with only one chair and some boxes. Terry offered Mac the chair and straddled a box. "Tell me about my parents."

"I've told you, over and over." Mac shook his head and raised his hands in confusion. "It hasn't changed."

"I don't want my lineage, my deep roots in tradition; I want to know about my mother's accident. You never talked about that very much."

Terry watched Mac divert his eyes around the room and then slip a chew into his cheek.

"When that happened, I worked for your grandfather, Charlie Lippard. He was a dominating and controlling man, but I respected him. I don't really think you want to hear what your grandfather or I thought back then."

Terry put his elbows on his knees. "Look, Mac, I need to hear this."

"Listen, my young friend, I love you as my own son. But there have been many miles in my life which transcend several generations of your family. No matter what judgments I may have had at a given time, those judgments have been tempered by further reflection. Regardless of your father's circumstances, I believe he was a good person. For me to digress to a past time and place might not be fair to him or to you."

"Mac, I'm twenty-one years old. It's time to start leveling with me... and why are you talking about my father? I asked you about my mother's accident."

Mac, looking sober and reflective, began. "Less than a week before your mother had her car accident, she called her father one morning, quite upset. She cried and said things were very wrong. Your grandfather pushed her for an explanation; I stood beside him shaking my head. He wanted to go over to her house and get to the bottom of it. I talked him out of it, told him Terri was a grown woman and to let her work it out. 'Don't treat your daughter like a business deal', I think were my words."

Terry straightened his back and placed his hands on his thighs. "Okay, good advice, and his reaction?"

"Your grandfather followed my suggestion and waited until the next day. He called your mom and some friend of your dad... what was his name... Austin Clemmons. Clemmons answered the phone saying he was feeding the dog and your mom and dad had gone off for the weekend."

"What dog? Not Sam?"

"Yep, barely a puppy. The next time we heard from anybody was the next day, the very day of the wreck. Your dad called to tell Charlie Terri was going to see a friend at Beaufort, North Carolina. Come to find out her friend wasn't even home and knew nothing about the visit. It didn't fit.

"Anyway, her car wreck near Morehead City left her comatose, never recovered. Her injuries were strange. We had dozens of doctors review her case. None could figure out exactly how the wreck caused the injuries, but none could rule the wreck out either. It's been so long, but there were some other odd circumstances about your mother's death."

"Tell me about them."

Terry listened intently about the nonsensical wearing of the overcoat.

"That could be the only explanation why seventy miles per hour into a seventy-eight-year-old oak tree wouldn't produce seat belt bruising. I know it sounds like I'm blaming your mother's death on someone else. It doesn't matter now. At first, I distrusted your father, but I came to believe he was a decent man."

"Why just decent?"

"I mean not malicious. He loved your mom, and he loved you. That's pretty decent."

"Yeah, short of honorable."

"The whole situation smelled. If Charlie Lippard had been ten years younger, he'd never have let the matter go. Somehow, he'd have gotten to the bottom of it. But his bad heart and Chip's dying pulled the life out of him. I don't blame your dad. The problem is I don't have a clue who to blame."

Terry sensed a renewed discomfort in Mac, as if he had gotten beyond trying to assign responsibility for the tragedy.

"Let me go back to your word honorable. In the end your father, in his own way, found honor."

"You think?"

"I know."

The room stayed quiet as Terry meditated until a stream of tobacco juice running down Mac's chin broke Terry's concentration.

"Terry, you've got the whole world ahead of you. Your company is in great shape. Do you want to come in to work tomorrow?"

"Eventually, I need to straighten things out around this new house of mine." Terry hugged Mac, thanked him for the talk, and said goodnight.

At 6:30, Terry's alarm rang. Excited to be spending his first morning in his new house, he started preparing for decorators and new furnishings. Terry brewed some coffee, poured a cup, and sat back in front of the Jack Daniels box. *Why is this nagging me so*, Terry thought to himself. Mac's comments last night left him with an uneasy feeling. How did all of these names, dates, and places relate to his mother's accident? The fire his grandfather may have lost started to burn deeply in Terry.

Digging through the box, he stumbled upon a hand-written chronology containing more names and places. It left Terry with far more questions than answers. He read the document repeatedly with no better results. He wrote out a narrative to clarify the events. The facts rolled into implications, turning his stomach. As he reviewed the details of what occurred mainly on September 4, 1980, a sensation resembling burnt flesh permeated his senses. Thoughts of evil, greed, and fraud melted in his mind, creating an inferno of wrongness around the mother Terry never knew.

A newspaper article said the incident occurred in Morehead City, North Carolina on 9-05-80. Terry thought about the chronology in his father's notes. *Who are 'they' and why did 'they' take my mother to F.I.?*

A separate sheet of paper detailed directions to Family Intervention. It appeared to be in the mountains near Boone, North Carolina. The next day Terry took Bonnie on a Sunday drive into the mountains. He mentioned nothing to Bonnie about the box or his growing suspicions. The F.I. directions committed to memory, he marked the mileage on highway 221. At the designated distance, on the left, stood a grand entrance-way to the subdivision of "Green Ridge Estates."

The sign by the gate showed a teal-colored mountain background and said homes started in the "150s." Terry asked Bonnie to play along as they went into the model sales home and met the developer, Joey Reed.

"How may I help you?"

Terry pointed to the miniature plastic replica of homes, streets, trees and people spread across a large table in the middle of the room. "Tell us about Green Ridge Estates, we may be interested."

Terry watched as Joey laid out the plans of the one hundred thirty-acre subdivision featuring one-half acre lots and eight different designs of home plans. As he began his well-prepared sales pitch, Terry interrupted.

"What was here before you built all this?"

"My father talks about some sort of manufacturing plant over in the northern section of the tract. In fact, I think he tried to sell the plant for years until he lost the listing. About fifteen years ago, an outfit bought it and tried to do the textile thing in the old plant, but it went bust."

"Okay, so how did you get to be the owner?" Terry asked, with a pinch of impatience.

"The bank took it in foreclosure, got no offers, and decided it was cheaper to tear it down. Finally, the bank wanted out of sitting on the land and sold it to my father and his two brothers ten years ago. Dad had a heart attack last year, so now I basically run this with the help of my two uncles."

"How could I find out who occupied this plant... say twenty years ago?"

"Heck, I don't have a clue. There's probably an old file that my dad may have kept at Mountain Ridge Realty in Blowing Rock, who knows? Hey, I thought you wanted to buy a house."

"Still looking, but we'll keep you in mind." Terry winked and held Bonnie's hand as they walked back to the car.

As Terry drove back to Greenville, he turned to Bonnie as she started laughing.

"Well, did you have fun entertaining yourself, Mr. Real Estate? Why are you asking about twenty years ago?"

"Like you say, entertaining myself."

Terry's curiosity continued. That night, going through the box again, he stumbled across a faxed copy of a check payable to Mountain Ridge Realty on an account called "The Children's Relief Center," dated August 15, 1980, about two weeks before "they" took Terry's mother to "F.I." *Maybe I'll visit Mountain Ridge Realty.*

CHAPTER TWENTY-FIVE

Bermuda
May 15, 2002

Sidney Wright sat in the huge dining room in his Hamilton, Bermuda home, his third house on the island. The structure rose from the city like a crown jewel.

He loved the island, in part, because of the challenge of an outsider having no chance of property ownership. Sidney managed to accumulate houses by finding disgruntled, arguing heirs of estates. He bought assignments of their interests and forced the others out.

Three butlers served dinner. Usually Sidney invited local escorts, high-priced prostitutes, to dine and fill his desires afterwards. He liked to pay for his pleasures. He demanded the circumstances be controlled, his instructions specific, an act of submission on his part, but with a clear understanding he had the final say. Once the service rendered and the account settled, the matter ended, no emotional attachment. He learned this concept at an early age and believed it served him well in later life.

Tonight, feeling his sixty-three years, he turned to the large mirror behind his chair and noticed his black hair graying slightly around the perimeters. Although he'd never lost his mental edge, he acknowledged even the great Sidney Wright can't defraud Father Time. Some might say it was a pity to have such an impressive house and no family. But his money was his family, and he could buy whatever company he needed.

Tonight, in a reflective mood, he considered how quickly twenty years had passed since he'd earned his fortune. At one time, he convinced himself he could walk away from the con game. Unfortunately, the game remained in his blood, causing difficulty giving up what he did best, making money. It felt more like entertainment than a vocation.

He continued to look at himself in the massive mirror behind him, appearing closer to fifty years old, a well-fit fifty.

He liked the awe his neighbors had for his mysterious wealth. He covered the mystery by making a big splash in some legitimate business ventures. One of his top prizes, Rafael Winery, stood as a virtual gold mine and Sidney, the largest shareholder, owned thirty-five percent of the company. Gross wine sales averaged several billion a year. Originally buying in at ten percent for one hundred million dollars, his investment return produced twenty percent annually. He violated his own rule by putting too much money in one investment. The next twenty-five percent really cost him. But he liked the risk, visualizing sales growing by thirty percent a year under the right management. Complete control could only be gained by a fifty-one percent ownership, and this lofty goal stood as an improbability, a challenge he sought, an inspiration.

But tonight, reflecting in the distant past, he had no regrets. Another might have regretted the termination of Barbara Simmons. Christopher Bonn and Jonathan Biggerstaff certainly had, but not Bobby Depew. In fact, Sidney assigned the deed to him.

Barbara fit the part like a glove. If Terri Rankin hadn't found the condom and given Josh the ultimatum, she would have caught Barbara and Josh Rankin in bed. Heck, the ultimatum simplified things for Barbara.

Why did Barbara soften while being away from her family and get sloppy? She knew to protect the identities of Level IV. She blew it and had to pay the price, and my murder/frame up was brilliant. It tied the loose ends into a nice knot around Josh Rankin's neck.

Sidney thought back through his development of Project "B." The target of the project, the Lippard fortune, became more attractive to Sidney when he learned of a cash sale to International Textile. But even with the intensity of his planning, no scenario seemed likely to work.

Then he stumbled across the complex character of Josh Rankin. Months of careful investigation brought Sidney to the conclusion Josh represented the perfect psychological profile. Josh's business failures, his self-interest, his fear of losing what he had, along with an incredible level of stupidity and gullibility, made him the manipulative dream in Sidney's eye. Sidney smiled as he pondered his calculated success.

The deaths of Christopher and Jonathan had weighed heavily in Sidney's mind. How could he not have known? For years, they were nearly his closest friends, both unwavering and dependably constant.

Yet I never really knew them, Sidney thought as he had slowly panned the faces of the dozen or more attendants at the funeral service. They were all men- some older- some younger. They each cried with an intensity of having lost a spouse, like each lost a part of themselves in Christopher and Jonathan's death.

Sidney's eyes were clear as he stood reverently at a distance from the grieving crowd. He felt no emotion as the mourners spilled tears upon each other. They formed a group hug while overlooking their lovers being lowered into the ground, as if they were all victims.

Mossback, Missouri, boasted a population of 2,600 people spread over thirty square miles of forest and farmland. For the most part, if you lived in "spittin" distance of Mossback, you either farmed or cut trees, no other industry, and not much law enforcement. People around Mossback had their own sense of right and wrong.

In the mid-1980s, the lush, rolling hills and virgin forests had attracted the group Christopher and Jonathan ultimately adopted.

The well-educated group had built a small community of houses in a remote area only accessed by a dirt road. The tranquil setting gave them privacy, quietness, and the freedom to practice their lifestyle in peace. The environmentally pro-active group only went into downtown Mossback to buy supplies.

From what Sidney could determine, Jonathan and Christopher had been made a public display against homosexuality in the spring of 1993. Sidney, after convincing the coroner he was sent by the State Police, leafed through the photos from the crime scene and autopsy.

Even Sidney slightly grimaced as the coroner outlined the evidence.

"What was dismembered and placed down each others throats... well... I thought I'd seen everything. But don't count on this case being solved. The Sheriff's Department will interview a few people, push some paper around, and call it unsolvable. That's unless you State boys do something."

Sidney took a walk by himself into the countryside thinking nearly ten years had passed since seeing either of his old friends. He knew they lived in the Midwest, but didn't care enough to ask about their lives.

How could they have been gay without me knowing? I read people; I know people. Maybe that's the problem. I look at eyes and read minds rather than looking at feelings and reading hearts.

Out of sympathy, he tried to justify his friends' life choices. Understanding wouldn't come, invoking emotions that avoided him. With a deep breath of spring air, he gazed into the blue sky. He raised his arms and allowed his body to go limp in some effort to let go of the emotional defenses he had constructed around himself like a fortress as a child. If ever he wanted a non-materialistic thought to come to him, it was then.

But a cool breeze caught his face and slapped him out of his compassion. He refused to deal with their chosen passions. But Christopher and Jonathan had participated in making Sidney a lot of money. *An obligation. A legitimate obligation.*

Sidney pivoted with resolve toward the oppressive town tolerant of the killing of his friends. He stared with a fiery determination as he charted his course of action, and left town without speaking to the group claiming the two as soul mates. *Their deal, not mine.*

A 1971 Ford F-100 pickup slid on the gravel as it parked by the Pork and More Barbeque Hut on the by-pass outside of Mossback. A chainsaw and climbing hooks bounced to the front of the truck bed as it came to a stop. The driver slowly walked in, took a stool at the bar, and ordered a bowl of hash. After the last bite, he wiped his sleeve across his mouth and spun his legs toward the mostly-full tables.

"The name is Pete, and I can climb like a monkey and cut timber better than a beaver. Anybody got some work?"

The next morning, he found himself in deep walnut forests outside of Mossback. The rate was ten dollars an hour, twelve if you had your own chainsaw, plus room and board at the harvest site. Wages were paid in cash. They worked ten-hour days until the purchased timber acres were cleared. After that, a cutter was on his own to find another forest and crew.

By noon, the other cutters couldn't keep their eyes off him.

"Man, he notched that hickory darn near perfect. It laid down softer than a cat's ass."

That night after supper, they sat outside around a huge iron pot of boiled peanuts while they chewed the fat.

"Pete, you play one hell of a saw. Is it you, or you got some magic in that old Homelite of yours?"

He chuckled. "Guess these ol' arms got a little life left in 'em. I'll see you fellows at sun up, I'm hittin' the hay."

Over the next week, the man called Pete continued to perform to the amazement of everybody. Nights were for talking. By the end of the following week, conversation turned to women.

"If I don't get some poon-tang perty soon, you guys better watch it bendin' over 'round me," said an overweight lumberjack after a couple of beers. The crowd laughed.

"You better bite ya tongue, or you'll be bitin' what them fruits got down the road." They all laughed again.

Pete had his eyes slightly closed as his head rested on a log during the conversation. He spoke slowly. "What you boys goin' on about?"

Pete listened as one of the lumberjacks told the story. "You guys did that?" Pete asked while sitting up straight.

"Hell, no. Ain't nobody in this camp that mean."

"So who's mean enough?"

Three around the fire seemed to know something. Pete watched them look at each other uneasily until one blurted out.

"Hell, half the sheriff's deputies know, and there ain't nobody gonna roll over on those two boys. The way folks figure it, the world is a better place with two less queers. But, if you're wanting to thank somebody, it'd be over in the Mills' camp, cuttin' over on the western side of the county."

Pete closed his eyes as he soaked up the rest of the "conversation.

I want to work for you," Pete said as he introduced himself to Henry Mills.

"Yeah, I already heard of you. What's it they say... yer reputation preceded you? But why do you want to work here? What's wrong where you are?"

"Mr. Mills, I need more pay."

"Look, twelve bucks is the goin' rate if you pack your own saw."

"I need fifteen."

"My cutters would go crazy if they thought you were gettin' fifteen."

"But I'll get out twice the timber of your cutters."

"Yeah, I've heard."

"Well?"

"Okay, Pete, but the extra three don't come to you 'till the end of the job. Just you and me... are we straight?"

"Straight as a Georgia pine."

"Then you start in the morning."

Within a couple of days, Pete sized up Lucas and Casey.

They grew up in Mossback and specialized in two things, loggin' and hatin'. Living a farm away from each other, they rebelled against their parents, teachers, and the "law." Hate bound them together, all they knew except raping the forests of trees.

"Stay the hell away from me, skinny boy," Lucas said.

"You got it," Pete replied.

But, by the end of the first day, Pete overheard enough to know he'd impressed even Lucas and Casey with his tree skills.

"Sump'n ain't right about that boy. What's he know we ain't figured?"

Pete patiently and slowly observed the pieces of the puzzle fall together as Lucas and Casey were overcome with his quiet, almost art-like, command of a chainsaw.

"I've been cuttin' timber my whole life... ain't seen nothin' like it... what's your secret?" asked Casey.

"Sharp blades and a good eye. You boys only look at the trunk. I look at the whole tree, even the limbs not growing quite right. I watch the little things. The small and powerless leaves will tell you far more than the trunk. If you want to know which way the wind is blowing and whether the tree is thirsty, the trunk won't tell you much. A tree is a little like life itself, a total package... weak, strong, straight, and not so straight."

"Damn, Lucas, if you had knowed all that shit, we could have logged everything from here to the Mississippi," Casey howled. Lucas laughed obnoxiously as Pete harbored silently the point missed.

"We'll be talkin' to you, Pete ol' boy."

The talk came a couple of nights later.

"Listen, Pete, you probably don't know this, but there's a virgin forest a mile south of here. It's got walnut trees you and me couldn't get our arms around. Straight walnuts big bring fifty bucks a foot right off the truck. We can get hold of a truck that'll pull four logs at sixty feet, twelve thousand dollars. Me and Lucas here split ten thousand since it's our truck and our idea and all. You get two thousand, more than you get here in a month. Problem is poachers got to be quick and good. We'll start mid-afternoon and be out 'fore we lose the last glimmer of light."

Pete raised his eyebrows.

"So are ya in?"

"Sounds risky, who'll know about it?" Pete said cautiously.

"Not one damned soul," Lucas said, as Casey nodded his head.

"Okay, boys, but we do it the way I say."

"You got it, partner."

A virgin walnut towered above the forest line. Its leaves glistened by the setting sun. A hundred years of Missouri nutrients fed through its roots. Its bark was richly colored, thick, and layered with years of character. The forest adjusted decade after decade, making room for the dominating tree, home to hundreds of animals, providing shade to thousands of plants, and dropping walnuts which brought forth saplings for nearly a century.

As Pete's hooks penetrated the bark with each climbing step, a long chain hung behind him. At forty feet, two massive limbs grew horizontally from the trunk, providing Pete with both a foot walk and a chest high support in which to ensure passage away from the trunk. At ten feet out, Pete produced from under his shirt a pulley that he secured to the top limb. He threaded the chain around the wheel of the pulley. The dimming light caused difficulty making out objects in the forest.

After climbing down, Pete told Casey to back up the truck. When he did, Pete attached one end of the chain to the truck hitch.

"How the hell do you plan to bring the tree down with all this chain mess?" asked Lucas.

"Come over here," Pete instructed with an authoritative voice. He positioned his partners under the limb by the chain. "Now, if you'll both look up along the trunk..." he said as he slapped the handcuffs around one ankle of each murderer of Sidney's friends.

The cuffs were suddenly attached to the end of the chain by a spring-loaded link.

"What the hell's goin' on?"

Sidney Wright quickly made his way to the idling truck and put it in gear as they shouted in unison and tripped over each other's feet. As the truck moved forward, the wiggling lumberjacks, dangling by an ankle, rose slowly, their noses pointed to the ground. Sidney heard their screams through the truck window. The tough and cruel exteriors of the men evaporated, and fear and desperation emerged. He turned the truck until the chain lay firmly against the walnut. He drove a metal stake through the chain which secured it to the trunk of the tree. With the truck parked and the ignition off, Sidney stepped out and stretched his exhausted muscles. Then he walked back and stood below their faces as the blood rushed to their heads. He listened, but he ignored their pleas and begging.

Sidney gave no words of retribution or judgment of their conduct. The names of their victims were never mentioned, but Sidney knew the score had been settled, the obligation met. The past month and a half of practicing the art form of lumber jacking back in a West Indies mahogany forest had served the cause.

Sidney unhooked the chain from the truck and left, never again to be seen in Mossback, Missouri. But as the dust clouded behind the spinning tires, he questioned himself once more, why, after years of doing business with Christopher and Jonathan, he never knew.

Sidney finally resolved he must have blocked his friends' relationship out of his mind. *What else have I blocked out?*

Invincibility, never a word or concept Sidney applied to his life. The lessons of the Starlight contradicted any such perception of self-value. But tonight, he relished in the undeniable success of his life. You could measure it by wins and loses or in terms of dollars. No matter the measurement, the result astounded him.

He took the crystal glass of his fifty-year-old brandy from the butler on the veranda, looking across the Atlantic Ocean in all directions. As he savored the evolved liquid, he gazed upon the clear sky of uncountable universal lights. In his mind, he weighed the vastness of the stars against the vastness of his accomplishments. He fell satisfactorily asleep before the results were tabulated.

CHAPTER TWENTY-SIX

Blowing Rock, North Carolina
May 19, 2002

Terry stood in front of Mountain Ridge Realty admiring the stacked gray stone facade. The front door, a wormy-chestnut, appeared to be original to the building. The charm quickly faded as he walked inside the musky old office with well-worn wood floors and peeling paint.

A secretary, sitting behind an old school desk in a cloud of smoke, greeted Terry. Overflowing ashtrays on her desk looked like an unfinished volcano project for elementary school.

"Would Joey Reed happen to be in?" Terry asked.

"No, he's over at Green Ridge. He doesn't come in much, but we'll call him if you need him."

"Not necessary, but maybe you can help me. Joey said he thought your company had an old file when you listed the Sun-Grill plant property."

"Boy, you're talkin' about a coon's age ago. I've been here eighteen years. We'd lost the listing by then, but I remember Joey's daddy saying selling someone leprosy would be easier than selling that place."

"Let me show you a copy of a check," Terry said as he handed the secretary the faxed copy of the check from "The Children's

Relief Fund." He stood over her as she looked at it between her yellowed fingers and shrugged her shoulders.

"I'm trying to find out if someone leased the property while you had the listing."

"If they did, I'd have no idea where the paperwork would be. There's a storage shed in the back, has probably forty years of old files in it. You know Joey's granddaddy built this place in nineteen-fifteen. Some around these mountains said it ain't been touched since."

Terry joined her in a hearty laugh.

"You're welcome to take a look around if you like, but you might be bit by a rat or get yourself lost in the dust and never come out."

Terry accepted her offer and she began rummaging through her desk drawer until she found an old "Tweetsie Railroad" key chain. She looked up at Terry.

"Did Joey say it was okay for you to do this?"

"I'm sure he won't mind."

Terry reached out and took the key as the secretary lit another cigarette. He jerked the tightly fitted backdoor, causing paint hanging off a pressed-tin ceiling to fall on his head.

Out back, he found a rusty lock securing the shed's door. He struggled with it until it popped open. As he opened the door, the rusty hinges squeaked loudly, and dust whirled in the room. He sneezed as he waited for things to settle.

It appeared no one had been in the structure for years. Terry spent an hour looking at various boxes. In no particular order, there were boxes of leases, listing agreements, and accounting ledgers. It all seemed not worth the effort until he stumbled upon a box marked "Sun-Grill." He pulled the box out of the shed into the sunlight. He found a listing agreement with the bankruptcy trustee, correspondence, notes of various property showings, and finally he spotted a thin file saying "Rising High." There he spotted several documents in addition to the copy of the check in the Jack Daniels box. He slipped the file underneath his shirt, closed the box, and returned it. Forcing the old lock closed, he muttered quietly, "Doubt they'll miss this before the next millennium."

"Thanks a lot," Terry said as he walked by and tossed the key on the desk.

"Find anything?"

"Mostly dust and rats."

Terry saw her cigarette bounce up and down in her mouth as the secretary laughed.

"I warned you."

Terry strolled out the door with the file, confident she hadn't noticed.

Back at home, Terry threw the file into the Jack Daniels box. He wanted to clear his mind of the matter for a while and decided tomorrow morning he'd go to the office and make Mac happy.

At six o'clock, Terry pushed the accelerator on his convertible through the streets of Greenville hoping to beat Mac to work. Driving into the executive parking lot, Mac's truck sat nearest the entry door. It looked awkward among the other executives' slick cars. Terry laughed at the dusty old pickup Mac had been driving for years, not one to waste anything. As Terry walked into his corporate headquarters, Mac smiled.

"Sir, I believe we will need to see some I.D. We don't let strangers in this part of the office."

"Where the heck do I get one?"

"New employees get Rankin Enterprises I.D. over at Human Resources. It might not be a bad idea for you to learn where that is."

Terry laughed out of a combination of humor and embarrassment. He knew too little about his own company.

All morning Terry pored over the details of Rankin Enterprises. Since Mac made all decisions as to profitability, he needed to catch up. Terry, anxious to get into the decision-making process, needed to learn what to grow and what to cut. He bounced several questions off Mac, who responded to each with a better question. He decided to listen. He sat silently, absorbing Mac's vast experience.

They were having a working lunch in office when Terry asked, "Mac, have you ever heard of 'The Children's Relief Fund'?"

Terry knew he had thrown Mac a curve ball as he paused at length, rubbing his chin.

"Yep, I couldn't forget that one, one of the five so-called charities paid out of your mother's estate." Mac went into great detail to explain the story. Terry could tell the whole thing greatly irritated him.

"Lawyers are idiots. We got only a minimum limits malpractice insurance policy out of that disbarred shyster. It costs us twice that to find out what he did."

"So what became of the investigation?"

"Basically, five dead ends. Don't waste your time worrying about what's now ancient history. You've got a company to run. It's all spilled milk... billions of it... it won't help to cry over it. And if a better cliché would clean out this clutter in your mind, I'd pound it into your ears."

Terry spent the rest of the week working hand in hand with Mac. The business theory he brought back from Wharton bled out of Terry in earnest, ready to put Rankin Enterprises on the leading edge of his theory.

"Mac, we can totally re-mold this department and get another three-percent return on it."

"That department is running well. When you milk something for an extra dollar, you better understand the consequences. A balance of taking a profit while giving your workers incentive makes for a smooth running department."

Terry decided to spend more time listening to Mac than preaching profit. The lessons became an inspiration to Terry.

Nights were harder. The disjointed circumstances of his mother's death created sleepless nights. Terry coped by reading the contents of the box, re-organizing and re-thinking names, dates, and places.

The "Rising High" file contained an application and a lease. Although the check contained Wilbur Brewer's signature, James Sexton signed the application and lease. Terry plainly saw connection between "the taking", the Sun-Grill Plant, and the estate payment to "The Children's Relief Fund."

Dad, why did you keep this information to yourself, in a box? As Terry reflected, he realized he'd been wrapped in a blanket of protection by Janelle and Mac, shielding him from his true circumstances, son of a convicted murderer.

The next morning, Terry again arrived at work before sun-up, finding the always dependable Mac well into his day. At the first opportunity, he approached Mac.

"I want to know more about the murder." Terry caught an unpleasant glance.

"Why do you want to go there? Let's leave it alone. If you want someone to vouch for your father, I'll do it. Somehow, I think he had a big heart, maybe part of his problem, couldn't control his emotions. There were times when, if you'll pardon me, I thought your dad down right stupid... not even close to having your smarts.

"But you know what? There were times I saw you cradled in his arms. I felt almost a jealousy to watch your father's eyes when they rested on you, as if the world didn't matter, a love for which I've never seen such intensity."

Terry shifted back and forth on his feet, hopelessly lost for words.

"When he held you in the courtroom after being convicted, I never felt more pain, for him or for you. I'll tell you this; he didn't kill that lady, my subjective opinion. But, if I'd never known your dad, and sat on the jury, I'd have convicted him myself.

"We did the best we could, got him the best lawyer, had bundles of character witnesses, he got a fair trial. My saying innocent is nothing but a gut feeling. I truly think you should let it go and focus on the future. This is nothing but a distraction to you."

"Mac, if he loved me that much, what's wrong with caring? I feel like I'm doing both myself and him a disservice by ignoring what happened. Please help me."

Terry looked at him with resolve, fully aware these old matters derailed Mac's best-laid plans.

"Fine, if you insist, I have a pile of stuff stored away in a file in my office. It won't be easy reading. Sure you want it?"

"Please."

After a few minutes, Mac returned. Terry took the file and tried to ignore the disappointment on Mac's face. "I need to look over these papers at home. Don't worry, I'll be back." Terry strolled purposely towards the exit but spotted Mac angrily shaking his head.

Terry lined the facts up in his mind. *Dad's name in her address book and the torn photograph looks like they snapped it of themselves at arms length. To look at it, I'd be a fool to think they hadn't cared for each other.*

Dad acted irate in the manager's office, the killing happened within a couple of hours, and three blocks from his house... my house. As he considered the wet blood on the side of his father's car, Terry realized the evidence had a snowballing effect and landed at the front steps of the "House of Guilty as Sin."

What's all this about the alias name of Angie Jenkins? Terry asked himself.

He read with interest the deceased's husband did not know what she did and admitted to a mysterious wiring of money into their joint checking account. There were too many strange circumstances. But for the web of conspiracy coming from the Jack Daniels box, Terry could have easily accepted the verdict based on the evidence.

Why am I doing this? It can't be the challenge. I've got a ship load full at my company, and Mac's getting tired of being the captain. So why? It's not a challenge. It's my family. I never knew 'em... I never loved 'em... nobody's left... only me.

CHAPTER TWENTY-SEVEN

Montreal
May 29, 2002

Terry's Cessna touched down in Montreal. Terry arrived unannounced and knocked on the door at 414 East Bank Street. An older man appeared at the door, overweight and wearing a bathrobe.

"What can I do for you?"

"Are you Isaac Simmons?"

"Right."

"My name is Terry Rankin. May I come in?"

"Whatever you're selling, I'm not interested."

"I'm not selling anything. I want to talk."

"Sure you do. Whatever you want to talk about, I'm not buying, so get lost."

"I've traveled all the way from South Carolina to see you. It's about your wife."

"Rankin? If you're the same Rankin that put a bullet in her head, you can head back south right now."

Terry calmed his voice. "I mean no harm, and I mourn your loss. Could I have a short minute?"

"It's been twenty years, there's nothing left to be said, and the mourning's done."

Terry conveyed the hurt look of a scorned puppy and watched Isaac scratch his head nervously.

Terry paused a moment. "I'm not your enemy. I suffer everyday of my life, not knowing why all this happened."

"Well, come in for a minute if you think it'll make you feel better."

Although the house was neat, it appeared to have been decorated over twenty years ago. The carpet and furniture upholstery were worn and dated. Terry took a seat in a harvest gold, woven chair, purposely looking sad and sober. Collecting his thoughts, he waited silently until Isaac spoke.

"What is it you think I can tell you?"

"Josh Rankin, my father, committed suicide in prison."

"Yes, I heard," Isaac said and, after some delay, added, "I'm sorry."

"Thank you, but I don't remember my father, being only three when he died. I want to talk to you about the year leading up to your wife's death, the year a bunch of unfortunate events took place. My mother died, my uncle died, and over four billion dollars stolen from my mother's estate."

"Did you say billion?"

"I did."

"Oh, I made some coffee. You want a cup?"

"Sure, if you're having one."

Isaac's interest seemed piqued as he handed Terry a cup and settled in the chair facing the television

"Do you hold your father responsible for the deaths and stealing of the money?"

"I'm confident my father didn't steal the money. It was already his, and he did everything he could to get it back."

"So what does that have to do with Barbara?"

"I'm not sure. There's something wrong with the way my mother died and how money disappeared. It had to have involved a network of extremely bright and well-funded people. I couldn't help but notice, reading old newspapers, you didn't know your wife was in South Carolina, what she did for a living, but got large sums of money wired to your bank account. She was also known by an alias name in South Carolina... Angie Jenkins."

"So what? Your father was guilty as the day is long, and if you don't think I ought to...."

Terry interrupted. "No, no, no! I don't. My father is dead, and your wife is dead. I'm not here to argue. Can you understand I think some outfit killed my mother, and those same people got my family's money? There's probably no connection between my mother and your wife's death, but I'd be forever grateful if you would talk to me about it for a few minutes. I promise I'll never bother you again."

"Well, what is it you want to hear?"

"Why did you not know who she worked for?"

"What the heck, it doesn't matter now, but she worked for the Canadian Government. Call her a secret agent, I guess."

"Did she get paid by the government?"

"I don't know who paid her, but fifteen thousand dollars a month would show up in our checking account, a heck of a lot of money back then, still is."

"Do you still have any bank records that far back?"

"Probably, but that's my business, not yours."

"Would you consider merely telling me the bank account number?"

Terry pleaded with his eyes as Isaac thought about it for a moment.

"No harm, I suppose, haven't used that bank in twelve years, hold on a minute."

When Isaac returned, Terry took an old blank deposit slip with the name of Royal Bank and Trust and the account number.

"When did the fifteen thousand a week stop coming to your account?"

"It's strange you asked that question, because the money kept coming even after she died, probably about nine months after we buried her before the money stopped."

"About the time they convicted my father, right?"

"Well, so what. Why should I question the money, complain to who?"

"I understand."

"You know, I hired a lawyer to sue your father for Barbara's death. Everybody thought he was loaded because he had inherited some textile family's money. Turned out all of the money was tied up in some kind of trust. My lawyer tried to break it up, but some guy... yeah, I can't forget the name... Mac, the trustee, and he gave us a damn fit."

Terry shifted in the worn fibers of the chair, trying not to grin.

"Irrevocable trust, I believe, they called it. We couldn't get to it. The money your father had was all spent on his lawyers and appeals. Since the fifteen thousand dollars kept coming, I figured our good government would take care of us. I guess I figured wrong."

"What about the names of people your wife worked with?"

"Oh, very secretive, she always told me not to ask her questions. I understood everything had to be confidential. But every now and then she might talk a little about her work being very exciting. She wouldn't say much, but you could tell she took pride in her job. She spent two months with us before the last assignment and was on top of the world."

"Think carefully, Mr. Simmons. Surely she mentioned somebody."

"She never used anybody's last name, but once I do remember a first name. I probably wouldn't have paid much attention except she seemed so damn taken with him."

"... and the name?"

"Sidney, I think. Yes, Sidney but, mind you, no last names."

"Is there anything else you can think of before she left for her last assignment?"

"No, her being gone so long, took a toll on all of us. Our son, Buddy, so young then, got only a weekly phone call from Barbara. He's thirty now. Would you like to see a picture of Barbara?"

"Sure... of course." Terry looked around, hoping to find more information, as Isaac left the room and returned with a large photograph.

"Wow." Terry sat in awe looking at Barbara in her mid twenties, strikingly beautiful. The torn photo, published in the old newspaper article, didn't do her justice.

"See what she meant to me?"

"Yes."

"She could've married anybody in our high school. Back then, I played varsity quarterback, and everybody thought I'd set the world on fire. Barbara, smart as hell, starred in all the school plays. Hot stuff, a match made in heaven, or so we thought. We married the summer after graduation. My career didn't exactly pan out, never got past assistant construction foreman at the company where I worked for twenty years. Had a beer belly by age twenty-two, but Barbara never gained a pound and looked as beautiful as this picture the last day I saw her."

Terry sensed Isaac relaxing as he watched him lean back into a worn leather chair, throw his legs upon the ottoman, and sigh.

"I knew she had to be satisfying her needs somehow during her long trips, and kept me around because we had a son."

Terry tried to be sympathetic. "Don't be so hard on yourself. It sounds like you've done a good job raising your boy, nothing wrong with the wife being the bread winner."

"A bum back knocked me out of work a while ago. I never spent a lot of money, and those weekly deposits really added up over the years. Even after they stopped, I had plenty to live on for years, but the money's about gone now. I really can't afford to live in this house anymore, no big deal since my son's grown, and I need a smaller place anyway."

"Why do you think she hid from you her alias name and where she lived?"

"It's probably none of your business, but after twenty years I guess it doesn't matter. She had her life, and I looked after Buddy. I always tried to believe this secret agent stuff but, you know, most of it didn't make sense. So now you know my story. Kind of strange, isn't it?"

Terry rose from the chair. "Well, thanks for the chat, Mr. Simmons."

"Sorry I wasn't much help. Hey, I meant it when I said sorry about your father."

Terry nodded. "Thank you." He walked out of the apartment feeling new optimism. The name "Sidney" quickened his heartbeat, though, at the time, he couldn't account for his emotion.

CHAPTER TWENTY-EIGHT

Greenville
June 2002

Sidney Wright's name, written on a single piece of paper, laid face up at the top of the box. Terry figured his father made the entry close to the end.

Terry, not one to flex his rich and powerful muscle, stood ready to move on the now closed bank account of Barbara and Isaac Simmons. From January 20, 1980 to May 21, 1983, monthly wires of $15,000 landed into the account. He began tracing the money through a series of transactions.

Some palm-greasing led to the originating account, in the name of Benevolences, Incorporated, from a Bermuda bank. Terry discovered the account, closed for fifteen years, had signature cards in storage, and he requested to do a search. The bank denied the request without much explanation. Terry waited.

Two months later, the Bermuda bank hired a new Vice President with an economics degree from the Wharton School of Business and one year with Chase Manhattan. Quincy Stevens quickly and skillfully blended himself into the fabric of the bank. His personality and banking savvy brought unity to the staff.

Quincy had access to all functions of the bank. No one ever questioned him when he inspected the archived records.

Benevolences, Incorporated had a board of officers listed on its account application with only one signatory, Sidney Wright. It didn't take long for Quincy to learn Sidney Wright, a resident of Hamilton, was a respected businessman with incredible clout. Although seen as a loner, his house and financial muscle were the envy of the island. The local newspaper frequently gave his estate the "Yard of the Month" designation.

To Quincy, he didn't sound like a man with extensive involvement in criminal activity, but no other Sidney Wright was listed as a resident for the past twenty years. From a local newspaper photograph, Quincy discovered Sidney used Pink Sands Landscaping and Maintenance Service for grounds and lawn care. Business was good at Pink Sands, and they were hiring.

Soon, Quincy announced he had accepted another position. Two weeks later, Quincy reported to his new job as CFO of a corporation located in Greenville, South Carolina.

Wharton School of Business had a mentoring program between seniors and freshmen. The arrangement grew into friendship and trust between senior Quincy Stevens and freshman Terry Rankin.

Mabry Barnes, a private investigator with the Anderson Agency of Atlanta, had extensive knowledge of security systems. As part of his assignment for Terry Rankin, he had recently turned lawn specialist and became a new hire at Pink Sands. He worked his way up to the better clients and regularly worked the grounds of Sidney Wright. After several weeks of investigation, he prepared to enter the premises. The problem for Barnes was Sidney spent a lot of time at the Bermuda house and had not left the island since Barnes' placement with Pink Sands. Finally, after three and a half weeks, Barnes learned Sidney left for South America and wouldn't return for four days. Wright never left staff alone in the house when he departed the island.

The security system, basic child's play to Barnes, made getting into the living quarters no problem. The mission clearly defined no evidence to be left of an unauthorized entrance. He sought documents of a criminal operation occurring 20 to 25 years ago.

Barnes worked mainly at night. Security stops by a hired service were as routine as the rising and setting of the sun. *These guys need to be fired,* thought Barnes. *Guess crime in Bermuda is like frost in Ecuador.*

He worked two full nights, going through all desks, files and other potential hiding places. Locks were easily opened, but he found no document resembling the targeted information.

On the third day, Barnes, working landscaping at the Wright property, felt tired and frustrated. At the noon break, he entered an unlocked basement room off the end of the house to cool off. A few of his co-workers joined him for lunch in the musty, cluttered old room containing mostly junk. Old rags, saw horses, and unused building supplies scattered the floor. The basement room sat underneath the main floor near the stairway.

Barnes had inspected under stairway and found only empty space surrounded by walling. But he noticed something unusual in the basement, a partial ceiling serving no obvious purpose. Barnes recalled some specialized training he received about eight years earlier at a Security and Architecture seminar. One of the concepts discussed was to design space underneath a stairway to deceive the human eye.

The deception occurred by altering the "V" through a gradual architectural process so the "V" ended at the second step instead of the first. This left a space the width of the stairway and the height and depth of a full step. In this situation, Mabry figured the space approximately 14 inches by 12 inches by 5 feet.

Once lunch ended, Barnes and the other workers returned to their landscaping duties. Barnes worked close to the basement room entrance. At the first available moment, he slipped back into the room and centered himself under what he perceived to be the location of the bottom step. The basement ceiling was about ten feet tall. He needed a ladder, so he casually retrieved one from the Pink Sands truck. With the ladder in place, he began to feel along the partial ceiling nailed directly into the bottom of the main floor joists. He inspected it with a flashlight finding no latches or hinges. As he rubbed his hand around the suspected area, he felt a small, nearly insignificant, gap. The line of the gap traveled about five feet and made a 90-degree turn for two feet and traveled back another five feet. *Bingo.*

A tightly-fitting board, two feet wide and five feet long, slid easily from the side, a tongue and groove board with a one inch thickness. Barnes removed it, set it to the side, and looked upward at his prize.

He released six latches and eased the heavy file cabinet downward. He struggled down the ladder and placed it on the concrete floor. A quick inspection showed hundreds of documents of many operations. Barnes' heartbeat picked up as he read a few pages containing the names provided by the client. They included Barbara Simmons, Austin Clemmons, and many others.

Barnes' concentration, interrupted by co-workers' voices coming toward his area, forced him to replace the board and hide the file under some old paint clothes. Walking out of the basement, he announced, "Let's mow some grass."

He waited that evening for security to leave and eased back into in the basement, feeling alive and excited. The documents needed to appear undisturbed. Barnes had enough film to process up to one-hundred fifty pages. Unfortunately, there were probably eighteen hundred pages, and he'd have to use some discretion. He focused first on the documents in which the familiar names appeared. The entire file seemed to be in chronological order.

The camera required some independent source of light. He set up a portable flashlight on a stand and placed each piece of paper on an old, flat piece of plywood, painted black. To get a quality picture, each document took nearly three minutes.

The first one hundred pictures covered most of the twenty-one to twenty-three year ago period. He took twenty-five additional pictures of those looking especially important and twenty-five dated the most recent. Barnes returned all documents to their proper place, latched the file in soundly with six latches, and replaced the board. He wore precision gloves during the whole process, which had taken more than eight hours. Barnes concluded his work at 4:00 a.m. and felt whipped.

The former employee of Pink Sands slept soundly as the Boeing 747 departed Bermuda for Atlanta on the 7:15 a.m. flight, with no plan to return anytime soon. Silent laughter jolted through his exhausted body as he recalled a couple of his Pink Sands co-workers' conversation when they thought he wasn't listening. Mabry Barnes loved their British accents.

"Mark my words, the new bloke will get the Employee of the Month. I must say, he is good... but been here less than a month... ah, the front parking space, and the extra change jingling in his pocket."

Guess I'll missed the honors ceremony, he pondered as he reclined in his First Class seat.

Once back at Anderson headquarters in Atlanta, he placed a call to Terry Rankin. "I think we got what you need."

"Did you get it all?"

"Nope, but hopefully it's enough."

"The film can be developed and printed by the end of the day. Care for our agency to take care of that?"

"No, I'll have a courier by your office in ten minutes. We'll develop it on my end. Nice work."

CHAPTER TWENTY-NINE

Greenville
November 2002

Terry reviewed the materials slowly and methodically. Clearly the written form, intended for Sidney Wright's purposes, contained abbreviations and symbolisms. Deciphering the words seized Terry like agents of destruction.

One document, labeled Project "B" Personnel List listed names with various codes to the right of each name. It appeared wrinkled compared to the others. Another list included Terry's father, mother, uncle, grandfather and Barbara Simmons. Beside the name Chip Lippard and Barbara Simmons he found the letter "T" with a date. Beside the name Terri Rankin and Charlie Lippard, the letter "D" with a date. Beside the name Josh Rankin, a "Self T" and a date.

These people had one thing in common, dead. The date matched the actual date of death. Everyone with a "T" died of unnatural causes. Terry inferred the "T" meant terminated, "D" meant died, and "Self T" meant suicide. Discovering this waste of life jolted through his body like a bolt of lightning. Then sadness came over him.

There had never been any mention of Uncle Chip's demise being anything other than an airplane crash due to pilot error. Terry went back and read the newspaper account of the heroin involvement. The airfield manager's comments about Chip's apparent sobriety were now given new meaning, and there seemed to be no end to the tragedy.

The other pages became easier to follow after Terry realized Sidney Wright had murdered Chip Lippard, Barbara Simmons, and might as well have murdered Terry's mother and father. It wasn't much of a stretch to factor all of this loss as a contributing factor to his grandfather's death.

Barbara Simmons definitely worked for the developers of Project "B." Eventually, the documents told Terry how much Barbara and the other operatives were paid. Some players were bigger than others, but the man in charge of it all was Sidney Wright, his plan, his money, and his control. The son and father both had to die before the daughter so Josh Rankin could inherit the greatest sum of money.

Terry's silent burden of shame, his father a convicted murderer, started to dissolve as he read. A sense of relief covered him like a warm spring afternoon. *My dad's no murderer.*

But as Terry learned the truth about his father, a new kind of shame took over. *Dad's hands weren't clean. His stupidity was no excuse to let them hurt Mom.*

Terry sat paralyzed as he scanned the pages showing the so-called mental erasement a conjured-up procedure with no basis in medical science. His father's ignorance and greed had been lethal.

Terry agonized through Sidney Wright's notes showing extensive background analysis of Josh Rankin. His anticipated proclivities for marital infidelity and weakness in character qualified him to be the central focus of Project "B." It sickened Terry.

Over the next month, Terry organized and carefully constructed the sequence of events. After calling in a couple of favors, Terry met informally with a federal prosecutor who discussed the facts on a hypothetical and confidential basis.

The prosecutor rejected Terry's argument. What seemed a clear and solid net of information was torn into pieces as Terry listened.

"How do you know when these notes were written? How do you know "T" means terminated and, even if it did, who committed the so-called termination? A man has already been convicted of murdering his mistress some twenty years ago. Do you know the difficulty in successfully prosecuting someone else after that many years?

"You've presented no proof, other than your father's notes, Wright ever left Bermuda. In a murder conspiracy, you at least have to identify a killer and work backwards. The only killer identified is your father, and your theory assumes he's not part of the conspiracy. Prosecutors like strong cases, fresh evidence and fresh witnesses, and your hypothetical falls short on all counts."

Terry attempted to argue the point, only to watch the prosecutor roll his eyes.

"I'll be happy to say whatever you want to hear, but it's my understanding you wanted this conversation to be candid and practical so you could get an honest, non-biased opinion on the chances of successfully prosecuting the case. I've now given that to you. If the hypothetical criminal lives in a foreign country and has lots of money, it compounds your problems further."

"Thank you," Terry replied. "I've heard all I need to hear."

He left, feeling shaken and frustrated. He was the last of his central family and knew exactly who caused him to grow up without parents. He also knew this man got the lion's share of four billion dollars and probably had more resources than he. *I've got to think ahead of this guy. He doesn't know I know. That's my edge. I'm going to bring him down,* he thought with an angry conviction.

The vast majority of Terry's time became focused on the last twenty-five pages, future information involving Sidney's obsession with his interest in Chilean ventures. Sidney did business by balancing the greatest gain with the least risk, and Terry smelled an opportunity.

Chile's great growing conditions are credited to its Mediterranean style climate. The climate is a combination of meteorological forces caused by the Andes, the Pacific, the Atacama Desert, and the polar ice caps. It has deep and fertile soils and a reliable source of water for irrigation. Sidney's notes concluded these natural conditions rendered Maipo Valley the best opportunity for investment compared to anywhere in the world.

Sidney presently owned thirty-five percent of a Maipo Valley winery called Rafael. It appeared from summaries he had extensively researched not only Rafael but also all other wineries in the region. Maipo Valley, located just south of Santiago, Chile's capital, offered some of the best growing conditions in the world for grapes. Land prices being much cheaper than in comparable regions such as Napa Valley, Bordeaux, and Burgundy, strengthened Sidney's interest

At Wharton, Terry enjoyed evaluating the worth of a company. From Sidney Wright's notes, Terry clearly saw Sidney intending to increase his ownership in Rafael. Terry quickly pulled together the public records on this company which traded on the New York Stock Exchange. He also developed documentation from knowledgeable sources. From a business concept, in Terry's opinion, the investment looked solid, even if Sidney paid the fair market value, something he had no intention of paying.

Sidney's apparent strategy consisted of buying off the main competitor of Rafael Winery to intentionally suffer financial losses. Companion Vineyards, who had about the same overhead per case, agreed to substantially lower its prices in the coming year. The vintage to be released had been a bountiful one. Each winery would release thousands of cases. The wine critics had been kind to Companion and rated its wines at several points higher than Rafael's, based on a 100-point scale. This meant a lot to the ultimate consumer, influenced by the critics. Terry sat in awe as he considered the impact of the plan affecting Rafael's ability to sell its product.

Companion, privately owned, had no shareholders to account to for the drop in revenues. Its owner, both the President and CFO, had Sidney Wright set up foreign accounts with sufficient certified funds to increase Companion's projected profits by five percent. Wright paid millions so Rafael's sales and profits would drastically fall, causing warehouses to be full of unsold wines with another vintage release rapidly approaching.

Companion should sell out of its higher-rated, lower-priced wines, and with Sidney's monetary cover, have greater profits than expected and empty warehouses waiting for the next vintage. Companion, being a private concern, could keep financial analysts from knowing its exact cost basis per case, while the private owner's bank account bulged with Sidney's extra money.

Terry frequently caught himself admiring the brilliance of the scheme until snapping back to the hate brewing inside. Terry knew the financial markets. Rafael's stock ratings, certain to be lowered, would spook investors into a selling frenzy. Sidney's plan predicted he should be able to pick up fifteen to twenty-five percent more of the company for a fraction of its value. As soon as he acquired the shares he needed, Companion would raise its prices and Rafael quickly normalize. Sidney's notes contained future plans for the critical judging of Rafael wines of the following vintage, another operation.

Terry digested and organized this information and developed a unique opportunity to deal with Sidney Wright. He spent the next six weeks on a countering concept, greedy and ruthless like Wright. Terry justified the means as a proper way to end the rampage of wrong.

Through intermediaries and holding companies, Terry acquired forty-five percent of a small, but well-managed, Chilean winery called Caberro. The agreement reached with management called for the new forty-five percent ownership to loan one hundred million to the company for the purpose of acquiring equity in other Chilean wine properties. The understanding gave Terry, if an exceptional value presented itself, the authority to buy shares, and place operations under the capable management of Caberro. One caveat subjected Terry's purchases to the advice and consent of the majority ownership as outlined in his contract with Caberro.

Upon release, as expected, Companion dropped its pricing, and Raphael's sales began to slow. Within a month, the publicly traded Rafael stock started to fall. Terry dictated Caberro should start buying at a fifty percent drop on a slow basis and start doubling up every subsequent ten percent dip. If the stock price reduced by seventy-four percent, they'd buy everything offered on the financial markets. Terry had the majority owners' verbal consent to the plan.

Working through a trusted securities broker, Terry began the counter-attack. He bought slowly, once the stock had dropped by fifty percent. The financial analysts, brutally pessimistic on Rafael, caused frantic selling and Caberro started beating Sidney Wright in acquiring shares. Terry knew from the last note Sidney planned to jump in when the stock fell by seventy-five percent.

Climbing in bed that night, Terry smiled broadly knowing he'd outmaneuvered Sidney to the fruits of his adversary's scheming. The phone rang at 5:45 a.m., and Terry listened as his broker nervously spoke.

"We've got a problem at Caberro. The work force, all the farmers, all the pickers and all the production people have walked out. This company hires its workers from the local people who make up the village of Esparanza. It's a tight community, and Jose' Fernando, President of Caberro, had the respect of the people. This respect had been earned over the decades. Fernando grew up about fifty miles away in the village of San Nicolas. Traditionally these communities are intense rivals. The two factions, a hundred years ago, were constantly at war. Over the past twenty-five years, these communities have been relatively peaceful, except for an unspoken distrust of each other. Jose' Fernando worked extremely hard contributing to the local Esparanza causes. He gave both his money and time. Until last night, he was held in high esteem."

"So, what the hell happened last night?" Terry asked impatiently.

"About an hour after sunset, a large group of the San Nicolas, in terrorist style, executed several high-ranking local citizens, burned the village church, and desecrated family burial grounds. There's a lot of evidence Caberro put up the money and orchestrated the attack. One captured militant, among his weapons, had an uncashed check, signed by Fernando himself, for twenty thousand dollars. The prisoner, after being pressured, confessed the whole operation was funded by Caberro's money, funneled through the militants.

Terry sat sweating in his pajamas. "Damn, so where does that leave us?"

"Well, Caberro refuses to buy any more Rafael stock. This is the least of their problems, and they think they'll need the money to stay afloat. Although we have a commitment for the stock purchase from Caberro, their advice and consent could be withdrawn under these circumstances. Listen, things are changing by the hour. Let me get back to you later."

Terry conversed with the broker three times that day, and the situation deteriorated. Looting by local citizens on the wine property caused one vineyard to burn, and Caberro had no dependable allies in the village, its fragile community standing shattered. The national government sent in troops to protect Caberro.

"Let's see how that goes," said the broker.

Hours turned into days and days into weeks. After four weeks, Terry took the final phone call.

"Looks like it's all over. Caberro has sold the land, wine, and all other assets rather than risk losing everything. Bottom line is your forty-five percent interest is worth only a fraction of what you paid. The holding company should get a check in about thirty days. I'm sorry, this should never have happened."

Terry paused for a moment. Then he asked the broker, "Who bought the assets?"

"That one you'll never believe, Rafael, the company whose stock had tanked. They paid cold cash. Man, if they are able to get the locals back to work and keep Caberro running, they'll make out like bandits."

Terry wanted to smash the phone through the wall, but regained his composure. "Before you hang up, do one more little thing for me. Check the current stock percentages of major shareholders in Rafael."

"Okay... sure... it looks like fifty-one percent is owned by a Sidney Wright of Bermuda. Five percent is owned by.... "

"Enough," Terry interrupted. "I'll talk to you later." Terry hung up the phone trying to reconcile his misery. *What am I going to do, go to the Chilean government and tell them about Wright's scheme? I'd go to jail if they discovered I decided to cash in on the deal for myself and, in all my greed, caused two communities to go to war and ruined a company in the process. My hands are tied, bastard won again."*

The two, in Terry's mind, were both illegitimate ships which had passed in the darkness of money. The winner had taken it all. The money could be replenished, but the disgrace not so easily erased. Defeat echoed through Terry's soul. He could think of nothing more personal.

I knew him, and I knew what he was doing. He doesn't know me and beat my sorry ass anyway. I underestimated him. Guess it runs in the family.

CHAPTER THIRTY

Greenville
February 2003

Terry, still angered and depressed, realized his neglect for Bonnie. Since their wonderful and passionate night on Grady Drive, his mind wandered, and he showed little attention to her. He knew this saddened Bonnie, but figured he'd make it up to her when he got his head straight. But time passed, and nothing added up. After days of stewing in his failure, he knocked on her door.

"Who's there?"

"Your pretty lousy friend. I'm sorry."

Bonnie's smile refreshed Terry as she opened the door.

"Don't ever be sorry, and don't look so sad."

He relaxed as she eased into his arms. Her firm breasts felt nice against his chest. He held the embrace for several moments, as stress of the past few weeks eased slightly.

"Are you hungry? I could fix you a sandwich."

Terry nodded his head. "I am kinda hungry."

He pulled a chair up to the kitchen table and watched her pull out some sliced turkey and mayonnaise and lay out two pieces of bread on a plate. He laughed as she dipped a butter knife deep into the mayonnaise jar and, as she pulled it out, a big glob dropped to the side of the plate. Terry dipped into it with his index finger. He spread the mayonnaise over Bonnie's well-defined lips, kissing her passionately while he collected the greasy substance on his own tongue. Plunging deeply in her mouth, he heard her breathing heighten and, as he pulled away, noticed her blushing slightly. He smiled as she took the knife and spread some on his ear, following it with her tongue, moving in and out. He sighed with lust and felt nothing but unguarded pleasure for Bonnie. He rubbed the oily, slippery substance on her neck, kissing along her curves with reckless abandon. His mental fortresses melted as soft as the mayonnaise as his temperature spiked. Then their tongues went everywhere. Terry gasped, he groaned, he spewed the tension of past weeks as she merged with his passion.

"Oh, sweetheart, I've missed you," Terry said.

Then he made the sandwiches, and they ate on her sofa while he looked into her loving eyes. Terry fell asleep in Bonnie's arms and rested hard and long.

The next morning, he awoke to her beaming face. "I could get used to this," Terry said.

"Me too."

As Bonnie toasted bagels and made coffee, Terry confessed. "Bonnie, everybody thinks I should be going to graduate school, and I'm having second thoughts. Maybe I've spent too much time reading business theory. This summer, I've done a few things that have got me thinking I know all too little about the real world of business."

"Why? Everything you've ever done has been a success."

"Maybe I'm not what you think."

"I don't buy that for a minute, Terry Rankin."

"Look, I've got a company, and I don't need another degree to run it. Mac is ready for me, and I couldn't find a better teacher. I don't do failure well; maybe I need a sure thing."

Terry felt defeated. "I need some time to think. Maybe I'll visit with my dad's side of the family in Ohio. I haven't seen my grandmother since last Christmas."

Terry started walking out of Bonnie's apartment, redressed in the same clothes, head down. He turned as she asked him to stop.

"Baby, none of us have all the answers, but I do know this, you're the most intelligent man I've ever known. Whatever is bothering you, you'll overcome it."

Terry sighed, not knowing if she was right and walked on to the car. On the way home, he passed the Cedar Grove Park and pulled up to the curb. It brought back wonderful childhood memories of the dog he grew up with.

Terry stepped from the car and walked, without purpose, along the trails he and his yellow lab ran upon carefree throughout his childhood. He laid his head under a large elm tree and remembering, at age fifteen, losing his pal in the summer shade under the same tree. Sam died peacefully in Terry's arms as they napped.

Terry snapped rudely out of his reminiscing, jumping to his feet, shocked and dismayed.

Over by that single picnic table is where the murder of my mother all started. It's clear in Sidney Wright's notes.

The horrible irony in the place of Sam's death tormented Terry as he drove home.

Josh Rankin's mother, now in her seventies, lost her husband twelve years before. Although Terry was not close to his grandmother, he had several fond memories of summer visits as a young teenager. Terry always felt he couldn't discuss his father with her, because she always became distant and changed the subject.

He hugged his grandmother at the door and helped her back to her chair in the den. He had asked Mac to help her buy the house a couple of months ago, and Terry felt guilty he had never bothered to look at it.

He helped her fix some tea, reclined on the easy-chair and relaxed while she questioned him. They talked about school, girls, and dating. He told her about Bonnie which really seemed to pique her interest.

"That's the one you should hold on to, stable and loyal, no better combination."

Then it hit him why he rarely visited her as the conversation turned to Terry's father, pain and shame.

"When was the last time Dad visited you before the... you know?" Terry asked.

She looked disappointed with the question, her eyes diverted to the window, but she cleared her throat. "He visited us shortly before your mother died. Your father, always so upbeat and optimistic, looked sad, hurt, like the weight of the world was crushing him slowly, with no one to share it with. I'd never seen him like that. We talked on the phone a few weeks later. I'll never forget what he told me."

"Please tell me."

"He said your mother was a better person than he could ever be, and his weakness had cost her life. He cried and I cried. But I didn't know what to say, because I didn't understand. You were only an infant then." She adjusted the back of her hair, rolled up in a bun, and looked Terry in the eyes. "He told me something else."

"What?"

"He prayed God to give you the strength of your mother. He loved you, Terry, and I'm so sorry for any shame our family may have brought to you."

As a tear fell down her cheek, Terry watched her fall asleep in her chair. He pulled a blanket over her, kissed her softly, and left.

He boarded his jet, took a seat beside the computer terminal and pulled up the most recent news from Chile. The lead stories all highlighted the recent problems at Caberro. However, the new ownership, Rafael, had already donated several million dollars to rebuild the damage caused by the terrorists, set up relief funds for all the victims, and offered a ten percent pay increase to all employees immediately returning to work. Caberro, back on track, looked to make the new owner rich. As Terry read, the utter brilliance of his adversary's turn-around wrenched in his gut.

In a related story, Companion issued a press release stating, due to accounting errors, recent price reductions were not sustainable and immediate price increases would be implemented. Due to the announcement, Rafael's sales stabilized, sending its stock price through the roof. Terry covered his face with both hands, rubbing furiously up and down.

The following week became an exercise in soul searching for Terry. His emotions varied widely between the disgrace of his defeat and the need for revenge to his self-perceived stupidity for engaging Sidney Wright in the first place.

How is this benefiting my family? My parents are gone, they were always gone. This is certainly not helping me. My stomach stays in knots, Terry said to himself, running his fingers nervously through his wavy golden hair.

It troubled Terry he'd not heeded Mac's advice to leave the past alone. His recent obsession with retribution cost time and money. He'd been no help to Mac, and it left Terry with a sense of emptiness.

Why can't I be thankful and content with what I've got? This hate I have for Sidney Wright isn't hurting him, it's hurting me.

He wrestled with these thoughts constantly, making him tired, sleepless, and lonely. *I'm living in the past. Why?* He pushed his face into his pillow. "Count your blessings, Terry."

CHAPTER THIRTY-ONE

Over the Atlantic Ocean
March 2003

Sidney Wright boarded his large private jet. The flight from Bermuda to Milan, seven hours, left plenty of time to focus. Rested, mentally sharp, essential at his age, and a mission at hand fueled his resolve. Too often, recently, he questioned his own degree of toughness, but not today, more alive than ever. It bothered him his criminal career could never be recorded in history. *A pity.*

Unimaginable this small winery, Caberro, started buying up Rafael stock, my stock, a curve ball. He'd researched all the Chilean wineries and found Caberro to be a well-run company, but with no cash. Never had Sidney worked so quickly to bring together militants, historical experts, and forgery artists. The circumstances could have wrecked him, but he reacted with brilliance. *Don't underestimate the Master.*

The power of money never ceased to amaze Sidney. He bought secrecy, military power, and labor bosses like desserts in a buffet line, but it wasn't cheap. As a result, now he owned majority interest of the largest winery in Chile.

His plane roared towards the coast of Europe, and Sidney entertained himself with thoughts of taking Rafael private and really shaking up the Napa Valley boys.

The original "J" phone, used for communication only between Level III and IV operatives, hadn't rung in two and a half years. Only five people ever knew the number. Christopher Bonn, the brilliant actor and communicator, had nailed the part of Dr. Sinclair. Jonathan Biggerstaff, with his air of confidence, sealed the deal on Josh Rankin's money. Christopher and Jonathan were Sidney's most trusted. But the "J" phone call couldn't be from either. Both were dead.

Rex Wilkerson, a non-issue according to Sidney's information, became a fisherman on the Pacific Coast. Barbara Simmons, twenty years in the history books. That left only one, Bobby Depew.

Sidney candidly admitted to his own weakness. The physical protection Bobby gave him in the early years or Bobby merely being the product of Sidney's own invention, might explain his dilemma, he wasn't sure.

Sidney, somehow felt obligated to include Bobby in Project "B", a risk. Placing him at the Pinkney Hotel with Josh Rankin, *a damned fool's choice*. Sidney worked with Bobby on his lines like a school play, a rough performance but, all in all, Bobby persevered.

The only analogy Sidney could draw upon, as to this weakness for Bobby, jumped into his mind while casually reading an entertainment publication. An author of a novel, turned screenplay, got a speaking part, even though he had no meaningful acting experience. After all, he was part of the family. Looking back, Sidney felt good including Bobby.

In fact, as he recalled, the only meaningful laugh Sidney had during the intense first days of the project was the massive clump of dried grits in Bobby's ear after he brought Josh Rankin in from the Pinkney Hotel.

"Bobby, didn't you think to wash it off?"

"The damn stuff's like glue."

But he hadn't heard from nor seen Bobby in quite a while. He couldn't figure out how he managed to blow the millions he earned in Project "B." During his last phone call, Sidney learned he was back in Birmingham, demoted to assistant manager at the same apartments, and spent most days drinking himself into a pickle. *Bobby can't handle life unless I'm there to direct him.* He reluctantly wired him a thousand dollars, knowing he'd convert it to booze. *I can't live his life for him.*

When the "J" phone rang two days ago, Sidney picked up the phone. "Hello, Bobby, old friend."

"I'm not Bobby, and definitely not your friend. My name is Isaac Simmons. You might remember my wife, Barbara."

Sidney sat in silence.

"You still there?"

Sidney slowly replied, "How did you get this number?"

"After my wife's murder, the Greenville Police Department gave me Barbara's personal items not used as evidence. I looked through them and stored most of it in a closet.

"I'm now in the process of finding a smaller place. Money is tight these days, so I'm having some yard sales. Going back through her things, I stumbled into a flap spread across the bottom of her gym bag. I pulled it up and found a very interesting note with this phone number."

"What did the note say?" Sidney inquired calmly.

"I'm not ready to tell you, but understand this; you're smack in the middle of my wife's death. Frying your rich ass won't bring her back, and I need money. I'll keep my evidence quiet if you'll start wiring $15,000 a month into my account, like you did before."

Sidney silently absorbed the facts and developed a list of options as he waited for Isaac to speak again.

"I've got your phone number so someone can figure out who you are and force you to explain Barbara's note."

Sidney shifted into his disarming voice. "Settle down, Mr. Simmons. I want you to know my name, Peter Miller. I had nothing to do with your wife's death, but don't want trouble. Perhaps instead of wiring money every month, I'll give you a larger sum in exchange for the original note you say Barbara wrote, call it even."

"How much?"

"Say two million American dollars, all paid in a lump sum. You'll be able to live on the interest alone. If you agree, my money's in a European bank account. I'll require the transaction done in person. I'm sorry about your wife, but it wasn't my doing. I'll explain it to you when we meet, but in order to resolve any misunderstandings, the money paid brings the matter to an end. Agreed?"

"Fine, but I don't have money to get to Europe."

Sidney, ready with his response, raised optimism in his voice. "Not a problem, give me your street address, and I'll overnight your round trip airline ticket and hotel accommodations. Today is Monday, and you'll get it Tuesday afternoon. Be packed and ready, because the flight will leave early Wednesday morning."

"Why should I trust you to pay me? What if I end up dead like Barbara?"

"If you really thought that, you'd never have made this call, Mr. Simmons. I've got the money in Europe if you want it. If not, I've done nothing wrong, so you'll end up with nothing. Take your pick."

"Okay, I'll take the money."

"Now listen. May I call you Isaac?"

"Yes."

Sidney heard a touch of greed in Isaac's voice. "I'll have to trust you. This is a lot of money, and I don't want anybody else to be a part of this."

When the conversation ended, Sidney felt Isaac's need of money would keep him true to his word. But safety nets would be erected.

Sidney Wright, an hour out from Milan, checked his secure e-mail and received a simple message. "Hog is loose." This meant Isaac Simmons had no visitors, made no phone calls, and left his house alone. This further confirmed he boarded the plane as scheduled and would be landing in Milan by 6:00 p.m., Piedmont time. Isaac's package contained round trip tickets, shuttle vouchers, and Hotel Continental accommodation confirmation. He should be checking into Room 218 a little after seven.

Sidney strongly considered using Bobby Depew to do the job, but he felt Bobby's recent instability too risky. Sidney could have set up surveillance, timed a walk in a remote area of Montreal, and Bobby taken Isaac out with his bare hands.

But who knows about Bobby anymore? Trust who you trust... me.

But then Sidney's thoughts shifted to the cost factor. *Hell, I could have bought the hit for what this plane ride is costing me.* But sometimes he liked keeping things "in house."

The hum of the jet engines miles above the European coast took Sidney's mind back to an earlier time and place. Sidney's expertise in aeronautics began in the late fifties in Birmingham. The I.F. Electronics' scam forced him to learn a lot. But his concentration intensified leading up to the demise of Chip Lippard.

As Sidney's aircraft approached the Milan air strip, he reflected on his success in the necessary removal of an heir to the Lippard fortune. Chip Lippard owned a vintage 1941 Boeing Stearman. This classic aircraft, a two-passenger open-cockpit, cruised comfortably at 70 miles per hour. September 14, 1980, Chip headed to Asheville, North Carolina, for a dinner date with his newest girlfriend. Sidney, dressed in the Greenville Municipal Airport issued mechanic's orange overalls, approached the Stearman, and found the gas tank to be half full, plenty of fuel for the Asheville trip. He professionally tightened screws along the wing as he waited for the field of vision around the aircraft to clear. Thirty minutes before Chip's departure time, Sidney poured exactly one gallon of water into the gas filler cap located on the wing. He placed a small chip, near the tail to work in conjunction with a global positioning system, allowing Sidney to monitor the plane from the ground. The equipment, state of the art, proved difficult to procure.

Sidney, not in the cab, imagined precisely what the plane would do and how Chip would react. He played it through his mind hundreds of times before that day and since.

The take-off would be smooth, and Chip would be airborne for twenty minutes before the water entered the injection system. The plane felt as if out of gas as the engine shut down. Time seemed precious and running out. Chip frantically tried to restart the aircraft fearing crashing into the Smokey Mountains between Greenville and Asheville. He'd check the level of the gas tank while trying to maintain the optimal speed and cruising level of the plane. The gage showed plenty of gas, so he shifted to checking the dual magnetos. Everything appeared to be in order, so he attempted to re-crank the engine. Sidney visualized sweat seeping from Chip's every pore as the engine failed to respond. In a matter of seconds, the plane nose-dived among the limbs of the native black locust trees with Sidney not far behind.

He had a twenty-five minute head start from the time Chip took off from the Greenville air strip. The fuselage soon came to rest near a farming road off Highway 25, within twenty-seven miles of where Sidney predicted. With the GPS he had obtained through military sources, he pinpointed the location of the aircraft and within eighteen minutes found Chip seriously injured.

The syringe contained a sufficient dose of pure heroin to kill a large horse. As the heroin rushed through the veins of the badly broken and bleeding heir to the Lippard fortune, the pain became masked. The heroin rush did not level off and continued at a frenzied pace until Sidney watched Chip draw his last breath. He drove two hundred miles, under the speed limit, before authorities found the plane.

After reflecting on what he labeled Project Smokey Mountain High, Sidney now focused firmly on the task at hand. He checked into the Milan Regalia, one block away from the Continental. He reset his watch, five o'clock, plenty of time to rest a few minutes, shower, and do the set up. Sidney's hired investigator sat in the Continental's lobby monitoring Simmons' arrival. Sidney intended to check in with the contact at 8:00 p.m., confirming adherence to the plan.

At 8:30, Sidney entered the Continental, strolled through the Renaissance-style atrium and headed to the stairwell. After climbing to the second floor, he quickly located Room 218. He knocked, knowing no one on either side would be disturbed. He had rented all three rooms.

Isaac spoke through the door. "Who's there?"

"Peter Miller."

Isaac unlocked the door, and Sidney walked in, briefcase in hand.

"May I sit?"

"Certainly."

"Where's the note?"

"Not until we go to your bank in the morning and get a certified check."

"Settle down. I have the money here." Sidney opened the briefcase slightly exposing mounds of American cash, and then closed it. "Now show me the note?"

Sidney read it, folded it, placed it in his pocket, and turned toward Isaac. He grinned knowing Barbara's husband's stupidity to be alive and well.

"You want to know about your wife? A whore, and I paid her well. Money you've lived well from. Her problem? Not keeping the trust, not keeping her mouth shut, just like you. You want to know who killed her? The same one who'll kill you." Sidney rose and pulled the silencer capped .38 from under his coat.

At that split second, Sidney's attention diverted to the door pounded open from the hall. Six Italian agents entered the room, guns drawn. In broken English the agents yelled, disrupting Sidney's focus.

"Put the gun down and lie on the floor."

He dropped the gun and, in calm and polished Italian, said, "Gentlemen, this man is an extortionist and has kidnapped my daughter. This is why I brought this money."

The agent bellowed. "Don't touch that briefcase, get down on the floor!"

As Sidney slowly eased downward, sizing up the room, Terry Rankin entered.

"Lying there on the floor like a worm doesn't seem consistent with an international business star, Mr. Wright."

Sidney looked up from his horizontal position on the floor and asked, "Who the hell are you?"

"Oh, my name is Terry Rankin, and you'll be hearing it a lot. Stay where you are, and within an hour we'll have developed some copies of pictures and play the video of your little charade and tidy confession.

"Mr. Simmons was wired and briefed before he called you in Bermuda. He communicated by e-mail from a computer in his closet. You should have rented the rooms above and below this one. We have coverage from every angle."

Sidney shouted in uncharacteristic anger. "You bastard," He rose up and made a move toward Terry. A right hook caught Sidney's jaw, dislodging it sideways. His conditioned mind blocked out the pain as the agents pulled him away.

He saw Terry holding his broken hand with a smile on his face as if pain never felt so good.

"That was for my mother."

"And who would that be?" responded Sidney, adjusting his jaw.

"The wife of Josh Rankin."

Sidney Wright's broken face turned a pale white. Facts and statistics roared through his mind faster than he could process them, a phenomenon not known to him. It wasn't fear, depression, confusion or pain, but rather a deterioration of control. He digested the facts between throbs resonating through his jaw, wondering how he'd changed.

Memories from Detroit jumped forward in Sidney's mind. *I don't like nobody gettin' in my face. Have I developed the mind-set of a Bobby Depew? Did Isaac Simmons 'get in my face'? Is that why I'm here? How did it happen?* Sidney questioned himself.

Within an hour Sidney found himself captive in an Italian prison. He promptly hired several of Milan's outstanding attorneys, and the legal games began.

Terry led the charge for U.S. extradition of Italian prisoner Sidney Wright but ran into a road-block. The Italian authorities were not persuaded the bare confession of a murder decades ago, under the circumstances of a sting operation, should justify extradition. Italian officials agreed, however, to hold him up to sixty days for an opportunity to provide additional evidence.

Terry flexed some political muscle at home, and a U.S. Senator called in some markers in London. At the request of Scotland Yard, British authorities in Bermuda became very cooperative. A search warrant was issued for the house and grounds of Sidney Wright in Hamilton, yielded nothing, until one of six British agents patiently gravitated toward the basement. Calling the other agents down he queried why someone would put a ceiling up on only an eight-foot square in the basement. Upon a careful inspection, grooves were found which led them to a secret compartment. The observant agent, handsomely rewarded from a private source, helped mark, copy, and seal the evidence.

Terry found twenty-six additional pages since exploring the file's contents. They contained plans to acquire Caberro, and a future operation targeting a wealthy Italian citizen. Strangely enough, the Italian authorities felt this an abundance of corroboration.

Unfortunately, Terry hit another snag when he learned no Italian prisoner, if extradited, could be subject to capital punishment. A U.S. agent broke the news to Terry.

"What do you mean 'no death penalty'? Wright caused more death than you can imagine," Terry argued.

"Doesn't matter. Europe's full of countries against capital punishment, think it's inhumane."

"I think it's spineless, give him what he gave."

"Mr. Rankin, it boils down to this. Either the U.S. agrees, if Wright's convicted, not to kill him, or he stays in Italy."

"So Sidney Wright's life is spared because of some damn political climate?"

"That's about the size of it, sorry."

Sidney landed back on American soil, and Terry watched months of legal maneuvering by Sidney's lawyers. Terry took comfort in a strong, unwavering judge, fair but not hesitant to call it like he saw it. Motions to dismiss, calling the evidence perished, stale, and prejudicial, were flung at the judge like baseballs from a batting machine. The judge skillfully hammered each one back to Sidney's lawyers.

Finally, Terry sat behind the prosecutor's table as Sidney Wright stood trial for murder and interstate racketeering. At times during the trial, evidence ripped like a knife through Terry's flesh. He hated Sidney's lawyers as they argued fabrication of evidence and claimed the real killer hung himself in prison. He agonized over the possibility a jury could cut this evil man loose.

When Terry finally took the witness stand, the case had been going on for weeks. Exhausted and worried, he placed his hand on the Bible, promised the truth and promised himself to open his soul and let the jury understand his life.

Terry told his story like heart-wrenching music, as if played from a sad violin. He saw jurors weep as they learned the truth of Sidney Wright.

As the Clerk read the verdict, Terry locked eyes with Sidney Wright. Behind the cold gaze, Terry saw an almost child-like sadness. It touched Terry in a way that made him uncomfortable, and he couldn't understand why.

The satisfaction Terry felt, as Federal Marshals hauled Sidney off in chains to spend the rest of his life in prison, was tempered by a curiosity of how Sidney got this way. Terry thought one day he'd like to know.

Terry filed for an attachment of Sidney Wright's assets in Chile and the U.K. as soon as the Italians arrested him. Terry reopened the estate of his mother, and as Personal Representative, brought a wrongful death action. The murder conviction completed the evidence puzzle needed to tie Sidney Wright to Terri Rankin's death.

The estate successfully brought to civil judgment an amount consuming the entire Sidney Wright fortune, Terry's legitimate inheritance. But money couldn't replace his parents.

Sidney Wright gone, Terry woke each morning fresh, alive, and ready to wrap his arms around work and those he loved. He bought Mac a mountain retreat miles away from Rankin Enterprises, demanded his retirement, and set up an annuity with more money than Mac could ever use. He moved his grandmother into a home near his with twenty-four hour nursing care and made legal arrangements that kept Isaac Simmons and his son in a comfortable quality of life.

CHAPTER THIRTY-TWO

The story of Mac and Janelle blossoms like a beautiful flower all because of an innocent child. The employment arrangement, after Josh's arrest, became one of necessity. Terry, the nourishment growing the relationship, bound them together.

Mac carried large arsenals of emotional defenses, and soon learned Janelle burdened her own load. Mac's business experiences tempered his distrust of the many seeking to squeeze out Lippard dollars. He spent a career watching those dollars, and in the beginning, watched Janelle through those same tempered eyes.

But Mac, amazed little Terry Rankin could break through the defenses surrounding him and Janelle, looked forward to coming home, hoping Janelle hung around a bit to talk about Terry's day. Sometimes he'd listen to the drama of Janelle's walks through the mine-fields of her reluctant love life. The disasters of many of Janelle's blind dates often made Mac laugh until he felt relief of the day's stresses.

Mac's romantic achievements weren't much better. Considering the money Mac controlled, hoards of available women threw themselves at him, but he held them off at a healthy distance, *gold diggers,* he thought.

Until Terry was eight, Mac and Janelle knew their roles and meshed them splendidly. Mac decided, even though Terry was listed internationally as one of the top twenty-five wealthiest people every year, he'd be raised modestly. In the back of his mind, he knew Terry's mother, but not Charlie Lippard, would approve. Maybe he owed Terri that. Since Terry liked living in his parents' house, Mac never moved from Grady Drive until Terry left for college.

In the early days, Mac enjoyed Janelle coming over for walks and picnics on weekends. He usually took Terry's dog Sam with them to nearby Cedar Grove Park. Mac cherished the unspoken bonding with Janelle as they watched the child joyfully playing with his dog.

Terry grew. One Friday, Janelle called Mac at work.

"He says he's spending the night with a friend. He acts like he's telling and not asking. What do I tell him Mac?"

Mac agreed to let Terry spread his wings. Mac, too stubborn to let her know, missed Janelle when Terry left.

By the time Terry reached puberty, got a driver's license, and started to date, Mac hardly needed a babysitter and started to feel Janelle slipping slowly out of his life. Mac caught Terry, sixteen, in an underage drinking incident. Mac acted disappointed, but the occasion rejuvenated him when he asked Janelle to come over and help him deal with the problem.

After dealing out the appropriate punishment and restrictions, he found her in his arms, awkward and wonderful. Their changed relationship predictably grew slowly. Mac felt like a kid several times when Terry caught them walking out of the house on Grady Drive at times when Terry wasn't expected. But Mac knew Terry didn't mind. Regardless of biological considerations, they were his parents.

CHAPTER THIRTY-THREE

Spring 2004

Terry Rankin asked Bonnie Freeman to marry him as she sat on limb hanging over the Nantahala River. They set September 22, 2004, as their wedding date. A week before, Terry flew himself out of the Greenville Municipal Airport in a westerly direction.

Pacific Fish Company, prospering for more than twenty years, started with the purchase of one fishing vessel, a dock, and a small office for the cash price of $48,000. With long hours and hard work, the owner ran the Oregon fishing operation, located west of Portland on the coast. After two years, the business expanded, and he borrowed enough money to build a three bedroom, two bath brick home in the hills. By the tenth anniversary, the business had a fleet of twelve fishing boats, and life was good for Rex Wilkerson, formally known as Austin Clemmons.

But the last six months had been a nightmare. His good people had been hired away, his buyers found better fish prices elsewhere, and his business bled cash at an alarming rate. He refinanced his home, but soon missed several payments, putting him into default and foreclosure.

He closed Pacific Fish Company, and his family left him. Faced with an Order of Ejectment, meaning move out or the constable would physically remove him, brought him to the end.

The front door of Rex's house stood open while he packed. His aging face had developed wrinkles through the jagged scar across his forehead, and he felt defeated. As Terry Rankin walked in, Rex looked up.

"If you're from the bank, don't worry. I'm getting out."

"I'm not from the bank. I received an assignment of your note and mortgage many months ago. In fact, I now own this house."

Rex stopped packing and rose from his crouched position. "Why are you telling me this?"

"My father didn't have many good friends. I believe you were once his best friend. He trusted you and respected you. You betrayed him and my mother. I believe you went by the name of Austin Clemmons back in Greenville. Remember that? Are you still playing racquetball?"

Rex's ulcerated stomach turned, and he took a step forward. "Are you Josh Rankin's son?"

When Terry nodded his head, Rex went limp, fell against a packing box, and slid to the floor as emotions came rushing back to him.

"Not a day has passed since I left South Carolina when I didn't regret what I did. Nobody ever told me people would die, a mere theft operation." Rex sobbed. "Go ahead and do what you came to do. Take my sorry life, there's nothing left anyway."

Moments passed slowly, and Rex, fearing death or worse, stayed seated, not caring to watch. Finally, after nothing but silence, he looked up at Terry's unsympathetic eyes.

"So why are you here, and what are you going to do?"

"Stand up."

Rex followed the demand made with indignation. Confusion added to his hopelessness.

"Oregon Bay Realty will be handling the rental of this house. If you go there by noon tomorrow, they will lease it to you for five hundred dollars a month. Downtown there is a center called 'Lost

Sheep'. I doubt you've ever heard of it. It doesn't put money in your pocket. It's a nonprofit organization specializing in helping children who have lost both parents. I have made a sufficient endowment to this center. There's a condition that you have a job, provided you work regular hours and make a difference. It pays you twenty-five thousand dollars per year which will cover your rent and expenses."

"Why would you do that for me?"

"Your wallet's not empty by chance; I did it. What I've done to you and your business is probably illegal but doesn't hold a candle to what you did to my family. Walk away from my offer and report me to the authorities. You won't win, and this community will see my documentation of your involvement in... what did you call it... Project 'B'? I know what you've done for the past twenty-three years. You made an honest living and, for some reason, I don't think you're one of them. I'm giving you a chance to make some right out of your wrong. Do you want it?"

Rex nodded his head.

"Good. Now you might want to start unpacking."

Rex stopped him as he walked away. "You have no reason to believe anything I say, but your father really loved your mother."

CHAPTER THIRTY-FOUR

Greenville
September 22, 2004

Terry walked under the massive limbs and stood before the grave markers of his mother and father in the Live Oak Presbyterian Cemetery. Deep in his heart, he felt they had joined one another in eternity and found a peace making the past forgivable. To their sides were Lippards, many Terry knew were somehow hurt by Sidney Wright. He'd never really known any one of them but felt bonded to them all.

A tear rolled down his cheek. "Momma, forgive Daddy. Weakness can be confused as badness. Daddy's heart was good, and he loved us, Momma." Tears flooded out of both eyes.

Terry felt Mac's soft touch on the shoulder of his tuxedo.

"It's time."

Terry turned towards him and smiled at Mac in his long tails and white gloves. "Yep, guess it's about time." As the sun set behind the cemetery, he grabbed Mac's arm as they strolled together towards the brilliantly lit church.

Bonnie never looked more beautiful to Terry as she walked down the aisle before him and wouldn't have traded her for any one of the hundreds of glamorous women watching enviously. The most significant Greenville wedding in decades, and Terry couldn't take his eyes off his bride.

Hours later they waltzed into the Pyramid Suite of Hotel Grande Rio De Janeiro, overlooking a magnificent landscape.

"The bottle you requested, sir."

Terry pulled the velvet down slightly uncovering only the neck of the bluish-green vessel, a red wine Terry carefully poured. He handed her the glass and watched as the nectar of the grape penetrated the curvature of her lips and engulfed her tongue.

"Tell me what you think." Bonnie didn't answer, and her eyes rolled back as the romantic fruit sensually caressed her senses. The surprise on her face, as the wine lingered, answered his question.

"I'm speechless. Where did it come from?"

"This is the first 100 point wine ever made in Chile. It's from your vineyard."

"What?"

Terry pulled the velvet off of the bottle exposing the engraving in the middle of the Rafael label, "Bonnie."

The honeymoon, like a fairy tale, lingered for fourteen glorious days as they relaxed, loved, and celebrated. No phone calls interrupted their days exploring the streets of Brazil, and nights and mornings exploring each other.

Bonnie showed him sensitive places on her body Terry wished he'd known earlier. *I know now, and I've got a lifetime to make it up to her.*

Outside their room, which consisted of the entire fifteenth floor, he rocked in a mammoth hammock. With Bonnie in his arms, Terry whispered. "Fortune in my life means nothing compared to you, sweetheart. You're my wealth, my happiness, my lifelong dream."

A tear fell from Bonnie's eye onto Terry's face.

"Oh, Terry, I want to have your children and be everything you need."

Terry felt complete, knowing only good things were ahead. Their lips touched, their tongues entwined, and Brazilian lust prevailed.

Beautiful sunsets punctuated the end of the day, each precious like a jewel, giving way to a brilliant moon, seemingly their own. Happiness.

The end of the honeymoon brought inevitable sadness. Terry spent the trip back on their private jet by the phone, holiday over, business to attend.

Off to work the next morning by six o'clock, a light kiss his goodbye to her. His mind was now preoccupied with Rankin Enterprises.

"What's all this?" Terry asked his administrative assistant while sitting behind a mountain of paper on his desk.

"It's from the legal department... something about restructuring all corporate enterprises under one blanket."

The first week back felt like walking naked into a hornet nest. With Mac being out of the loop, Terry felt strung out in all directions.

Work days were long, and he arrived home in the evening later and later, exhausted. Bonnie seemed to tolerate it fairly well, although Terry could see a fraying around the edges of her patience. He wanted to fix it but had too much patching-up to do at work.

Months passed, and Terry unintentionally pushed Bonnie from the center of his attention, nearly removing her from his playing field, as work became his obsession. Returning from a business dinner, Bonnie commented, "I'm nothing but window dressing."

Distracted by his work thoughts, he casually replied, "The company's a big window, and you dress just fine."

The riveting glare she gave him hammered home his growing lack of sensitivity, and he rationalized work leveling off and he'd rejuvenate their relationship, a concept he quickly forgot.

On a rainy December afternoon, Terry suddenly realized his career dwarfing his attention for Bonnie. He pushed the tons of work aside and left for home. He entered the house, quiet except for a noise in the kitchen. He walked softly towards the noises. The volume gained with each step, sounding strange, like jerking emotion.

This can't be good, Terry thought as he entered the room. He found Bonnie sobbing at the kitchen table, her eyes swollen. "What's wrong sweetheart?"

Bonnie acted startled. "Oh, nothing, but a little cry, how are you doing?"

Terry sat down at the table, caught by surprise. "How often do you do this?" Bonnie waved him off. "Talk to me, Bonnie."

Bonnie turned, her piercing stare focused on Terry.

"Like when is there time?"

Tears again started rolling from her eyes, and Terry felt like a fool.

"I do this every day, helps me cope. I'm not part of your life.

"I don't know what to say. You're right. I'm over my head with work, with stress, with everybody else's problems."

"It's okay."

"It's not okay."

"That's your job, what you do, Terry."

"It sneaks up on me. None of this means what you mean to me. But when I work, everything personal gets pushed aside. It's like, if I don't fix everybody's daily dilemma, I've let them down. These people work for me. I don't love them, and they're not my family. But somehow they get better from me than my family does... than you do. I need to do better."

Terry watched nervously as Bonnie rose from her chair, walked over to him, and slipped into his lap. Her lips on his cheek comforted him, and stress seemed to melt under her softness.

But Terry could feel her frustration and felt responsible. He took time off for Christmas. They shopped, caught a couple of movies, made love, and became best friends again. He forced himself to push work to the back of his mind. *Bonnie's my life.*

On Christmas Eve, Terry held Bonnie in his arms in front of the roaring fire. She whispered something unexpected in his ear.

"Would you like to have a child?"

They'd talked about children abstractly, a distant time and place. Bonnie sounded like the future knocked on their door. He hugged her tightly. "What do you want to do?"

"A baby would be nice if it's okay with you." He held her in silence, contemplating tomorrow, and fell asleep as Christmas Day arrived.

Bonnie and Terry always enjoyed the annual Grand New Year's Eve Ball to benefit the Heart Society, a big social event in Greenville. Bonnie, already back from appointments for her hair, nails, and dress alteration, sat in front of her makeup mirror doing the final touches. Terry read over financial reports.

Looking at his watch, he yelled across the room. "What time do you want to get home tonight?"

Bonnie's voice, obviously tense, echoed back. "Who cares?"

"Is there a problem here?" he asked, folding up the work.

"Listen, Terry. It's been a week since we agreed to have a child. You haven't mentioned it since, like you don't care."

Bonnie's caustic look stopped his quickly formulated explanation.

"Remember, having a baby takes a little thing called sex. We aren't having much of that lately. I guess you don't want to know about timing or cycles, because you haven't bothered to ask. Maybe you flat changed your mind."

Bonnie sobbed heavily as Terry stood helplessly with nothing to say.

"Now I'm ruining my makeup. Look what you made me do."

Terry suppressed his desire to laugh, already in enough hot water. He took a deep breath. "I haven't changed my mind, and we do need to talk. We'll have all day tomorrow."

Terry had a blast mingling with the crowd, Bonnie at his side, a proficiency that Mac could never manage. Terry and Bonnie, over the years, developed great dance steps. As the band played the old Glenn Miller classic, "In the Mood", they stole the dance floor. Their spins, pivots, and dips were enviable.

Terry contained his laughter for the second time as he overheard a boisterous couple seemingly in awe of his dance steps.

"All that money, and the spins to go with it," he said. "Um... I wonder if he has those same moves in bed," she replied.

At midnight, two cases of sparkling wine donated by "Bonnie's Vineyard" were served to the guests. Terry pulled her closely, toasted her beauty, and kissed her. "I love you."

She looked speechless, intoxicated by the evening. Terry smiled. "Maybe this time next year we will be checking in on the babysitter." They both laughed, and a great evening got greater.

Terry loved the first few nights in January in his wife's arms. But then the sex became work, with failed results. An M.D. prescribed fertility drugs and drew blueprints for love-making like a construction project. The whole process wore on Terry's nerves, and he felt like the doctor was in bed with them. The results were as barren as their patience.

Terry's required appearances were cutting into his work. He silently harbored ill-will. Bonnie seemed more frustrated than he. The tension began to stretch the boundaries of their tolerance. Sex seemed angry, and arguments became frequent.

"If you're that unhappy, why don't you find someone who'll make you happy?" Bonnie said.

"You're so prickly about everything. It's like trying to live with a roll of barb-wire. I can't breathe around you."

"Well, there's the door. Go find some air."

The next New Year's Eve came with no child. Jousting became an assignment of fault, which Terry sensed was becoming an enemy to their relationship. When the anger subsided, they went back to the drudgery of mandatory sexual intercourse. Spontaneity became a forgotten art, and monthly disappointment the expected. The failure distanced him from Bonnie, but the distance gave him space to reflect. He took faith in the strength of their love for each other and prayed for hope.

Terry, working at a rapid pace at the office flipped through his calendar and discovered it was Valentine's Day. He thought, *I've got to keep things in perspective.* He called Bonnie. "Hey, Valentine. How about the two of us leaving town? Maybe we could drive out into the country and get away."

"Okay, sounds like fun."

The day became relaxed, and he rejuvenated in her soft humor as she laughed at his navigational skills.

"Where the heck are we going?"

He didn't have a clue. He'd been paying attention to Bonnie, not the road.

"We're going wherever Highway 9 goes," he said as the road marker flashed by the car.

By sunset, they passed an old but dignified looking hotel, the Lake Lure Inn. "This place sounds familiar," Terry said, but couldn't remember why. Seeing no bell service, Terry carried their overnight bags through white stucco arches into the large wooden doors leading to the reception desk.

The clerk handed him a large, rustic key, and they climbed the steps to find what the owner called the *Valentine Suite*. The room overlooked the lake and Bonnie found it charming.

Almond-glazed trout, caught in a local stream, and wine were served in their room. The bitter winds of a lingering winter, stealing entry through the old drafty windows, made the quaint fireplace in their room cozy and romantic. The distance from Greenville, coupled with the warmth of the wine, gave him a mellowed feeling.

For the first time in months, blood ran to the core of his erotic being. Bonnie's heat flowed rampantly, covering Terry's throbbing with a whirlpool of ecstasy.

The next morning, still embraced, rushing hormonal cravings took over again. As his heartbeat leveled out, he said, "Ooooh!" It made him feel special, realizing Bonnie had not recovered her breath.

The surprise came on the Ides of March, as Terry got the news from Bonnie.

"You'll be the best father."

Thrilled and humbled, he kissed Bonnie and bowed his head.

On November 3, 2006, Terry took no chances as Bonnie labored in Greenville Regional Hospital, among an army of medical people. At four o'clock p.m., Terry heard a nurse announce

Bonnie was at four centimeters. Terry held her hand, spoke softly, and guided her through breathing.

His heart soaked up the miracle of new life as a six-pound, two-ounce boy entered Terry's world. He cherished the moment and felt inadequate for the joy lifting him to a place beyond happiness.

Terry wept as he looked down on the face of his beautiful, beautiful wife.

"Oh, Terry, we got a gift."

"We got a gift, and you're still my gift."

Terry found Mac waiting patiently in the hall, but noticed Janelle looked quite impatient. He considered them as grandparents, and he knew they had waited longer than Bonnie's folks and were every bit as excited.

"Well, do you have any news?"

Terry blurted out the specifics like the proudest of all fathers. "He's not big, and he doesn't have much hair, golden, maybe wavy, definitely wet."

"So, did you give the child a name?"

Terry blushed. "We'll call him Josh," he said with pleasure. "It's actually Charles Joshua Rankin. Is that okay with you, Mac?"

"You bet, but I wish they were both here to share it."

Terry invited Bonnie's family in and asked Mac to bring the child's great-grandmother up in a wheelchair. Terry stood in the corner, admiring his new son and knowing he would always be loved. This child enriched and nourished his deepest feelings for Bonnie.

Terry purposely sought to avoid excesses in their lifestyle, partly to set an example for Josh as he grew, partly from a strong desire to get away from the meaningless glitz afforded to those of privilege, a lesson Mac taught him.

Terry grew to understand being a good husband a necessary part of being a good father. He looked at his son as a seed he'd planted. He intended to nourish him, care for him, love him, and hope his efforts would bear fruit.

He often found himself in awe of the tremendous emotional sensation that came over him when in his child's presence. He had always been consistently analytical. He mentally tried to quantify Josh's impact on the quality of his life. Nothing he had learned at Wharton applied. Raising Josh, an investment of time, somehow taught Terry the investment itself was its own dividend. A void in Terry's life was that he had never known his parents' love. Time molded Terry into a caring man, and fatherhood partially filled the void of never knowing his own parents' love.

Terry pondered these things deep in his soul. He talked to Bonnie a lot about life, time, and priorities. Hand in hand, they pushed Josh around the lake at Cedar Grove Park. As a warm summer breeze blew over the stroller and into their faces, they resolved to dedicate their lives to their son and to each other.

"I could never ask for anything more in my life," Bonnie whispered to Terry as he gently squeezed her hand.

Terry fought his most loyal advisors on the issue of security. "My son doesn't need a bodyguard; he needs a father."

Before his first birthday, Josh scaled the quartz rock of a high peak in the Appalachian Mountains, west of Greenville. He negotiated Shining Rock in his father's backpack, a bit dangerous, but a day richer than money. Terry posed, and Bonnie took the picture.

The enlarged photograph sat on the mantle above the grand fireplace of the newly-constructed Rankin mansion, located on the western edge of Greenville County. Terry figured, long after Bonnie and he left this world, the photograph would be a treasure to Josh.

In proper Presbyterian fashion, a tradition inherited from the Lippard side of the family, Terry carried the newest member of the Rankin family, clothed in a two hundred-year-old christening gown, carefully down the natural finished oak stairway of their home and left for the church.

Bonnie amused Terry as she discussed the event with the Reverend the previous week.

"Is this Sunday still convenient to do the christening?"

"My dear, the term is baptism. You christen a ship, not a child", the Reverend explained.

Terry, filled with exuberance, drove his family to church. For a change he basked, not in his own success, but rather a milestone for his child.

"Bonnie, today is a celebration of many to come, his first step, first word, first everything, a lot to teach him."

"You'll teach him how to care about others. You've got a big heart, Terry Rankin. Open it up, you know how, and let Josh see the love, all our son needs."

The packed pews at Live Oak Presbyterian was a tribute to the family being honored. The unplanned spontaneous tears, choked back by Terry, made him blush and added to the enrichment of all who watched. The pre-baptismal sermon by the aging minister caught Terry by surprise.

"A few of you here today remember this child's great-grandfather. Most of you don't. A half-century ago, our church had problems... money problems, quite frankly, or so we thought.

"Charlie Lippard asked, in the midst of our difficulties, to address our church leadership. We all thought he'd be our salvation and bail us out of our financial woes. He didn't. Rather he established a desperately needed church on the other side of town, becoming a mission of this church. It made us, as leaders, look at the people and areas of this community we previously ignored, touching our hearts.

"As a church we decided we weren't so bad off. It became a rallying point. Our financial problems were cured, because our members always had the resources. Charlie Lippard merely showed us the importance of our mission."

Terry held Josh as the Reverend dipped his hand into the water.

"I'm honored to baptize his great-grandson in the name of the Father, and of the Son, and of the Holy Ghost."

Most of the congregation gathered outside the front of the church, a tradition. The weather pleasant, skies blue, Terry watched the movement through the stained-glass window of the church's narthex. The ceremony was nearly over, and they needed to greet their loyal friends gathered outside of the church but planned to spend Sunday afternoon alone with each other. Centering his attention on Josh felt awfully important to Terry.

"Is your momma ready?" Terry mumbled to Josh while nibbling on his ear.

"Yes, yes, let's get this over with," Bonnie said.

As they exited the church, a thousand pair of eyes turned towards them. With Josh in his arms, Terry laughed, "My goodness, is this Greenville?" They walked gracefully down the forty-three steps leading to a simple van. Terry wanted a common touch. He had no say in the gown draped over his son, making him look like a girl.

Hundreds negotiated their positions to shake the hand of South Carolina's wealthiest businessman. Terry eased Josh over into Bonnie's arms, smiled and began shaking hands as fast as they came, hoping soon to get home.

The cross hairs had followed the baby's head since the family exited the church. The shooter selected a single shot from his .223 caliber rifle, blasting the bullet at a speed of 2,900 feet per second, ripping through its victim before one could hear the sound of the rifle. Although the polished projectile measures only a fraction, upon impact the tiny metallic instrument of destruction tumbles and separates. The high speed fragments eat through flesh as if they each had a life of their own.

The baptism of the child was an irrelevant fact in the shooter's mind. The steadfast hands gripping the weapon and a cool focus on the target were all that mattered. He watched through the magnified lens of the scope as the father nodded his head in agreement to a well-wisher. Bonnie's warm personality beamed over the crowd.

The calm and collected right index finger pulled gently on the trigger, sending the revolving highly-developed bullet precisely toward its victim. He'd polished it himself. The roar of the congratulations muffled the crack of the firing weapon.

As the bullet entered the cranial cavity of the precious and newest member of the Christian faith, skull shattered. The bullet tumbled, fractured, and exited the rear of the child's head. Brain matter followed and splattered onto his mother's face. Particles of the bullet continued their course into Bonnie's neck. The killer, pleased with his shot placement, had no time to dwell on it.

Love is to lay down your life, give up a body part, swap places in order to spare your child. A devoted parent can appreciate an unquestioned and unreserved willingness to make ultimate sacrifices when the life of a child is at stake, an opportunity the man behind the scope stole from Terry Rankin, and the shooter knew it. He'd stripped Terry of any forewarning to move his only child from the path of the bullet, jerked away his chance to take the bullet himself. These were details the assassin pondered once distanced from the hit. But he had to keep these thoughts way back in his head while working. It complicated things.

The split second between euphoric life and murderous death passed mercilessly by Terry. The emotional pain from the sudden slaughter of his child felt endless. It flowed from within, and there were no boundaries. The shock rolled in waves of agony, grief, heartache, and fear. A numbness, a blur, a hole with no bottom stirred within him, a wretched hell for which he had no preparation.

Terry eased his arms under his son and cupped Bonnie's head into his hand. The saturated christening gown felt like a blanket of blood as it flowed over him. With each beat of Bonnie's heart, blood spurted from her body where a bullet fragment entered.

He sensed the shock and fear of friends many fleeing the scene as if expecting more bullets. Others stood by, a look of horror in their eyes.

Terry sat on the bottom step with what remained of his family, a blank stare on his white face. His eyes jerked back and forth without tears or cries for help, as the remaining crowd appeared spellbound. He spotted Mac and Janelle looking frozen and useless, and felt outside of himself.

Sirens rose on the horizon, as Terry watched Mac cautiously approach him.

"We need to get some medical help. Let me take Josh, and you hold on to Bonnie."

He let go of his son into Mac's grasp and looked down at his wife, gasping for air. "I don't know how this could have happened, baby. Please don't leave me." He quivered when Bonnie couldn't respond.

He released Bonnie to a couple of EMTs when they arrived and watched them haul her to an ambulance. He continued in a motionless position on the bottom step. He ignored the minister's attempt to offer comfort, and the minister began weeping. Terry felt no concept of time or place. He hesitated to move or act, his mind not functioning. Numbness invaded his entire being.

Although people moved around at a frenzied pace, he felt alone. His eyes, fixed on the pool of blood around his feet, sensed a dark cloud moving across the sky, casting its shadow over the steps. He could hear Mac barking orders to the ambulance people and explaining to the police when they could talk to Terry.

"He'll talk when he's cleaned up. He doesn't need an ambulance, I'll get him home."

Finally, Terry motioned for Mac to come over. "I'm going to the hospital."

"You're covered with blood. Let's change clothes. We'll monitor the hospital from the car and get you over there in a few minutes."

"I don't care about the blood, Bonnie and Josh might need me."

"Listen Terry, they'll be in surgery for hours. Let's try and get a handle on things."

"No. We go to the hospital first."

Terry grabbed Mac and Janelle's bended arms, eased up from the step, and steadied his feet on the cobblestones, without direction.

Mac eased him forward. A sensation of this father figure, guiding him as a child, blurred the years in Terry's mind. He rode in silence in Mac's car.

Terry, about to explode, spent an hour moving from the E.R., to operating waiting rooms, to administration offices, not finding answers. Mac strolled several steps behind him and finally spoke, softly.

"Let's go home for a few minutes. You can wash off and we'll make some calls, get some direction."

"Ok, but I'm coming right back."

Terry, his new house quiet, nearly vacated by his staff, stood in the foyer trying to clear his mind. He looked down at his legs and arms, covered with blood, dried to a crust. He held Janelle's arm as small, uneven footsteps took him to the bottom of the staircase.

"Do you feel like cleaning up a little?" Janelle asked.

Terry said nothing, but he grabbed the handrail and slowly climbed the steps. About midway up the staircase, he collapsed into a sobbing heap of a wrecked man.

"What have I done to deserve this, God? Why have you taken everything?" He screamed through the tears remoisterizing the blood splattered upon his face.

He watched Mac slowly and timidly climb a few steps and sit below him.

"We never get answers to those questions. Right now, I'm at a loss as to what to say, but know Janelle and I love you very much. We must pull together for Bonnie; it looks like she may make it. She'll need you more than ever."

Terry reached down the steps and put his hand on Mac's shoulder. "I'm going to get cleaned up."

The shower reminded him of just hours ago. The baby wash he'd used that morning while bathing Josh still had its lid off. The hot water from the shower head mixed evenly with his warm tears of anguish. Small pieces of his family's blood circled in the drain and disappeared. As he reached into the linen closet, he stopped and turned to the still slightly damp towel he'd dried Josh with earlier. He held the towel to his face and smelled his son's sweet scent.

He dressed slowly and without purpose, seeing no light at the end of a monstrous and evil tunnel. Fear and agony struck deep in the pit of his stomach.

He entered the kitchen and found Janelle, Mac, and a police detective sitting at the table. He waved off the plate of food Janelle offered. As the detective rose to introduce himself and start collecting information, Terry put up his hand cutting off the officer.

"Right now I need to see my wife. Mac, will you phone one of our drivers and ask him to pick me up out front?"

Terry listened as Mac smoothed the detective's ruffled feathers and Janelle called one of the limo drivers. He rode with Mac back to the hospital where, months before, Josh had entered the world. When they arrived, Bonnie was still in surgery. They sat together in the waiting room in silence. After thirty minutes, Terry saw an aggressive hospital representative rapidly approaching.

"Sir, I need to review the details about the death certificate of Josh Rankin."

Terry turned his head away as Mac rose from his seat.

"Young lady, I can assure you this is not a good time. If you have any questions, you take it up with Fred Hardwood, president of this hospital. His office, in case you don't know, is in the next building which you might notice is called "Rankin Hall." You tell Mr. Hardwood I'll contact him when we're ready to handle the details and not to send anybody else this way."

The hospital representative looked shaken as she left. Terry laughed. "Calm down Mac, I could've handled that." Mac grinned back; they locked eyes for a moment and returned to their silence, grief, and thoughts.

By midnight, he met with the surgeons.

"The bullet fortunately missed her spine. There is a lot of tissue damage and several blood vessels had to be repaired. She lost a lot of blood, but we had a good supply of her type. Everything went as well as could be expected.

"There is one fragment from the bullet which diverted toward Bonnie's spine. It lodged itself in an area which causes too much of a risk to remove it. In my opinion, the fragment poses no current danger, and it should not impede the healing process. Hopefully, she will live a long life, Mr. Rankin. She's a strong patient, and Lady Luck smiled down on her."

Terry breathed a sigh of relief. Bonnie meant too much to him, and the night had been unbearable with the thought of losing her.

"She's in recovery now. By midmorning, you should be able to see her. She'll be alert but will have problems speaking because of the wounds."

Terry thanked the doctors and, as he turned, spotted a man in a white lab coat, stepping meekly towards him. As he spoke his voice sounded nervous, his sentences choppy.

"My name is Dr. Elroy. We tried everything to save your son... the damage, so severe... never really any chance. I met him at the back of the ambulance when he arrived. He had no pulse, no blood pressure, and no breathing signs... I took him into surgery anyway, knowing no better than a one-in-a-million. I thought you'd want me to try. The entire staff worked very hard but, in the end, nothing helped."

He took the doctor by the arm. "I know you did everything and more. You look very tired, Doctor. Please understand your efforts are appreciated more than you know."

Sleeplessly, Terry stretched out on a sofa outside Recovery the entire night. He passed up a private room set up for him. At 5:45 a.m., he followed them as they transferred Bonnie to a private suite. Terry waited patiently at her side. Nervousness layered itself over his grief, knowing he'd have to tell her Josh died.

About nine o'clock Bonnie startled Terry as she began moaning in pain, and a nurse increased the morphine drip set up for management of the inevitable. He watched Bonnie's eyes open and shut several times over the next twenty minutes. Finally, her eyes stayed open in line with Terry's.

As she attempted to speak, the pain seemed overwhelming. "Shhh. Don't try to talk," Terry whispered. "I think you're going to be okay. I've been praying a lot, and I think God means for you to outlive me by about thirty years." He rubbed her hand gently. He couldn't think of what to say next. His weak smile faded as tears welled in his eyes. Her eyes pleaded hope for Josh. Terry simply shook his head and saw shock come over her face, and her body started to quiver.

"No!"

Terry tried to comfort her as nurses and doctors rushed to her side. He felt ill when she began to shake violently, and the staff injected her with medication causing immediate sleep.

"This is going to take some time," a nurse said.

He sat by Bonnie's side for hours. Exhaustion finally kicked in, and his head rested by her arm. He awoke to a soft rubbing of fingers through his hair. Bonnie was awake and seemed peaceful.

"I wish I could understand and help you understand our tragedy. All I can think of right now is you, and how much I love you, and how happy I am to still have you in my life. We have the rest of our lives to try to figure this out. Right now we need for you to get better. I'm here and will stay here as long as it takes until you can come home."

In Bonnie's tear-filled eyes, Terry saw a broken spirit, and he struggled for an answer to spare her.

CHAPTER THIRTY-FIVE

Greenville
November 2007

"Sidney Wright," Terry said emphatically.

"Yeah, you've told us, repeatedly, Mr. Rankin."

Terry squirmed in his leather wing-back chair in front of Detective Al Olson, not accustomed to people disputing his evaluations. Getting used to the barking of questions of the Greenville P.D.'s investigator made him uncomfortable.

"We know Sidney Wright sat in a federal prison in New Jersey when this happened, still is. I questioned him two days ago. He's not our shooter. Besides, from the best I can tell, the guy is broke. If he's broke, he's got no clout on the outside. Please don't take this the wrong way, Mr. Rankin, but rumor has it, you cleaned this guy out of every penny he ever had after the conviction."

Terry, unconvinced, heard the detective sigh.

"Listen, Mr. Rankin. You own and run a major corporation. Everybody in your position has enemies, it goes with the turf. I need you to open your mind, to think whose ass you kicked lately in the business world, what 'crazy' has been barking up your tree, who thinks you're the burr under his saddle. I can't get a decent lead without you giving me some direction on this."

Terry waited silently until Detective Olson finished. "I could buy into your thought process if I'd been the hit. I may be a tough businessman, but I follow a personal code of ethics. I can't think of anyone I haven't beaten squarely in a business deal. There's no one my path has ever crossed I believe would take the life of my son over an earned or lost buck."

Al seemed to ponder this and leaned in Terry's direction, eyes stern, focused.

"You know, Mr. Rankin, motives come in many different flavors. I hate to ask you this, but have you licked the candy off the tootsie pop of some lady, not ready to call it quits when you were? Or maybe some mad as hell husband found out you and his wife had a little on-the-side, you-do-me and I'll-do-you arrangement? Sir, this is murder, and if there's some secret looming out there, put it on the table, get to the truth."

Terry sadly chuckled. "Detective, before I got married there were many women in my life, all single. I treated them all with decency. Some wanted more commitment than I was willing to offer, but they accepted the relationship's end. I can't think of a single person who has shown any animosity. When Bonnie and I married, my oats were sown, and I haven't wanted another woman, still don't. There's no one else, Detective."

"I don't underestimate your opinion, Mr. Rankin. This is a difficult time for you, and it's police business to me. What may be clear in your mind is not clear in mine. For many reasons, I'll need to interview your staff. People like your secretary, assistants, and managers may know of some person you never knew about who had a score to settle, okay?"

Terry nodded. "Of course. I'll see that you get full cooperation."

"In this crazy-ass world, we see all kinds. Some head-case might have read an article in a business magazine and decided to fulfill his bizarre craving by killing your child. You can't list suspects based on common sense principles you and I carry around in our heads. There are nuts out there and some beyond nuts."

"I understand, please feel free to interview my staff. Look at my business deals. Check out independently if I have had extra-marital flings, check the nut box, and then the more-than-nuts box.

When you get finished, we'll get together, and perhaps you can do a proper focus on Sidney Wright."

"Fair enough, I'll be in touch."

As the detective headed toward the side door of the Rankin's mansion, with a small touch of sarcasm, Terry added, "Yes, you will."

Albert Olson, under the gun, felt extra pressure from the Department to solve the murder, a lot at stake. The Mayor and his Police Chief wanted decisive results, showing Greenville as a top notch, state-of-the-art city taking crime seriously. On the other hand, if Al didn't get the job done, Greenville would look like a red-neck southern town. At the moment, he couldn't care less about Terry Rankin and his billions worth of clout. He did care about his reputation. And a dead child.

Al grew up outside of Austin, Texas. He played baseball, skillfully batting fast balls out of the park. He was an "A" student, happy, and well-liked in his neighborhood. But at age fourteen, his family was forced to move to Greenville when his father lost his job.

Without a lot of money, he grew up in the public school system and attended a local community college. He never had a teacher who didn't comment he needed to be in a more challenging academic environment. Money being tight, he simply excelled without special opportunities.

He got involved in police work during a summer intern program at Greenville Community College and spent the summer with beat cops. By summer's end, he knew the beat, the players, the action, and could think circles around his mentors. He found the work exhilarating and decided to stick with it.

Officer Olson worked his way through the basics, graduated number one at the State Police Academy, and showed the same aptitude at Greenville P.D. His shining moment came when, on a hunch, he silently worked the backside of a so-called murder-suicide case. The evidence, from the standpoint of every detective whose voice counted, pointed to only one conclusion. Fingerprints, the position of the bodies and other forensic evidence lent themselves to one meaningful theory; he shot her and then himself.

He had an unsettled feeling about the case. His investigation showed the owner of a small, white-water rafting operation had fallen head over heels for a young blond coed who worked the river for this owner as a guide. By autumn, the owner convinced the guide to live with him in a secluded cabin just inside Greenville County, less than twenty minutes from the Chattooga River. The coed, to the displeasure of her parents, didn't return to school.

In late October, the owner and his new roommate were found dead in the cabin, along side the murder weapon, a shotgun. It wasn't the stuff of a good romance novel, but it seemed consistent for an eccentric, older man who probably found out his new lover planned to leave him, case closed. But something in the file didn't make sense to Al. Being a rookie in the detectives' division, his senior colleagues turned a deaf ear.

A l, not a local, found it difficult to ease into working the banks of the river. He quickly learned river people liked simple questions and didn't like their answers questioned.

For several weeks, Al picked up bits and pieces of an old and intense dispute. It existed between the deceased rafting company owner and an owner of a fleet of dilapidated vans used to shuttle people and rafts between the entry point in the river and the take out point. Locals called the owner of the vans Shuttle Man. Al spent the following summer, after the so-called murder-suicide, rafting the river as a tourist, and learned Shuttle Man had stepped into the deceased rafting company owner's shoes and took fees from one end of the river to the other and back, a motive.

The deceased owner was generally considered as a peaceful man. Nobody along the river banks had known him ever to hunt or talk of firearms. On the other hand, Al chatted with several folks who hunted with Shuttle Man and described his shotgun, a match.

Al approached a number of detectives at Greenville P.D. who he thought would support a solid theory. He found no allies at the department.

"You don't open an old case already solved. We've got newer and bigger fish to fry."

Al set up residence on the river bank. He worked the case on his own time and in his own way.

The only watering hole in the area, located off the banks of the river and operated by an old broad named June, went by June's Rapids. Shuttle Man patronized the bar regularly and that summer Al did too.

Al, who'd often laughed at Shuttle Man's jokes, pulled up a chair one night. By that time, Al had learned the lingo and knew how to talk rapids.

"Hell, looks to me like the guys driving all these friggin' tourists, puttin' 'em in and takin' 'em out, are the real ones doin' any work. These lazy-ass rafting companies are gettin' rich off the drivers."

"You damn right they is," claimed Shuttle Man as Al watched him take another long drag off his draft beer. "I've been tellin' you this, ya jest do like I did, and git yah own raftin' company, and do ya own drivin'. Do that, and ya don't need to worry if ya gonna have no beer money come night."

Al replied, "How much ya gotta pay somebody for a raftin' company?"

"When the owner ups and kill himself, it don't cost nothin'. Hell, move in."

Al bought another round of beers, and the conversation turned to hunting. Al picked up an imaginary shot gun, pretending to shoot it in the air and said, "You knowin' anybody havin' land with some whitetail waitin' to get picked off?"

Al continued to shoot as Shuttle Man took another chug and belched loudly.

"Listen, ya wanta do some huntin', stick with me. I'll finds ya some split tail."

Al took him up on it. The more time he spent with Shuttle Man, the tighter they got. By September, Shuttle Man acted as if Al were his little brother.

In mid-October, they were poaching on land a couple of miles off the river. They bagged a bunch of the local deer. Al wielded a pretty good skinning knife for a Texas boy. He laid open a buck and two doe and packaged enough venison for the next year. Shuttle Man seemed impressed. While Al had done all the work skinning the deer, he saw Shuttle Man was getting pretty liquored up. As the evening wore on, they settled into their campsite and put their feet up by a blazing fire. Al asked Shuttle Man about his favorite shotgun.

"My best shotgun done got gone. She wuz a Remington 1100. She had the best feel of any shotgun 'fore or since then."

"Where the hell is she?" Al questioned as Shuttle Man laughed loudly.

"Reckon she's a sittin' in some evidence room somewheres."

"What-da hell you goin' on 'bout," Al said with a fake slurred speech.

"Member the sum-bitch who killed that purty blonde over a year ago?" he replied.

Al broke air and laughed. "Oh yeah, the guy who takin' ya to the cleaners on them rafting trips. You doin' all the work, and he keepin' all the money."

"You're gotdam right, sum-bitch wouldn't go fifty/fifty on the money. But I figure I fin'lly took care of his ass."

"Sounds to me like you entitled. When a man screws 'nother man of his hard earned cash, he gits what he gits," said Al with indignation.

Then Al sat up smiling. "Alright, so how did ya fix his ass?"

Al watched Shuttle Man stick his head high in the air and look around as if somebody might be listening.

"Listen here, you gotta keep ya damn mouth shut."

"We tight, man. You shit's safe with me," Al assured him.

Shuttle Man then spilled all the beans right into Al's lap. By the time Shuttle Man had passed out by the fire, Al had names of everybody on the river knowing his secret. He learned the location where Shuttle Man took his competitor out with his Remington 1100. He heard details on how Shuttle Man had broken into the cabin, blew the chest out of the coed, and dragged the owner's body from the spot in the woods where he'd made the owner swallow buckshot. Shuttle Man wiped all the fingerprints clean and put the shotgun into the hands of the older man.

Shuttle Man's mouth kept moving even while falling asleep. "Figure my only regret wuz not gettin' that 1100 back... it wuz a fine..."

Al and a couple of curious detectives found fragments of the owner's remains under the new fall leaves in the woods where Shuttle Man murdered him. The scratches, notches, and discolorations described by Shuttle Man matched to a "T" with the Remington 1100 being held as evidence in Greenville.

Once the river people knew Shuttle Man's goose was cooked, they fessed up. They didn't want to go down on what Al threatened as accessories after the fact.

Al shook his head in disbelief when he heard Shuttle Man hired a notoriously ineffective lawyer with an office beside June's Rapids. Al figured the cheap retaining fee made Shuttle Man's decision easy. Al, during his patronage at June's, remembered the lawyer frequently coming in, getting drunk, and bragging about "whoo-doin" insurance companies in car wreck cases.

The case went to trial, and the best Shuttle Man's lawyer could come up with was nobody should believe Al because he killed doe during bucks only season and poached on another man's land. Al sat in silence as he watched Shuttle Man catch a life sentence and hauled out of the courthouse.

Al had some explaining to do in the department, after working outside the system and communicating with no one. Al considered hanging his supervisors out to dry for not listening to him, but decided to be graceful.

"You know, I probably should have done a better job of going through channels, but you guys, at the time, were under a lot of pressure to solve bigger cases. I got lucky."

CHAPTER THIRTY-SIX

New Jersey
Federal Prison
2007

Sidney Wright, drained of every penny to his name by Terry Rankin, leaned against the cold, steel bars restraining his body, but not his mind. At least, that's what Sidney knew everybody thought. A German bank account containing eighteen million dollars sat an ocean away from Sidney's prison cell.

Decades back, Reinhardt Hallman, the owner of a small automobile parts manufacturing company in Germany, became part of Sidney's safety net. The company had a thriving business in the early 1970s. Its primary product, a wiper blade refill, standard fit for millions of European vehicles, represented eighty-seven percent of the company's business.

In the mid-1970s, a competitor set up a factory shop in Poland. Its owner, a ruthless man named Russell Vonet, using cheaper labor and stolen materials, nearly squeezed Reinhardt's company out of the market. Reinhardt stood virtually broke and ready to quit, until he met Sidney Wright.

Sidney spent years watching Vonet and launched elaborate schemes against Vonet's, business interests all over the world. Sidney smelled blood, and knew Vonet would not have money or credit to continue any of his business interests. Vonet's downfall would cause a gushing running river of profit into Sidney's hands.

Part of Vonet's demise, the inevitable closing of his plant in Poland, gave Sidney an opportunity. Sidney met with Reinhardt Hallman, offered him help, promising Reinhardt an end to Vonet's ruthless competition. "Trust me; your old customers will come back.

"Why save me? What's in it for you?"

Sidney responded, "You don't need to know all the details, but you have my word your company will be prospering within four months. I'm not asking for anything from you. All I want is your trust; see if I deliver on my word. Perhaps I may need a favor one day. I tend to think you're a person of honor."

Reinhardt Hallman's company went from the brink of bankruptcy back to the glory days enjoyed in the early '70s. Vonet, out of business and out of his life, Reinhardt recognized his indebtedness. Sidney had done nothing to personally help Reinhardt except to announce the inevitable and take credit.

The return of the good deed came several years later, when the proceeds of Project "B" blossomed. Sidney thought it prudent to have funds set up in an account untraceable to him, a small safety net he figured he'd never use. *Diversification. I can afford it.*

After Sidney's conviction, he found little access to anyone on the outside, like he had a disease nobody wanted. He fought desperation of prison life, and patiently developed his contacts within, slowly and carefully. Prisoners were quarantined to roam only in their immediate cell block, and "lifers" filled Sidney's block.

Sidney found an exception. Any prisoner wanting an opportunity for bible study could access both reading material and study groups. Sidney understood the outside political system has a "law and order, or lock them up and throw away the key" mentality. But the concept of redemption, in Sidney's mind, stood as a human weakness, a rationalization. Man's judgment over man is necessary but the Judeo-Christian faith, which dominates the American political system, demands of itself not to interfere with the ultimate judgment between a prisoner and his God. Thus is the basis of liberal rules for a prisoner's faith development.

Therein, Sidney Wright found the small opening he needed for interaction. He dismissed the grace of God. God abandoned him by age six. Sidney's salvation happened only by the grace of his own doing. God never lifted a hand when men molested him with the acquiescence of his own mother, never lifted a hand when Bert Keller beat him mercilessly.

He thought of Sister Mary, telling him to cry out to God, and as often as he cried, as often as he prayed, his pleas stood unanswered. Sidney's faith was in himself. He took care of everything God failed to deal with.

"God exists just as Sister Mary existed, she was merely wrong about Him."

Circumstances dictated a change, and he sprung into action announcing publicly his new-found religion and decision to repent. Sidney, so well read in most subject matters, retained more religious theory than the chaplains or hundreds of inmates participating in the program. Sidney became a model prisoner, likeable, obedient, never violating prison rules. He developed a degree of trust with the local prison guards who stayed preoccupied with fighting, deviant sexual practices, and other multitudes of disobedience prisoners contrived. Sidney, a refreshing calm in the sea of chaotic behavior, sensed opportunity.

Sidney respected by of most prison authorities, also impressed the various chaplains who conducted the bible studies. Sidney laughed to himself watching the emotional aspect of worship. Speaking in tongues and other rituals worked inmates into a frenzy, reaching upwards, expecting God to pull them into an eternal life of leisure.

Sidney recited biblical facts from memory. Maps of holy lands focused in his mind before the chaplains could draw them on a chalk board. He used discretion assisting the chaplains and fellow inmates, never being rude, but as seen more often the teacher than the student.

As time progressed, Sidney convinced the chaplains to divide the more than one hundred inmates into smaller groups to increase the "learning's of Christ." Sidney worked tirelessly, organizing the groups based on what he marketed as "level of study." Slowly, Sidney began categorizing the multitudes of inmates for his own purposes. With chaplain approval, he kept records in his cell.

He set an objective, having meaningful access to inmates with outside connections. Many had appeals pending, with access to their lawyers. Others enjoyed visiting privileges, according to the security level of their cell blocks. Inmates came from families of varying degrees of economic standing, social connections, and moral integrity.

Sidney's expensive trial attorneys failed in defending lawsuits focused on depriving him of his assets. He made numerous transfers, trying to hide them. None of his efforts worked, because Terry Rankin's legal team relentlessly tracked down every transfer and found every asset. Other than the German account, Sidney didn't have a dime, leaving him with one lawyer who feared he'd soon be working pro-bono. Sidney watched his attorney's optimism over the appeal evaporate as soon as the money ran out. Sidney distrusted the lawyer and decided not to chance discussing the eighteen million.

Sidney easily handled the hardness of prison, but he couldn't sleep over how he got there. His victories had richly layered themselves around him like a coat of invincibility.

Then came Terry Rankin. The name tormented Sidney during waking hours. He dreamed of Terry Rankin most nights. A twenty-three-year-old kid had taken down perhaps the most brilliant career in modern times. Rankin had cost him billions and beaten him at his own game. He worked the facts through his head at least ten times a day. Pieces of the puzzle didn't fit.

Isaac Simmons could've never touched me. Even if I needed to deal with Isaac Simmons, I had a dozen contacts who could have taken him out. I should have hung up the phone and watched my back. Somehow that little bastard Rankin knew I'd do it myself. But how? I got rushed into thinking the note had to be dealt with immediately, like I didn't have time to hire it out properly. What note? Rankin made it up, wrote it out himself. These thoughts played back in Sidney's mind like a broken record.

The task in front of Sidney Wright was formidable. Statistically the chances of an escape, less than one percent, became further diluted if you factored in recapture rate, federal prison and murder conviction. Computing the odds of a successful and final escape put Sidney's mind to the test. *Hell, I'd have better odds of publishing a novel.*

Although the possibilities were remote, Sidney's objectives were simple. Get out, get money, and get hidden. Sidney agonized with himself when his mind would drift from the simple objectives to the complexities of revenge.

Damn Terry Rankin... forget him.

But during times when he did focus on revenge, he knew of no better alibi than being locked down in a federal prison.

Sidney studied inmate Brent Davis, an "A" block prisoner, convicted of bank fraud and doing a four-year term. His family had money, and an appeal was pending. The issues involved the admission of certain hearsay evidence.

"Brent, the Court's bound by law to cut you loose. The only evidence of your involvement was that bank teller saying you admitted doing it. Problem is you didn't tell the bank teller, your wife did. Since your wife wouldn't testify, your admission turned into hearsay, and the government's case falls like a house of cards."

Sidney became Brent's good friend and developed a brainstorming method where the bible group of eight would consider biblical issues in four groups of two and report its findings back to the group as a whole. Sidney's partner was Brent. They talked about Brent's lawyers, Brent's family, and Brent's connections. Sidney took charge of reporting their undiscussed theological findings back to the group.

In time, Sidney convinced Brent to solicit the lawyer to place proper postage on a letter with no return address to a "Reinhardt Hallman."

Dear Reinhardt,

You have certainly heard by now of my recent charges and conviction in America. I am presently incarcerated. I trust you will recall my degree of character when I helped you put your company back into a profitable position.

You trusted me and I delivered for you. I have that same trust in you. Please transfer the sum of 1.5 million American dollars to the Bank of Paris, Account No. 2286432C. Please continue holding the balance of my funds per your prior commitment.

Regards, SW.

The vast majority of projects Sidney Wright had orchestrated involved no deaths. Killing, messy and complicated, raised the stakes. He resorted to it only when necessary.

Although Sidney knew the reputations, skills and results of most hit men in the international community, he'd hired only one, Tom Connor, an Irishman. Sidney first met him in Cairo while Sidney was setting up a political power play which necessitated taking out a political figure. Sidney's plan called for an ally to assume the political position and approve a controversial building project being handled by the development group controlled by Sidney.

Sidney was impressed with the clear, calm eyes of Tom Connor. Connor didn't drink or smoke. He reminded Sidney of a great heron who could stand frozen until striking its victim. He liked what he saw and hired Tom for the hit, successfully completing the project. Sidney earned a healthy profit when he checked out of the development group.

Sidney admired the way Connor always worked with the greatest of secrecy, monies always paid in advance, details of the hit never shared. Connor disappeared after each successful mission. As the cautious relationship grew, Sidney convinced Connor to use a separate account at the Bank of Paris for Sidney's deposits. Sidney knew the contract fee schedule and would transfer the funds to the account for the benefit of Connor. Once the funds were in place, Sidney called a secure answering machine leaving the time and number for Connor to call him for the object of the hit. By agreement, the return phone call would occur twenty-four hours after Sidney left the message, a system which always worked well.

The hit, not necessary, haunted Sidney. More importantly, it put no money in his pocket at a time when he needed money most. The hit violated his code, but times had changed. His deepest inner being demanded revenge, needed to bring him peace.

The substantial challenge, communicating with Conner, required a wireless phone. Due to interference by the concrete walls and steel incorporated into the prison structure, the call would have to be placed in the activities yard.

Sidney became well acquainted with a fellow inmate, in for third-offense stalking, unable to come to grips with the fact his wife had left him. After two convictions for constantly following her, the stalker confronted her at the post office where she worked and cried for her to come home. The boss was not impressed, and the judge gave him eighteen months.

The stalker fit well into Sidney's religion program. He acted quite emotional and believed God still, somehow, would return his wife to him. Sidney had prayed with him, given him words of comfort and assured him God's coming justice would one day reunite them. He substantiated all of it with scripture.

The stalker, three months from his release date, participated in the job-training transition period. The transition program had a daily work release, and the stalker took a job in a sandwich shop beside a discount phone store. Each day the inmate returned to the prison. The stalker, more than willing to help out with Sidney's dilemma, agreed to the plan. Sidney had no phone privileges without warden approval and only under the strictest of supervision.

Sidney explained, "My mom is ninety years old and, for the most personal reasons, I've harbored hate for her for the past thirty years. I haven't talked to her for nearly half my life, and I can't die with this hate in my heart. Jesus wants me to tell her I love her, but I need a phone and some privacy."

Sidney hollowed out a compartment in one of the stalker's shoes, large enough to conceal a small cell phone.

"Here's how you save my life. Ask your family when you call them tonight to leave a hundred bucks in a paper bag under the bush we talked about. Leave your shop when the boss takes his morning constitutional, pick up the bag, and quickly buy the prepaid cell phone. You'll be back before you hear the toilet flush."

Sidney retrieved the phone from the shoe by sunset, ready to put his plan in motion. He grabbed one of the regular chaplains by the arm asking to speak to him in a quiet place. The chaplain quietly slipped out to the activities yard and escorted Sidney to a bench. Sidney said a solemn prayer and thanked the chaplain for allowing him to work with the other prisoners. Sidney explained faith gave meaning to his life and strengthened his belief in the concept of forgiveness.

"The problem is, Reverend, no one has ever once told me I've been forgiven." Sidney hung his head low and humbly.

"My son, I'm honored to affirm God's forgiveness of you, and you should feel it deep in your heart."

Sidney held his hand to his heart, slightly above the cell phone, as the chaplain left him in silence to meditate.

The moment the door clicked behind him, Sidney pulled out the telephone and dialed Connor's number from memory. The answering machine activated, beeped, and Sidney spoke softly and quickly. "Hello, Connor, Sidney Wright here. It's 7:48 p.m. Eastern Standard Time. Your fee should already be in the Paris account." He left the number and pleaded for Connor to call in exactly twenty-four hours.

With two pieces of duct tape he had salvaged from a closet in the bible class, Sidney secured the phone under the bench.
Sidney promptly walked back into the common area between the cell blocks.

"You know you're not supposed to be out there without a permit," the guard said patting Sidney down. "You're clean. Now get out of here."

The next trick, getting back in the yard in twenty-four hours, posed complications if confronted by the same guard. But Sidney knew the schedule, and the problem guard should be off and another more laid back one on duty near the door leading to the field. He needed complete privacy when the phone rang and nervously hoped for some luck.

At 7:40 p.m. the next day, Sidney, in his group of eight, figured the guard on duty would probably let him go out into the yard and retrieve the bible he supposedly had left that afternoon. At 7:46 p.m. he strolled toward the guard and stopped cold. Sidney stood looking at the one who reprimanded him the night before and felt frustrated for the miscalculation.

He needed a diversion and hurriedly returned to the group pulling Brent Davis aside.

"Brent, I need a big favor, brother. Just fall down on the floor, hold your stomach, and scream like you're in pain."

"Are you nuts?"

"Please, don't question me. Do it now."

Brent fell to the floor in agony while Sidney ran to the guard. "Can you help him?" The guard rushed in as Sidney looked at the clock, hanging on the wall, showing 8:49. He exited quickly to the yard and heard the phone ringing. "Connor," he said through rapid breathing.

"I thought you were in a federal pen, my friend."

"I am. Pretty good alibi, wouldn't you say?"

Sidney heard Connor chuckled. "I wouldn't expect anything less of you. I got the money. Who's the target?" Within one and a half minutes, Sidney concluded the call, taped the phone back under the bench, and returned as Brent was recovering.

"Must have been gas. Sorry to alarm everyone."

The guard started returning to his station, and Sidney caught his scorned look.

"Some damn emergency."

Many weeks went by, news coming slowly to those in prison. Sidney's first indication of Conner's activity was a visit from a Greenville detective named Olson.

"We had a right awful killing down in Greenville County last week. A sniper's bullet ripped through a child and his mother, both Rankins. Mr. Wright, have you ever heard of a Terry Rankin?"

He looked at the detective. "Sir, I spent quite a bit of time in court before coming here, heard the name all the time. What of it?"

"We find it quite coincidental you're the only person on the face of this earth with the motive to execute the child of Mr. Rankin."

Sidney put on the face of astonishment. "Is it not enough I'm spending the rest of my life in this prison with no privileges? If you'll bother to check, you'll find I've had no visitors and no phone calls. How could you accuse me? You might not know it, but I have turned my life over to God."

"Yes, Mr. Wright, I've checked that all out. Still, somehow I'm not convinced. Do you know of anyone, other than yourself, wanting to see a Rankin dead?"

Sidney, in all truthfulness, said, "I think not." The conversation ended. *Two for the price of one,* jingled in Sidney's head as he walked in chains back to his cell. *Now Rankin can live with his torment.*

CHAPTER THIRTY-SEVEN

New Jersey
Federal Prison
April 2008

There were seventeen chaplains who worked the New Jersey prison, and Sidney came to know all of them. He studied their movements, how they walked, and how they held their heads. He knew their schedules and practiced their accents.

Only one fit Sidney's mold, Chaplain Horton, a retired Methodist minister and nearly identical in size to Sidney.

For weeks, Sidney studied every aspect of his mannerisms. He knew how he greeted the guards coming and going, and he considered the man a model of consistency.

Sidney earned the trust and companionship of Chaplain Horton through many conversations about John Wesley's impact on the Protestant faith. Sidney learned what kind of car he drove, where he parked, what guards were nice, and what guards irritated him. He discovered Chaplain Horton had not been searched by prison officials coming or going in over six months.

Sidney took care to observe his skin color. Chaplain Horton worked his garden and carried a bit of a tan. Sidney took a new liking to the direct sunlight during activity yard time and sat close to the spot where he'd buried the cell phone.

On a mild but rainy August evening, the tanned, slightly shaking right hand reached towards door number 18 and hit the speaker button. "This is Chaplain Horton, leaving for the evening." The electronic door lock clanged open. He pushed the door, and slowly walked to the next of four checkout points.

He wore a raincoat and hat, still damp from when they were worn into the prison hours earlier during a thunderstorm. "God bless you, my fine officers," he said as he passed the first security station.

"Night, Chaplain Horton."

By the final checkpoint, Sidney felt like the chaplain himself. His constant practice of his accent, his slight limp on the left side, and the way he cupped his right arm when he walked were all part of the reproduction. As he passed and greeted the last guard before exiting the front gate, he heard the guard shout.

"Hold it."

A shiver went up his spine.

"You tell that Mrs. of yours you don't have to work the garden tomorrow. It'll be too wet."

The familiar chaplain laugh came out of Sidney. "Yes, I'll surely use that excuse." Sidney stepped onto the asphalt of the parking lot, freed. With keys in hand, he found the car right where it should be. As he cranked it, he mumbled, "How much gas? Three-fourths of a tank... good." He drove away, cautiously, refusing to look in the rear-view mirror.

Sidney usually took comfort not having any emotional tie to his victim. He pushed to the back of his mind Chaplain Horton possessing not a shred of evil, clearly the only man Sidney ever met with no character flaws. The chaplain, purely a combination of compassion and love, was nearly a sister Mary.

A metal wire from a brake cable sliced through his vocal cords as Sidney Wright supported the back of the chaplain's head with his knees. He got the cable from the automotive shop with the help of a fellow bible worshiper. The sawing motion of the weapon, held between Sidney's hands, brought silence quickly. Handles at the ends of the wire, constructed from rolls of leather taken from the back cover of an old bible, rolled tightly into balls, fit nicely in his hands.

The deed took place in the bible supply closet off a study class. The body, along with towels which caught the blood, was stuffed on a large upper shelf. The closet, designed by Sidney with building approval from the warden, was large and the only substantial square footage in the prison that wasn't monitored by cameras.

CHAPTER THIRTY-EIGHT

Greenville
2008

Despite the healing of bullet wounds, Terry could see the emotional wounds Bonnie carried were still raw and inflamed, seemingly never to completely heal.

The week following the shooting, an emotional roller coaster for Terry, pulled him in all directions. The unceasing questions of the police authorities, the funeral arrangements, and Bonnie's need for support sucked hours from the day like the air from an untied balloon. The responsibility for a multi-billion dollar business, along with the see-saw dilemma of sorrow and revenge, stretched the limits of his emotional tolerance.

Hardly a dry eye watched the funeral of Charles Joshua Rankin, sadness replacing the joy that prevailed in the same sanctuary days earlier. Security forces surrounded the perimeter of the church. Terry held Bonnie as they exited the service. Reaching the bottom step, standing in the exact place where his family's blood spilled, brought pain rushing back to Terry. He could see the memory overwhelming Bonnie. He caught her as she lost consciousness realizing the length of the recovery road before him.

Opening the backdoor of the building, abandoned for months, was child's play to the professional shooter.

Connor scouted out dozens of sites for the hit, the abandoned warehouse across from the church the clear choice. He waited patiently for the Rankins to attend. After several Sundays, they did. The drama of the hit occurring after the baptism was not planned. Connor himself attended the early service and spotted the baptism announcement in the bulletin, not a Sunday to be wasted.

The maze of buildings behind the warehouse offered excellent cover for his escape. He left the spent shell casing and rifle at the place of the shooting. The firearm, not traceable, had no prints. Within four minutes after the shooting, he was two blocks away and entering the car he rented in Atlanta under a fictitious name. By the time the first police vehicle arrived at the church, Connor headed south on I-85. When the sun rose the following day, he sat comfortably in a café near the airport in Paris, sipping a latte. Connor lived modestly. A million and a half would go a long way.

The next few months didn't get any better for Terry. Bonnie started seeing a psychiatrist, and her treatment program called for Terry's participation. Therapy caused Terry to hesitate, distrust, and hold his thoughts to himself. He had gotten along his entire life without someone telling him how to think, but it became clear to him it wasn't simple for Bonnie. She needed help, *his* help.

At first Terry found the sessions an invasion of his privacy. The doctor opened their lives, like a surgeon repairing a ruptured organ, laying them out to analyze. Their loss, their pain, their agony stared back at them. Terry justified the invasion if Bonnie could get better.

As sessions progressed, Terry surprised himself. Something happened while he built emotional support for Bonnie. Their emotions were linked: to help Bonnie was to help himself, he hoped.

Terry and Bonnie had a beach house on Kiawah Island, south of Charleston. Terry announced he'd take two weeks there by himself. The psychiatrist caught Terry off guard when he objected.

"This is no time to be by yourself. You need to be open with your feelings. Being alone tends to bottle up the pressure."

But anger started overtaking the hurt Terry suffered. Right or wrong, doctor's advice or not, he needed to deal with the anger in his own way.

"I'll be okay, Doc. You keep working with Bonnie. I'm about counseled out."

"Well, if you must go, you need to dwell on the positive aspects of your life. Think about whom you love, and who loves you. Focus on the natural beauty at Kiawah. Take walks on the beach, let the water's movement calm you, and the night sky amaze you with its vastness," the psychiatrist said.

The two weeks at Kiawah couldn't have been more different. He focused not on past pleasantries, but rather revenge. As the sand sunk beneath his feet with each step, his hate for Sidney Wright erupted like a roman candle in his gut. He wanted a solution, and none would come to him.

But the trip did afford him time to finally ask himself some questions. They came in a rambled manner.

Did I kill my own boy by not having better security?

How could Sidney Wright have possibly set it up?

Where did the money come from?

How do I get some attention from a cop willing to nail Wright's ass for this?

Who the hell shot up my family?

He left the island, empty for answers but filled with a mission to find out who shot Josh and to make sure Sidney Wright would never breathe freedom. Terry returned home, greeted with a loving and gracious hug.

"Welcome home, sweetheart."

They chatted a while, catching up on the past two weeks. Terry claimed the Kiawah trip had rejuvenated him and had gotten rid of a great deal of bitterness. But the insincerity in his words reflected back at him off Bonnie's face.

"How are you on dealing with this Sidney Wright thing?"

"Hey, I'm not worried about him. He'll spend the rest of his life in some federal hell hole."

He watched Bonnie raise her eyes suspiciously, but she said, "Good, then let's just forget about that monster."

Terry spent the next couple of hours reviewing mail and checking voice messages. There were a couple from Al Olson which sounded a bit urgent. He had left both his office and home phone numbers. Terry called him at home.

"I've got some bad news from the federal prison in New Jersey. Sidney Wright escaped," Al said.

"What in the hell are you talking about?"

"I got the call this morning. The bastard murdered a prison chaplain, put the chaplain's clothes on, and walked out of there like he owned the place. Heads are rolling left and right up there. I've never seen so much mud-slinging. The Feds are all over the place, and the Governor's office is involved. Everybody's trying to save his own ass. The warden has already been fired. It's a bloody mess."

Terry screamed, "What's wrong with you people? The guy is a convicted murderer, and you let him walk out? I told you five weeks ago Sidney Wright killed my baby, and you didn't bother to tell the Feds to lock him down tight? What do I have to do to get some attention?" Terry slammed down the phone.

Defeat jerked Terry's heart towards his stomach, a hurt combined of sadness for his dead son and humiliation of his flattened dignity.

A l Olson gently hung up the phone. *He's right. I'm part of the system failing him,* he thought to himself. Al made a commitment at that very moment to never retire until he solved the case of the murdered Rankin child. *Even if it takes the rest of my life.*

CHAPTER THIRTY-NINE

New Jersey
Outside Federal Prison
April 2008

F orty-six dollars sat in Chaplain Horton's wallet. Sidney estimated the body would be found by nine o'clock the next morning. He carefully considered what could become problematic over the next twelve hours as he drove. The vehicle, once found, would be the origination point for a nationwide search.

Get out of New Jersey...the deceased was its man of the cloth, and I'm its crazed man on the loose. Avoid establishing a direction. If the vehicle is found in the South, the investigation will be tightly contained. Who the hell would care along the Pacific coast?

He needed a plan to ditch the car, find a place to sleep and food to eat. He took the shortest route to escape the state, picking up Interstate 95 at Linden, and heading south. A quick stop depleted his assets by twenty dollars for gas and fifty cents for a pack of peanut butter crackers.

The year 1951 registered in Sidney's mind. He was twelve years old with considerably more money in his hidden box than he had at the moment. *How that pendulum swings,* solemnly crossed his mind.

South of Fredericksburg he left I-95 and traveled west on Massaponax Church Road. The country drive provided many prime opportunities to dump the vehicle off the side of the road, but nowhere to walk. He needed sleep badly, and his head bobbed as he drove in the blackness. He finally passed a motel with a neon sign blinking "$19.95," in his budget.

Carefully, he did a U-turn and retraced the road to a spot seen one-quarter mile earlier. It was five o'clock in the morning, and he hadn't seen traffic in the last forty-five minutes. He pulled off the side of the road and surveyed the terrain. *Nothing better than kudzu.* He re-entered the car and drove it to the edge of the road. With his left foot on the dirt shoulder of the road and his right leg extended into the open driver's door, his right foot tapped the accelerator. Chaplain Horton's vehicle edged toward the cliff. Sidney didn't know if it was his lack of sleep or an actual occurrence as the car seemed to perform an acrobatic flip and turn, as it lost itself in the jungle of green and expansive kudzu. The landing, not loud, seemed almost a peaceful crunching of nature.

He dragged his exhausted sixty-nine-year-old body back to the $19.95 accommodation, and slept like Chaplain Horton. Sidney abruptly awoke seven hours later, the equivalent of a homeless man. He couldn't afford the fare of another night at the roach infested motel. He had no car, no home, and no clothes. In his pocket was five dollars and thirty cents, and he lacked a clear plan as to his next move. He humored himself with the idea that food, shelter, and clothing waited for him back at the federal pen.

When he eased into *The Coffee Pot*, a greasy spoon next to the motel, Sidney knew he'd entered a critical time frame. His picture could be posted nationwide any minute. He watched the morning news on the television behind the restaurant counter, no report. Seven hours of sleep had done wonders for Sidney's defense mechanisms. Slowly, he considered a single man sitting in a booth.

"Is that your rig out front?" Sidney asked, with his best Southern accent.

"Hell, yeah, I got to make St. Louis by tonight and Omaha by the end of tomorrow. It's going to be hell. But, hey, I'm a driver and that's what I do," the trucker said.

He eyed the trucker's plate containing one egg and bacon. He turned his head towards the menu board on the wall behind the counter, and figured that, with coffee and tax, a total of three dollars and five cents, leaving him with two dollars and twenty-five cents.

Sidney slid into the booth across from the trucker, picking up his tab. "I got that. My name is Wilbur Barnhart," Sidney reported to the trucker, "and I'm in a hell of a mess. For the last year I've been standing on Capitol Hill down in Carolina with my rebel flag. It's heritage, not hate. My ancestors died in the War of Northern Aggression, and I think the South ought to honor its own."

"Amen, brother," the trucker yelled.

"My old lady told me to let it go. When I wouldn't, she let me go. I hitch-hiked up here. I'm about out of money and need a change of scenery."

The truck driver sat up straight. Sidney thought he was going to salute him. The trucker's eyes resembled what Sidney thought might be the eyes of a dedicated Confederate soldier starring into the face of Robert E. Lee himself.

"There ain't many left like you. This damn country don't have a fuckin' clue. A man's got to make his own way. The gub'ment got no right to play favorites."

Sidney's hook set, he was soon in Omaha. Before he and the trucker parted, they had become comrades in the "war against the oppressed white man." Sidney walked away with a fifty-dollar loan.

"Pay me back when you can. Use it for the cause."

The trucker looked as if it had been his greatest benevolence.

In Omaha, he read the first headlines of the national outrage through the plastic front of a newspaper box. Hostility bled from the law-abiding public, and he needed his money. Banking on Reinhardt Hallman's further cooperation resembled luck, not a commodity Sidney trusted.

Had he known Chaplin Horton's body wouldn't be found until they smelled his decaying body, he could have already made it to the Pacific Coast. Omaha was not where he wanted to be. Anything he did had to be low profile. He invested twelve dollars for a pair of scissors and some hair dye. He cut back his normally three-inch black, but graying, hair to one inch and dyed it autumn red. Sidney Wright now sported, for the first time in his life, the start of a full beard. He found an old pair of sunglasses and a sweatshirt in a trash dumpster and bought a one-way bus ticket headed west.

CHAPTER FORTY

Greenville
April 2008

From the time Terry slammed the phone down on Al Olson, he focused on nothing but Sidney Wright. After several days, he regained his composure, called Al, and apologized.

"I don't blame you, Mr. Rankin. I can't imagine how I'd have reacted if in your shoes."

They agreed to meet the following afternoon at Terry's office.

Terry began. "So where do we go from here, and how can I help?"

Terry watched as the detective's eyes roamed the plush, expensive interior of his office at Rankin Enterprises. It seemed the detective soaked up the room as if it were a crime scene. Terry couldn't help being impressed with the meticulous way his eyes shifted from the gold leaf wallpaper to Persian rugs and across leathered furnishings. Finally, the detective responded.

"We've completed our interview with your staff and followed up on every potential lead. We did a due diligence search for anyone who would have a motive to injure you or your family. You were right, nothing panned out. We rechecked the crime scene... clean as a whistle... a real pro. We're still running all of our local contacts to see if there's anything on the street about the shooting. I doubt anything'll shake out. The shooter's too polished to be from these parts."

After a long pause in the conversation, Terry broke the silence.

"How much do you know about professional contract killers?"

"We studied the practice at an FBI seminar the department sent me to a while back. Assassins are an intriguing bunch. There are those who do sloppy work and those who seem to move around with the transparency of a ghost. Quite frankly, until you lost your son, I've had no reason to investigate a contract killing. I may be able to get some help out of D.C., but we have no money budgeted for that kind of thing."

"Why don't you let me help you? I've worked with the Anderson Agency in Atlanta in the past. With your permission, I'll hire this firm to consider that aspect of the case. Perhaps every hit man has a unique method or style, like a fingerprint."

"Of course, I'd welcome the help."

Terry looked at Al until he addressed the question they both were pondering.

"Okay, you're probably correct about Sidney Wright. I'd go back and re-interview the son-of-a-bitch, but I don't have the luxury of that, do I? There's not been a single sighting of him. The car he stole hasn't shown up, and he could be anywhere. For the first few days, the murder caused a news media buzz all over the country. Now the frenzy has died down. The average guy on Main Street has mostly forgotten about it, and unfortunately, time is on Wright's side.

"You know, Terry, I have been back through the trial file of Wright's murder of Barbara Simmons, a crime nothing less than brilliant, framed your father like nobody I've ever seen. The man who pulled that off and then walked out of a federal prison has got to be some kind of genius."

"He is a genius," Terry said bitterly. "And you don't know the half of it." Over the next two hours Terry mesmerized Al with the remarkable story of Terry's mother and the company known as "Family Intervention."

"Do you think Sidney Wright master minded the crime by himself?"

"Not a doubt," Terry said as he observed a look of guilt on Al's face.

"You know, I don't sleep well at night."

"Why?" asked Terry.

"Don't spare my feelings. You made it clear Sidney Wright orchestrated your son's death, and I failed to listen."

"So why aren't you sleeping?"

"This guy, Wright, won't get out of my head. He's the soil from where my nightmares grow."

Terry laughed sadly. "Join the club."

The two men sat in silence considering the depth, gravity, and baseness of the mind of Sidney Wright. Terry, again, broke the silence. "He's more vulnerable than you think. I got him once before. The trick, I believe, is to get into his mind and think like he does."

"A scary thought."

The two agreed to get back together in three days. Terry's drive and determination, making him so successful in the past, now burned brightly in his soul.

Terry was greeted by Russ York in the posh Atlanta offices of the Anderson Agency. Terry had worked with him previously on the Bermuda matter and knew he had personally selected Mabry Barnes to be the point man. He trusted Russ.

"It's been a long time," Russ said as Terry settled into the flame stitched, upholstered chair in his office.

"What can I do for you?"

"Did you, by chance, hear of my son's assassination?"

"Of course we did. It shook up everyone in the agency. Sorry I missed the funeral, I was out of the country. Please understand we grieve for your loss."

"Thanks, but I'm not here for your sympathy. I'm here for results."

"How can we help, Mr. Rankin?"

"Find the killer."

"I had a feeling the hit-man stumped your local police, and I've been checking around. It's a tough request and might not be cost effective."

"Listen, I wouldn't be here unless you were tough enough to get it done. You worry about being effective, and I'll worry about cost."

"Fair enough. We'll need some cooperation from the Greenville authorities. We need access to all police files, including interview notes and forensic evidence. We don't have many requests such as yours, but we have a very good contact in London who understands what makes contract killers tick. He also knows many of the players. Once we develop a mode of operation from the Greenville files, we'll lean hard on our contact and see what shakes out."

He gave the phone number of Al Olson to Russ and assured him of Detective Olson's full cooperation. Terry requested a preliminary report in two weeks and left the agency feeling more confident. He stepped into his limo, waiting to return him to Greenville, with new hope.

Terry found himself giving more authority to his company managers, since all of his businesses were running efficiently. Josh's death weighed so heavily on him, work seemed unimportant. He spent days giving Bonnie the support she needed and dealing with details on the Sidney Wright investigation.

Terry coped well during waking hours, but nights were different. Fear replaced purpose. He had a sensation of falling as he slept. Terry, always a sound sleeper, fought the psychological demons attacking him ruthlessly.

"Baby, what is it you're dreaming about?" Bonnie asked as Terry realized he had jolted from his sleep.

"I don't know. I can't turn it off."

"Turn what off?"

"Being scared."

"Please don't say that."

"Then why did you ask?"

"Terry, you've always been my strength, what gets me through losing Josh."

"I didn't say I wasn't strong. But at night, when everything is quiet, I have this fear of not knowing what will happen."

"What do you mean?"

"Bonnie, I don't want to scare you, but I have no control over this Sidney Wright. He seems to manipulate my life, even when behind bars. Where is he, and what's he doing now?"

Terry gently pulled Bonnie's head over to rest on his chest and combed his fingers through her hair as he silently pondered their future.

An overhead projector, set up to facilitate Russ York's presentation, sat among several large briefcases full of materials in Terry Rankin's conference room. Terry invited Detective Al Olson to attend. The world of murder for hire felt strangely fascinating to Terry as he listened to Russ.

"The profession goes back in history, nearly as far as the oldest profession itself. Although prostitution has always been dominated by women, hired killing is dominated by men. The mentality of this breed is complex and bizarre."

"Why?" asked Terry.

"They're all different. The only common thread among them is the desire for money. A hit man is devoid of emotion for his victim. The lack of motive and personal involvement makes the killer difficult to track."

"Right, this guy was so slick it looked like the rifle picked itself up and took Mr. Rankin's son," Al said.

"Typically, only the person hiring can connect the shooter to the crime. For that reason, methods of communication and payment are used which maximize distances between the hirer and the hired."

York handed the two a laminated piece of paper, and Terry scanned the written list containing the names of over a hundred people. He felt repulsion for each.

"Most names are probably not ones you'd find on a respective birth certificate. They are code names, trade names, if you will. They are broken down into various categories. A large number are nothing more than thugs. There's nothing splendid about their methods. They usually reside in countries where there is little police presence and often kill with basic techniques and with minimal concern about who witnesses the event. They protect themselves by intimidation. In other words, no one in their right mind would report them."

"Our guy's not likely to be one of those, right?" Al asked.

"Correct... which brings me to the next category called "blue collar hits." The price of these services might range from eight hundred to eighty thousand dollars. The victim has no notoriety, status, or power. Although the shooter has to take reasonable precautions, he doesn't have to worry about a nationwide manhunt. The government won't spend the money for it."

Terry cut his eyes over at Al. He could almost see the wheels of injustice turning in the detective's mind... finding the killer of the unprivileged has to involve a cost analysis.

"The final group is a small number representing the elite of contract killers. I caution you these names, all fictitious, are labels for highly paid killers who take extreme precautions to remain anonymous. Even the made-up names are only known to a handful of people with both financial credibility and a proven past of protecting the identity of the hit men. This group contains fourteen names along with what is presumed to be their home base. These killers use various methods. Some plant car bombs, some prefer to use a blade to the throat in the dark of night, others use poison or drugs to effectuate the kill. Firearms of different shapes, calibers, and sizes are used by some. Shotguns are messy and don't always deliver a kill. Handguns are easily concealed but need to be used at close range for accuracy. Rifles have the potential for long range take-downs, but the target needs to be reasonably still, and a prior set up at an advantageous angle is necessary."

Terry digested the information as fast as it came. He asked a number of questions pointedly targeted at the long-range rifle candidates who fetch a high price.

"My agency believes the shooter had to come from the elite group. In analyzing the investigative material from Greenville P.D. and comparing the MOs of the elite group, we are prepared to predict the killer to be one of these five people."

Terry watched the overhead projector screen as the names appeared.

Toby Willingham - United States

Soon Lay - Japan

Carlos Playa - Spain

Tom Connor - France

Phillip Code - Australia.

Terry gazed intently at the names as Russ concluded his comments.

"Gentlemen, if I gambled, I'd bet heavily our killer is one of these five. This process has been an inexact science at best. We have shaken the trees, but nothing has fallen. We've gone through an exhaustive process with our contacts. They touched base with their contacts, and so on. Nobody has heard of a legitimate rumor, very quiet out there."

Terry stared at the list of five, one his son's killer, who never knew how precious Josh was, only money. He thanked Russ and explained he'd give him a call after he'd processed the information. Russ left, and Terry turned to Al.

"Where do you usually eat lunch?"

"Mr. Rankin, my regular place is Watson's Grill. It's the best grease in town, but not your kind of place."

"Exactly my kind of place, and besides, the name is Terry," he said as he removed and threw his tie into the corner of his office.

CHAPTER FORTY-ONE

Oregon
April 2008

Sidney Wright knocked on the glass storm door of the modest Oregon home. Sidney observed the familiar scar across the forehead of Rex Wilkerson as he slowly approached. Sidney focused, knowing the first few seconds would dictate his level of trust for his former associate in crime.

"Hello, Rex. It's been a long time, and you probably don't remember me."

"Well, I'll be damned, it's Sidney Wright. I'd a never recognized you with red hair after all these years, but your voice is hard to forget. How ya doin?"

The smile on Rex's face seemed sincere, and Sidney accepted his invitation into the home. Patiently, Sidney waited as Rex fixed some sandwiches and a pot of coffee. He sat across the kitchen table from his host.

"Old friend, you might have heard about me being in jail and recently escaping."

"Yep, matter of fact I did, but you know, Sidney, I pretty much keep to myself out here. For the most part, I stay out of trouble and don't get into anybody else's business. You're okay here."

"Listen," Sidney continued, "I need somebody I can trust. After all these years, as far as I can tell, you've never rolled over on me, something I appreciate."

"I remember your trial last year, back in South Carolina, over the murder of Barbara Simmons. I kept my mouth shut. I'm sorry you went down on that one, but at least you know I didn't cause any trouble for you."

"I know. But like every time before, I don't ask anything from you without seeing you're well paid for it." Sidney spent the next hour and a half chatting with Rex about different things. Precious time was wasting, but he had to be sure Rex would stay true to him. Besides needing help out of the country, he would eventually have to have one person as a dependable contact, once he established his new residence. Reinhardt Hallman, one option, had been dependable in the past, but Sidney had no history with him except for the money. He might have to trust Rex.

Sidney contemplated these matters as he rested on a small bed in Rex's guest bedroom. He fell soundly asleep. The aroma of sausage woke him six hours later. He got up and walked into the kitchen.

"Are ya hungry?" Rex asked.

"Starved."

The country breakfast was a feast to Sidney. As they ate, Sidney talked.

"I have over twenty million in a German bank account. I've got to get there. In order to do this, I need you to get hold of eighteen hundred dollars. You'll use it to purchase a one-way flight ticket to Frankfurt in the name of Robert Parks Wilson. I'll need to borrow another couple hundred dollars, some clothes, and a carry on bag. You'll go to the Portland Airport and buy the ticket. On the way back, you'll stop at the business address written on this paper. A guy named Joe will set you up with a passport and Oregon drivers' license for seven hundred fifty dollars. Here's a recent photo I had made before coming here. Get the first flight out with enough time for you to drive thirty minutes from the airport to Joe's, spend an hour and fifteen minutes with Joe, pick me up here, and drop me off at the airport.

"Now, before you say anything, I want to tell you what I'm going to do for you. You have my commitment I'll wire to your bank account one million dollars. Give me a copy of a deposit slip that has the bank and your account number. I'm doing this, because you'll have earned it. You know damned well you'll get the money, because you're the only person who knows when I leave and where I'm going. You'll know about my passport and my drivers' license. You could own me, a matter of mutual trust."

Sidney's confidence rose, as Rex's eyes widened.

"A million bucks? Things have been a little tight lately. Hell, I could get my fishing business back into operation."

Rex left the house, withdrew the funds from his bank account, and departed for the airport. He purchased the ticket and reviewed the business address on the back of an old delinquent utility bill Sidney had written upon. Not knowing its location, he stopped by a gas station and found a city map of Portland. Three miles later, he pulled up to the curb in front of Friendly Pawn and Jewelry, a rough section of town. He walked through the glass front entrance. The man behind the counter didn't show Rex his eyes. "Is Joe in?"

"Don't know a Joe around here. Unless you got something to pawn or got cash to buy something, you got no business here."

Sidney warned him of this situation. Rex walked up to the counter, laid out seven one hundred dollar bills and a fifty. "Mr. Wilson sent me."

He watched the man pick up the cash without hesitation. Suddenly, his eyes were alive.

"Follow me."

Rex found Joe, a cigarette hanging from his mouth, in the smoky back room. With no introduction, he gave Joe the essentials. Within an hour, the documents were done. To Rex's amazement, the drivers' license and passport looked like government issue. In the new plastic appeared the name of Robert Parks Wilson, a red-headed man from Portland, Oregon.

Rex thought about his life on the drive home. Deep in his heart loyalty was important, and his continued dedication to it gave him a sense of comfort. He returned home with the ticket, passport, and drivers' license and handed them to Sidney.

These instruments of travel would serve Sidney's purposes, but seven hundred fifty dollars didn't buy the quality he liked. Time and resources didn't permit his preference.

He packed up a carry-on suitcase with two outfits of clothing. The clothes were slightly large for Sidney's frame but close enough. He enjoyed Rex's company on the drive back to the Portland airport. They chatted about old times and the nearly extinct concept of loyalty. They laughed about the resourcefulness of Rex's old character, Austin Clemmons. Sidney confided the details of his final destination to Rex and stepped from the car onto the airport's front curb, bound for Frankfurt. He firmly shook Rex's hand and looked hard into his eyes to confirm the trust he was betting on.

True to Sidney's word, Rex received by wire a million dollars into his account in Oregon. For the first time in a long while, Rex had the opportunity for long term financial stability. It had been a long drought since Terry Rankin jerked the rug out from under his feet ruining his prosperous fishing business. The sole responsibility of knowing Sidney's plans caused a mixture of emotions, particularly since he suspected he'd never see Sidney Wright again.

CHAPTER FORTY-TWO

Frankfurt
April 2008

S idney Wright shared a bottle of one of Germany's premier Rieslings with Reinhardt Hallman at a traditional German restaurant in downtown Frankfurt, finally his money within reach. He listened as Reinhardt explained how well his business had done over the past decade, giving Sidney much of the credit.

Reinhardt humored Sidney continuing to believe he single handedly was responsible for the turn around of Reinhardt's business successes. He graciously acknowledged the appreciation. He still liked to think his instincts superior to most.

The lunch was great, but Sidney had plans to implement.

"Where will you go, Sidney?"

"New Zealand. You'll have to come visit me after I get established," Sidney said, knowing it could never happen.

The bank documents were then all executed, and he rode with Reinhardt to the nearest branch of the German Bank. Sidney was pleasantly surprised his friend had steadfastly kept the money compounding in interest. The bank converted his money into negotiable documents as Sidney requested, except for several million he left in the account. Sidney said his goodbyes as Reinhardt dropped him off at a rental car lot.

Sidney reclaimed the name of Robert Parks Wilson and rented a "C" class Mercedes, paying cash and presenting his credentials. Over the next month and a half, Sidney reworked through the details of his new life. After some investigation, he located a DC-3 at a private air strip, adequate for his purposes. He negotiated a cash offer with its owner. He would take a nine-hour flight without refueling and land on a dirt airstrip.

The weather would be quite warm, year around. During the weeks before departure, he purchased at a local mall several wardrobes of clothing. His destination had no malls. A healthy hair-cut took care of the remaining red dye.

Before taking off, he returned the Mercedes to the closest rental outlet. Robert Parks Wilson needed to leave Germany in good standing.

Very early in the morning, before his departure, Sidney entered cash money in a pay phone and called the office of his old apartments in Birmingham. The last he knew, Bobby Depew still lived there. For some reason Sidney wanted to hear Bobby's voice again since he'd be cutting ties with his oldest friend. The apartment manager answered.

"I'm Earl Fallow, and I'm trying to get in touch with Bobby Depew. Does he still live there?" Sidney asked.

"I'm very sorry, sir. Bobby had been with us a long time, but he died a couple of months ago."

"From drinking himself to death?"

"No sir, he actually got shot by the husband of a lady living in the next apartment."

"What reason?"

"If the old-big-guy was your friend, I hate to be the one to tell you, but Bobby wouldn't leave this lady alone. She was a looker, and your friend never could get it through his head she was happily married."

"Was Bobby happy?"

"I think he was. You never know for sure. He was a fixture here. My parents bought these apartments decades ago and somehow had the understanding that Bobby was part of the deal.

Bobby would take off unannounced at times but usually would return and do simple maintenance and help collect rent. We had some laughs over the years watching Bobby keeping the tenants in line. But my folks are both dead now. With Bobby gone, there's nothing left but me and these run down appartments.

Sidney slowly hung up the phone. He thought back to days in Birmingham where Bobby had lost his mind over Paula. Sounded like nothing much had changed. Sidney felt saddened but smiled. Somehow Bobby going out with a gun blast seemed more fitting than vegetating with a bottle.

Sidney felt elated after takeoff, the last leg of a journey taking him to a world of rest, peace, and security. As he ascended above the cloud cover over Germany, the scattered sunrays seemed full of promise.

Hours later, Sidney's future hovered below the plane. He dropped skillfully, kicking up dust behind his landing gear and stopped short of the tree line. Walking out of the plane with hands full of the accepted currency, he introduced himself to some locals as Robert Parks Wilson. The suspicious look on their faces melted away as he passed out cash and asked for information.

Brava Island, part of the Cape Verde Republic, located off the coast of Africa, has warm tropical breezes year-round. The temperature is mild, ranging between 68 degrees in the dead of winter to a high of 83 degrees in the heat of summer. This May afternoon felt particularly pleasant as he talked with the locals.

The island, having a population of less than a thousand people, seemed to Robert Parks Wilson a paradise having all the elements of anonymity. The inhabitants were primarily Creoles and various people of African ancestry. The other inhabitants were mostly monkeys, wild goats, and exotic birds.

In less than a week, with some well paid help, Sidney found a nice cottage to occupy. He insisted he wanted to live away from any human noise. The cottage was a good mile away from the so-called commercial area, primarily a general store dealing with most all forms of commerce the island had to offer. Even though it had been under new management for the past few weeks, the general store had been in existence for nearly eighty years.

His cottage, secluded among the palms and the orchid plants off a dirt road seemed peacefully forgotten. At first he stayed close to his cottage, lost to the island and the world. The sustenance he brought on the plane tided him over for a couple of weeks. Soon he harvested the local produce that grew naturally in the trees and ground around his new shelter, but sweet potatoes, coconuts, and dates could sustain him only so long.

Robert Parks Wilson made the daily mile walk to the general store and cautiously became a customer. The first few visits he made purchases with no small talk. As weeks passed, he'd patronize the store about twice a week. Although the solitude a welcome change, Sidney found himself looking forward to his general store visits affording him a little human interaction.

The manager, a likeable fellow named Hallie Lumas, had long hair and a gruff look. Sidney sensed his love for the store and his life on Brava. He soon learned Hallie had checked out of his twenty-year career as a pipe fitter in Alaska.

"The work hard, weather mostly bitter, but the money's unbelievable. In twenty years, I saved up a small fortune.

"But my wife hated Alaska from day one, left me flat before I got the first paycheck. I became an ice oyster. The money kept layering up until I had a pearl of a stash.

"No kids, no wife, and plenty of money. I bought a forty-four-foot boat and started sailing the seas. I pulled into hundreds of ports between Alaska and the southern tip of Africa and found this island to be the best. The rest, for better or worse, is the history of Hallie Lumas."

Hearing his hearty laugh, Sidney couldn't help but laugh with him, almost as if he had known Hallie before. Robert Parks Wilson became Hallie's best customer. He didn't question prices and tipped generously. Ten-fifteen each morning became a ritual. He'd walk in and take a cup of coffee made from island beans milled right in the store.

It bothered Sidney this simple pleasure becoming, as he pondered each night, *necessary.* But he had no doubt he'd selected the ultimate hideaway, only a question of what degree of social interaction met his needs. *But what needs?*

At times he couldn't get the people in prison out of his head. The inmates he controlled, the guards, even the chaplains came to mind when he only wanted to look to the future. *I don't need people.*

"What do you do around here at night?" Sidney asked Hallie one day.

"Ever play poker, Robert?"

"Not a great deal, but I remember the game a little," he said as his heartbeat jumped a couple of notches.

"We start a little game around sunset on Thursday evenings... just four of us. If you want to play, bring a pocket full of money... no such thing as credit with these boys."

Credit, Sidney laughed to himself. The offer truly made him introspective. Thoughts of poker took him back to a place and time in Alabama. He reflected on fifty-two cards, the faces, and the probabilities.

"I'll think about it, Hallie old boy, and let you know next trip."

He rested while rocking on his porch hammock, knowing his answer. The cottage had one bedroom, a kitchen, and a large living area. Screened windows surrounded the exterior walls of every room. The breezes cooled slightly at night, offering a peaceful break in the temperature, and kept the insects at bay. Sidney had porches on three sides of his cottage. The furnishings were simple but were padded with local materials and were remarkably comfortable. His favorite chair backed up to the window in the living room and caught breezes from every direction. This low back chair, well constructed, fit Sidney like a tailor-made suit. It faced the only entrance in the cottage and had a magnificent view of the green luscious tropical vegetation going toward the road.

The next morning, Sidney sipped on his coffee and chatted with Hallie, trying not to appear anxious. "Are you sure you wouldn't mind me joining your group for a little card playing?"

"No problem, Robert, but remember I warned you. I'm a push over, but a couple of these guys will empty your pockets in a flash."

"Oh, well, I'm sure it'll still be fun," Sidney said as he was leaving. "I'll be here on Thursday."

The general store had a much darker appearance out of the direct sunlight, dimly lit by four exposed one hundred-fifty watt bulbs hanging by lamp cords from the ceiling. One hung directly above the poker table set up in a back corner between the beer cooler and the snack selection.

Robert Parks Wilson introduced himself, and the games began. The former skills of Sidney Wright came back quickly. He played conservatively at first and lost a couple of hands at five bucks a piece. He gripped his sides to keep from laughing about the expertise Hallie had described of two of his adversaries. *Easy pickings.*

As the hours passed, he frequently reminded himself this island, now his home, rendered these half-baked card players as close as he might come to a social structure. But, eventually the competitive nature of Sidney Wright took over. By the end of the night, the only pockets not empty were those of Robert Parks Wilson. He'd wiped them out.

"Guess I got lucky. You guys will win it all back next time."

"Yeah, yeah, you can count on it," they said.

Sidney grabbed a cold beer out of the cooler and tossed Hallie a more than generous fare as he left to return to his cottage.

The clear sky, filled with what seemed to be a billion stars, all shined down on him as he walked home. He basked in his victories of the poker game and felt satisfied in his choice of island. He slowly returned to the cottage as refreshing night breezes blew through his light cotton shirt. He stepped upon his wooden porch hearing only the mild hum of his portable generator.

"Hello, Sidney," came from the other side of the room after he closed the cottage entrance door. Sidney looked in the direction of his favorite chair, a dark figure in it. The person reached for the only lamp in the room and turned it on.

The yellow hue from the lamp cast itself across the face of the uninvited visitor. Sidney knew him at once. Defense mechanisms flew into his head before he noticed a pistol steadily focused.

"Why don't you have a seat?"

He watched Terry Rankin rise from the chair and take careful aim at his chest. Sidney took a seat in a small wooden chair to the left of the door. The usual options going through his head didn't fit. The man pointing the pistol at him didn't need money, a bribe laughable. Promises of power, women, or success would have no impact on this man.

"How did you find me?" he finally asked of Terry.

"I found you here because I started thinking like you do. The first thing I did after you murdered the preacher and escaped was to call my friend Rex Wilkerson. It occurred to me you'd need a little help. You got there quicker than I figured, but the plan was already set. My biggest concern, you entrusting Rex with your final destination, caused me hesitation, but Rex handled that one pretty good, wouldn't you say?"

Sidney processed this new information quickly through his head. He had difficulty believing he'd misjudged Rex.

"If you knew I was headed to Rex's place, why not take me out there?"

"There's a time and place for everything. This is better."

"Rankin, torture doesn't seem your style, and I can't imagine any other way you could have gotten my details from Rex Wilkerson."

"I figured you'd think that. The difference between you and Rex is he has seen the bad in himself and found a way to make it right."

"Good and bad have nothing to do with you and me, its business. Surely you ought to understand better than most," said Sidney, sensing some emotion that might get him out of this mess.

"What I understand is evil grows in you, it nourishes your soul, and it's inseparable from your existence."

Sidney, tired of the lecture, but his options few, thought it better to go along. "Okay, let me make it right."

"That's exactly what I'll let you do."

"Rankin, this island is too quiet for you to ease back to my place and not be noticed. Who helped you?"

"I set up here over a month before you landed your plane on this island. As brilliant as you might think you are, you're actually quite basic and predictable. Your new beginning is over, ended."

"I think you want something, or you'd have already killed me. What is it?"

As Sidney considered his next move, Terry paused. "You had somebody to kill my son. Who was it?"

"Okay, what's in it for me? If you want information, let's deal."

"You're in no position to bargain. I'm ready to blow your brains out right now. It's one of five people. I know every name. Tell me a lie, and you won't take another breath."

Sidney thought about it. At this point in time, what difference could it make, might buy him time.

"The name is Tom Connor, and I can tell you more."

Sidney could see Terry now knew the shooter. "You know I've told the truth; how can we work this out?"

"You don't get it. Four generations of my family victimized by you, and I should ask you why. I can't. No answer could give me comfort or understanding. What explanation could justify robbing Bonnie and me of our child?"

Sidney sensed the anger throbbing in Terry's heart, catching him off guard. "Now I want you to do something for my mother."

Sidney looked at him with uncertainty.

"There's something under your chair. Get it."

Sidney's extended hand felt a cold metal object. As he pulled it from under the chair, he noticed a cord running back toward an electrical outlet in the room. The drill contained a bit the diameter of a toothpick.

"You take the drill and put a hole right in the middle of the back of your head, the brain stem, the way you first thought my mother should be raped of her life, before you stumbled upon the gamma-knife."

Sidney laughed. "You're crazy as hell."

"My heart has ached every day since I read an entry in your notes."

"Which note?"

"You wanted to 'manipulate Terri Rankin's brain only to the degree necessary', right?"

Sidney watched tears rolling down Terry's face and, for a moment, thought of his own mother breaking his heart. Quickly, he shook it off and smiled at Terry. "She wasn't supposed to be hurt."

A shot rang from the barrel of the pistol and produced a gaping hole in the side of Sidney Wright's left calf. Blood spewed profusely.

"Drill, murderer, you've told your last lie."

Sidney cried out in pain as he grabbed his leg just below the wound. He slipped a precision-throwing-knife from its taped position. A split second flip of his wrist set the knife spinning toward Terry Rankin. He watched the blade catch him directly in the shoulder on the side of his shooting arm. The blade ripped through muscle and tendon as it embedded itself deeply. The disturbance gave Sidney Wright the time he needed to bolt through the door, dragging his injured leg.

Sidney made it to the tree where he had hidden a nine-millimeter pistol for backup protection. With a jerk and a snap, the pistol was ready to fire. Sidney thought, *come here, you annoying piece of failure. I'm ready for you.*

He could see Terry pulling the blade from his shoulder. Terry's silhouette looked almost animated in the yellow hue of the cabin. Sidney steadied himself on the side of the tree, taking aim, all very fitting to take out Rankin, a thorn in his side. Killing Rankin would erase the indiscretion of throwing out Conner's name. After this, he'd find another island, but he had a plane to accomplish the move.

As the whites of Terry's eyes were appearing, a disturbing noise arose behind the tree that steadied his aim. Sidney turned slowly around to the direction of the sound. A baseball bat with a home run swing behind it caught him square across the left side of his skull. Sidney fell toward the ground in a spinning motion. A flash of terror swept through his mind from an earlier time as he landed on the rich island soil. As his body twitched, his emotional soul reached out in revenge, and then all slowed. He was dying.

Glimpses of Chaplin Horton, a bible shredded for a weapon, perfectly understood psalms, all ignored, came to him. A blurring thought of Josh Rankin, not totally unlike Bobby Depew, plucked by Sidney from his own weakness, misused, abandoned, much like Rosie Murck had treated her own son. Torment raged in his dying realization he'd become his mother.

A light appeared. The face of Sister Mary, unscarred, pure, loving, smiled at Sid Murck. He saw in her eyes every second chance in his life for redemption. He smiled back, not a single thought of success, a settled debt or revenge. As his last bodily function abandoned him, Sid's heart changed. Too late. And Sister Mary cried.

The baseball bat had come from the inventory at the general store. The swing behind the bat was that of Al Olson. Al managed the store for its silent owner, Terry Rankin, for over a month. He played the role of Hallie Lumas relatively well for a cop. Longer hair, two-month-old beard, and a sailor's accent covered up his visit to the Federal pen nicely. Al tended to the shoulder of the man who had become his best friend. Al thought nothing of taking a ninety-day leave from the Greenville Police Department. His flagship piece of detective work was no longer Shuttle Man. Somehow, the broken system of justice became fixed for the moment and his commitment to Terry fulfilled.

Terry's success came by becoming the student of the teacher, Sidney Wright. His entire strategy came from the lessons pouring out of Sidney Wright's files, obtained after the arrest in Italy. Since Sidney's trial, Terry, sparing no expense, investigated Sid Murck's story back to his childhood.

Terry stood over the carnage of the most incredible mind he had ever known. There was no joy, the finality ungratifying. As death settled around Sidney, it appeared to Terry, through Sidney's eyes, final judgment opening its arms to a six-year-old child in the back room of the Starlight, attempting to understand his mother and the men to whom she surrendered his innocence.

An outward extension of Sid Murck's arms stood out in Terry's mind. He didn't realize Sidney reached for a pillow he abandoned in Chicago. Sidney's wide open eyes had a different look. Terry could feel power in a repenting gaze better than he understood it. But somehow, beyond the hate, Terry connected as death took over his enemy. *What would I have become if I had grown up in this man's shoes?*

CHAPTER FORTY-THREE

Oregon
September 2008

"I have been a broken man. Since the age of two, I've had no mother and no father. You'd think by now it wouldn't matter. But it does matter. I look at you and share your pain. You have no parents either. Do you wear it on your sleeve? No. Do you let it control your life? No. Does it matter still the same? You bet.

"At the age of twenty-one, I became obsessed with revenge, learning who killed my mother and father. I guess you could say the score has been settled, but, in fact, it was never a score.

"The man haunting me from the age of twenty-one is really no different from me. He had no parents. You see, when a parent refuses to act as a parent, there's not much difference. But when I look into your eyes, I can see a difference because somebody cares what happens to you, and that, my friends, makes all the difference in the world.

"As a child, a man and woman cared about how I felt, what I was, and where I was going. They took a special interest in my life. The fact that someone cared made me care about myself. If that's not the soul of a parent, what is?

"We break this ground and dedicate this facility to the honor of caring. All of you who will live and work here should look beyond the brick and mortar and into the heart of the "Terri

Lippard Rankin Center for Caring." Have no doubt her heart and spirit beats and breathes in this site. Have no doubt our mission here will succeed. Everyone standing on this site will be a part of our success. This Center is not to put a roof over your head. It is for you to understand you have a future, and if you care as much for yourself as we do for you, good things will come to you."

The crowd, between its joys and tears, erupted with applause. The words of Terry Rankin reached out to the hearts of Mac and Janelle. Their love and nurturing of Terry had come full circle.

Terry looked from the podium in the direction of Rex Wilkerson. Their eyes met, and Terry motioned for him to join him on the podium. Terry saw grateful eyes as Rex shook his head. He could feel what Rex thought, his deepest sense of justice dictated he had no right to claim credit on this wonderful occasion. His past, his participation, his part in the death of Terri Rankin could never be accounted for.

No one had asked or made a suggestion. The new center was not the idea of Terri Rankin's son. The million dollars in Rex's account could have meaningfully changed the way Rex lived... and it did. The job Terry had created for him years earlier had changed his perspective on the meaning and purpose of life. Terry was proud Rex's drive became the success of the parentless children's center. By the time Sidney Wright escaped from prison and dropped by Rex's house, the enrollment at the Center had doubled. Terry personally witnessed nearly a hundred children get their lives together.

The Center would now become a model for the nation, and its director was Rex. Another twenty million had been added to the mission of the Center by virtue of an anonymous donor from overseas accounts. Terry understood the reluctance of Rex to join him. But Terry could see straight into his chest. The heart beat warm and proud, knowing Terry had forgiven him.

Kiawah Island
Spring 2009

The mild Kiawah winds blew soothingly across the expansive ocean side porch of the Rankin's beach house. The oversized hammock rocked gently as if in time with the breaking waves. Their eyes faced the Atlantic Ocean, and Terry, at peace with the world, slipped his arms around Bonnie, satisfied, at this moment, to rock in the hammock for an eternity. Terry's hands softly rubbed the smooth skin along her curves, slowly, sensually. His fingers tenderly caressed her lips, ears and neck. All the pain of his past vanished as her pleasure heightened.

With heart-felt passion, he whispered into her ear. "I'm ready to have a baby."